# No Place Like You

**Also by Jillian Meadows**

*Wreck My Plans*
*Give Me Butterflies*

# No Place Like You

*A Novel*

# JILLIAN MEADOWS

AVON

*An Imprint of* **HarperCollins***Publishers*

Without limiting the exclusive rights of any author, contributor, or the publisher of this publication, any unauthorized use of this publication to train generative artificial intelligence (AI) technologies is expressly prohibited. HarperCollins also exercise their rights under Article 4(3) of the Digital Single Market Directive 2019/790 and expressly reserve this publication from the text and data mining exception.

This is a work of fiction. Names, characters, places, and incidents are products of the author's imagination or are used fictitiously and are not to be construed as real. Any resemblance to actual events, locales, organizations, or persons, living or dead, is entirely coincidental.

NO PLACE LIKE YOU. Copyright © 2026 by Jillian Meadows. All rights reserved. No part of this book may be used or reproduced in any manner whatsoever without written permission except in the case of brief quotations embodied in critical articles and reviews. For information, address HarperCollins Publishers, 195 Broadway, New York, NY 10007. In Europe, HarperCollins Publishers, Macken House, 39/40 Mayor Street Upper, Dublin 1, D01 C9W8, Ireland.

HarperCollins books may be purchased for educational, business, or sales promotional use. For information, please email the Special Markets Department at SPsales@harpercollins.com.

Avon, Avon & logo, and Avon Books & logo are registered trademarks of HarperCollins Publishers in the United States of America and other countries.

hc.com

FIRST EDITION

*Interior text design by Diahann Sturge-Campbell*

*Tulip illustration © itsmeemi/Stock.Adobe.com*

*Paw prints illustration © satou koma/Stock.Adobe.com*

Library of Congress Cataloging-in-Publication Data has been applied for.

ISBN 978-0-06-341620-8

Printed in the United Kingdom

26 27 28 29 CPI 10 9 8 7 6 5 4 3 2

*To my brother and sister. Thank you for loving me,
encouraging me, and helping me heal when I needed it most.*

Hello friend,

I'm so excited to share this book with you. Fable and Theo's story has been swirling in my mind for years, and it's finally their turn in the spotlight.

Before we start, though, I'd love to tell you a little bit about what you'll find inside these pages.

When Theo was first introduced in *Give Me Butterflies*, he popped into existence fully formed. He came strutting into my mind with his friendly personality, his backward cap, his crush on Fable . . . and his traumatic history.

In a lot of ways, I thought I was the perfect person to write Theo's story because it is a journey I know well. I know exactly how it feels to have an abusive parent. Exactly how it affects everyone else in the family. Exactly how the wounds still impact my life years and decades later.

But once it came time to write his story, digging into that part of myself proved more challenging than I expected. So I want to thank you for being patient while this book came together. Through many rounds of rewrites and edits and tears, it's finally a story worthy of Theo. And his sister.

And me.

There are no moments of abuse described on-page, and you will not meet the abuser in this story. In fact, you don't even learn his name because he doesn't deserve that much attention. I wanted our focus to remain on Theo, his sister, and his mother.

Despite the heavy moments, I hope this story brings you a sense of comfort. I hope it's a warm blanket and a steaming mug of tea and a reminder that you deserve to be loved exactly the way you are. I hope Theo's journey reminds you that healing is not linear, and sometimes even though we think we're "okay," it's absolutely normal to need help again.

Thank you for bringing my characters into your heart and for spending time in the town of Fern River. It's a place of found family and open arms, kindness, and inclusivity, and I hope you feel right at home there.

Love,
Jillian

**CONTENT WARNINGS:**

*No Place Like You* is intended for adult readers (eighteen or older) as it contains explicit language and on-page sexual content. While I wrote this book intending to make you smile, there are a few subjects addressed in it that may be upsetting for some readers.

- Grief from the loss of a grandparent and mention of Alzheimer's
- Mentions of domestic and child abuse (off page, in the past, no reappearance)
- Alcohol use

## NOTE TO READERS

If any of these topics are difficult for you to read about, please protect your heart, dear reader. I hope I have portrayed them with the care they deserve, but your mental health is important to me. Feel free to reach out via email or social media if you have any specific questions.

Also, just so you know ahead of time, all the animals you meet in this story remain happy and healthy, living their best lives forever and ever.

# No Place Like You

## Chapter 1

*Fable*

"Come *on*," I mutter, yanking on the handle of Gramps's old Bronco.

Even six months into driving it, I still haven't mastered opening the door, which has me seriously questioning why Gramps trusted me with his beloved vehicle. I watched him open it hundreds of times. Maybe thousands. He'd pull mostly from the left edge, making sure to press his thumb into the top at the same time until he heard the faint *pop* of success.

When he was teaching me how to drive, I'd never get it on the first try. Or even the second. Gramps would circle the hood with his trademark grin, drop a kiss to my forehead, and position his fingers on the handle, nodding for me to place my hand over his as he worked his magic.

"Be easy on her. Baby Blue's got her own timeline," he'd say, casting a tender, reminiscing look toward the sky-blue Bronco. "You'll get there."

"When, exactly, will I be getting there?" I grit out, jiggling the handle again and stubbornly ignoring his advice to be easy on her. The urge to kick the tire jolts through me before I can stop myself, and the tip of my boot hits the dirty rubber with a light thump.

I immediately regret it. Shame curls in my chest. Baby Blue has been quite the diva over the last few months, requiring more attention and repairs than I was prepared for, but she doesn't deserve to be kicked when she's down.

"I'm sorry," I whisper, placing my palm on the hood. "I didn't mean it." I drag in a deep breath and close my eyes, visualizing his fingers under mine as I try again. Slowly.

This time, I hear the *pop*, and the handle releases. "Got it," I announce to a quiet Main Street, pulling open the door to the familiar smell of old leather and the wood shavings caught in every corner and seam of the interior. I toss my Hawkins Hardware shopping bag onto the cracked leather seat—thank you, employee discount—and shut the door again (very gently to make up for the tire kicking).

The cool, misty evening dampens my cheeks as I walk through downtown Fern River, toward the Branch, where my order of coconut chicken tenders should be waiting by now. I pass back by the hardware store, then the dark windows of Wildwood Bakery—home of the best chocolate chip scones to ever exist. I swear Mrs. LaGrande is baking up magic in there.

My phone buzzes in my back pocket, and I pull it out to find a text from my best friend illuminating the screen.

> **Mia:** Have you seen this photo? How have we never noticed she is the spitting image of human Ursula????

Pausing under the awning for the thrift store, I click the link she sent, and a social media post pops up. My already-empty stomach hollows out even more.

The engagement isn't a surprise. I heard about it last week (and promptly downed an entire pint of Ben & Jerry's chocolate ice cream). But this photo of Philip and Samantha still leaves me unnerved.

It's a cruel sort of message from the universe when the man you were sleeping with six months ago is now engaged to your polar opposite. I stare down at her perfect raven waves. And perfect red lips. And the perfect pink nails pressed against her fiancé's jacket.

Philip Anderson, owner of said jacket, is all movie-star blond hair, sharp jawline, and flawless suit. His teeth are alarmingly white as he beams toward the camera, effortlessly confident, like the world was made to do his bidding. He looks every bit of the future politician his parents have groomed him to be, and now he has the flawless wife to stand by his side.

They're days away from a wedding in Greece, then a whole new life in Portland. A power couple. They'll probably drink red wine right on their $100,000 white couch while they talk about crypto and other things I don't understand.

Maybe high school Fable would've been the ideal match for him. Valedictorian, captain of the girls' soccer team, big dreams of becoming a doctor, voted Most Likely to Succeed.

But now . . . my gaze dips down my body, to the Hawkins Hardware logo on my shirt, where the *H*s are designed as hammers and screwdrivers. A layer of dust coats my jeans from where I knelt in aisle three for the last hour, organizing the bins of pipe fittings. I glance at my bitten-off nails and the callus on my palm from helping Dad clean the horse stalls yesterday.

While Philip and Samantha are picking out evening gowns and tuxedos, going to galas and probably shopping for yachts, I'm living in my grandfather's old A-frame, sleeping on a mattress I've had since I dropped out of college. I'm on my fifth job in the last two years, and I spend my evenings in an empty living room, hunched over a puzzle, listening to an audiobook or a true crime podcast, cuddling with my six-month-old kitten, and shoveling spoonfuls of that night's dessert into my mouth.

We're in completely different worlds, and I'm not sure I could've ever made it in theirs.

Shaking my head, I shove the phone back in my pocket without replying and cross the street to the flickering orange sign of the Branch. A cacophony of voices spills out as I open the door, confirming that half the town is here for coconut chicken tenders night.

I've just stepped inside when a sudden, rowdy *whoop* of laughter echoes above the noise, sending a chill up my spine.

As if my thoughts have summoned him, Philip stands in the center of the room with a group of his friends. I recognize a few of them, but all their faces and names blur together—same guy, different font.

Dammit. I scan the restaurant and assess my options, searching for a way to avoid him seeing me. I could duck back out the door and forget dinner. The bowl of cereal waiting for me at home is nothing compared to coconut chicken tenders, but I'll survive.

Or I can brave the path toward the bar and get my food. I'll have to skirt around Philip & Co., but he likely doesn't want to acknowledge that he knows me anyway, so I should make it without an issue.

There's also the option of begging the floor to open up and swallow me whole. Someone would surely remember to feed Knocks—

The universe intervenes. The door swings open behind me, propelling me forward.

Option two it is, I guess.

My boots stick on the linoleum floors as I thread my way through the crowd. The bar is so close that I can practically taste the crispy coconut, but right as the owner, Ethan, makes eye contact with me, Philip's group moves to block my path. I come to an abrupt stop right on the edge of their huddle, then step to the side, trying to get around them, but with tables bracketing the group, I can't get by.

"Which bridesmaid should I go after, man?" Chad/Brad/Ben—something like that—asks, beer sloshing over the edge of his glass and plopping to the ground.

Philip shifts to stand in front of me, not looking my way. "Don't care as long as you stay away from Kate."

The room narrows around me. I watch the side of his face for a beat, trying to remember what I liked about him. But under the yellow-hued bar lighting, I can't recall a single thing.

All I remember is four months of sneaking around and to-go containers and back roads. He wanted our situationship kept a secret, and I'm ashamed to admit I willingly went along with it, hoping that maybe his attention meant something. If the mayor's son had an interest in me, then surely I wasn't a complete failure. Right?

While his group gets even louder, I keep staring, willing him to acknowledge me. *Good to see you, Fable* would be simple enough. It's a hello and goodbye all wrapped into one.

Instead, he looks over me, around me, everywhere but *at* me.

"Fuck you. I'm not going after your sister, you idiot." Chad/Brad/Ben pushes Philip right in the center of his chest.

Suddenly, his broad shoulders seem closer, and he's stumbling back toward me. I barely have time to register what's happening before I lift my hands to stop his momentum. But the effort is futile.

The overbearing scent of his cologne hits me first. Then his back collides with my hands, and the force of it knocks me off my feet. I'm toppling sideways like a bowling pin, Philip falling with me, and I'm sure we're about to land in a heap on the floor.

But instead.

A strong arm snakes around my waist, tugging me off course. With a startled yelp, I land on a firm thigh and watch as Philip crashes at my feet. He's a pile of khakis and red polo, groaning on the linoleum in a puddle of his own spilled beer, and I can't help grinning down at the sight.

My grin falters, though, when I realize there's a hand on my hip and a heady scent in my lungs. Like the woods on a warm summer afternoon. It flashes me right back to sunshine and childhood and sticky Popsicle-covered fingers and splashing into the pond at the farm.

My traitorous brain recognizes it immediately, and I turn to find a pair of gorgeous mocha eyes on me.

The sight of Theo Nikolaou wrenches all the air from my lungs.

"Hey there, Fabes," he says, his deep voice practically vibrating through me. A dark gray baseball cap sits backward on his head, his chestnut hair peeking out around the brim, and a blue plaid flannel stretches across his broad shoulders, rolled up to his elbows.

The loud bar muffles to a faint murmur as an arrogant, lopsided smile curls slowly over his lips. Dimples pop out on his tan cheeks, and my heartbeat goes annoyingly unsteady.

That's the smile that makes me feel like I'm ten years old again, whirling on a theme park ride until my stomach flips. It's the same smile he had when he beat me by one vote for president of the Ecology Club in eleventh grade. The same one he flashed when his baseball photo was plastered on the front page of the school paper. And the very same cocky smile he's worn anytime we've seen each other since.

Sometimes I want to slap it right off.

Other times . . . well, other times I don't know what I want.

The space between us crackles with years-worth of tension until an annoyed grumble echoes from the floor, and Theo's attention snaps in that direction. He reaches around me to fist the collar of Philip's shirt. "What the fuck?" he growls sharply. "You could've hurt her, you fucking asshole."

"Let go." Philip tries to swat his hand away.

My heart rate jumps at the flicker of Theo's jaw. The flare of his nostrils. The darkening of his eyes.

"Hey." A calm voice murmurs from across the table. Theo's best friend, Maddox, places a hand over Theo's fist. "She's all right."

Maddox's eyes don't leave Theo's as a silent conversation passes between them. It looks like one they've had before, no words necessary. Then, slowly, the fist in Philip's shirt loosens.

Theo blinks a few times and tugs me closer, as if to keep me from falling. His chest rises with a deep breath. "You okay?" he asks softly.

There's a commotion beside us as Chad/Brad/Ben helps Philip to his feet, but I can't pull my attention away from Theo.

"I don't know," I answer honestly, because right now I don't know much of *anything*. Basic math skills would be a challenge. One plus one equals Theo's dimples.

His gaze sharpens, and he wraps his free hand around my elbow. "Are you hurt?"

I open my mouth to answer, but my focus drifts to Philip as he stands beside the table.

Chad/Brad/Ben barks a laugh. "Dude, you got something on your pants."

Philip whips around, checking his slacks. "Dammit," he spits, pushing his friend and storming away. "These are *new*."

My lungs squeeze as I watch his retreating form. That asshole didn't even acknowledge me. Literally ran into me, and I *still* wasn't worth a glance.

Warm fingers settle on my chin, and Theo turns me toward him. His proximity has my mind spinning. I haven't seen him since he moved back to town two months ago, and even before that, when he showed up to a get-together with our families, we were never this close. We're barely even in the same room if I can help it.

But tonight, I'm close enough to see the tiny flecks of gold in his deep brown irises and the small scar across his eyebrow from a bike wreck when he was eleven. His smile lines have deepened over the years and a dark five-o'clock shadow now dusts his jaw, but everything else is exactly as I remember.

His eyes hold the same playfulness they did when I met him on the first day of fifth grade. I took my assigned seat in math class beside him, and an hour later, he sent over a folded note: *Do you want to be my best friend? Check yes or no. [ ] yes [ ] no*

We were always together after that, comparing answers and sharing a pencil sharpener for the entire year. He introduced me to his sister, Mia, a fourth grader, at recess one day, and our mothers became friends shortly after, weaving our childhoods together in intricate ways. Along with my sisters, Millie and Tessa, we built forts in the woods behind my parents' farm, spent summers swimming in the pond and picking thimbleberries in the back fields.

The five of us were inseparable.

Until everything changed.

"Hey," he whispers. "Want me to track him down? You say the word. I'm ready."

I shake my head. "He's not worth the jail time for murder."

His chuckle is easy and rich. "I was thinking we could spill something else on his fancy khakis, but by all means, I'll let you take the reins on this."

I feel a smile curve my lips, which is a completely foreign sensation when it comes to Theo. And it's enough to snap me out of whatever trance I've fallen into.

Sucking in a breath, I stand abruptly and busy myself with straightening the hem of my T-shirt, needing something to concentrate on other than the man before me.

Theo blinks up at me. "Chicken tenders night?"

I need to put some distance between us, physical and otherwise, so I quip, "Obnoxious lumberjack night?"

Those dimples are on display again, some inside joke I'm not privy to dancing through his eyes. "Is it the flannel?" He looks to his best friend. "It is, isn't it?"

Maddox snorts. "Definitely the flannel. Every time I see you, you're a little more lumberjack. If you have an axe under the table, Fable and I are calling an intervention."

"Lucky for you"—Theo gives him a withering look—"I left my axe at home." He turns to me. "How are you, Fabes?"

"Fine," I reply quickly. It's a generic, boring answer, but it's as much as we've given each other over the years. Between his sister and our mothers, I've gathered bits and pieces about him, but *fine* and *good* are as deep as our responses usually go.

"Everything going okay at the hardware store?" Theo tries.

Either my shirt's giving me away, or he's been told a few things about me as well. "Yep."

"And how about at the farm?"

"All good."

"How's your grandpa's A-frame?" Maddox wonders. "Are you still working on fixing it up?"

"It's a learning process." I bare my teeth in what I hope can pass for a smile. "But I'm figuring it out." Currently, "figuring it out" means "watching endless YouTube videos and trying not to break anything," but I leave those details out.

Theo folds his arms over his chest. "You'll give him full sentence answers, but not me?"

"Yep." I look around for Ethan, hoping to find a way out of this conversation.

Maddox huffs a laugh. "I get the feeling she *really* hates flannel."

"On second thought, I do have that axe. I just wasn't expecting to have to use it on my best friend," Theo says, eyes narrowed on Maddox.

Against my better judgment, I'm grinning. I try to bite it away before Theo notices.

"You'll back me up, right?" Maddox asks me. "I think the two of us could handle him. When we're done you can take the axe to the flannel if you want."

"Deal." I reach out to shake his hand, and Theo blinks back and forth between us, that classic smile still plastered in place.

"Here you go," Ethan interjects, setting a paper bag on the table. "Fable's chicken tender special. Extra ranch."

"Thank you." I fumble into my back pocket for my debit card.

"It's on the house tonight." He tips his head toward Philip's group. "About to ask that crew to leave. You okay?" Concern pinches his expression.

Gripping my bag of food, I assure him, "I'm fine. Thank you."

"If you want to stick around, someone just ordered soft pretzel sticks," Ethan says with a fond smile. "We've got Billy Joel all cued up."

Last year, he started a tradition to honor his late wife. When someone orders her favorite appetizer, Ethan plays her favorite song, "Just the Way You Are," by Billy Joel, and everyone flocks to the dance floor to celebrate her.

Theo stands and reaches out a hand, a smirk tugging at his lips. "Come on. Those chicken tenders can wait four minutes."

My pulse *whooshes* through my skull, panic racing in my veins along with it. I can still feel the imprint of his palm on my hip and smell his woodsy scent, and it's all too much. If I spend any more time with him, I'll start missing him. And if I start missing him . . . well, my heart already hurts too much for that.

"I've got, uh . . . I have to go," I blurt and beeline for the door, not looking back.

## Chapter 2

*Theo*

"Arthur?" I call, quietly opening the back door to the clinic.

No answer. I glance over my shoulder to check that it's really his car in the employee parking lot, and yep, it's hard to mistake that DRDOG vanity plate. Normally, he's more likely to stroll in around ten, after his two-eggs-and-pancakes breakfast at Kevin's Diner. And honestly, I don't blame the guy. When I'm seventy-four, I hope I get to mosey around at my own pace and show up to things whenever I want. Garrett, the clinic's other veterinarian, and I handle everything fine without Arthur anyway.

My ears perk at the sound of shuffling papers, and I follow the rustling to . . . *my* office. Arthur is hunched at my desk, sliding files around, mumbling to himself. It's likely he didn't hear me come in, given the fact that he refuses to wear his hearing aids when his wife isn't around to make him.

"Morning," I greet loudly from the doorway.

He peers up at me over the top of his glasses. "Theo. Good morning."

"You're so early I thought I might be hallucinating," I tease.

As he reaches for a file, his elbow bumps my cup of pens, sending them rolling across my desk. A low curse falls from his lips.

"Can I find something for you?" I ask, helping him gather them back up.

"Need to look at the financials," he mumbles, opening Grover's file like the Saint Bernard's vitals and test results might be hiding what he's looking for.

"Remember, Jenna helped us get all of that digitized last month?"

"But I need to see it in my hands," he explains, spreading them wide. "I don't know how to find it on the computer. I need paper."

I hide my smile. "I can help you."

Garrett and I have some version of this conversation with Arthur several times a week. He has been struggling with the digitization of our files since the beginning, no matter how many times we take him through the process of accessing things on his computer. The man is still using a flip phone, so it might be a hopeless case.

"I can print whatever you need," I offer, pointing to my computer. "Let me hop in that seat, and I'll pull it up."

He groans as he rises from my chair and moves to the spot by the door. While my computer boots up, Arthur stares at the two pictures on my desk. There's a framed photo of my dog, Layla, and I at the coast last summer. I'm snapping a selfie as her gritty tongue licks my cheek, a thick layer of sand covering her white-and-tan muzzle. Next to that is my favorite snapshot—I have an arm around my sister, Mia, on one side, and my mom on the other. We're all laughing in our matching penguin pajamas on Christmas morning, our image tilting to the side as the phone fell right when the self-timer ended.

The computer's welcome chime rings through the room. "All right, what are we printing?"

"Any financials from the last three years. I'm meeting with my lawyer later this week."

My fingers trip over the keys as I type in my password. "Lawyer?" I scan the screen and click open the spreadsheets I think he's looking for.

He shoves his glasses up his nose. "I'm getting old, Theo. About time I sold the practice."

I straighten my shoulders. "Really?" I've been wondering when this day would come, hoping for a chance to prove myself as the perfect person to buy it.

He nods. "Garrett and I are going to talk about it after I meet with my lawyer."

My stomach drops like I'm on an elevator falling thirty stories to the bottom. "Garrett? Why Garrett?" I croak. *Why not me too?*

His head tilts. "What do you mean?"

I swallow the lump in my throat. Fidget with the mouse in my grip. "I thought . . . well, I'd hoped to be considered as an option, I guess."

Arthur shifts in his seat. "Garrett has the experience needed for something like this."

Copper brushes my tongue as I bite the inside of my cheek to stop my words from spilling out. Since I came back to town Garrett and I have been running this place together. We've been splitting duties right down the middle. After-hours calls, opening early, leaving late.

*Together.*

Maybe it's irrational to think I stand a chance, but I'd love to at least discuss the option.

"Susie and I are ready to move closer to the kids," Arthur

informs me, face pensive. "You know, I have a new grandbaby due to arrive this summer, and I think it's about time for me to retire. I want to leave this place in the hands of someone stable and committed to this community, and Garrett's proven he is. He and I have similar styles, and I can see him running this place the way I have. He can keep the legacy alive."

I clench my jaw so hard I think I might crack a tooth. This clinic is running smoothly because Garrett and I balance each other out so well. "I'd really love a chance to be in the mix. I think Garrett and I could be a great team. Heck, we already are."

He offers me an apologetic smile. "Theo, I appreciate all you've done over the last two months. You're a hard worker, but you left this practice high and dry once. Who's to say you aren't going to do it again? Garrett's been here consistently for almost ten years."

Shame coils in my chest. My shoulders drop. He's right. I did leave, hardly more than a year into working here. I'd come back after college, thinking I was ready to build a life in my hometown. Fern River is where I grew up, made friends, and started to learn about myself. It's where most of my happy childhood memories are held.

But it's home to my worst ones too. It's the place where my dad's uncontrollable anger multiplied. It's where that anger trickled down to me, resulting in a very public screwup at the town parade—effectively ending my closest friendship. It's where I got in too many fights in high school and pushed away everyone I cared about.

It was painful to be in this town, reminded of every detail on a daily basis.

So when my grandparents' health started to decline and they asked for help, I jumped at the opportunity to move to their house in Oregon. It felt like the perfect way to escape the memories that were haunting me in Fern River.

Arthur sighs. "I don't want any bad blood between us, but my gut is telling me that Garrett is the right choice for this."

Clearing my throat, I open a few files on the computer. "I know I haven't been here as long as Garrett, but I've helped a lot in the time I have been." It feels ridiculous to beg, but I'm going to try anyway. "It's right here in these spreadsheets. Even adding in my salary, I've found ways to lower our overhead costs. I've increased the number of patients we can see every day and the amount of money we can donate back into the community."

He shakes his head. "And I appreciate all of that. This isn't to say you can't keep working here. I'm sure Garrett would love to have you on staff. But I've never gotten the impression you were settling down in Fern River permanently." Arthur waves a wrinkly hand across the hall, toward Garrett's closed office door. "This is his home, his community. He's not going anywhere."

I picture Garrett's office wall. It's a mural of memories. Photos of pets, hand-drawn art from kids, framed pictures of his work in the community—all hard evidence of the life he has built over the last ten years.

My office walls are bare. Stark white.

With a resigned sigh, I open the rest of the documents he needs.

The printer whirs to life in the hallway, and he stands. "You're a great vet, Theo, but this clinic is my life's work. It means the world to me. I need to know I'm leaving it in the hands of someone who will take care of it. Hopefully you'll understand one day." And with a pat to the doorframe, he walks out.

All the oxygen in the room leaves with him, and I deflate in my chair, staring at my desk in a daze. Distantly, I hear the back door open and footsteps in the hallway. Our office manager, Jenna, tosses me a greeting, but I don't even have the energy to respond.

Leaving Fern River years ago was an impulsive decision, but it felt like the only right choice in the moment. I don't regret the time I spent with my grandparents—those years were invaluable to me—but I ended up staying in Oregon longer than necessary. Even after they passed away, I spent two more years there, avoiding Fern River and the emotions that come along with it.

Life in Oregon was lonely, though. I had never let myself get settled there—never made friends or had relationships that lasted longer than one evening. I felt like my life was on pause. I was holding my breath, waiting for something I couldn't identify.

Then, a few months ago, Mom called. She was going on about work she needed done on the house, the gardening technique she wanted to try, her book club's pick that month, and giving me updates on the Oaks family. All mundane things we chat about regularly. But somewhere in that conversation, an overwhelming sense of homesickness washed over me. *Home* was calling to me in a way that it never had before. When I started looking for jobs, this position with Arthur immediately popped up, and it felt like a sign. I had a gut feeling that it might be time to try again.

I don't know what's different now—maybe it's the town or maybe it's me—but something seems fresh this time, like a clean slate. I finally feel ready to settle. Put down roots. I want to rejoin the Volunteer Fire Department, get involved with Little League, and make a permanent place for myself here. I'd love to heal my relationship with this town and make new memories to snuff out the bad ones.

But unfortunately, it might be too late to convince Arthur of that.

My phone buzzes on the desk, and my sister's face brightens the screen.

I try to sound like nothing's wrong as I bring the phone to my ear. "Hey. How are you?"

"Has Mom made it there yet?" Mia asks in a rush.

My brows furrow. "What do you mean? I'm at work."

"Yeah, I know. I am too." I roll my eyes, picturing my sister *at work*—which means she's curled up in the corner of her couch with her laptop, in her most comfortable loungewear. There's probably an iced latte nearby. "She's not there?"

"No. Should she be?"

"Perfect. I want to hear what happens when she arrives."

I rub my temple. "Mia, what the hell is going on?"

"What's going on," she replies, sounding annoyed, "is you're keeping secrets from me, and you better believe I'm going to get you back for this."

A familiar voice echoes from the clinic's lobby. "—need to chat with him before his first patient," Mom says, and I can't make out Jenna's reply, but then Mom's voice sounds closer as she adds, "Thank you!"

"She's here," I announce warily.

A squeal of excitement leaps through the phone. "You're in deep shit, big brother. Now put me on speaker and pretend I'm not here."

I follow her instructions (mostly because I'm too curious not to at this point) and set the phone on my desk right as Mom appears in the doorway.

"Theodore Alexander Nikolaou," she says sharply.

Oh shit. My middle name. Must be serious. "If this is about the gutters, I promise I'm going to get to them this weekend."

She crosses her arms and glares down at me, looking exactly like she did every time she found out I'd gone to detention for fighting. But I haven't been in a fight in . . . well, I guess I almost was last night. If Maddox hadn't been there to calm me down, I think I would've really enjoyed the crunch of Philip's nose against my fist.

Instead, I found his phone under our table—where it must've fallen out of his pocket when he tumbled to the ground—and being the mature, twenty-nine-year-old that I am, I turned the phone off and hid it behind the dumpster at the bar. A sick sort of pleasure warms my chest at the thought of him searching for it. Fuck him for crashing into Fable and not even bothering to apologize. I couldn't stand him in high school and turns out I still can't.

"You know exactly what this is about." Mom's eyes narrow. "When were you going to tell me you're *dating Fable*?"

My brain stumbles. I open my mouth. Then shut it. Then open it again. Surely, I heard her wrong. "*What?*"

"You and Fable. Together."

Standing quickly, I pull her farther into the office. "Mom, I don't know what you're talking about."

"Cathy sent the photo an hour ago," she explains as she sits down. Cathy? What does that busybody have to do with this? "I tried to give you time to tell me yourself, but I called your sister, and *she* had no clue."

"Hold on. I'm lost—"

"Then I called *Mary* and she didn't even know!"

I shake my head. "You called Fable's mom before you called me?"

"Well, of course. We've been dreaming of this for years."

I drag a hand down my face. "There's apparently been some sort of mix-up."

"Show him the picture," Mia calls through the speaker.

Mom's expression softens. "Aw, is that my baby?"

"Yes. Hey, Mama. Hand him your phone."

She pulls it out of her purse and offers it over the desk. I type in her passcode, and the screen immediately reveals the image.

It's a grainy shot, taken in the bar last night, but there's enough detail to make out that it's clearly me, with Fable in my lap and my fingers on her chin.

My mind transports me right back there, where I can see every freckle across the pink apples of her cheeks. That sparkle of the gold hoop decorating her nose. Those honey-blond strands framing her face. The way her hazel eyes snared mine. The feel of her in my lap, her jean-covered hip against my palm. That tiny glimpse of the flowers tattooed on her wrist.

We look . . . fuck, we look like we're together. It must be the lighting.

"I should've FaceTimed," Mia grumbles. "Mom, what is he doing?"

"Smiling at the picture," she replies, and I immediately clear my throat and hand the phone back.

I don't know what's going on here, but I need to rein in this situation before it goes any further. "I haven't been keeping any secrets."

Well, that's a slight lie. The crush I had on Fable managed to stay a secret. For the last eighteen years, that information has stayed locked inside a cage in my chest. More like in a cage, in a vault, hidden behind a brick wall. Or two. I figure if I don't give it any attention, it won't come back to life.

Arthur's voice trails in from the hallway. "Theo, I was hoping—" He stops in the doorway. "Oh, hello, Eva. How are you?"

Mom grins proudly. "I'm great. It's a wonderful day, isn't it?"

As I study her expression, I'm suddenly—terrifyingly—aware of what she's about to say. It's like I'm watching in slow motion as a wildfire jumps the firebreak and spreads.

"I just found out my son is dating Fable Oaks." She clasps her hands under her chin. "We've been waiting so long for this day."

Yep, there it is. Fuck.

I look to Arthur in time to see a flicker of movement in his brows. It's subtle, but I've spent enough time with him to know he's processing something. He looks to me. "I had no idea. You and Fable, huh?" There's that flicker of his brows again. At first, I don't know what to make of it, but then he says, "Well, I saw Dave last night at our birding club. How dare he not tell me? That's great, Theo."

And the puzzle pieces seem to slip into place. *The Oaks family.*

You'd have to work pretty hard to find a more beloved family around here. Dave and Mary Oaks are pillars of this town. They're involved in every community event, are first to volunteer anytime someone needs a hand, and according to my mother, they're a part of countless group activities. I don't know how they have time to run their farm in between.

Their oldest daughter, Tessa, is the outgoing organizer. She ran the entire holiday festival at the age of fifteen—when the original committee leader came down with the flu—and has been doing it ever since, even though she lives in Chicago. Millie, the middle daughter, started a pollinator garden in every park in town and makes a point of checking on all of them when she comes to visit. And Fable, the youngest, the town sweetheart. Could usually be found with her nose in a book or a soccer ball at her feet. Sometimes both. She's the only Oaks sister who lives here now, and everyone knows her. Everyone loves her, exactly as they have since we were little.

They're an integral part of the community.

The community that Garrett has put roots into.

The same community that matters so much to Arthur.

I only have half a heartbeat to decide how to respond. It's not enough time to fully process what I'm even saying before the words are already coming out of my mouth. But when Arthur steps farther into the room and offers me a "Congratulations," I don't correct him or set the record straight.

Instead, I say something that immediately makes me wonder if I'm losing my mind. Something Fable will probably kill me for.

I reply, "Thank you."

\* \* \*

THE CLINIC IS a mad rush for the next few hours. Garrett and I see patients back-to-back, then we work together on an emergency surgery through lunch. And all the while, I'm scouring for a few spare minutes to try to get a hold of Fable. I don't even know if she'll answer my calls, but I need to get to her before Arthur runs into her somewhere. Or my mother does. Or her mother does. This has probably already spread further than I meant it to.

I'm jogging back to my office to finally grab my phone when Arthur calls my name, and I skid to a stop.

He's sitting at his desk, the papers I printed spread out in front of him. "Come on in." He pulls off his glasses and points them toward the empty chair.

The seat creaks as I drop into it, nerves prickling beneath my skin. "Everything okay?"

"I've been thinking about what you said this morning. Looking over all of this." He sweeps the papers into a neat stack. "And you're right. Things have improved since you started working here again. The office is running more smoothly thanks to your work with Jenna on the schedule, and I'm seeing the evidence of it in the financials."

"Thank you," I reply, unsure what else to say.

He gives me a stern look, hands folded together on the desk. "Please be honest with me. Are you staying in Fern River? Is this where you want to be?"

The questions surprise me. I hold my breath, gauging my answer. *Is this where I want to be?*

I used to be sure it wasn't. I used to take every opportunity to be somewhere else.

But this time, something's different. This feels like the closest I've ever been to finding *home*.

"Yes. Yes, sir." I nod. "It's where I want to be."

He studies me for a long moment. Finally, he says, "I'll consider allowing you and Garrett to buy the practice together. But nothing is decided yet. I want to know for sure that you're sticking around here. I'll be frank, settling down with Fable is a great start, but I need to know you want to stay permanently. I don't want to leave Garrett in a bind by trusting you."

A tentative spark of hope ignites in my chest. "Right. Absolutely."

"I'd like you and Garrett to take charge on the adopt-a-thon next month. Coordinate with the shelter. Plan the events and get involved in the community part of it. Show me you can be a good team, then I'll decide about the practice."

I nod. "I can do that."

"I'll talk to Garrett," Arthur says. "Make sure he knows the plan."

"Thank you." I stand and reach across the desk to shake his hand. "I won't let you down. I promise." That spark of hope flares brighter. I might have a chance with this.

But as I leave his office, the reality of how I got that chance settles like a lead weight in my stomach. Accepting his congratulations about Fable was one thing—but this suddenly feels much bigger. I've just fabricated an entire relationship to make myself look better in his eyes.

And my only chance at making this right involves talking to Fable. And crossing my fingers she doesn't try to murder me for what I've done.

## Chapter 3

*Fable*

"Knocks, I think we're cursed." I nudge a bucket under the dripping pipe. Every time I think I've finally managed to stop this leak, I run into a new problem.

My tortoiseshell kitten nudges at my elbow, trying to worm his way under the bathroom sink to see what I'm doing.

"No, buddy. I actually don't need your help for this." I drop the pipe wrench so I can set him back a few feet behind me. He gives me a sassy *meow* in response. "You're already on my naughty list after the shit you pulled with my phone cord. I don't need you making this worse."

His dark eyes blink once, completely unapologetic about the fact that my phone is now dead because he chewed through the charging cable.

I pull my laptop onto my thighs and press play on the video. The man on the screen explains the steps to cut and replace the piping while I make a supply list on the back of a receipt. When the video ends, I walk outside to shut off the water to the A-frame. At least while I'm at work today, I don't have to worry about that small leak turning into a flood.

On my way back down the hall, my feet pause in front of the

downstairs bedroom door. I take a deep breath, bracing myself for my routine check-in as I turn the knob.

Dust particles dance through the sunlight streaming in from the window. They drift over the stacks of boxes, a sheet-covered armchair, and the table that sat in Gramps's kitchen for as long as I can remember.

This room is a time capsule, holding memories for me that I'm too afraid to examine closely. Opening any of these boxes—seeing his books, blankets, puzzles, Christmas ornaments—would hurt too much. So they stay tucked in this room. Frozen in time. Undisturbed.

He's still everywhere in and around this cabin. In the kitchen, where he used to make me and my sisters cups of tea every afternoon. In the living room, where he read me stories while I did puzzles. In the dining area, where we labeled jars of his fresh thimbleberry jam. On the back porch, where we sat, watching the seasons change.

After Gramps died two years ago, my sisters and I spent a weekend here, putting everything in boxes until Dad could decide what to do with it. When our parents started having conversations a few months ago about how run-down the property had gotten, they hinted at selling it, and I couldn't let that happen. The thought of someone else owning this place made me nauseous.

Knocks brushes my ankle as he steps two paws into the room. "No, no, no," I whisper, pulling him back. "This isn't for you." It isn't for me, either—touching anything in this room would feel like poking at an infected wound.

I scoop him up and glance over everything for one more long moment before carefully shutting the door.

"He would've loved you though," I murmur, nuzzling my cheek against Knocks's head as I walk to the kitchen to make tea.

While the kettle heats up, I pluck the to-do list from the fridge and add a few items to it. The list seems to be growing instead of dwindling. There are some bigger, safety-related items that need to be done as soon as possible, like fixing the broken steps, replacing all the smoke detectors, leveling the house, and stabilizing the railing on the stairs.

Then there are things that would be nice to fix, like getting some insulation under the house before next winter and figuring out why it takes about seven years for the water to get warm in the shower.

Last, there are items on the list that I think would be fun. Like painting the hallway to brighten it up and removing the wall that Gramps always talked about taking down to open up the kitchen. Those are bonus tasks that I dream about getting to accomplish.

Altogether, this is a huge project. But I'm determined to tackle it. I need to prove to myself that I can accomplish something.

High school Fable was successful. Motivated. Top of the class, full of plans, and executing them to the highest degree.

Then something happened. A switch flipped during my first semester of college, and all that motivation vanished.

For years, I haven't been able to find the path I'm meant to be on, and that has led to many failed attempts along the way.

My family has rallied behind me for every new idea I've had. Going to college? They got bumper stickers and helped me move in. Dropping out? Mom found me an apartment and searched job pages with me. Going to be a waitress? Family trip to Seattle to visit the restaurant. A barista now? Perfect, we have a new spot to get coffee. The flower shop is hiring? That's amazing, we love flowers! The hardware store? Here, you need your own tool belt!

They show up every time. Full excitement. They've helped me move to and from Seattle, paid out the rest of my lease when I couldn't, let me live with them for the last two years, reassured me, "This is the right decision," every time I switched jobs. They help me clean up the mess, sweep it under the rug, and we move on like nothing happened.

And I love them. *God*, I love them so much.

But every time they pick me back up, there's this *look* on all their faces. It's a knowing, we-saw-this-coming look, and I don't even think they realize they're doing it.

*That's all right. Don't worry about it. Life happens, sweetie.*

My self-confidence crumbles in the face of it. I'm chaotic, unsuccessful Fable—moved back home because I couldn't get my life together. And even though they've *never* said those words, that's exactly how it feels.

The truth is, when it comes to this A-frame project, something feels *imperative* about it. It's fundamental. Foundational. I can't move on until I've done this and seen it through to the end. It may not be perfect or easy, but I'm determined to keep trying for Gramps. He deserves my greatest effort.

I add *fix bathroom sink piping* right under where I'd crossed it off last night, thinking I'd resolved it for the second time. I pin the list back on Gramps's vintage sage-green fridge beside the only picture I have displayed in the house.

My ten-year-old smile and Gramps's sixty-seven-year-old smile shine back at me from the grainy photo. We're crouching beside the flower bed in front of the A-frame—where his pink, orange, and yellow tulips blossomed every spring. He has that sparkle in his eye that was reserved just for his granddaughters.

That sparkle began dimming a few years ago, when he was diagnosed with Alzheimer's.

"Can you read to me?" Gramps would ask, and I would. *The Hobbit*, *My Side of the Mountain*, and *Julie of the Wolves*. All books he introduced me to. His favorites.

"Remind me again about the bookstore we're going to open," he'd say, and I'd recount every detail he'd lined out for me over the years. The cozy chairs in the back corner, the plants in the front windows, the free books on the stoop, because in his words, "everyone needs a story."

"Tell me about my Hazel," he'd request, and even though Grandma passed away when my dad was a child, I'd tell him every story I'd heard over the years. About her favorite flower, the tulips he tended in her honor. About their wedding in the mountains, with only their parents and the birds to witness their vows.

Slowly—heartbreakingly—Gramps began to forget those tulips, forget his favorite books, forget the secret to opening Baby Blue's door, until we were left to carry those memories.

But no matter how many memories there are, it's not enough to fill the giant hole left behind by his loss.

The kettle squeals, and I startle, blinking to clear my vision. Making Gramps's perfect cup of tea soothes my heart a bit. I let it steep for a few minutes, then add a tablespoon of cream—exactly how he taught me.

Then I lift my warm mug toward the photo on the fridge. "Cheers." I swallow a sip and close my eyes, doing my best to recreate the little hum of contentedness he used to make. "Happy Birthday, Gramps."

\* \* \*

I'M STOCKING THE shelves with a million types of light bulbs (Why the hell are there so many different options?) when I realize I left the supply list at home. It's probably still sitting on the bathroom floor. Unless Knocks has found it and shredded it by now.

I reach for my phone to find the video again, only to remember it's still dead. "Fuck," I hiss quietly. Pushing the cart of light bulbs to the side, I walk toward the front counter in search of a charger.

"You doin' okay?" Logan, my boss, pops into my path at the end of the aisle, concern etched across his face. The overhead lights glint off his glasses as he tilts his head. "Heard you say *fuck*. Did that handle get you again?" He reaches for my hand to examine the scar on my palm. A sharp piece of metal cut me last week, and he had the first aid kit out in half a second and was dragging the cart away once I was bandaged up.

Logan is known around town as a grump, but he's been nothing but a softie to me my whole life. When I walked in here a few months ago looking for a job, he had me working twenty minutes later, no questions asked.

"No, I'm fine." The bell at the front of the store jingles as someone opens the door. "My phone is just—" I start, but my brain-to-mouth wires get tangled when Theo appears around the corner.

He's wearing navy blue scrubs that look perfectly tailored to his muscular frame. If there was a trophy for Sexiest Scrubs, those would win, hands-down. His chestnut hair is a little messier than normal, like he's been running his fingers through it, and somehow his presence seems to take up so much *space* in here. My gaze dips down his frame, and the sight of his wide chest and strong thighs make me irrationally angry.

I hate that I notice any of it.

I hate that I've run into him two days in a row now.

I hate that I can still feel the ghost of his palm on my hip from last night.

I hate that every time I see him, my heart picks up the pace and something fluttery happens in my stomach.

But mostly, I hate the fact that I don't actually hate that feeling at all.

"Fabes, thank goodness you're here," he says, stopping beside Logan and letting out a relieved breath.

I'm caught off guard for a moment. He's here to see *me*? Why?

"This is where I *work*. Of course I'm here. What are *you* doing here?"

Theo looks to Logan, then to me, then back to Logan, before turning and grabbing the nearest item off a shelf. "I was uh . . . looking for these."

Logan smothers a snort of laughter.

"Do you think I could ask you a few questions about"—Theo peers down at the package in his hands—"magnetic drill adapters?" He widens his eyes and tips his head toward the next aisle, clearly requesting we chat privately.

Logan glances at his watch. "I was about to head over to the coffee shop. Fable, you want your usual?"

"Yes, please." I bite back my knowing smile. He really thinks I haven't noticed his frequent trips to visit a certain employee next door. "Is Mabel working today?"

"Not sure," he says, doing an awful job at pretending he doesn't have her schedule memorized by now. He rounds the corner, and the bell jingles over the door as he leaves.

"Logan and Mabel, huh?" Theo whispers as we watch Logan through the window, tucking in his shirt and turning toward the coffee shop.

"His coffeepot is 'on the fritz,'" I explain in my best imitation of Logan's voice.

"Suspicious." Theo shoves the drill adapter back onto the shelf. "But cute."

When his gaze meets mine, an uncomfortable silence stretches between us. I don't know why he's here or what he wants from me, but being alone with him is . . . unnerving. There's a tense feeling beneath my skin when it's just the two of us, and I'm already too aware of it.

That's when I notice his cheeks are rosy and he's breathing heavily. The vet clinic is on the opposite side of town square, which isn't very far for a man who goes on five-mile runs every morning.

Not that I know about that or anything.

"Did you run here?" I ask, suspicious.

"No, no." He runs a hand through his hair. "Definitely didn't run."

My eyes narrow. "Then what's wrong with you?" It comes out harsher than I intended, but I don't take it back. I need answers. Now. Before this uncomfortable feeling has time to sink any deeper into the pit of my stomach.

A smirk plays on his lips. "That's a great question. How much time do you have?"

A growl sneaks out of my throat before I can control it. Is it too much to ask that we just get to the point? I don't have the time or the patience for his teasing. Or his annoying grin. Or that mischievous look in his eyes. "Just let me know when you're ready to check out," I grumble, turning back toward the cart of light bulbs.

## Chapter 4

## *Theo*

*I* need a plan here. Running over on a whim wasn't a plan, but that seems to be a trend with me today: making decisions before I've thought them through.

As Fable slides boxes onto the shelf, my gaze wanders, sweeping over her pink cheeks and long lashes. Her hair hangs in a braid down her back, and a Hawkins Hardware shirt sits above a pair of loose jeans, their legs rolled up above her black Converse sneakers.

Goddamn, she's beautiful. This happens every time I'm around her—I lose track of what I'm supposed to be doing and just end up staring and fumbling over myself.

We'll start slow. Ease her into a full conversation. Maybe that will get me back on track. I grab the next box from the cart and offer it to her.

"If you're here for a job, I don't think handing me light bulbs is going to impress Logan. Especially when he's not even here." She gives me a droll look but takes the box.

"No, not here for a job." What the fuck *am* I doing? I probably should've practiced with Maddox or something.

The bell dings over the door, drawing our focus as Mr. Garfield, our high school calculus teacher, steps inside.

"Then hurry up, because I'd like to keep mine," she hisses. Then her expression transforms into a bright customer service smile as she greets Mr. Garfield.

"Two of my favorite students," he says warmly. "Although I can't say I've seen you together like this. Have you finally put aside your differences?"

Fable lets out a sarcastic snort under her breath. "Not at all," she says at the same moment I tell him, "Absolutely."

Poor Mr. Garfield really saw us at our worst. By the time we entered his class in twelfth grade, our rivalry had reached its peak. There were many days where he had to stop Fable and me from arguing about the best way to solve a problem, even though both of us had ended up with the correct answer.

I flash him a wide smile. Maybe the way to endear myself to Fable is to remind her how much fun we had competing. "I've totally forgiven her for that point-one GPA win. And she has forgiven me for the fact that everyone laughed way harder at my graduation speech."

A haughty *humph* sounds from beside me. "They did not."

"Did too," I insist.

Fable grumbles something incoherent under her breath.

Mr. Garfield is rightfully confused, his gaze bouncing between us. "Well, okay," he says with a forced grin. "Good to see you both. I need to find some painter's tape."

"Aisle two." Fable directs him.

"Thank you," he calls, disappearing from view.

When I hand the next box over, she glowers at me and snatches it with more force than before. Okay, apparently the competitive angle didn't work. I'll try a straightforward approach. "So, you know the picture of us from last night?"

Something startles behind her eyes. "What picture?"

"The one everybody's talking about this morning?"

She cuts a look my way. "What are you saying? My phone has been dead all day."

"The picture." I pull out my phone, swipe to the image, and turn it in her direction. "This one."

She goes still, lips parted. Her gaze bounces all over the image before she grabs my phone and zooms in. Her pulse flickers rapidly in the column of her throat as she scowls at the image.

*Damn, I don't think she's seen this yet.*

I try to lighten the mood. "We look pretty good together, huh?"

She ignores my question. "Let me guess, Cathy took this?"

"Yeah. She sent it to our moms."

The corners of her mouth tighten. "For fuck's sake, Cathy."

"Excuse me." We both jump at the sound of Mr. Garfield's voice. "Where can I find the spackling paste?"

"Uh, aisle four," Fable replies distractedly, turning to give him a quick grin.

When she whirls back to me, she shoves the phone into my chest. "This is fine. Annoying, but fine. It's a stupid picture of a moment I'd love to forget. I don't think you needed to run all the way here to show me." She tips up her chin stubbornly and reaches for another box.

Objectively, this isn't going well so far. We're getting further and further from any sort of conversation that leads to *Hey, so what if we pretend we're dating for a bit?* What *does* lead to a conversation like that? How do I even bring it up with someone who's so clearly annoyed by my presence? Competitive memories didn't help. Practical and straightforward didn't help. Maybe I flirt with her?

It's worth a try. I'm pretty good at it, I think.

"*Love to forget*, huh? Because that flush on your cheeks is telling me a different story." I playfully nudge her elbow with mine and she lets out a small growl before stalking to the end of the aisle.

Fable turns to whisper-yell over her shoulder. "My face is red because I'm pissed that you're here."

Well, that may be true. She seems to operate in a constant state of pissed at me, but fuck me, I love every second of it. "You missed an epic dance party last night," I say, following after her. "We were having so much fun that Ethan played the song twice."

"Cool." She rounds the corner, pacing quickly down the paint aisle.

"It's okay. You can owe me a dance next time."

She whips around fast, and I stop just in time for her finger to land in the center of my chest. "How is it possible you've gotten more annoying over the years?" Her hazel eyes spark as she glares up at me.

My heart beats faster. "How is it possible you've gotten more stubborn?"

Her eyes burn even brighter, and the air seems to vibrate between us. She's all sass and freckles and fire, and it's adorable. Irresistible. Her finger digs into my chest a little farther, and I'm not sure if it's because I'm leaning closer or she's pushing me back.

The bell over the door breaks our stare, and she shakes her head, dropping her finger. "Please go back to your own job. I've reached the maximum amount of time I can spend with you without losing my mind."

Well, the flirting didn't work, but it was the most fun. Noted.

The customer strolls slowly down the aisle, so I lower my voice. "There's more I have to tell you."

She crosses her arms. "You have one minute."

"Um." I grab a paintbrush, so I have something to hold as I stumble through my next words. Time to go all-in, I guess. "Arthur is selling the practice, and he was originally going to sell it to Garrett. Because I guess he doesn't trust that I'm going to stick around long enough. He doesn't think I'm planning to stay."

"Okay." Her tone asks, *Why are you telling me this?*

"Sooo." I drag out the word, trying to find my angle. I move closer, giving her my best smile—the one that I know brings out my dimples. They've worked to my advantage in the past, and I need all the help I can get for this harebrained idea. "This morning, Mom showed up with the picture, going on and on about how happy she is that you and I are together."

"Together?!" she shrieks, so loudly that the customer a few feet away lets out a startled *yelp*.

"I'm sorry," I whisper to the customer, who scowls at Fable. Then I see Mr. Garfield peering over the top of a shelf. I reach for Fable's arm and steer her toward the back corner of the store.

"Me and you?" She motions between us, a disbelieving look on her face.

"I mean, yeah." I stop us beside the boxes of nails. "You saw it. That picture looks . . . pretty convincing." She groans up at the ceiling, and I steal the opportunity to blurt out the rest of it. "So, here's the thing. I didn't correct her and then kind of also let Arthur believe it. Sort of accidentally."

There's a silent pause where the earth stands still. Neither of us moves or breathes, and I'd bet Mr. Garfield and the other customer are holding their breaths to listen too.

Then the earth snaps back to life and Fable's eyes go wide. "*Together?!* We aren't even *friends*!"

"Ouch." I pretend to pull something from my heart and hold it out to her on my open palm. "Here's your dagger back."

She stares up at me, unblinking.

"We're . . . friends." I rub my hand over the side of my neck. "Or at least friend*ly*."

"On what planet?"

*Wow. This is going great.*

"Okay. Jeez. I get it." I rack my brain for a time I might've done something friendly. "What about when I brought your favorite wine to your parents' holiday party?"

She rolls her eyes. "That's your mom's favorite too."

"What about when I drove you to the airport a few years ago?"

"Mia had a flight too. You were basically our Uber driver."

I tip my head back and forth. "Unpaid, but I guess that's fair since you both sat in the back seat anyway." Shifting on my feet, I try, "Oh, what about last summer at your mom's birthday party. We played Catan with your sisters and Finn? We were friendly then."

"Do you not remember me yelling at you across the table? I almost knocked you out of your chair when you blocked my settlement."

"I remember." I smile fondly.

Another person enters the store and Fable groans. "My god, there have *never* been this many people here." She looks over her shoulder, and we both spot the new customer at the same time.

"Cathy," we whisper.

Fable turns back to glare at me, and I know this is my last chance. While I'd love to give her more time to process this information, time is a luxury I don't have.

"Fabes, listen. What if we . . . pretend we're in a relationship? I'm fighting an uphill battle here, and I need all the help I can get." She looks taken aback, but I keep going. "I'll seem more settled and like I'm putting down roots around here. Because, hell, you're practically Fern River royalty. Everyone loves your family." Her lips part, a rebuttal forming quickly, but I power through to the end. "I'm willing to help you somehow in return. Just name your price."

Her head shakes immediately. "Theo, that's ridiculous. And I don't need anything from you."

Behind Fable, I see Cathy turn our way. I only have seconds left to seal the deal. "*Please.*" Suddenly, inspiration strikes. "I could help with the A-frame. I worked in apartment maintenance all through college. I can do pretty much anything you need."

For three long seconds, she just stares at me. Then she asks pointedly, "Why don't you just find yourself a *real* girlfriend?"

The list of reasons why I don't do relationships scrolls through my mind. *Because I won't let myself. Because it's not safe. Because I can't repeat what my dad did.*

But none of that is going to come out of my mouth standing beside the nail selection at Hawkins Hardware. "I can't, Fabes. I don't do relationships. That's why you might be the only solution here."

Her head tilts. Unease twists in my stomach. She's either considering it or debating how she's going to kill me with the nails beside her. "No," she finally decides, lifting her chin. "You and I can barely be in the same room without bickering. No one would believe it. And I can fix the A-frame on my own. I don't need your help."

"But—" I start, my voice coming out strained.

Mr. Garfield comes into view beside us. "I found the spackling, but you all seem to be out of scrapers," he says, headed our way. Fable doesn't give me a second glance before she turns and leads him toward the next aisle.

She's already out of sight when I finish, "But what if I need *your* help?"

## Chapter 5

*Fable*

"Let me know if those work." I slide the box of screws across the counter to Cathy. "If they don't, call us and we can special order some."

She got me into this mess with Theo, and I can tell her blue eyes are glittering with questions. I saw her stalling as she walked around the store, waiting for her chance to press me about Theo. But I've refused to indulge her. I've done my own stalling, hoping Logan will walk back in and rescue me. He has very little patience for nosy people and even less patience for Cathy. When there was a rumor of a feud between Logan and Diana, who owns the thrift shop, apparently Cathy pestered him for details until he got so frustrated that he shouted, "For fuck's sake, Cathy!"

That was very offensive to her delicate ears, but it's become a secret motto around town.

"I appreciate your help." Cathy leans her hands on the counter. "Again, so sorry for interrupting you and Theo—"

Logan slips into view just in time, with two to-go cups from Coffee Cottage. Cathy presses her lips together, tips her chin up, and walks toward the exit. Logan tucks one cup into his elbow to grab the door for her.

"Logan." She stares down her nose at him as she leaves.

He dips his chin in greeting and once the door shuts behind him, we both murmur, "For fuck's sake, Cathy." We have matching grins as he hands me a cup.

"Thank you. What did you get today?"

"Some lavender honey shit." He brings it to his lips for a wary sip and shrugs. "It's not half bad."

"Mabel really knows what she's talking about, huh?" For a man whose office coffeepot looks like it was made fifty years ago, Logan's been awfully adventurous with his drinks when Mabel's serving them. Last week, it was some sort of mango-flavored concoction and yesterday he came back with what he called a rainbow latte.

I'm starting to wonder is she's pranking him at this point.

His cheeks flush pink and he clears his throat. "She's good at her job."

"She must be. Got you trying all kinds of stuff." I hide a smile behind my cup.

He takes another sip. "What's that look for?"

"You know, just thinking about how much you're visiting Mabel lately."

One brow arches. "I see. And how often is Theo going to be visiting now?"

I choke on my tea, spewing it across the lid. "Not at all!"

"Oh, don't kid yourself, Fable." He shakes his head, turning to walk toward his office. "You're smarter than that. That boy was fumbling all over himself in front of you."

"No, he was scared of *you*," I call after him, but he just chuckles.

With a huff, I drop onto the stool behind the counter and stare out across downtown. The long, open park has a gazebo in the center, where carolers sing in the winter and kids eat drippy ice cream cones in the summer. A farmers' market fills the northwest corner every Saturday from May until the end of October, and when there's a festival, the whole block comes to life right before your eyes.

On the other side, at the far corner of downtown, I can just make out the blue-trimmed building where Theo works. It's not that I sit here watching for him, but I do happen to see him coming or going through those doors occasionally. Sometimes he has lunch or a coffee in his hands and sometimes he's walking a dog in the park.

I can't help but notice him. It's the same tic that makes me look for him early in the mornings when he runs by the A-frame. And the same one that made me hyperaware of him every day of high school. It's a homing beacon in my brain that won't shut the hell up when he's around. It makes me want to get as far away from him as possible so I don't have to hear it.

My stomach twists when I remember his idea. *Pretend to be together?*

It's insane. Ridiculous. No one in town would even believe it after the parade incident.

The moment that changed everything for us.

We were fourteen—the summer before freshman year—and newly assigned to our high school athletics teams. It was my first event with the girls' soccer crew, and I was nervous as hell, hoping to make a good impression. Football, baseball, soccer, golf, and swim team were all walking in the parade just before the marching band.

Theo had been quiet all morning—uncharacteristically broody and closed off. Mia and her mom were notably absent from the event, and all of it together had my nerves prickling. Something was going on, and I had no idea what it was. And no time to ask him.

As our section of the parade reached downtown, Theo was

walking beside me, arguing with Todd, one of the guys on his baseball team, about who knows what. All of a sudden their argument escalated. To this day, I don't know who started it or how it happened so quickly, but before I could fully focus on it, Theo's nose was bleeding, and he was throwing a punch back at Todd.

Everything got out of hand in an instant. Todd stumbled back with a shout. I tried to get out of the way and tripped over my soccer ball, rolling my ankle in the process. And as I tumbled to the ground, I remember thinking that the marching band sounded really good together.

That was until the front row tripped. Over me.

They toppled. Fell like dominoes around me—trombones, baritones, French horns, trumpets. Instruments were colliding, loud honking sounds blasting out of them as their momentum came to a stop.

There were people shouting, music still playing from a parade float somewhere, and plenty of laughter, but all that faded away when I looked up at Theo from the ground. He had blood running down his chin and a wild look in his eyes. I watched his lips shift around my name, and then he was gone. Running without a single glance back.

Within days, the photos and video had spread. People found it hilarious—the contrast of the adorable, small-town parade, floats and balloons and flowers everywhere, the angry teenagers fighting in the middle of it, and the girl who brought the entire thing to a screeching halt. *Good Morning America* cohosts were commenting on it, Kevin's Diner was hanging a poster-size image of the incident on the wall, and it was the talk of the town for way longer than necessary. It was so public, so *seen* by everyone, that there was no way to escape it.

Of course, the most embarrassing moment of my life would happen right before I started high school. The girls on the soccer team brought it up at every practice that summer, teasing me about the incident and stoking my fury with Theo over the whole thing. It was humiliating to be the laughingstock of the team I'd worked to be a part of, and Theo's temper had been the cause of it.

The day after the parade, my parents told me Theo and Mia would be spending the summer with their grandparents in Oregon, and I didn't see them again for months.

It wasn't until school was about to start in the fall that my parents explained what was happening in their family. I was angry, hurt, and devastated and had no idea how to sort through those feelings when it came to Theo. It took Mia and me only minutes to get back to normal when we reunited. But Theo and I never recovered. He came back to town with a dark shadow around him, two fresh scars on his nose and jaw, a new long-distance girlfriend in Oregon, and no comment about the parade.

And I couldn't forget the fact that he'd deserted me. He'd caused the entire scene and ran away. Left me to deal with the fallout.

Now I can put together the pieces and see how hard that summer must've been for him. I can forgive him for the fight and the parade—he was going through a lot at the time—but we've never made it back to our friendship. We're on opposite sides of a giant ravine. Over the years that space has filled with snippy comments and avoided conversations. Angry glares on my part and arrogant smirks on his. Our rivalry in high school became a self-fulfilling prophecy at some point—egged on by everyone around us.

Which begs the question, Why would anyone even believe Theo and I could be together now?

\*\*\*

From my spot on the ground, I watch the light-gray clouds slip across my view. The raised wooden garden beds on either side of me fill the air with the earthy smell of fresh soil. My parents wander the garden around me, having some sort of mild disagreement about the placement of the cabbage versus the broccoli, but Dad will give in eventually and push full steam ahead with Mom's idea.

They didn't bat an eye when I wandered into the garden and plopped myself in middle of the walkway. They didn't gasp when I explained the story behind the photo of me and Theo, and they didn't give me a look when I mentioned my phone has been dead since last night.

They didn't ask any questions beyond, "Are you okay?"

A noncommittal hum was my only response. I'm not sure exactly what *okay* means.

*Okay* can encompass a whole slew of feelings. *Okay* can be sad, happy, scared, and being *okay* doesn't cancel out any of those. *Okay* can still hurt really bad, but even two years later, the grief of losing my favorite person in the world feels very *not* okay.

Sometimes that grief is a storm cloud I can feel looming right behind me. Other times, it's a heavy weight on my chest that spreads out to my limbs, and those days, it's hard to get out of bed and fake my way through a customer-service smile.

That's how it feels today—like the memory of Gramps is pressing me down into the earth, making my muscles difficult to move.

"Look at this one." Dad proudly thrusts a seedling into my view.

"So cute. What is it?" I ask, trying to add some enthusiasm to my tone.

"Little kale plant!"

"Kale chips!" Mom cheers from the other side of the garden.

"Oh, wait, look at *this* one." Dad holds up another plant.

## *No Place Like You*

A few clumps of soil fall onto my shirt. "Looks exactly the same."

"Nah, this one's about an inch taller. Healthy little guy. Spring is officially here."

One of my parents' dogs, Maple, curls herself up next to me. "The tulips still haven't sprouted," I announce, my voice somber. I've been checking every morning, hoping to see a hint of green in the flower beds in front of the A-frame. They never appeared last spring—almost like they were grieving the loss of Gramps too.

"I bet they show up soon," Mom assures me. "The weather is getting a tad warmer every day."

"Have you added any compost into the soil?" Dad asks.

"Yeah. Hopefully the bulbs are okay."

"We can get some new ones. Your dad and I are heading to a gardening store in Wilhelmina in the morning. We can look there."

"No thanks." I sigh. "I want to keep trying Gramps's original bulbs."

"Okay, sweetie," Mom says soothingly. "Want to come with us tomorrow? We're staying to see the girls after they get out of school. They have soccer practice."

"I wish I could, but I have work." I grin, imagining my nieces in their little shin guards and cleats. "I love that they're playing soccer."

Dad laughs. "Millie says they dance around the field for most of the game."

"Well, they are *six*," Mom points out. "I'm sure that competitive streak will come, especially with Finn and Millie around." She sets a basket of garden tools down beside me. "Sorry we won't be here for dinner tomorrow, though. You'll be on your own, but there's leftover casserole from last night, if you want that."

I close my eyes, assessing this new low I seem to have dropped into. My parents apologizing to me—their twenty-eight-year-old daughter—for having plans. It's pretty pathetic, when you think about it. Here I am, star-fishing in their garden, waiting for them to finish so we can go inside for dinner.

As a kid, my twenties felt like this shiny time I couldn't wait to get to. I'd be going to parties, surrounded by friends. I'd have a job I love, an adorable apartment straight out of a Nora Ephron movie. I'd be jet-setting somewhere on a whim and have a camera roll full of hilarious memories. Living the dream.

Now, I'm turning twenty-nine in a couple weeks. Which is basically thirty. Which is basically middle-aged. Menopause is on the horizon, and I still don't have my life figured out.

"How's everything at the cabin?" Dad asks, interrupting my spiral.

"Great." A lie.

"Need help with anything?"

"No, I've got it." Another blatant lie. My voice is pitched too high. There's probably A Look passing between them right now.

Dad clears his throat. "You know, if the A-frame is getting to be too much work . . ." A pause. He totally heard the truth beneath my lies. "We can sell it. Gramps wouldn't want it to be a burden."

The solid ground beneath me wobbles. A sharp pain shoots through my stomach. I place my hands over it like that might help.

"He would understand," Mom adds. "His memory lives in our hearts, even if the A-frame doesn't make it."

My breath stops altogether at those words. They're completely contradictory to how I feel. He doesn't live in my heart . . . he's in that house.

They're offering me an out. Just like they always do when I run into difficulty. *It's all right, let us pick up the pieces.* It's so easy to say yes. But, goddamn it, I'm tired of quitting things and running away from my problems. I'm sick of giving up when shit gets hard. So frustrated with looking in the mirror and not recognizing my reflection. I've been coddled and taken care of through every failure, and I'm *done*.

It's a struggle, but I muster the strength to sit up. Dad is two garden beds over, dark soil caked up to his wrists. Mom turns on a hose, showering her herbs.

"I'm not giving up," I announce. This is one project I plan to see all the way through. I'm going to accomplish something Gramps would be proud of.

## Chapter 6

*Theo*

$\mathcal{E}$very morning, I run a five-mile loop through Fern River. Rain or shine. I wake up early, restless and jittery, and if I stay still too long, give my brain too much time to think, I'll spiral.

So, I run, music blasting, until my muscles are tired and it's time for work.

My path leads through the small neighborhood where I'm renting a house on the edge of town and then down Main Street. I'm usually there in time to wave to Hal while he opens the market, say hi to his husband, Omar, as he unlocks the door to Coffee Cottage, and Mrs. LaGrande waits by the window to call out which scones they're baking up that day.

It's lemon poppyseed this morning—Mom's favorite.

Once I get through town, I take a left down the road where Mom, Fable, and the Oakses live. Fable's cabin is hidden in a grove of trees and only visible for a moment, but I always look. I can't help it. A few weeks ago, I glanced over and spotted her standing on the front porch with a mug in her hands, dressed only in a long T-shirt and tall green socks, her thighs and knees on display, hair in a messy bun atop her head, early-morning sunlight playing over her frame. She looked sleep rumpled and soft, so unlike how I normally get to see her.

I haven't been able to get the image out of my head.

Now, as I pass, I peer over in time to see the porch and dark wood A-frame—but no Fable today. Another drop of disappointment joins the deep well in my chest from yesterday.

I had a secret, last-ditch-effort hope that she'd say yes. The stars would align. Pigs would fly. I'd catch her on a good day where she might want to do me a favor.

But I don't blame her. It was a wild idea.

So, it's time to move on to the rest of the plan: Project Settle Down in Fern River.

First thing this morning, I'm calling Cathy, who (despite her full-time job busybodying) happens to be the best Realtor in town. I want to trade my rent for a mortgage, and hopefully she can help me. Then I'm contacting Maddox, who's been trying to convince me to rejoin the Volunteer Fire Department since I moved back. Finally, I'm going to get in touch with the man who runs Fern River's Little League program, to find out if they're looking for coaches this spring. Maybe I can put those years of baseball to good use.

The music fades out of my earbuds as a call comes through. I slow myself to a walk and tap my AirPod. "Hello?"

My panting breaths fill the silence before Mia squeals, "Ew. What is wrong with you? Do not answer the phone in the middle of whatever you and Fable are doing!"

"Running," I groan, dragging a hand down my face. "I'm *running*, Mia."

"Oh god, okay, please never answer if you're . . . *busy.*"

On that note, my mind betrays me with an image of how Fable

and I could be *busy*. Her hair fanned out on my bed. Her flushed cheeks. Those hazel eyes bright with lust—

"You still there?" Mia asks.

I turn around and squint into the rising sun, hoping the glare will burn away the image. "Yeah. I'm here," I grit out. "Why are you awake so early?"

"Bree had to be up for court. She has to go put the bad guys in jail, you know?"

"Superhero shit." I walk until the road curves, and Mom's property comes into view.

"We love her for it." She yawns. "Might go back to bed in a minute though."

"Don't let me stop you." I laugh, turning down Mom's driveway.

Her little house is nestled between the woods on one side and her garden on the other, and if I know her, she's already out there, tending to it with her second cup of coffee.

"Wanted to check on you," Mia says. "I tried calling Fable all day yesterday, and it went straight to voicemail every time. Figured I could call *you* to check on her now."

My face pinches. I'm going to have to admit the truth. I managed to avoid Arthur the rest of yesterday, but I can't keep lying to my own family. "First of all, she mentioned her phone was dead."

"Ohhh. And second of all?"

My tongue presses into my cheek. "Hold on. I just got to Mom's. Let me put you on speaker so I can tell both of you."

"No," Mia groans. "Do not tell me there's already trouble in paradise."

I find Mom kneeling beside the ferns lining her patio. "Oh, Theo!" She brushes back a few strands of her long gray hair and leaves behind a streak of dirt on her cheek.

"Morning, Mom."

"You on your run?" She reaches out a hand and I help her up. "I've got coffee going. Let me get you some."

"No, no. You sit down." I wave toward her patio table. "I'll get some coffee; you say hi to Mia." I shift the call to speaker and shove my earbuds in my pocket.

"Oh, hi, baby!" Mom says when I hand her the phone.

The kitchen door squeals as I pull it open and duck inside. Mom bought this house after her divorce was final. It's small, just big enough for the three of us back then, but she got to turn it into her personal oasis over the years. I'm obviously much older now than I was when she bought it, but I still feel like a kid inside these walls—safe, cozy, and warm. It was exactly what we needed after years of our home feeling unstable.

Mr. Maxwell, mom's old pit bull mix, groans from his spot on the couch, stretching out his legs, and trying to decide if he should get worked up about whoever has come into the house. Mom rescued him from the shelter about a year ago. He had an awful injury to his eyes, and after a few surgeries to help his pain, he's doing much better, despite having lost his vision.

"It's me, Mr. Maxwell," I assure him, letting him sniff my hand before I pet him. Mom says he prefers his full name, so we're not allowed to shorten it to Max. His tail thumps against the couch and he rolls over to let me rub his belly. "Not the early morning gardening type, I see."

After a kiss to his muzzle, I pour coffee into my favorite mug (which has a picture of Mr. Maxwell with sunglasses on the side), pour another mugful for Mom, and step back outside.

Mia's voice filters through the phone as I sit down. "We're thinking about coming down for Fable's birthday. I miss everybody."

Mom pats my arm. "Do you and Fable have any plans for her birthday?"

Staring at the phone on the table between us, I admit, "Actually, I need to come clean about the whole me-and-Fable thing."

"What do you mean?" they ask at the same time.

"I sort of lied about it. Well, not *sort of.* I did." I shake my head. "You came into the office, all excited about the photo, then Arthur followed, and there's all this shit with him selling the practice. And I don't know, I got carried away, and didn't correct it. But Fable and I are not together. At all."

Stark silence. No one moves.

Then Mia croaks, "What the actual fuck, Theo?"

"Language," Mom scolds, but her eyes stay on me, concern etching her features. "Why did you lie?"

"I'm sorry." Guilt bleeds into me. "I panicked. Arthur had just told me he wants to sell the practice to Garrett. He's worried I'm not *settled* enough here and that I'm going to leave again. He wants it to go to someone who has roots down in the area and isn't going anywhere." Cupping my hands around my mug, I sigh. "And when you told him I was dating Fable, he looked . . . happy about it. So I didn't correct him." I shrug. "Now, as I'm saying it out loud, it sounds ridiculous. But in the moment, I didn't have much time to think it through."

"So . . . the photo?" Mia asks.

"She fell. That guy, Philip, collided with her and knocked her into my lap."

"That fucker," Mia hisses, and Mom doesn't scold her this time.

"What did Arthur say when you told him the truth?" Mom asks.

I wince. "I haven't. Yet."

Mom swats my shoulder. "Theodore Alexander Nikolaou!"

"I will today!" I add hastily. "But he did say that if I can prove that I'm sticking around here, he'll consider Garrett and me buying the practice together. I just need to figure out how to do that without Fable."

Mia hums thoughtfully. "That picture, though. You two have always had this . . . *thing* between you. I don't know what to call it other than tension."

My lips twitch. I know that tension well. I don't know if it's fueled by hatred or annoyance or chemistry, but it doesn't matter. Fable's her normal feisty, sarcastic self to everyone, but as soon as she looks my way, she turns up the volume. Her eyes get all fiery and her cheeks flush pink.

I love every fucking second of it.

Mom gives me a knowing look. "Mary and I did always hope you two would fall in love, and there'd be a wedding and babies in no time."

Immediately, something clogs my throat. I can't swallow around it. "We've talked about this. There's never going to be a wedding and babies for me," I say as gently but firmly as possible.

Sadness pinches her expression. "Theodore, just because *he* hurt us doesn't mean *you* will."

Pain burns in my stomach as I watch her eyes turn glassy. I shove my hands into my lap and squeeze them together.

The truth is, I have hurt people—including Fable.

Mia sighs. "You're not him, Theo."

I can hear their words, but they don't make it past the barriers in my mind. They can't get through the doubts and deep-seated fear that terrorizes my thoughts of having a real relationship one day.

My father's rage was unpredictable. We never knew when it was coming or what caused it. Even as a child, I could see the obvious signs—the shouting and slamming doors and throwing things across the room. But I didn't know what was happening when I wasn't there. I didn't know he was hurting Mia. The smallest of us. The easiest target.

I'm haunted by pieces of his reflection when I stare into the mirror. We have matching eyes, the same bone structure. And that reflection distorts how I envision my future. When I picture myself years from now, every image holds *him* in my place, like we're interchangeable.

As a teenager, when a flash of anger hit me, I let myself succumb to it. I was so mad all the time—at my father, yes, but mostly at myself. For not seeing it. For not protecting Mia and Mom. For not standing up to him when I should've.

Over the years, I've worked to find other ways to dissolve my anger, and I'm proud to say I haven't been in a fight since my college days. But I'm still terrified *his* violence is lurking beneath the surface of my skin, waiting for me to let it out. Show my true colors.

I've seen the damage that man left in his wake—the pain he caused my sister and mother and the emotional tolls they still carry—and I never, *ever* want to subject someone to that.

So, I won't be the one to get married and give my mom grandchildren to spoil, but I've mastered a different role over the years: distraction and deflection. It's my self-appointed job to brighten up the mood when Mom and Mia are struggling. It can be hard to keep it going when my own thoughts creep darker, but I have to make sure they're happy. It's the least I can do at this point.

"Let's go get breakfast." I put an arm around Mom's shoulders, forcing a grin. "Mrs. LaGrande is making lemon poppyseed scones today."

"Theo." Mia's voice is soft, concerned. "Don't push this away. Have you been going to therapy?"

Mom's gaze warms my cheek, and I can practically feel Mia holding her breath for the answer. "Sometimes," I reply, even though I've canceled the last few months' worth of appointments. We all went for years when we were younger, but it doesn't feel like a priority right now. Besides, it was Mia who endured the worst of it. She's the one I'm worried about.

"It might really help with all this," Mia says.

"I'm okay. Promise." I stand and stretch out my legs. "But I really need to move a bit after that run. I didn't have much of a cooldown."

"When I come to town then?" Mia asks. "We can talk about it?"

"Sure," I mumble, knowing full well that I'll find another way to change the subject when the time comes.

## Chapter 7

*Fable*

"Are you kidding me?" I stare at the newly broken step, my tailbone throbbing. The board slipped forward as I stepped down, then the railing swayed under my weight, and my poor tailbone took the brunt of the fall. This makes two unusable steps in the last two weeks, and if it keeps happening at this rate, soon I won't be able to reach my bed upstairs.

*I'm not giving up.* I remind myself of my words from last night in the garden. This is fine. A minor setback. I simply have two boards to replace now. Okay, well, maybe I should replace all of them, really? But I'm trying to stay positive, so let's not focus on that.

I take extra precautions on the rest of the way down, trying to stay on the inside edge. At the kitchen counter, I blink at the red notification bubbles on my phone. I missed twelve calls and forty-three texts yesterday, and honestly, the thought of catching up on all that—especially when most of it is probably about Gramps's birthday or the photo with Theo—sounds rather exhausting, so I tuck it into my pocket. Maybe I shouldn't have stolen a cord from my parents after all.

With a warm mug of tea in my grip and Knocks on my heels, I head to check on the bathroom pipe I fixed last night. Without the list at work, I had tried my best to remember what I needed, and although I was missing one piece, I think I made it work. When I turned the water back on after, I didn't see any leaks, so third time might be the charm.

I'm one step into the hallway when I come to sudden halt. There's a puddle filling the space—soaking into my socks—and the faint sound of trickling water coming from the bathroom.

"Shit, shit, shit," I shout, my body bursting into action.

I throw open the bathroom door to find a stream pouring from the cabinet beneath the sink, pooling on the floor and running into the hallway. With a slew of incoherent curses, I set my mug roughly on the counter and run outside to shut off the water to the house. On the way back in, I grab an armful of towels from the dryer, tossing them over the puddle in the hallway as I make my way to the bathroom.

"Dammit. Really?" I groan when I find Knocks ears-deep in my abandoned mug.

He prances away, tail whipping sassily as I yank off my wet socks, almost falling on my ass in the process. Thankfully, the water has stopped flowing, so I spread the rest of the towels across the bathroom floor, then lean against the door to catch my breath. I'm staring at the damp towels in the hallway when I suddenly realize the water is reaching all the way under the spare bedroom door.

My knees go weak. With a soft cry, I open the door and cross the threshold into the room. The entire space is flooded with about half an inch of water, but as I maneuver around Gramps's boxes, it gets even deeper. The house must be more unlevel than I thought, because it's already seeping into the drywall in the back corner of the room.

Pulse skyrocketing, I turn to the left and scan the nearby boxes. BOOKS is written across each one, in Millie's handwriting. There are five stacks, three or four boxes high, and every bottom one is soaked on the edges, cardboard swollen with water.

Panic races through me. *Not the books. Anything but the books.*

"Please, no," I cry out, reaching for a box at the top of the nearest stack. My throat tightens as I traipse through the water to take it to the dry living room, my tailbone aching the whole way.

The towels in the hallway are soaked, so I hurry upstairs (carefully avoiding the broken steps) and grab everything I can find in the upstairs bathroom. It's still not nearly enough, but hopefully it'll make the path safer while I move boxes.

One at a time, I heave them into the living room, lining the wall. I'll never judge Gramps for his love of books. He gave me the same obsession—right down to my name, which he recommended to my parents. I was fated from birth to love stories. But as my arms start to feel wobbly from exertion, I at least wish I had an assistant. Knocks sure isn't helping as he leaps from box to box like I'm building him a playground.

Every time I reach a bottom box, I lift it onto Gramps's table in the spare room and move to the next stack, until I have all five damp boxes safe from the water. With a steak knife from the kitchen, I cut the tape on the first one and open it.

Armful by armful, I pull out the dry books and carry them to the living room. The first box has swollen woodworking magazines at the bottom, which in the grand scheme of things, is all right. My attachment to them is pretty small.

But when I find his favorite sci-fi trilogy at the bottom of the next box, with water damage on all the corners, my throat tightens with sadness. "I'm sorry, Gramps," I whisper, setting them aside.

## No Place Like You

In the next box, I find history books that I never actually saw him read, and in the fourth box I discover a latched blue metal tin that appears to be fine. But time slows when I see what's at the bottom of the final box—his collector's editions of *Jurassic Park*, *The Count of Monte Cristo*, and *The Hobbit*.

"Oh no," I gasp, pulling them out.

Stepping over sopping towels, I carry the waterlogged books to the living room and lay them out on the couch, kneeling to examine them. My vision blurs. The corners are soft, the pages swollen and stuck together.

Six of his favorites, damaged because of my screwup.

He loved all of them, but it's the sight of *The Hobbit* that makes tears finally fall past my lashes. This is the book—the one that started my love of reading. This exact copy, which he would read aloud to me, with characters' voices and sound effects. I'd been struggling to read for years, always feeling like my eyes were bouncing three words ahead.

"Let's fall in love with *stories* first," he'd said, opening to the first page. He always had something for me to do—a puzzle, colored pencils and a notebook, small wooden animals he'd whittled—anything to keep my hands busy while his calming voice transported me to faraway places.

Pulling *The Hobbit* into my lap, I lean back against the couch. Carefully, I peel the pages apart to the middle of the book. The printed words look okay, but Gramps's handwritten notes are blurring on the edges. He loved to keep commentary as he read, sometimes on pieces of paper, and sometimes right in the margins. He'd mark spots where we laughed or scenes that were so enthralling that I wouldn't let him stop reading.

I quickly swipe away a tear with the back of my hand. It's been a long time since I read a paperback—two years, to be exact.

I shoved all of mine into boxes after Gramps died. Everything from the feel of the paper under my fingertips to the weight in my hands to the nostalgic smell of the pages . . . it's all so full of Gramps's memory that I can't touch them. Now, all my books are sitting alone in Mom and Dad's attic, waiting.

Something feels like it's fracturing in my chest as I stare at the wet pages, and I don't know how to prevent it. I lift my watery gaze to the room around me. This place is falling apart—the pipes, steps, railing, even the siding is peeling, and I feel helpless to stop it. If I could keep this place going, keep this cabin alive, keep his books safe . . . then the memory of him would be safe too.

But everything I touch ends up in failure.

My phone vibrates in my pocket, but I ignore it. Knocks curls himself up at my ankles, apparently willing to take a break from mischief to comfort me. After a momentary pause, the vibrating starts again.

I let out a sharp breath and wipe my tears away before pulling out the phone. Millie's name illuminates the screen, and my shoulders loosen. If it was our oldest sister, Tessa, I'd probably let it go to voicemail, because she'll sniff out any difference in my voice and start questioning me. But Millie is more likely to let me take my time with telling her things, and as I sit here, surrounded by sadness, I think borrowing a little of her warmth—even through the phone—might be nice. Might help me feel less alone in this heartache.

"Hey, Mills." I try to keep my tone steady.

"*I knew it*," Tessa squeals. I pull the phone away to check the name, but it still says Millie. "You ignore my calls, but answer Millie's? What the hell?"

"She was probably busy," Millie replies, a smile in her voice.

*Great.* Both of them on the line. I don't stand a chance.

"Five seconds before *you* called?" Tessa grumbles. "I'm not buying it."

"Aaaanyway," Millie says. "Hi, Fabes. Mom said your phone was dead yesterday—"

"Which is awfully convenient after that photo of you and Theo was making the rounds," Tessa chimes in, and my heart tumbles over itself. "But Mom told us there was a bunch of confusion about it?"

Millie sighs and redirects. "We *actually* called to see how you're doing. A little sister check-in."

I swallow. Clear my throat. Sit up straighter in case any of that will hide the fact that I've been crying. But dammit, my words still wobble on the edges when I say, "I'm doing all right."

Tessa immediately detects something's off. "What's wrong?"

I press my lips together, but my chin quivers anyway. "I'm just . . . not having a great morning."

"What happened?" Millie's voice is full of concern.

"A lot," I admit hollowly.

There's a moment of silence before Tessa says, "You've got to tell us so we can help."

Resistance seems futile at this point. My sisters have a way of drawing information out of me like no one else, and my guard is crumbling by the second.

Taking a deep breath, I ignore the broken step incident and leaking pipe and focus on the worst part. "Some of Gramps's books got wet."

"Oh, no," Millie groans. "How bad is it?"

"Six books, which I guess in the grand scheme of things isn't that bad." I scan the dry boxes in front of me. "Especially when you look at how many he had."

"Okay, hold on," Tessa interrupts. "This website says there are things you can do. I'm sending you a link. Do you have paper towels? And a fan? Like a big one?"

My phone buzzes with the text as I turn to the kitchen and spot my empty roll of paper towels. "No. But I can get everything at work today."

Tessa sighs. "This says you need to get started on drying them as soon as possible. Be right back. I'm calling Dad."

"No, it's all right—" I start, but her line clicks.

"Give Tessa a task and she'll figure it out from half a country away," Millie says with a laugh.

I close my eyes, tipping my head back to the couch cushion. "How is everybody there?" I ask, needing a distraction.

A content hum. "We're good. I'm having coffee with the girls while Finn makes scrambled eggs. Here, say hi."

She puts me on speaker, and Eloise and Avery squeal, "Hi, Aunt Fabes!"

Despite my morning, their sweet voices make me smile. "Hi! I miss you!"

"Oh, Tessa's already beeping in," Millie interrupts.

"Bye, girls! I love you!" I call before she adds Tessa back in.

"Dad didn't answer," Tessa huffs.

"He and Mom are on their way to Wilhelmina," I tell her.

She scoffs. "And they don't even have same-day delivery services in Fern River . . ." She trails off, probably emailing the CEO of Instacart to tell them how frustrated she is.

"I'm fine." I try to make myself sound as confident as possible. "I'll get what I need from the store to see if I can save the books."

"Are you sure?" Millie asks.

"Positive." I might not be sure, but maybe I can fake it for them.

"Is everything else okay at the house?" Tessa probes. "How are the renovations going?"

I glance around the living room—the broken steps, the leaning railing, the smoke detectors in pieces on the kitchen counter, the pile of pipe-fixing supplies sitting in the hallway.

It's a shit show. "Yep. Everything's totally fine. Great, really." I cross my fingers, hoping it worked.

There's a long beat of silence before Tessa says, "I'll call you back," and her line clicks again.

Millie chuckles. "She's either tracking Dad's location or something came up at work."

I roll my eyes. Sometimes, when I'm unsure about life, I like to think to myself, *What would Tessa do?* or *What would Millie do?* My sisters have very different responses to most things in life. Millie tends to quietly think—or overthink—and weigh all the options. Meanwhile, Tessa is a doer—ready to act in a heartbeat and barely giving anyone time to catch up.

I'm almost positive Tessa is in the process of pushing her nose further into this situation, but I don't even know how to prevent it. She's been a fixer for everyone else her entire life. She can't help it.

"Oh. Oops. It's okay." Millie says, a little muffled through the phone. "Fabes, I gotta go. We had a little milk spill."

"Love you, Mills."

On the other line, I hear Eloise giggling as she says, "It's okay. Pepper's cleaning it up . . ." before the call ends.

Suddenly exhausted, I curl my body into a ball, giving myself a few moments of stillness. The urge to quit creeps into the corners of my mind. I could run—pack up Baby Blue right now and hit the road. Leave everything behind. Take the easy way out. Let my parents sell the A-frame and all the memories that live here.

I'm really good at giving up. An expert, even.

A distant knocking sounds from the door a few minutes later. I reluctantly lift my head, and through the front window, my gaze lands on a lopsided smile and a pair of irritatingly charming dimples.

Theo lifts a package of paper towels and a large box fan into view, and I groan.

*What would Tessa do?*

Apparently call the last person on earth I want help from.

## Chapter 8

*Theo*

She glares at me through the glass, gorgeous hazel eyes narrowed, lips pressed into a flat line. Honey-blond wisps of hair have escaped the two buns behind her ears and curl at her cheeks. Her arms fold over the most adorable pair of light denim overalls, and her hip cocks to the side.

She looks ready to give me hell.

I'm here for it.

My smile hitches wider. "Tessa told me to bring supplies. Wanna let me in?"

"Not particularly," she shouts.

"She thought you might say that."

My attention drifts behind her to the hallway, where it appears wet towels are sitting in a heap, then to the couch, where a few books are spread out on the cushions, then to the haphazardly stacked boxes on the wall.

This looks like way more damage than what Tessa described.

Fable steps forward quickly, blocking my view, and opens the door a few inches. "Just leave it on the porch."

"Excuse me. What happened to, 'Hello, Theo, my knight in shining armor. Thank you for coming to my rescue!'?"

She gives me a bored stare and says in a monotone voice, "Hello, Theo, the scoundrel in ugly scrubs. I didn't need rescuing. You can go now."

Laughter bubbles out of me. "You don't like my scrubs?" I set the fan down to turn in a circle. "These are my favorites. Admit it, they look pretty good, right?" Her expression hardens, almost like she's fighting the urge to look down. I could've sworn I saw her checking me out yesterday in the blue version of these. But when her eyes don't budge, I change tactics. "Okay, I really am here to help. I promise I'll behave."

"You've never behaved a day in your life," she responds, unimpressed.

"I'm turning over a new leaf. This is Theo 2.0, at your service."

She rolls her eyes. "Shouldn't you be at work?"

"Told them I had to run to an emergency. Garrett's handling our first two appointments."

She chews at her bottom lip, analyzing me. "Thank you for bringing what I needed. It was . . . nice of you."

*That* is officially the most complimentary thing she has said to me in a long time, and I don't want to push my luck. I'm walking a very thin tightrope right now, and one wrong step could get a door slammed in my face.

I point to the books lining the couch. "It was *The Hobbit*?"

Her lips curve down. "Yeah."

My heart sinks. She loved that book growing up—carried a copy of it to school for an entire year.

"Can I see it? Tessa told me how to help."

She thinks for a moment, glancing between me and the fan and paper towels, but finally, slowly, she opens the door wider. I grab the supplies and step inside, where Knocks gives me a much warmer greeting than his owner, rushing to my feet.

I set down the fan and scoop him up, feeling Fable's eyes on me as he curls into my neck. "You're cute as hell, aren't you?"

"He's actually a menace."

"Ah, so we're a scoundrel and a menace. Two peas in a pod." Knocks's purr rumbles against my chest as I sit on the hardwood floors beside the couch.

"Except I actually *like* one of you."

I crack a smile and peer down at him. "Aw, she didn't mean that. You'll grow on her. Just give her time."

"I'm going to kick you out now."

"No, no. I'll be serious." Setting Knocks in my lap, I grab a copy of *The Count of Monte Cristo*. "From what I saw in the link Tessa sent, we're going to put a few paper towels every ten to twenty pages and press them down to soak up the water. Then we'll put them up in front of the fan for the rest of the day."

Fable sits in front of me and sets *The Hobbit* on the floor between us. I watch her carefully peel apart the pages. Her eyes are a little swollen, like she's been crying this morning, and my chest pinches at the sight.

"Are you okay?" I ask gently.

"I'm fine." She reaches out a hand and I tear off a few paper towels, helping her line the page. Lifting onto her knees, she applies pressure.

"You sure?"

Wordlessly, she nudges *The Count of Monte Cristo* toward me, and I get the message. Whatever is going on, I'm not in the club of people she wants to share it with. As usual.

We work quietly for a while, and when Fable reaches the end of her book, she starts over at the beginning. I'm really trying not to focus too much on the state of the cabin around me, but it's hard not to. It's sparse, only a couch and boxes in the living room, along with random tools. My gaze snags on the pile of smoke detectors on the kitchen counter and . . . a couple broken stairs? *What is happening here?* She assured me yesterday that she could fix everything on her own, but judging by . . . all of this . . . I'm thinking there might be more to that story.

"How'd the books get wet?" I ask.

She blows out a sharp breath. "A minor bathroom leak."

"How minor, exactly?" I nod toward the towels in the hallway. "Because those are soaked."

"The house is unlevel," she grumbles, locking her elbows and pressing down on the book. "All the water went straight to the bedroom."

"Not very minor, then."

"No, not very minor," she concedes, emotion coating her voice.

Her gaze crashes with mine, and there's no fire in their hazel depths. For a moment, I can see right through to the sadness underneath. "I'm sorry."

She stares down at *The Hobbit*, gliding her fingers along the edge. "Me too."

We fall back into quiet work, punctuated by the sounds of ripping paper towels and her tiny grunts as she presses all her weight onto the book. She tugs her white sleeves up to her elbows, revealing the thimbleberry flowers tattooed on her left arm. They curl from her wrist, trail up under her sleeve, and all the way to her shoulder.

The first time I saw the tattoo was a few years ago. I was in town for the weekend, helping Mom install paving stones through her garden. I'd taken a break to get some things from the market for dinner, when in walked Fable in a black tank top and cut-off jeans shorts.

I froze, holding a jar of spaghetti sauce, while I tried to take in every detail from across the store. The setting sun was dancing through her wavy hair and illuminating every dark line imprinted on her arm, and *I couldn't breathe.*

My sneakers are still stained from the marinara that splattered across them when the jar plunged to the ground.

"I think that's as good as I can get this one," she says after she has gone through *The Hobbit* three times.

I hand her my book and motion toward an empty corner of the living room. "Can you set them upright over there, and I'll get the fan?"

She balances our books with the pages spread out while I plug in the fan and point it in the right direction, the gentle hum filling the cabin. The pages are still too damp to move much in the air, but hopefully in the next couple of hours they'll dry.

Nodding, I step back and scan the room. "So, I was thinking."

She grabs *Jurassic Park* and kneels on the floor again. "Did it hurt?" she deadpans.

A surprised laugh tumbles out. "Jeez, Fabes, stop flirting with me."

"I'm not flirting with you. I'm *insulting* you."

I hum wistfully, hoping I can get her to crack a smile. "My heart can't tell the difference."

A grin creeps into the edges of her lips before she stifles it. "You're incredibly annoying."

That tiny grin feels like I've just won the lottery. I tuck the memory of it away for safekeeping.

"I was thinking," I start over. "That I could take a look at the pipe?" Her movements pause. Eyes shoot up to meet mine. Her lips flatten, and before she can make up some reason why she doesn't want me to, I add, "I'll only look. I won't touch anything you don't want me to."

I can practically see the thoughts running through her head as she debates letting me into her life a little more. "Just *look*. Don't try to fix it."

"Yes, ma'am." I salute, turning toward the bathroom.

What I discover there is . . . a mess. Wet towels, channel locks, a handful of smaller wrenches, some quick-dry PVC glue, and a few sawed-off pieces of PVC litter the floor. I kneel beside the supplies and assess what might be going on.

There's an old shutoff valve lying under the cabinet, along with several quick-connect fittings, and some smaller chunks of pipes. She obviously tried a few different ways to fix this, and I guess none of them have worked.

"What exactly happened?" I call, picking up the pieces in the cabinet to move them out of the way.

"The shutoff valve was leaking," she replies, her voice coming closer. "The first time, I took the valve off and tried to replace it." I glance up to find her leaning on the doorframe. "When that still leaked, I cut the pipe to cap it off. But then that leaked, too, so I bought those shark teeth-looking things because the internet claimed they were 'easy,'" she says with air quotes. "But then the house flooded overnight."

"Well, I have good and bad news. The *good* news is, I think we can fix it with what you have here."

She crosses her arms. "And the bad news?"

"I mean, it's only bad news for you."

There's that unimpressed glare again. "What is it?"

"You'd have to spend a few more minutes with me while we get it done."

Her teeth tug at her bottom lip. She glares back and forth between me and the cabinet. "How annoying are you going to be?"

I smirk at her. "My baseline is incredibly annoying, I hear."

She sighs, casting a long look over her shoulder to the bedroom. When she turns back to me, she asks, "Why are you helping me? I said no to your pretend relationship thing."

I tilt my head. The answer seems obvious. "So you don't have any more house floods for the foreseeable future."

Her features soften the tiniest bit. Our eyes lock, and I can feel her gaze burrowing beneath my skin. I don't know what she finds, but it must be good enough, because she turns to leave and tosses over her shoulder, "Fine. Fix it." After a beat, she adds, "Please."

Chuckling, I call after her, "Wait! Get back here!" She returns with a scowl, but I only smile wider. "Fabes, *I'm* not fixing it. I'm teaching *you* to fix it."

## Chapter 9

*Fable*

"Push in a little farther. It'll fit," Theo assures me. Molten lava floods my cheeks as I follow his instructions, pushing until the quick-connect slides into place. "That's perfect."

The back of my neck prickles with warmth, and I'm going to blame it on how close we are. With both of our heads inside the small cabinet, our knees pressed together, and our arms brushing every few seconds, it's a wonder I'm even hearing his words at this point. If I don't get some distance between us, I might overheat.

I tried holding my breath for a while, to avoid inhaling his summer-sunshine scent, because it's doing weird things to my brain—like making me wonder what kind of soap he uses and if I can buy the same one—but then I felt even more lightheaded.

I'm doomed either way. Letting him into this house might be my downfall.

"Looks like you had just enough pipe left to make it work." He slides his fingers over the connection, his forearm flexing a few inches from my face. I have the irrational urge to sink my teeth into it.

"Yep. Great," I chirp, clearing my throat.

Mocha eyes lock with mine in the dim cabinet. "We should be good to go this time. Where's the main shutoff to the house?"

"Outside." I slide back and gulp down some fresh, not-Theo-drenched air. But when I go to stand, he places a hand on my knee.

"You stay. Make sure everything looks good when I turn it back on."

While he's gone, I collect the scraps of PVC from under the sink. Turns out I'd made so many cuts to the pipe coming out of the wall that we barely had enough left for the new shutoff valve. If I'd cut any more, the next step would've been to take apart the drywall behind the cabinet and replace the whole pipe in the wall.

So admittedly, maybe letting him in here *wasn't* my downfall.

As long as I don't have to spend any more time with our faces three inches apart.

"How's it looking?" he calls, walking back down the hallway.

I peek under the sink. "Good."

He plants his hands on the doorframe. "Use your fingers. See if it's wet."

The lava is back in my cheeks. I lean under the cabinet before he notices. "Everything seems good."

"Perfect. Then turn the valve to let the water through." He kneels beside me and reaches over my body to the faucet, and for a moment all I can see are gray scrubs and strong thighs. A stark reminder that I was 1,000 percent bluffing with the ugly scrubs comment. I swallow, snapping my attention back to my task.

Water flows softly through the pipe and Theo says, "Okay, check for leaks. Even the tiniest bit."

I touch everywhere I can and listen closely, but everything seems dry. "I think we're good."

When I slide out from under the cabinet, that lopsided grin is aimed at me, dimples on display and hair curling playfully at his temples. He sits back on his heels, his broad shoulders taking up most of my tiny bathroom, and I'm painfully aware it's only the two of us here.

"You did it," he says brightly.

"*We* did it," I correct. "Thank you."

He glances behind him dramatically. "Did you just . . . thank *me*? Has the world ended? Are you really Fable?" He grabs my shoulder desperately. "Are you being mind-controlled?"

I roll my eyes, but I can't stop my smile. "I take it back then."

"Oh, no you can't." He stands and reaches for my hand, helping me up. "I'm treasuring that *thank-you* for the rest of my life. Getting it embroidered right on these scrubs you love so much."

"It's truly extraordinary how quickly you can shape-shift from *decent* to *infuriating*."

"I have a gift," he muses.

Together, we fill the shopping bag with trash and set the tools on the counter, then he follows me out to the living room. I walk quickly toward the door, hoping he won't ask any questions about the state of the rest of the house. If I'm lucky, he'll mosey right out and go on his merry way.

But my luck is shit these days.

"What's the story with the stairs?"

I turn to find him surveying them. He picks up one side of a broken board and examines where it's still partially connected to the frame. When he sets a hand on the railing to lean closer, it falters under his weight. He pulls back. "Shit. Fabes."

"I know." I busy myself with rearranging the books in front of the fan.

Rounding the steps, he stares up at them from underneath. "I think every single one needs to be replaced." Dread sinks

## No Place Like You

heavily in my stomach. That was a lovely two-minute span of feeling like I'd made progress on the to-do list. "Did Gramps build these?"

"No. I think they're original."

He wiggles a few of them, standing on his tiptoes to reach higher, and that's when a *pop* and *snap* echoes through the cabin. It ends in a bleak silence. We both freeze, Theo with a newly loose board in his hand and me with a waterlogged book in mine.

All I can do is stare. This place is crumbling right before my eyes. That fissure in my heart splits wide open.

As if he can hear it happen, Theo walks toward me, brows dipped with concern. "I'm sorry. I didn't mean to break it."

I blink back the burn in my eyes. "Not your fault." My voice cracks on the edges. "It was bound to break anyway."

His hands fold around my shoulders, and he lowers his head to meet my gaze. "It's okay, Fabes. I can fix them."

I swallow back the emotions bubbling up my throat. "No. This is my project. I can do it. I need . . ." I straighten my spine. "I need to do it myself."

Theo's expression sharpens. His gaze tracks over my eyes, my cheeks, my mouth, and down to where his hands still cup my shoulders. It feels intimate in a way that should be uncomfortable. I should be pushing him away and asking him to leave.

But there's something safe and nostalgic and warm in the small space that separates us, and I can't find it in me to step away.

"Let me help you," he whispers.

A hollow feeling worms its way into my chest when I remember the words I heard him say at the hardware store. The words he probably didn't mean for me to hear.

*But what if I need* your *help?*

I didn't let myself acknowledge it at the time. I shoved it far away, under a rock, in the next county, where I didn't have to think about that soft plea threading through his voice.

But it comes crawling back to my mind now.

He needs my help.

And when I needed his this morning, he showed up—left work, got supplies, and was here in a handful of minutes. He dropped everything for me.

Glancing around the cabin, I catalog all the work that needs to be done. The railing, steps, hallway, the now-soaked drywall in the bedroom. Between needing to do the labor but also needing to be at work to pay for supplies, I can't keep up. I'm spinning in circles. But with two of us working on it . . . maybe it's feasible.

It could be mutually beneficial. It doesn't have to mean I'm *letting* him fix everything for me. I'm basically paying for it with my time. I think? It's not the same as my parents cleaning up my messes because he's getting something out of it. This time, I would be working for the help. Right?

I meet his gaze. "Do you know anything about insulation?"

He releases my shoulders. "Some. Why?"

"What about drywall?"

"I'm decent."

"And stair railings?"

He turns to look at it, then back at me. "What is this about?"

I wait for a beat. For a sign from the universe—a divine voice, a lightning strike, or the ghost of Christmas past—*anything* to warn me this is a bad idea. But it never shows. "And what did you tell Arthur about . . . us?"

Pink stains his cheeks. "I haven't told him yet. He wasn't at work yesterday afternoon, but I promise to tell him the truth today."

I walk to the kitchen and fill the kettle, needing something to do with my hands while I gather possible plans.

Theo joins me. "What are you thinking?"

"I'm thinking . . . about a trade of sorts." Turning the knob on the gas stove, I watch it ignite.

"What kind of trade?"

I wave a hand around the room. "A-frame work for . . . girlfriending?"

Hope flares in his eyes. His answer is immediate. "I'm in."

"Well, *I* don't know if I'm in yet. I'm still thinking." Blowing out a breath, I reach for my spiral notebook on the counter. "What exactly does the fake girlfriend role involve?"

"Um . . ." He leans back against the counter, crossing his arms. "I hadn't really gotten that far into it."

"What was your plan then?"

He drags a hand through his hair. "I didn't have one yet."

The kettle squeals and I grab my hand-painted cat mug from the drying rack, dropping an Earl Grey tea bag inside. Theo opens a few cabinets until he finds a forest-green mug and sets it beside mine. I give him a tea bag as well.

We work in silence making tea together, and once our mugs are ready, I motion toward the living room. "Come on. I have ten minutes before I need to leave for work."

After moving the rest of the wet books, I nestle into the corner of the couch, tucking my legs under me. When Theo sits sideways on the opposite end, I tighten my grip on my warm mug, hoping it'll calm my racing pulse. Whatever I'm on the precipice of right now, it feels big. And slightly terrifying.

Maybe I'm just nervous that someone is here at all. I've kept this place to myself for months, not wanting anyone else to see that it's a husk of what it used to be when Gramps lived here. It's a space for grieving. Being alone. Thinking. Letting the darkness swallow me up sometimes.

But now Theo's here, sitting across from me in this quiet,

barely furnished room, beside piles of unfinished projects and haphazardly stacked boxes of books, with a cup of tea on his bent knee. Morning sunlight floats through the wide windows at the front of the A-frame, reflecting off his smooth, sharp jaw and making his eyes shine even brighter.

And this place somehow feels less lonely with him in it.

Knocks hops onto the couch and curls himself up on Theo's lap. I take a sip—to avoid looking at how adorable they are together—and end up burning my tongue. "Okay. How are you going to appeal to Arthur?"

"Well, after you said no, I moved onto the rest of the plan, which involves settling into the community a bit more than I have been." He trails a hand over Knocks's back. "Sign up to coach Little League, rejoin the Volunteer Fire Department. Look into buying a place."

"A little performative, don't you think?"

"This whole concept is essentially a performance." He sips his tea, eyeing me over his mug. "But they're all things I've been wanting to do anyway. This is just my push to get them going, I guess."

"And you can still do all that, even if you and I make an . . . arrangement?"

A slow smile curls over his lips. "You'll be the icing on the cake, Fabes."

For some reason, my ears feel hot. I blame the tea and set it on the ground. Pulling the pen from the spiral of my notebook, I flip past at least eighty-seven pages full of random lists and turn to an empty one. "So *if* we were going to do this fake relationship thing, what would it look like?"

He thinks for a moment, fingers tapping on his mug. "A few public outings? We'd have to make it believable to the town, I think—not just Arthur—but with the efficiency of the Fern River gossip train and phone tree, I don't think it would have to be much. Not to mention the fact that it's *us*," he says pointedly.

"Us?" As soon as the word leaves my mouth, I realize what he means. "Oh."

The kids from the incident that put this town on the map. The kids who spent four years publicly competing over class elections and GPAs.

He shrugs. "It's bound to draw some attention."

"Right." I nod. "What kind of outings?"

"Like . . . dates?"

"Dates," I repeat solemnly. I haven't been on a real date in a while. Everything with Philip was very secretive—nothing public at all. His parents definitely wouldn't have approved of their future politician son dating an unemployed college dropout, and my confidence was too shaky at the time to protest.

Theo jerks his chin toward the notebook. "How 'bout this? You make a list of the things you need help with around here, and then we'll fill in my part second."

I tap my pen against the blank page. There's so much that needs to be done, but safety-related tasks are the priority.

First, I write, *fix bathroom pipes*.

Theo leans forward to read it. "But we just got that done."

"I still owe you something for it."

A muscle ticks in his jaw. "That's not why I did it or why I'm offering to help." He blows out a sharp breath. "I can't deny that I'm getting something out of it if we follow this arrangement. But I'm willing to do whatever it takes to know you're safe here. Write as many things down as you can. It could be five house tasks for every one date, I don't care."

His eyes pin me in place. Unyielding. I try not to let that statement—*whatever it takes to know you're safe*—weave its way into my heart.

I reach for my tea and take a sip, then I hold his gaze with matching resolve. "This has to be a fair exchange of services. A contract. A business arrangement. That's the only way I'll do it."

After a few quiet moments, he dips his chin once, conceding.

Down the left side of the page, I continue the list: insulation, stairs, railing, bedroom drywall, paint hallway.

When I run out of things to write, I hand him the notebook. "How's this look?"

His gaze slips over the list. "Great. I can help with all of that."

I pull the notebook back. "Then let's make a list of a few things I can do for you."

He hums, thinking. "The adopt-a-thon is next month. You could come with me to that." I write it down. "And we could go house-hunting together if you want?"

"With Cathy?"

"Only choice, really."

"Fuck's sake, Cathy," I murmur, and he chuckles as I add that to the list.

He takes a sip of tea, then asks, "How about a dinner at Maddox's, for practice? He invited me over this weekend."

I chew on my bottom lip while I consider it. Practicing sounds smart for two people who've barely spoken to each other for years. "All right." I count both sides of the list. "We're still three short for you."

"We could leave those as bonus events—dealer's choice."

I give him a skeptical look. "Who's the dealer here?"

"Open-ended events that *either of us* can claim." There's a playful glint in his eye.

"As long as they follow the plot," I amend, adding three *free space* spots to the list.

"Yes, ma'am."

As I read over the page again, one question looms at the front of my mind. "Are you sure you don't want to find a real girlfriend instead? It seems like it would be a lot easier." I shrug. "Less manual labor at least."

His gaze flickers to the window, and he's quiet for so long that I think he might not answer. Then he says, "I don't do real relationships, Fabes. I don't trust myself in them. No-strings situations have worked out fine in the past, but beyond that . . ." His focus shifts, trailing over my face. "People have gotten hurt around me before. I can't let it happen again."

His tone is laced with regret and pain. It seeps into his expression, tightening his lips and wrinkling his brows. And the way he's looking at me, I know we're picturing the same moment. Me on the ground, surrounded by chaos, him with a bloody nose, running in the opposite direction.

This is the closest we've ever gotten to acknowledging that moment. There were times in high school when I thought we should, but the further we got from the incident, the less I wanted to. I could see the heartache in Theo at school, and it always felt like the wrong time to bring it up. Why would I want to start a conversation about something that would only remind him of more pain?

I can't even imagine what he must've been feeling that morning at the parade—he'd just found out about the abuse the night before and his entire life was falling apart.

At the time, that moment was humiliating for me and changed the trajectory of my high school years. The grudge was easy to hold on to.

But now . . . now I wish I could give that fourteen-year-old boy a hug.

I have so much to say about that day—both of us do—but it's a bigger conversation than we can dive into right now. We watch each other quietly for a few moments before I do us a favor by changing course. "So, I'm the chosen one?"

His grin is only a fraction of its usual size, but I'll take it. "In a way, you're the perfect candidate. One: This rumor has sort of fallen into my lap, so to speak. Two: You're getting something out of it too. I can help you with the A-frame. And three: You understand this isn't real. We can fake date until Arthur believes I'm sticking around and feels comfortable selling me the practice. Then you're free to dump me. In fact, that might be your favorite part."

My stomach swoops with a feeling I can't identify.

"I won't be lying to him about the other aspects of this," he continues. "I'm staying in Fern River and putting down roots in the community. I plan to make this my home in every way that counts."

A hint of jealousy trickles through me. It sure would be nice to have that kind of certainty about where I'm supposed to be.

I nod, processing his points. "Okay. I'll do it." Grabbing the pen again, I draw two lines across the bottom. I sign my name over one before passing it to him. "Sign here, please."

He smirks, taking the notebook and tilting it up out of my view. He writes way longer than necessary for his name, then hands it back to me. Above his signature, he's written: *Do you want to be my fake girlfriend? Check yes or no. [ ] yes [ ] no*

Something shifts in the air, tugging my memories back to that first day of fifth grade, when he came into school wearing a shirt from *Homeward Bound* and green cargo shorts. His hair was sticking up on one side, he had scabs on both of his elbows (from what I later learned was a Rollerblading fall) and his backpack was half open, a notebook about to tumble out.

With all the confidence in the world, he turned and smiled my way. "Do you like Starburst?" he asked, offering me a red one in his palm.

My heart aches at the memory. I miss that kid more than I let myself realize.

Blinking away the image, I place a check next to *yes*.

* * *

### Oaks Folks

**Fable:** Update for all my nosy family members.

**Tessa:** I'm waiting with bated breath.

**Fable:** Theo and I are pretending we're together for now. If anyone asks, we're a thing.

**Millie:** That squeal you just heard from Wilhelmina was me.

**Mom:** Do I activate the phone tree?

**Dad:** What kind of "thing"? Is this a newfangled term I don't know?

**Tessa:** I'm freaking out. How long? Is there kissing involved? Can I see pictures?

**Fable:** NO PHONE TREE.

**Fable:** I won't be taking any questions at this time.

## Chapter 10

*Fable*

"What the fuck do I even wear?" I grumble to Knocks, tossing a jean jacket onto the Mount Everest of clothes on my bed. He immediately pounces, pawing at a button.

A text comes through on my phone, and I grab it off the nightstand to find a message from Theo.

> **Theo:** You still up for dinner? Need me to make up an excuse to cancel?

> **Fable:** Depends on the excuse.

> **Theo:** Sorry, we can't come. Fable got arrested for murder.

A choked laugh bursts out of me, and I start to reply, but more excuses come through.

> **Theo:** She's taking her boating exam.

**Theo:** She's writing an essay about why Aragorn was her first crush.

**Theo:** That last one is the most believable.

**Fable:**

**Fable:** I'm going to dinner. That insulation isn't going to install itself.

**Theo:** I'll pick you up at six. It's a date.

**Fable:** It's a work dinner.

**Theo:** It's a dating work dinner.

*This is business. These are work events.* That mantra has served me well for the last three days, and I'll keep a grip on it until my nails bleed. No matter how much Theo teases me about it.

With a frustrated groan, I swipe out of the text chain and open my contacts. My first instinct is to call Mia for fashion advice. She's been curating my clothing choices since ninth grade, when she called an intervention because I'd been wearing my soccer jersey to school every day. (*You're a spring*, she told me, flipping through her mom's color analysis book. *You look like a corpse in this shade of red.*)

However, aside from a few texts back and forth—Mia: omfg Theo told me you're fake dating??? Fable: It's more like a business arrangement. Mia: Debra Messing and Dermot Mulroney had a "business arrangement" in The Wedding Date, and we all know how that turned out 👀—we haven't had our usual once-a-week, catch-up-for-hours phone call. And I don't have the time or stamina to argue with her about how this is nothing like Debra and Dermot.

I scroll to my next best option.

"Cute bra, but you forgot a shirt," Tessa points out when she appears on my screen, lying on her couch, a charcoal mask smeared over her face, and a purple Popsicle in her free hand.

"That's why you're here." I prop the phone up on my nightstand and step back until she can see me from the knees up. "What the hell does a person wear to their fake boyfriend's best friend's house for dinner? I need my most fashionable sister's advice."

She points her Popsicle at me. "I'll help if I can tell Millie you gave me that title."

"I'll put it on a mug. Now, how are these jeans?" I turn for her to see the full view of how the black denim hugs the curves of my hips.

"Literally perfect. Bring a towel though, because Theo's going to be drooling all night."

I laugh that off, even as the thought settles low and heavy in my stomach.

"I know you're going to cover up that bra, but just so you're aware, that would kill him."

Glancing down at the emerald-green lace, I smile to myself. Lingerie is one of my favorite forms of self-care. I love how the silky, delicate fabrics are just for me—simply because they make me feel beautiful. Sexy. Strong. It's not really something I have the budget to indulge in lately, but I found this matching set tucked into the back corner of my dresser and thought it deserved an outing. And even though no one—well, except Tessa, I guess—is going to see it, it makes me feel pretty.

"This is a *work* dinner. We're not trying to kill anyone."

She lets out a skeptical "Mm-hmm," then asks, "Where is that sage-green sweater you wore to dinner in Wilhelmina last month?"

I turn and scoot Knocks out of the way to rifle through the mess until I find it. Pulling the sweater onto my shoulders, I fold the sides across my body and tie the string to hold the wrap in place.

"That's the one." Tessa bites off a chunk of Popsicle and crunches through it a few times. "You look hot. Leave your hair down, add your sexy leather jacket, and *bam*. RIP, Theo."

Stepping toward the phone, I examine my reflection a little closer. The neckline brushes smoothly over the top swell of my breasts, then dips down to a vee in the middle, giving away a subtle hint of cleavage. The fabric hugs my stomach and ends right at my high-waisted jeans.

I'll be honest, I'm not trying to *kill* Theo, but the thought of him being a little . . . *tortured* tonight sure does make my insides all warm and fizzy for some reason.

Tessa finishes another bite and asks, "How are the books?"

I reach for a wad of clothes on the bed and start to put them away. "They seem okay." After a full day in front of the fan and two days in some sort of clamp-press thing Theo left on my porch, all six books have mostly recovered. The only big loss is the fact that I can't read most of Gramps's notes in the margins anymore.

"That's good. Still waiting for my big *thank you* for sending reinforcements."

I scowl at her over my shoulder. "Those reinforcements were an absolute pain in the ass."

"But did he help save the books?" When I don't reply, she

snorts. "Exactly. Pain in the ass or not, he didn't even need to hear the whole story. I said, 'Fable needs help,' and he said, 'I'm on my way.'"

My fingers flex around a hanger. I can't look in her direction as my mind slips to a memory from my senior year of high school—me and Mia hiding in a bathroom, right before midnight at a New Year's Eve party. Theo was at his own party but answered on the first ring. "We need help," Mia whispered. I can still hear his gravelly, rushed, "On my way." He was there in minutes, and I get chills when I think about the way his sharp gaze tracked the tears on my cheeks and his gruff, "Wait in the car," as he stalked farther into the party.

I told myself he showed up because his sister had been the one to call, but I've never been able to forget the sight of his broken and bloody knuckles on the steering wheel as he drove us home that night. Or the sight of my cheating ex the following week at school, with a purple bruise circling his eye.

Swallowing down the emotion in my throat, I turn to the phone. *"Thank you, Tess."*

She tucks the wooden Popsicle stick between her teeth and smiles. *"You're welcome,* Fabes. Now how do we make sure it doesn't happen again? We need to get those books out of boxes and somewhere safe. Where are Gramps's bookshelves?"

"Pretty sure Millie got them when we were divvying up furniture."

"So, you need new ones." I can practically hear her plotting already. She's going to be on the IKEA website as soon as we get off the phone.

I give her a stern look. "If you deliver a bunch of shelves to this house, I *will* tell Mom and Dad about the Paramore concert."

That sufficiently shuts her up, and I let her go so I can finish getting ready.

Twenty minutes later, I'm sitting on the front porch—mascara on my lashes and leather jacket on my shoulders—when headlights coast down the driveway. There's a hint of nausea in my stomach, and I'm not quite sure what to blame it on, but blaming things on Theo works great, so I try that.

The truck motor dies off as I walk down the steps, then look up to see Theo skidding to a stop at the tailgate.

All the oxygen in the state vanishes at the sight of him.

The last bits of sunlight are clinging to the tops of the pine trees, but even in the looming shadows, his eyes gleam bright as they slip slowly down my body. I *feel* it like a hot trail that dips over every curve, all the way to my toes and back up.

"Damn," he whispers, so soft that maybe he didn't mean for me to hear it.

A dark gray shirt stretches over his broad chest, layered under an open blue-and-gray flannel. His hair is styled perfectly like he took the time to fix it for tonight. Dark jeans are molded to his muscular thighs, and I'm starting to wonder if it's not actually the scrubs making them look so delicious.

My nails bite into my palms in an effort to stop me from reaching out to see how soft that shirt is. Or how hard the muscles are underneath.

He shakes his head as he steps closer. "You look gorgeous, Fabes," he breathes, voice thick and husky.

The compliment burrows into my chest. It finds a cozy spot, to burn like an ember, warming me from the inside out. It's dangerous—so fucking dangerous—how much I enjoy that feeling.

"Thank you." I tilt my head, searching for a way to get us back on track. I'm off kilter. This night was supposed to be RIP Theo, and instead, it's about to be RIP me. Murdered by the sex appeal oozing off my fake boyfriend . . . I mean business partner. I settle for: "You look like you thought this was a date."

His grin is cocky. "I think that's a compliment, because I look *good* for dates."

Dammit, I'm sure he does. I give him a simpering smile. "Is that what those poor women told you?"

"Aw, is someone a little jealous?" His eyes glitter, and I fight the urge to pinch him. "Your blush is giving you away."

Rolling my eyes, I turn away and walk toward the passenger door. "I'm *pretending*," I reply haughtily. "Isn't that the point in this whole escapade?"

A dark, taunting chuckle sounds behind me. "Ahh. Didn't know we were performing already."

There's no way I'm jealous at the thought of him on a date with someone else. I've seen him with girls when we were in high school, and I'm sure he does very well for himself in those no-string arrangements he was talking about. Objectively, he's an attractive guy. Devastatingly attractive, really. I'm sure he goes on lots of dates.

I'm not jealous at all.

It's just warm tonight.

Yes. That must be it.

*This is a business partnership,* I remind myself. *You're an actor, taking on the role of a lifetime, but instead of an Academy Award, you're getting insulated floors. Do not blush around him. Maybe don't even look at him unless you have to. Period. He sees all of it as a win.*

And I refuse to let Theo Nikolaou win anything tonight.

## Chapter 11

*Theo*

"Are you going to give me the cold shoulder all night?"

My question goes unanswered as Fable glares at the window in Maddox's front door.

I poke her shoulder and wince. "Ouch. So cold."

Her lips twitch. Only a millimeter, but I'll take it.

In theory, tonight should be a piece of cake. Maddox and his wife, Vivian, know this is a charade. So, really, Fable and I are practicing spending time together. It should be relaxed. Easy. A little chaotic (knowing the usual state of Maddox's house), but fun.

If I can get Fable on board.

"Do you mind telling me *why* you're ignoring me? You know, so I can write it in my journal later?" I lift an imaginary pen and pretend to write on my other palm. "*Reason number 8,975 why Fable isn't speaking to me . . .*"

"I'm mentally preparing for the performance I'm about to take part in," she says primly, but I can tell she's fighting a grin. "Pretending I like you requires a lot of effort, but once that door opens, I'll be *on*."

Perfect. I ring the doorbell again. "Let's get this show on the road, then."

Footsteps echo on the other side of the door, and she lets out a long-suffering sigh, her lashes fluttering to her cheeks. Then her hand slides into mine.

For a moment, all I can do is stare down as she laces our fingers together, a bolt of electricity zinging through me. Her palm is warm and soft, and I'm not sure why she felt the need to hold my hand but fuck if I'm going to question it. She fits perfectly there.

When Maddox swings open the door, Fable *transforms*. Her eyes open brightly, a smile stretches her cheeks until little brackets appear at the corners of her mouth. It's like she's flipped on a light switch, and as I watch it happen, I feel myself frown. She doesn't smile like *that* for me.

*Damn Maddox.* He's been there for everything—my one true friend since we met freshman year of high school. I'd take a bullet for him, his wife, or his sons.

But watching Fable smile his way? Makes me want to kick him in the shins.

"Welcome," he says, looking frazzled but happy.

Fable's hand leaves mine as Maddox hugs her quickly, then waves us inside. We follow a trail of yellow footprints on the tile into the kitchen, where Vivian is washing two-year-old Miles's yellow-tinted feet in the sink. Four-year-old Carter is running circles around the island, leaving more footprints as he goes, and their chocolate lab, Chewie, in lying on the floor, yellow staining her paws as well. A puddle of what looks like paint is pooling near the back door, the stove is pulled away from the wall with a row of tools spread out on top, and animated dogs are singing on the television.

Pure chaos. I love it here.

Maddox scoops up Carter and tosses me a package of baby wipes. "Mind cleaning Chewie's feet?" he asks before dunking Carter's feet under the faucet.

Carter waves. "Hi, Uncle Theo." Then he squints at Fable (who looks surprisingly unbothered by what we've walked into). "Who are you?"

"I'm Fable." She side-eyes me as she hangs her jacket on a barstool. "Your uncle Theo's"—a swallow—"girlfriend."

Surprise flickers through me. Did I forget to tell her that Maddox and Vivian know the truth? Surely, I told her. Right?

"Welcome!" Vivian says, tossing her braids over her shoulder and out of the way. "Sorry for the mess. Miles thought it would be funny to dump an entire bottle of paint on the floor." She smacks a kiss to his cheek. "*Hilarious.*"

"At least it wasn't red." I yank a baby wipe out of the package and squat beside Chewie to clean her paws, careful not to step in any paint. "Then it would like *blood*." I use my best creepy voice and Carter giggles.

"Blood," Miles repeats as Vivian sets him on the couch with a cup of snacks.

Maddox plops Carter next to his brother before grabbing a mop. While the boys watch a show, the four of us work together to erase all the evidence of yellow footprints and paw prints from the house.

When Maddox returns from taking the trash out, he washes his hands and eyes me across the counter. "In addition to all this," he says, waving toward the boys, "the oven crapped out on us this afternoon and I can't figure out how to fix it myself. So, how's pizza sound?"

"Perfect," I assure him.

"*Pee-zah!*" Miles screams.

As Maddox pulls out his phone, Carter hurdles over the back of the couch and runs to his dad. "Extra pepperonis!"

Vivian uses the dish towel to soak up a puddle on the counter, then leans against the surface. "I could use a glass of wine. Want one?"

Fable settles into a barstool. "Yes, please."

While Vivian heads to their wine fridge, I glance down at Fable—at the perfectly torturous view of the way her sweater dips to her cleavage and that adorable freckle that lives right in the soft swell of skin.

The first time I noticed that freckle, we were seventeen, and she and Mia were getting ready for a trip to the river. Fable breezed in the kitchen door. Bright orange bikini top. Cut-off jean shorts. Sunglasses in her wild hair. And so much bare skin.

My heart forgot how to beat.

All I could see were her sensual curves. Strong thighs. Tiny orange straps. Freckles cascading over her collarbones and down her chest. Then my eyes landed on one freckle in particular, bigger than the rest, sitting low enough to be hidden from the world normally.

My attraction to Fable has always felt like a living, breathing thing inside me, but most of the time I can ignore it well enough. That day, however, it *roared* behind my rib cage. My subconscious said, *Mine. That freckle is mine.*

I have no right to it, obviously, but that hasn't stopped me from looking for it every time I see her. I'm in for a long night with that freckle on display. A long night of wondering what it would feel like to press my lips there. How sweet her skin would taste on my tongue.

"You're staring," she whispers.

"Hard not to," I admit.

Voice dipped low, she murmurs, "People in real relationships aren't *constantly* staring at each other. You're going a little overboard."

I'm undeterred, still staring, following the cascade of pink as it flows over her cheeks and down her neck. I can't help myself—I lean into her ear and whisper, "You're blushing again."

Her lips tighten. "That's annoyance you're seeing."

"I don't think so," I tease.

Fiery hazel eyes meet mine. "I *will* murder you." She pastes on a smile when Vivian walks back in, but out of view, she reaches over and pinches my side. Hard.

\* \* \*

"They were in rare form tonight." Maddox drops into the empty seat beside his wife and starts disassembling the magnetic block tower that Miles insisted we have on the table for dinner. "Carter was convinced I needed to kiss every stuffie good night before he could go to sleep."

"And you did it, right?" I ask, running my hand over Chewie's head in my lap.

"Hell yeah, I did," Maddox confirms. "Anything for bedtime."

"It could be genetic," Vivian says, slouching in her chair and propping her bare feet on Maddox's thighs. He abandons the blocks and rubs the arch of her foot. "When I was a kid, I had to tell every single one of my Beanie Babies good night. There were at least thirty. It was a long ritual."

My lips curve up. "Fable and Mia were obsessed with Beanie Babies too."

"We were," Fable admits with a sigh. "Had quite the collection. I even adopted all my sisters' once they were tired of them."

"They wouldn't let me play with them," I add. I still remember the orange construction paper sign they'd tape to Mia's door.

A little stick figure me, with wavy *this-boy-stinks* lines coming off it.

Fable rolls her eyes. "You're just jealous."

"Of course I was. You were my friend first!"

That comment seems to surprise her. Maybe she meant that I was jealous of their Beanie Baby collection, but no. I was jealous every time she gravitated toward Mia and left me out. She was my first friend in a new town, and half the time, I lost her to my little sister.

I can feel Fable's gaze as I steer us back in the right direction. "I would dress up in a badass ninja outfit and try to sneak in and steal them."

"Did you have the one with the secret pockets?" Maddox asks.

"Yeah! I could fit like six Beanie Babies in there." I mime sliding them into pockets at my sides. "I took my job very seriously. Drew out plans for my attacks and everything."

Maddox snorts. "Irritating your siblings is a full-time job."

"He'd hide them from us," Fable says, appealing to Vivian now. "Mia never found her lobster."

I whisper to Maddox behind my hand. "That one got put in the river."

The women gasp. Fable turns to me with wide eyes. "*You did not.*"

I shrug. "It needed water."

"It was a Beanie Baby!"

"It was a lobster!"

"The tag was still on!"

I roll my eyes. "I was *eleven*."

Her eyes pinch. "Annoying little shit."

"You're not wrong. I did use my allowance to replace it though."

Vivian lifts her glass in cheers. "We're all thankful you grew out of that annoying-little-shit stage."

Fable murmurs, "Did he though?" She dips her chin to hide her smile, but I catch it anyway.

"Do you still have Beanie Babies covering your bed?" I ask.

There's a beat of silence. Her eyes flare with meaning, but I'm not sure why. "Obviously you *know* they're not covering my bed." She clears her throat. "Since we sleep together and everything. Since we're in a relationship." I smother a laugh as she turns to Vivian and Maddox and very unconvincingly adds, "He sees my bed all the time. Like every day. No Beanie Babies."

Huh. I'm starting to think I forgot to tell her they're in on this. Maddox and Vivian exchange a confused look, and listen, I have two choices here.

One: Tell her they know. Two: Play along.

And obviously—being the *annoying little shit* that I am—option two sounds way more fun.

Reaching down, I grab Fable's chair leg. It skids across the hardwood floors as I drag it next to mine. She lets out a little yelp, planting her hand on my thigh to balance herself. With a shameless grin, I curve my arm around her shoulders.

"We can get some if you miss them," I offer. "I promise not to take any to the river this time."

"You'd be dead meat," she threatens, her nails digging into my leg. "You think I don't know how to hide a body? I listen to a lot of true crime podcasts."

I slide my fingers through the ends of her silky hair. "Wouldn't doubt you for a second."

Our conversation turns to the Volunteer Fire Department (apparently Chief Harver is very excited about me returning), Vivian's day at the hospital (where a woman delivered a baby right in the emergency room waiting area), the budding romance between Logan and Mabel (word on the street is, there's a townwide betting pool for who everyone thinks is going to make the first move).

We're on our last sips of our drinks when Maddox asks, "Have you heard back about Little League?"

I shake my head. "Nah, no one's called me back yet."

Vivian's gaze bounces between Fable and me. "Are you two going to coach together?"

"Fabes is more of a soccer girl," I say, squeezing her shoulder.

"Used to be," she corrects. "That was a long time ago."

It may have been, but I remember every detail of her on that field. I was supposed to be there cheering for Mia, but Fable had most of my attention. Her fierce expression. The quick, powerful movement of her legs. Those two braids swinging at her back as she ran. Her whoop of excitement when her ball made it past the goalie.

A force to be reckoned with.

"She still has the division record for most goals in a season, girls *and* boys. And she set it as a *sophomore*," I announce, and Fable shifts in her seat. "You should've seen her on that field. Once she set her mind to something, she was unstoppable. She'd blow right past the other team and make it look so easy."

Fable stiffens. There's a flicker of emotion in her eyes as she peers up at me. I don't know what to make of it, but it's almost... strained. My fingers fold around her shoulder, offering comfort for whatever's going through her head.

"Damn," Vivian says. "Do you still play?"

She lets out a bitter, uncomfortable laugh. "No. I peaked in high school. Haven't kicked a soccer ball since my first year of college."

An awkward quiet hovers over the room—like none of us know what to say next—before Fable clears her throat and stands, excusing herself to the bathroom.

\*\*\*

"Think they bought it?" Fable asks as I come to a stop in front of her cabin.

"Bought what?" I pull the key from the ignition.

"The relationship. Even with your slipup about seeing my bed, you were surprisingly convincing. Getting me refills, dipping your pizza in my ranch like you do that all the time. So casual."

My lips twitch once. Twice. And then before I know it, I can't hold back my laughter anymore.

"What?" she asks, suspicious.

*Fuck, I have to tell her.* "Um. I thought I told you about this . . . but it seems like I didn't." I wince. Her face is full of shadows, but I can still make out her wary look. "Maddox and Vivian know the truth—that we're just faking it."

A beat of stunned silence stretches between us. Her lips part, shut, part again. Then she opens the door and is out of the truck before I can blink.

By the time I round the tailgate, she's stomping up the steps to the porch. "I let you put your *arm* around me! I lied to a *child*!" She gasps, glaring over her shoulder. "I shared my ranch with you!"

"I'm sorry." I follow her up. "Didn't I text you about it?" I could've sworn I was typing that out at work yesterday—*oh, shit*. That was right before we were called out to that emergency at the animal shelter. I must've forgotten to finish it.

"Better watch your back, Theo."

"Noted. *Reason number 8,976.*"

She stops at her door and turns. "It's truly a miracle I've made it through your presence this long without murder. That insulation is the only reason you're still around."

My gaze travels from her narrowed eyes to her flushed cheeks to her crossed arms. "You know, sometimes I think you actually enjoy my company. More than you want to admit."

One side of her lips curves up. Sassy and sexy. "Expert-level faking it."

I'm not buying that. "You mean every time your cheeks turn that pretty shade of pink and your eyes go sparkly—it's all fake?"

"You're not as irresistible as you think," she insists, but I don't miss the way her gaze flickers to my mouth.

My pulse thrums in my ears. "I don't believe you." I steal one step forward, and her back hits the door.

Moonlight shines on her wide eyes. Her throat works on a swallow.

"Are you faking it right now?" I ask, planting my hands on the door beside her arms and leaning in until her scent fills my lungs. Fresh spring air and flowers and Fable. I *inhale* it—breathe her in like my life depends on it.

"Yes," she whispers, her quick breaths warm against my cheek. Her tongue darts out to wet her lips, and I fight my hands not to touch her. "I'm actually plotting where I'll bury your body when this is over."

"Oh, yeah?" I drift closer until my lips nearly brush her ear. "So, the way your breaths are coming faster—that's for show?"

"Mm-hmm," she hums, low and smooth, and it shoots straight to my blood.

"That's *really good*," I whisper, my voice thick.

She makes a soft, smug sound. "Are you faking it right now too? Because your voice is abnormally deep, Theo."

I almost choke on the way my name sounds from her lips, this close and intimate. But I'm having too much fun with this little game to let her win that easily. "Yeah, I have a lot of experience."

"With women *faking it* around you?" She tsks. "What a shame. Thought you'd be better than that."

"Mmm." I breathe in her scent again, letting it drug me, lull me closer to the inevitable high. "So you've been thinking about me," I murmur, way too pleased at the idea.

A little growl of annoyance bursts out of her, and in a flash, she ducks under my arm and steps away. Cool air rushes back into my lungs.

She whirls to glower at me, half-dazed and flustered in a way I've never seen her.

A heady thrill zips up my spine. I've either royally pissed her off or she's more affected by me than she wants to admit. Either way, it's a win and I'm going to savor it.

"It'll be the manure pile in the back field," she decides, crossing her arms and tightening her jaw. "That's where I'll bury you."

# Chapter 12

## *Fable*

**Oaks Folks**

**Tessa:** Fabes, how'd the dinner go? Was Theo drooling?

**Fable:** Yes. Over a dog named Chewie.

**Tessa:** . . . you know that's not what I meant.

**Mom:** What did you mean?

**Tessa:** Fabes looked hot last night. I told her Theo would need a towel for his drool.

**Millie:** Why didn't we all get a fit check? I want to see!

**Fable:** The day I start sending you all outfit photos, you know I've been possessed.

> **Dad:** <selfie in muddy jeans and T-shirt> fit check!

*I* slept horribly last night, and there are three words to blame.

*That's really good.* Husky and deep. Vibrating across my skin.

All night, I tried to forget them. Tried to pretend they were about something completely different. Unsexy and boring. *That's really good broccoli casserole. That's really good laundry detergent. That's really good use of the Pythagorean theorem.*

Turns out, however, anything can be made to sound sexy when I'm imagining Theo saying it softly, right against the shell of my ear.

That asshole is currently taking up way too much space in this house. Acting like he lives here with music playing from his phone, a water bottle sitting on the kitchen counter, a bag of tools in the hallway, and a load of "fire clothes" in the dryer that he needed to wash before his first meeting this afternoon. This is his first day of A-frame work, and he's acting like he's moving in.

Knocks is hanging out with him in the downstairs bedroom while he replaces the wet drywall with a few sheets I found in Gramps's shed. He talked me through cutting and replacing the first piece, but I made up an excuse about needing to clean the kitchen cabinets to avoid being in that room with him any longer. Because if he says *that's really good* one more goddamn time, I might lose it.

I'm four cabinets in, sweat beading on my temples from the effort, and at an especially creepy part in a podcast, when I turn to find Theo in the doorway.

"Shit," I cry out, ripping my noise-canceling headphones off and standing.

The flannel he showed up in is long gone, leaving him in a navy T-shirt that's barely containing his giant shoulders. His hair's a little mussed, curling at his ears, and he has a big smile on his face. There's a stack of pictures and a metal box in his hands—the same one I discovered during the bedroom flood.

"What are you doing?" My voice comes out harsh.

His smile falters. "I found these in the bedroom. Have you seen them?"

My heart squeezes. I don't know what's in that box, but I know it was Gramps's. Which means it needs to be put back. Locked. Kept safe. Exactly where he had it.

I snatch the box and set it on the counter, then hold out my hand for the pictures. "Give them back. They're not yours. Or mine."

Theo watches me carefully as he hands them over. The second my fingers wrap around the photo paper, a sigh of relief rattles out of me. I press them to my chest and silence blankets the room.

After a few beats, Theo says, "Have you seen those photos?" His eyes are full of sympathy, like he can sense everything I'm not ready to say out loud. "You should look at them. They're of Gramps and—"

"I can't." I press the pictures harder into me, like I might absorb them and end this conversation.

Too late, I realize that choice of words reveals more than I'd like. *I don't want to* would be straightforward. But *I can't* implies something different.

A difference Theo doesn't miss. "Why can't you?" he asks, tilting his head.

*Because it would hurt too much. Because I'm afraid of how I would feel after. Because I have an unexplainable, looming sense that if I look, something will fundamentally change.*

He steps closer, and my first instinct is to push him away. Create distance between us. I can feel something destabilizing inside me, and I don't know what it is or how to stop it. I only know that he needs to be far away from it.

But when his fingers graze my elbows—the touch barely there, but warm—and his scent envelopes me—woodsy and sunshine and *comfort*—my heart settles a little. I draw in a slow breath.

"You're in them." His smile is gentle. "Just look."

Emotion clogs my throat. Something burns behind my eyes. And when I finally lower the photos, a choked sob bursts out of me.

The top image shows Gramps and me in front of an empty building. I'm probably seven or so, short blond pigtails, denim overalls, and an ice cream cone in one hand. Gramps is kneeling on the concrete beside me, an arm around my shoulders, a twin ice cream in his grip. The redbrick building behind us has a For Rent sign in the window.

I know exactly what this is, but I flip over the picture to confirm. And there's his messy, loopy script. *Our Bookshop, Seattle, Washington.*

Tears spring to my eyes. I feel Theo shift to stand behind me, his head curving over my shoulder as I go to the next photo.

This one, we're both in raincoats, a little younger, standing in front of a gray-walled, empty shop. *Our Bookshop, New Meadows, Idaho.* I flip through more pictures. A small white house. A corner spot beside a plant shop. A tiny airstream camper. All of them with Gramps and me, smiling in front of potential bookshop locations.

I don't remember every spot, but I remember Gramps in each one. He's so full of life in these photos. Kind, patient eyes. That wide, toothy smile. Those newsboy caps he wore everywhere.

He always traveled with us, every family vacation we went on, and he'd get so excited when he saw somewhere he thought would make the perfect location for his dream bookstore.

"Pull over! That's the one!" he'd say. We'd peek in the windows—he'd point to where the reading nook would be, the best location for the register, and how he'd lay out the shelves. "It's perfect. I'm tellin' you. We're gonna do this one day."

I can still hear the steadfast assurance in his voice. Blinking rapidly, I try to stop the tears gathering at the edges of my eyes. He was so sure we would get to do that one day, but now a stack of pictures in a metal box is all that remains of that dream.

Theo reaches around me to point to the top photo. "Look at your little umbrella. It's adorable. And Gramps's hat." His breath of laughter caresses my cheek. "What's the story behind these pictures?"

It takes me a few moments to make the words form. "It was always his dream to open a bookstore. Ever since he was a kid. But Grandma died when Dad was young, and Gramps was working full-time when they moved here. And I think his dream just never became a reality." I flip to the next picture, where we appear to be standing in front of a barn, and I choke on a watery laugh. He could see his vision anywhere.

Distantly, an awareness comes over me that I'm leaning back against Theo. He's a sturdy wall behind me, holding me up, warming me all the way through. I feel soft and vulnerable—not at all how I normally am in his presence. But for some reason, I can't bring myself to slip away from it. One of his hands lifts to slide up my arm, and I don't push that away either.

A tear slips down my cheek and I catch it with the back of my hand. "Once he'd spread his book obsession to me, it became *our* bookshop. He'd mention it everywhere we went. We'd talk about what it could look like and every time we read a book we loved, he'd make a note that we needed to stock it. And I guess he was collecting these pictures along the way." My shoulders shudder with a deep breath. "It was just a pipe dream."

I leaf through a few more pictures, some of them familiar and some I have no memory of. But I don't even make it all the way through before I realize tears are streaming down my cheeks.

My face crumples. Something has unwoven, and all my insides are spilling out. There's nothing left to fight against. I don't know if I've ever cried like this—as if the sadness is coming from some bone-deep reservoir inside me. Like I've been storing up all my grief for this very moment.

Before I know it, I've turned and pressed my forehead into Theo's chest. He wraps his arms around my shoulders, and I shake against him, letting my tears wet his shirt. As much as I've tried to keep a wall between us, his presence feels *good*. His hug is safe. Warm. Familiar.

He rubs my back. Presses his cheek to the top of my head. Murmurs soothing words I can't understand, but it's enough to *feel* them.

When my hiccuped sobs have slowed, I pull back to meet his eyes. He cups the sides of my face, slipping his thumbs over my cheeks to catch the dampness there. His gaze sweeps over my face, soft and searching. My own self-consciousness follows the path. I'm probably a mess—swollen-eyed and red and puffy.

I briefly consider hiding behind my hands or running to the bathroom, but my body is too drained. It's a wonder I'm still standing at all.

Slowly, the world around me comes into focus and I realize there's a distant ringing in the cabin. I give him a questioning look.

Theo's hands drop from my face. "That's my alarm that I need to get going," he says but doesn't move to leave. "For what it's worth, I don't think you should say that the bookshop is a pipe dream. If anyone could do it, it's you."

I scoff. I'm about as qualified for that as I am for space travel.

"I meant what I said at Maddox's." His voice is measured and deliberate. "Once you set your mind to something, you're unstoppable."

Just like last night, those words make me want to hide under a rock. He has no idea what he's talking about—that couldn't be further from the truth.

I set down the photos and wipe my eyes. "Theo, that's . . . not true at all."

His alarm is still ringing in the bedroom, but he doesn't seem to care. He cups my elbows, capturing my gaze. "Do you remember when you were eleven and your parents put up that rope swing over the pond? Your sisters, Mia, and I played on it all day, and the entire time, you stood on that platform, trying to work up the nerve to jump."

I frown. "Yeah, I was . . . *am* afraid of heights."

He smiles softly. "But even after we'd all gotten out and dried off, you were still up there."

All four of them lined the dock in their towels, eating hot dogs on paper plates, waiting for me. I was terrified—feet sweating, palms clammy, heart racing—but I wanted so badly to be able to jump. Just like them.

Millie and Tessa tried to convince me to come down—said it was okay if I couldn't do it. Mia whispered that she wouldn't tell anyone at school. Mom brought me a plate with a hot dog that sat untouched. Dad told me he'd build a slide instead if I thought that would be easier.

But Theo didn't give me an out. *You can do it. Just take a deep breath and jump*, he coached from the dock, patient and steadfast.

His thumbs glide over my arms. "And what did you do?" he prods.

"Jumped." I can still feel that stomach-dropping, breathtaking leap. The way the cool water crashed over my head, and I squealed beneath the surface, bubbles dancing in front of my face. When I got out, Theo was beaming.

He is now too. "I knew you would. Once you set your mind to it, it was a done deal."

That unwavering confidence makes my stomach twist, and it's not entirely uncomfortable. However: "You can't compare a rope swing jump to starting an entire business. They're not on the same playing field at all."

"And yet I believe in you even more now," he insists, sounding so certain that it's almost convincing. "You just need the right motivation."

"And where do I find that?"

With a cocky grin, he gestures to himself. "Isn't that the role we were playing for each other in high school?"

As I study his mocha eyes, something shifts in my worldview. All through high school—the prime of my life as far as accomplishments and achievements—Theo was there, pushing me to keep going, whether it was intentional or not.

Our only interactions back then were full of sharp looks and verbal jabs. We were subtly and not-so-subtly celebrating and gloating about our wins. But, in a way, it became addicting to see the light that sparked in Theo's eyes in those moments. The rest of the time, he looked like he was going through life in a fog—barely awake and distracted constantly. I used to watch his hollow expression and wish I knew how to get through to him.

When we were sparring over grades and class elections, though, he was *there*. Alive. Engaged. He seemed like himself again for those short interactions.

Maybe I was motivating him somehow too.

"I need to go," he says with an apologetic half grin. "But I did get the drywall done. Later this week, I'll work on the finishing touches."

"Okay," I whisper, my emotions raw and bumbling. I watch him leave the kitchen, then the alarm quiets in the bedroom. Knocks curls himself around my ankles as I place the pictures back in the box and shut the lid.

When Theo makes it to the door, his clothes from the dryer tucked under one arm, I walk toward him. "Thank you for . . . everything." It feels a like an inadequate statement, but I try to make my eyes say the things my mouth isn't.

*Thank you for letting me cry on you. For helping me with the A-frame. For believing in me more than I believe in myself.*

His soft gaze travels all over my face, like he can see everything I left out. "Anytime."

## Chapter 13

*Theo*

**Fable:** Things you left at the A-frame:

**Fable:** <photo of red water bottle>

**Theo:** In case you get thirsty.

**Fable:** ew

**Theo:** We're a couple. We can share drinks.

**Fable:** <photo of blue flannel>

**Theo:** So you have something to sniff when you miss me.

**Fable:** ew

**Fable:** <selfie scowling and flipping off the camera>

"Come back in next week and we'll see how that hot spot is doing," I tell Hal and Omar as they follow me out of the exam room. Their beagle, Elphaba, is wrapped in a blanket in Hal's arms, a giant plastic cone circling her head.

Omar sticks out his bottom lip and pets her muzzle. "Got the cone of shame, baby girl."

"She'll be out of it in no time," I assure them.

Hal shakes my hand. "Thanks for fitting us in."

"No problem." I'm waving goodbye when Garrett rounds the corner with a wide grin.

He has a paper bag with a Ladybug Café logo in one hand and two large drinks tucked into his other arm. "I got us lunch. You still like their Italian sub? No tomatoes?"

Surprised, I reach for the drinks. "Yeah. Perfect. Thanks."

I follow him into his office, where my gaze immediately cuts to his wall of pictures. He and his wife, Piper, moved here after college, and they've been an active part of this community ever since. If I didn't like the guy so much, I'd be jealous of his ability to fit in here so easily. But it's hard to hate him when he's exactly the kind of guy I'd love to go into business with. Thoughtful, patient, respectful to anyone who comes through those doors. Instead of being jealous, I admire the hell out of him.

He empties the bag on his desk and nudges my sandwich toward me. "Here you go."

"Thanks. You really didn't have to get me lunch." I take the seat across from him and open my container.

"Thought it might make our planning meeting more fun," he says, blue eyes twinkling. His chair creaks as he reaches behind him to grab two papers out of the printer. "I typed up everything I have already for the adopt-a-thon, but I was hoping we could chat about making this year's event a little bigger."

"Absolutely." I scan the full page, my throat going dry. There's already so much here. Vendors, volunteers, donations from local businesses. "This is . . . Wow. You've made a lot of progress."

He nods, peeling the wrapper away from his sandwich. "Since it's happening the same weekend as the Thimbleberry Festival, I wanted to get a head start on reserving things." He chews through a bite. "I'm in a bowling league with Carl, over at Premier Rentals. So, we started talking the other night about tables and chairs, and he volunteered to bring some over that morning. Then we ran into Mrs. LaGrande at the diner the other night, and her team is going to make like ten dozen scones for us."

I blow out a slow breath. "That's great." And by great, I mean shitty. Because I've officially done nothing to help with this project, while Garrett has already handled most of it. I'm at a disadvantage without the same community connections he has built over the years.

Historically, the adopt-a-thon is a small event. They set up a few portable fences in the town square and let the animals lure in the parade attendees. From what I hear, the timing has worked out well in the past, ensuring they have a great turnout, and Garrett says last year, every single pet got adopted. But this list—with tables, chairs, food, a few sponsors—seems a lot more extensive than in the past.

Garrett sets his sandwich down and wipes his hands on a napkin. "How do you feel about reaching out to some local rescues and shelters in neighboring towns to try and get as many animals adopted as we can? Might run into some issues with transporting them here, but if we can coordinate enough volunteers, it could work out."

I grab a pen from a cup on his desk to write down the rescues and shelters I know off the top of my head. "Sounds great. I can get that started this afternoon."

"We could also use some advertisements in local towns." His shoulders lift. "I'm not great with social media, but maybe Jenna can help with that."

"Yeah, I'll chat with her. Get as many people here as we can."

While we eat, we brainstorm a few more rescues I can reach out to.

Then Garrett surprises me when he asks, "Is Fable coming to the parade?"

My heart trips over a beat. The adopt-a-thon is included in our contract, but I didn't register until this moment that it was right after the parade. And given our history, I don't know the answer to his question.

It was an embarrassing event for both of us for different reasons. I was a loose cannon that morning and had no business getting into a fight in the middle of the parade. Shame coats my throat every time I remember it. I wish I could go back and change a hundred things about that day.

Standing to watch that same parade with Fable—I don't know if I can do it.

"I'm not sure yet," I reply before taking the last bite of my sandwich.

\* \* \*

BUMPER-TO-BUMPER TRAFFIC ONLY happens in downtown Fern River on three occasions. When Lou's Pizza is hosting their annual three-for-one sale, when Santa visits the square in December, and every Friday afternoon, from three thirty to five, when the Volunteer Fire Department gets together for a group training circuit.

Cars line both sides of the road. Today seems to be particularly popular with the misty, damp April air making our shirts cling to our bodies like we're competing in a wet T-shirt contest.

Maddox grunts, pushing a kettlebell into the air. "I know it's your first day, but we tend to actually work out. Quit smiling for the cameras."

Beside me, Lizzy and Brooks snicker as they copy Maddox's movements.

"I can do both." I pick up my water bottle and spray it in my best friend's face before he can block the stream. He barks a laugh, lifting the bottom of his shirt to wipe his forehead. I think I hear the sound of brakes squealing on the street.

"Cathy. Ten o'clock." He jerks his chin toward where she's crouched on the ground with a camera pointed our way. A hand smacks my stomach harder than necessary. "Look alive. Fable might see these pictures," he teases, and I return his stomach smack. "How is she?"

Instead of answering, I grab my phone off the bench and show him my new background photo. Fable's sitting on her couch, her knees tucked up to her chest, hair wild and wavy like she just woke up, with a sleepy little scowl and her middle finger pointed at the camera.

She looks absolutely edible.

He squints at the photo, then me, and chuckles. "Oh, so you're down *bad*."

"Says the man who was rubbing his wife's feet for an hour the other night."

"There's no shaming me for that," he says, shaking his head. "I'd do anything that woman asked me to, with a smile on my face. Put it on my grave: *This man was down bad for his wife since the moment he met her.*"

"I'll be sure it says that," I promise as my phone rings. An unknown number appears on the screen, and I swipe to answer it. "Hello?"

A man's voice asks, "Is this Theo Nikolaou?"

"Yes?"

"Hi, Theo. This is Drew over at the rec center."

"Oh!" I step away from the fire crew to hear better. "How are you?"

"I'm good. Got your message about coaching Little League this season." His voice dips like bad news is on the way. "But here's the thing. We don't have any spots open."

Disappointment slumps my shoulders. "Okay, I'm—"

"However, I do need a soccer coach."

I wince. "I played baseball—"

"Listen," he interrupts, sounding exhausted. "I had a guy drop out. His shifts got switched around and he's not gonna be able to do it. So I have a team of five- and six-year-old girls who desperately need someone—anyone—who can show up for them. And they won't give a hoot if you've never played soccer, I promise. We're not talking about the Olympics here. They're out there to have fun. What do you say?"

## Chapter 14

*Fable*

"Do you think I'm having a midlife crisis?" I ask Mia as I lean my elbows on the counter and peer around the empty hardware store.

She hums through the phone. "Have you already given yourself bangs?" Her keyboard clacks in the background, and as usual, I'm thoroughly impressed with her ability to multitask.

"Nooo." I drag the word out, my gaze straying to the old metal scissors in the cup beside the register. *What would Tessa do?* She already pulls bangs off beautifully. My face is a little rounder than hers, but I've never tried. Who knows? Maybe they'd look—

"Don't touch the scissors," Mia snaps.

"Fine," I grumble, dropping my head to my forearm.

She snorts a laugh and stops typing. "You're required to think about it for ten to twelve business days before you make any drastic hair decisions." After a short pause, she asks, "This midlife crisis isn't Theo's doing, is it?"

*Is it?* I've had five days to process his words. *Once you set your mind to something, you're unstoppable.*

It's not necessarily those words that have me feeling restless. It's the possibility behind them. It's the kernel of *what if* that's been rattling in the back of my mind ever since. I want to pop it open and see what's inside.

"I don't think so," I admit, my voice muffled against the desk. "Life is . . . a lot right now, and I can't quite figure out if I'm where I'm supposed to be. Or if I should be pushing for something different."

She's quiet for a moment. "What kind of different?"

My sigh is nearly a groan. "I don't know. I like my job here. It's easy, Logan's great, it doesn't really involve any stress." I stand, restless. "But I can't help wondering if I'm supposed to be reaching for something more fulfilling. Or if my true calling is somewhere else—in another town or another state."

"You're unsettled," she says.

"I'm always unsettled," I agree, walking down aisle two. "But I don't know if that actually means I need to *choose* to be settled. Quit looking elsewhere for a feeling of contentment. Stay still. Live in the moment." I straighten the front row of spray paint cans. "Or if I'm supposed to follow that unsettled feeling and reach for something else. I can't tell."

A few things clatter around through the phone before her espresso machine whirs to life. "Maybe it's like dating. What if you were with a partner who's pretty nice, but there's no passion? Say they know how to load the dishwasher, but when they kiss you, there's no fire in your heart. Do we settle?"

"No?" I ask, unsure. I've never experienced what she's talking about, so I have no clue if fire in my heart is a good thing.

"Right."

"So, my job should give me heartburn?"

"Not literally. But it should at least be something that gets you excited. Even stronger than butterflies . . . *dragons*. We want fire-breathing dragons in your heart, Fabes."

"Ouch." I wince.

"You'll understand when you feel it. You'll find a career that lights you up, then you'll come running back to me." Her voice pitches up in some Valley girl impression that sounds nothing like me. *"Oh my god, Mia, you were so totally right!"*

I mimic the tone. *"Someone, buy me some antacid because this heartburn it's, like, totally killing me."*

We both laugh as I curve around the end of the aisle and approach the glass windows at the front of the store. My gaze drifts over the street congested with cars, out to the grass, where there seems to be a lot of people milling around. And is that Cathy crouched on the ground with a camera?

*Oh.* It's Friday afternoon, which can only mean one thing. I turn toward the firehouse and—

*"Holy. Shit."* I nearly drop the phone.

The usual volunteer fire crew is there, but the newest member steals all my attention. Theo's front and center, doing a move I don't know the name of, but whatever it's called . . . it's . . . well, those biceps are working overtime with the weights in his grip, and I don't hate the sight of it.

Not even a little bit.

"What?!" Mia gasps.

"It's, um . . ." I wince, not about to tell her it's the view of her brother that just knocked the wind out of me.

My brain stops working when Theo pulls his sweat-soaked shirt off and tosses it aside. Someone in the community park squeals loud enough to make it through the glass. My eyes are greedy as they trail over his body. It's hard to make out every detail from this far away, but my imagination has no trouble filling in the blanks. Firm abs, bulging pecs, broad shoulders. It's already too much, but when he squats and those tree-trunk thighs flex, I'm done for. Something warm and achy pools in my blood. I think I make a choking sound.

"What's wrong?" Mia asks.

The only response my brain comes up with is: "Hot."

Distantly, I hear Mia yammering about how she doesn't know what I'm saying, but all I can concentrate on is her brother. He pauses, hands perched on his hips, chest heaving from effort, and my stomach flips over on itself. I want to climb him like a koala and bury my face in his neck. Sweat be damned.

The sight of Theo from a city block away is getting me more hot and bothered than Philip ever did up close. This is not normal. I should not be having this many feral and unhinged thoughts about *Theo*. Sure, he's attractive—so irritatingly attractive that it's hard to pull my eyes away sometimes. But this is a new level. My hormones must be completely out of control. I may be unwell. I should check my temperature.

"Want me to get you some binoculars?" asks a voice at my shoulder.

I squeak, whipping around to find Logan, who somehow made it all the way back from the coffee shop without me realizing it. My face bursts into flames.

Without a goodbye, I hang up the phone. "I was checking to see if . . . uh, there was . . ." I scrunch up my face. Damn my brain. "I don't know."

"Mm-hmm. Sure you were." He doesn't sound like he believes me at all.

I've been caught—red-cheeked and guilty. My best defense is to turn this around on him. "I saw you staring out the window when Mabel walked into work today."

His grin is shameless. "Difference is, I'll own up to it."

\*\*\*

I'VE TRIED EVERYTHING I can think of.

Deep-cleaned the kitchen. Wiped down the baseboards. Swept the front and back porches. Organized my closet by color. Vacuumed the couch. Scrubbed the inside of the fucking washing machine, for crying out loud.

I'm now on my second cup of tea, trying to calm myself from the inside out, and I'm still no closer to smothering the achy, wanting feeling running rampant in my body.

We're not going to *blame* Theo for this, because that would make it sound like he's the reason for it. But did the sight of him outside the fire station exacerbate the problem? *Yeah, fine, it did.*

Maybe if I get it over with, it'll be much easier to be around him. I won't constantly be thinking about him and his *that's really good*, all moan-y and deep right in my ear the other night.

"Fine," I growl, horny and angry about it. Grabbing my headphones, I practically stomp up the stairs, grateful when no steps break. I strip out of my work clothes and stand in front of my full-length mirror, surveying my lingerie. Today it's pale pink—a lacy see-through bra and matching thong. I feel sexy as hell in them but slip them off because the thought of getting into my softest pajamas is too good to pass up.

The creamy fabric glides over my body as I slide the tank top over my head and pull the loose shorts up my legs. I snag my vibrator from the nightstand and tug the headphones over my ears. They fit snugly, giving me just the right amount of noise-canceling to help me focus. I sit in the middle of my bed and press the icon for my erotic audio app.

At the top, a banner appears. *Today's new audio: Did someone call the fire department?*

"Oh my god," I blurt, swiping away from it as quickly as humanly possible. *Hell no. Absolutely not. I'd rather die.*

I settle on a guided session from a narrator I've listened to before. It's firefighter-free, praise the audio erotica gods. As soon as his deep, raspy voice hits my ears, relief loosens my tense muscles.

"Hey, there. Are you alone?" he asks. Chills race over my bare shoulders and arms as he lets out a low, gravelly groan. I set the phone on my nightstand and fall back against the mattress.

"Have you been a good girl?" He hums softly. I squirm, heat already pooling between my thighs. "Yeah, I know you have. You need some relief, don't you?"

I try to picture him in my head. Maybe he has long black hair, pulled into a bun, and dark blue eyes. He watches me slide a hand up my shirt. Soft whimpers drift from my lips, but all I can hear is the narrator's voice in my ears as he guides my movements, telling me exactly how he wants me to touch myself.

My other hand slips inside my shorts, and I glide my fingers through my arousal. All it takes is one gentle touch to have my hips twitching up to seek more pressure. I'm keyed up and agitated and desperate for relief.

I fumble beside me for the vibrator and press the button before sliding it into my shorts. My eyes squeeze shut, and I writhe into my hand as it pulses against my clit.

"You're doing perfect," the narrator says.

I imagine him watching my every move.

*Black hair, blue eyes.*

*Black hair, blue eyes.*

I repeat it to myself as my body surges with pleasure and my heels dig into the mattress. The wave builds, and I throw my head back.

*Black hair, blue eyes.*

*Brown hair, mocha eyes.*

A cry hiccups out of me when Theo appears in my fantasy. He studies me from the foot of the bed, his gaze burning with need.

*That's really good.* The words echo through the headphones, but it's Theo's voice I hear.

*No. No. Please no. I can't.*

"Theo," I whimper helplessly, unable to stop it from leaving my throat.

Pleasure forges up my spine and through my limbs, pulsing into every nerve ending. It's so close, it's *right there*.

But I cry out, desperate to stop it in its tracks.

*I refuse to come with Theo in my head.*

With a frustrated moan, I shoot my eyes open at the last minute—

. . . to find that mocha gaze blinking back at me from the end of the bed.

Rage and embarrassment claw their way up my throat. My scream is jagged, and I throw the vibrator with all my remaining strength.

Theo's lips are parted. He watches it hit his chest, and all I can do is groan, hurling myself to the side in humiliation and anger.

*Thud.* My head collides with the corner of the nightstand, and I crash to the floor as everything goes dark.

## Chapter 15

*Theo*

"*T*heo."

Her voice is desperate, making my heart pound as I run up the stairs to find . . . My knees buckle. I grip the railing, but it sags under my weight. My vision whirls, trying to make sense of what I'm seeing.

Tiny blue shorts. An ink-covered arm disappearing beneath them. Long, smooth legs writhing on a pale green comforter. Peaked nipples under thin fabric. A low, husky moan.

All the blood in my body rushes south. My mind wars with itself. *Get the fuck out of here! But she said my name.*

No, I have to get out. One last glance, then I stumble back to leave. But as my feet shift, her eyes snap open and crash into mine.

Everything freezes. The whole world halts like someone hit the pause button.

I'm officially fucked.

The silence pulses around me before her scream shakes the entire cabin. She hurls something in my direction. As it hits me square in the chest, I realize what it is. The pink vibrator tumbles to my feet, gives one more faint *buzz*, then quiets. For a heartbeat

I'm too stunned to move. Too turned-on to function properly. But then I crouch to grab it—because what the fuck else am I supposed to do—and have to bite back a groan when I find it slick with her arousal.

Fuck me, she's going to kill me. And that's fine, honestly. What a way to go.

A loud thud echoes across the room, followed by a tumbling crash. My breath stops as I drop the vibrator and rush around to the side of the bed, only to find her limp on the floor.

Despite the panic flooding my veins, my medical training clicks into place. I kneel and scan her body, making mental notes along the way. Eyes pinched closed. Small line of blood and swelling on her forehead. Lips parted. Lashes fluttering open—

"F . . . Fabes," I stutter, touching her shoulder lightly. "Are you okay? Where does it hurt?"

She yanks her headphones off and drops them to the floor. "Fuck . . . you," she mumbles slowly, pressing a palm to her forehead.

"Let me see." I move her hand away gently to find the trickle of blood running into her eyebrow. I stretch the bottom of my shirt out to catch it. "Did you hit the nightstand?"

"Fuck. You," she repeats.

Guilt is a heavy weight on my shoulders. I shouldn't have watched her, even for those few seconds. She's hurt again because of me. "I know. I'm sorry." I tilt her chin slightly to check for any other injuries. "I really am, but I need to make sure you're okay."

She scowls. "Fuck. You."

My fingers graze her skin, brushing the hair back from her face. "I think you might have brain damage. You can only say *fuck* and *you*."

Her eyes are the most fiery I've ever seen them, but she lets me help her sit up and lean against the bed. Then she fists the collar of my shirt, and—with a wince—tugs until my ear is an inch from her mouth. *"Fuck you,"* she growls, then pushes me back. Two middle fingers are thrust in my direction. "I hate you."

Ah, so she remembers other words. I bite the inside of my cheek to hide my smile. "You're allowed to hate me, but I'm your best choice right now for a ride to the hospital."

She scoffs. "Hell no. I'm not going *anywhere* with you."

"I have to take you, Fabes." It feels imperative. "You hit that nightstand pretty hard. Maybe even blacked out for a second."

"No shit, Sherlock," she grumbles, dragging the back of her hand through the blood. "I just bumped my head. It's nothing."

My heart stutters at her words. They catch in my brain, sounding all too familiar. Too identical to things I heard Mia say in the past.

The world tilts around me, the energy in the room shifting abruptly. Something squeezes around my throat, fear racing through me. I can't breathe.

*No, no, no.* "You . . . you don't understand." I swallow, my chest caving in. "I need to . . . I have to . . . make sure you're okay." My hands tighten on my knees, knuckles bleached white. "I can't do nothing. I have to do *something*."

Too many times I didn't know. Every bruise, bump, scratch—for years I did nothing. I can't do nothing again. *I can't.*

Her gaze searches my face. She looks momentarily taken aback before her expression softens. "Theo," she whispers. "It's okay."

"I can't do nothing." I don't know what else to say. Too many thoughts are fighting for space in my head. She's hurt because of me, and I can't run away like I did last time. I couldn't live with myself. I have to fix this the only way I know how.

She seems to hear everything I leave out. Her hands fold

around my wrists, fingers against my pulse. My grip on my knees loosens under her touch.

"Okay," she says softly. Gently. "Let's go."

\* \* \*

SHE LET ME carry her downstairs and watched carefully as I helped her into the flannel I left at her house. With shaky hands, I buttoned it down to her thighs, then scooped her up again. That time, she tucked her head against my chest—almost like she knew I needed it—until I got to the passenger side of the truck.

When we arrived at the hospital, they checked her vitals before questioning us separately. I gave the nurse every detail, probably more than she wanted to know about the room arrangement and shape of the nightstand. But I need them to have as much information as possible. There weren't enough questions asked when Mia was younger. Not enough people searching for details.

So I told the nurse *everything*.

"I need her to be okay," I said, dragging a shaky hand through my hair.

The older woman's eyes creased with a smile. "She's okay. I promise."

Now, I watch through the glass as Fable sits cross-legged on the hospital bed, talking and laughing with Vivian. She looks all right—just a small bandage beside her hairline—but that hospital band around her wrist has guilt gnawing at my stomach lining.

I should've left the second I found her. After my workout, I came over to ask if she wanted to help me coach soccer. When she didn't answer the door, I opened it, and as soon as I heard her call my name—

The scrape of the glass door startles me. Vivian steps out and gives me a hug—a long, knowing hug, like my emotions are written all over my face.

"She's okay," she whispers. "You did good."

An ache burns in my throat. "Thank you for taking care of her."

She pulls back and turns to watch Fable down the rest of her cup of water. "You should watch out for nausea or vomiting, dizziness, confusion. Anything out of the ordinary, really. But other than that, she should be totally fine."

"Got it," I confirm as Fable shuffles out, my flannel swallowing her frame and two little disposable hospital shoes on her feet. "I'll keep a close eye on her."

Fable tips her head toward me, her nose ring glinting under the hospital lights. "And I'll keep a close eye on him."

A silent conversation passes between them. Then Vivian gives her a hug, whispers something I can't make out, and waves her goodbyes.

"Sorry I forgot to grab your shoes." I set my hand on her lower back as we walk toward the exit. "Want me to carry you?"

She gives me a look. "I let you carry me in. I think I can walk myself out."

"Sorry," I say again.

The automatic doors slide open, and Fable loops her arm through mine. "Don't be. It was very *knight in shining armor* of you."

"No more scoundrel in ugly scrubs?" A warm breeze brushes against my cheeks, and I draw in a deep breath. Let it out slowly.

She pats my forearm. "Not tonight."

Once she's settled into the passenger seat, I stand in the open door, my heart beating an unsteady rhythm from the last couple of hours. Swallowing around the heavy lump in my throat, I whisper, "I'm sorry. I was excited to tell you something and burst in your door. Then I heard my name and ran upstairs, and *fuck*. I should've turned around immediately. I know I should've, but you were so . . ." I swallow thickly. "I didn't mean for you to get hurt. I never would've wanted that, and—"

"Theo." Her hands bracket my cheeks, and my words stop. She pulls me toward her, and I lean into the cab, planting my hands beside her thighs. Her palms are warm. Her scent fills my lungs. Calms my mind.

With only a few inches between us, her eyes hold me captive—firm and soft at the same time. "I'm okay. You're okay."

My jaw tenses. "You got hurt because of me."

She shakes her head, adamant. "*You* didn't hurt me. You would *never* hurt me."

I breathe in the words. Try my best to let them soak through to my bloodstream. The ache in my chest loosens a little.

Her thumbs glide in a slow caress over my cheekbones, and her lips curve up in a small grin. "Now, I could really use some dinner."

## Chapter 16

*Fable*

"This isn't the way to my house." I glance sideways at Theo. "Are you kidnapping me?"

A passing streetlamp illuminates his smirk, and it soothes my heart a bit. He's slowly coming back to himself.

"Not kidnapping," he says, turning onto the road he lives on. "But if I'm going to stay at your house, I need to bring Layla with me. She can't be by herself all night."

My eyes go wide. There's no way he can stay in my house. After everything he's seen tonight, I think some personal space might be for the best. "You know who *can* stay by herself, though?" I ask, pointing at myself.

"Vivian told me to keep an eye on you. I can have her on the phone in five seconds if you want to hear it straight from the doctor herself."

*Dammit, Vivian.* "I'm fine though. I have to be up early to help Dad fix the goat pen anyway, so I'll go to sleep right away and by the morning, I'll be good as new." Another idea dawns on me. "Or I can sleep at my parents' house . . ." My words fade away when I realize I'll have to explain the wound on my head. Maybe a hat will cover it.

A sharp turn into his driveway, then he pushes the gearshift into park and angles his body my way. "Let me take care of you. I'll cook you dinner, keep you company, tuck you in. Think of it like you're doing *me* a favor." His eyes are tender. So full of concern and warmth that all the fight leaves my body.

And that's how I end up with a large dog planting slobbery kisses on my cheek all the way back to the A-frame. She's truly adorable—white fur with splashes of fawn spots all over her body, three long legs, and enough excited energy that I wonder if she'll be able to sleep tonight.

When we arrive, Theo insists on carrying me inside. He sets me on the couch, fluffs the pillows, steals the duvet from my bed, and nestles it around me before handing over my phone from my nightstand. Then he pats me gently on the head, leaving me in a cozy cocoon. I even have built-in entertainment as I watch Layla's attempts to climb the boxes of books while Knocks sits at the top, tail whipping sassily. Only a cup of tea would make this better.

The audio erotica app is still up when I open my phone, and I swipe away quickly. The last thing I need is that replaying with Theo here.

Henceforth, that moment never happened. My brain is going to completely block that from the memory bank. No vibrator. No Theo. Definitely no thinking about the fact that it was *his* face that popped into my head right before the pivotal moment. That was a dream (nightmare?) and nothing more.

"Where are all your groceries?" he calls, opening and shutting cabinets.

"Don't have any." I scroll through my missed texts in our family group chat and heart all the pictures of Avery and Eloise at their school program. "Wait. Did you see the cereal?"

"Fabes, cereal isn't dinner. How are you surviving on no food?"

The kettle squeals, and I hide my grin behind my phone. Gotta give the man credit—he's actually great at this caretaking thing so far. "Hold on. It's a miracle. Found the stuff for grilled cheese. Knight in shining armor strikes again!"

I roll my eyes. "Don't push it."

He rounds the corner with a mug, dimples on show. "Milady," he says, offering me the tea.

I peer down at the creamy brown hue—the perfect color. When I lift my gaze to thank him, he's leaning closer to inspect my bandage. His fingers are featherlight against my forehead, brushing my hair back. My focus glides over his throat a few inches away. I could so easily press my mouth right there, where his pulse flickers rapidly.

Something in my stomach clenches. Yearns. Aches.

"Is it sore?"

I swallow. Let my eyes fall shut. "Mm-hmm."

A slow exhale. "Might be for a few days." His hand smooths over the top of my head. "I'll keep a close eye on it."

* * *

"This is actually delicious," I tell Theo, my mouth full of grilled cheese perfection. Crispy crust and the perfect amount of cheesy goodness. I wish I'd asked for two.

He tucks himself into the other corner of the couch, burrowing his feet under the edge of the duvet, his grilled cheese balanced on a plate on his lap. "You're saying 'actually' like you're surprised." Layla sits beside him, already begging for a bite, and he offers her a piece of crust.

"Well, the last time I saw you cook, we were thirteen, and you added crushed potato chips to the pancake batter."

"Wait, I forgot about that! Those were pretty damn good." He nods several times like he's proud of that idea. "Salty and sweet. We should try it again."

I make a gagging sound. "I'll pass. The texture alone was awful."

"Your loss." He laughs, chews through a few bites, then: "We should talk about the fact that you leave your doors unlocked."

"Trust me, I'm locking them constantly now. May even install two more locks, just for kicks. Keep out any unwanted guests."

"Totally. We don't want them coming in here."

My eye roll doesn't seem to bother him. "I don't remember inviting you."

"I came to tell you that the youth sports organizer called. They have an open coaching position starting next week." He tips his head back and forth, looking like there's more to the story. "Only problem is . . . it's not Little League. It's soccer."

I snort a laugh. "You don't play soccer."

"But my *girlfriend* does."

"I do not."

"Maybe not anymore, but you *did*. And you'd make an amazing coach."

"I would not."

That stupid, lopsided smile is back. Dimples carve out on his cheeks, and dammit he looks charming. Boyish and excited. "Come on . . . they're five- and six-year-old girls. It'll be fun!"

"No way," I insist, even as I picture what it would be like to coach Avery and Eloise. Their big smiles and pink cheeks. Clunky shin guards and baggy uniforms. Those two are adorable out there, and if I'm being completely honest, coaching girls their age does sound kind of . . . moderately . . . maybe a little . . . *fun*.

"Imagine being a six-year-old and finding out your coach is the high school record holder for most goals in a season." He looks and sounds like I've won five Olympic gold medals.

"Or the woman who finally got a ball past Nora Lopez—the greatest goalie in the state that year—*and* the player with most assists her senior year!"

My brain shorts out. I'm a computer that's been given too much information and can't fully process. I stare at him, fingers clamped around my plate. How does he remember all that?

"Orrrr," I counter, "their coach could be the guy who captained his team to the state championships two years in a row."

One brow quirks up. "You keeping tabs on me, Fabes?"

"You were first."

His piercing gaze burrows under my skin and makes me lightheaded.

I have to look away from it, so I set my empty plate on the ground. "How could we compete without keeping tabs on each other, right?"

That's the only thing that seems to make sense. Why else would he know all these random facts about a sport he wasn't in?

He's quiet for a few moments. "Do you ever wonder what it would've been like if we hadn't been bickering and competing all through high school?"

An unsure smile flickers over my mouth. "We wouldn't have been valedictorian and salutatorian, that's for sure."

My rivalry with Theo may have been my biggest motivator as a teenager. Everything changed after I left for college. I was alone, dropped into a world of options, trying to figure out my life in a strange city, surrounded by new people, and I couldn't figure out how to keep myself motivated.

It started with blowing off a class here and there. An unfinished assignment. A missed meeting with my adviser. A skipped soccer practice. Staying in bed was so much easier. So much less mental work. I didn't have to see my teammates playing better than me or other students making higher grades. If I stayed in bed, no one was beating me because I wasn't in the race.

If I quit trying, there's no risk of losing.

"Sometimes I wonder if it's the only thing that kept me on track back then," Theo admits softly. His mind seems far away as he stares out the dark window behind me. "It's no secret that was a hard time. I felt like I was walking around in a dark shadow most of the time. My anger was festering beneath my skin and making everything hurt."

I pull my knees up and wrap my arms around them, at a loss for words.

Emotion coats his voice as he continues, "But when you were there—urging me to keep going, pushing me to do better, giving me shit—I felt . . . like I could take a deep breath. Like my chest wasn't so cold. I had a goal and something to work toward."

I blink back the burn behind my eyes. He seemed so distant during freshman year—he'd pushed all his other friends away and folded in on himself. It was heartbreaking to watch, but I had no idea how to change it. His trauma was so much bigger than anything I knew how to fix.

As I watch him across the heavy silence between us, my mind slips back to the first week of freshman year. Dad had given us a ride home from school, and since Ms. Nikolaou had moved down the road from us that summer, Theo and Mia were in the minivan too.

Millie had promised to make snickerdoodle cookies, and everyone had dashed into the house to await them, leaving Theo and me outside alone. We hadn't said a word to each other since they'd gotten back from Oregon a week ago, but when he turned to walk home instead of coming inside, I broke our silence.

"Wanna come in?" I'd asked tentatively.

With his back to me, he'd frozen in place, shoulders tense. He had changed over the summer—he was taller, broader, and more muscular than when he'd left, like the weight of his world had grown heavier, and he had to adapt to carry it. Six months ago, we'd been laughing together about Tessa's first boyfriend and making fun of her for spending hours on the phone with him, and now Theo had a girlfriend, who Mia reported was calling every night.

The friendship we'd built seemed like it belonged to different people.

Several long heartbeats passed before he replied. "I need to get started on that English assignment. You heard Mrs. Stephens—it's going to count for fifty percent of our grade this semester."

"You mean the project that isn't due until November?" I forced a bitter laugh. "Are you sure you're not just running home to call your *girlfriend*?"

He finally turned to look back, his dark eyes sharp as they narrowed on me. "Maybe you should worry more about your grades and less about my love life."

And then he stalked away, igniting something in me I didn't recognize—the need to beat him at that project. To beat him at everything, just to prove he wasn't right.

Layla sets her head on his lap, as if she can sense he needs it, and he slides his hand over her ears. "It may not have been the kind of relationship we had before, but maybe it was what I needed to keep me going. I had to rein in some of the anger if I wanted a chance at beating you."

My heart feels like a fist is wrapped around it, squeezing. "I missed what we had, though. I missed you."

His face contorts in a deep frown. "I missed you, too, but I thought I deserved that after hurting you at the parade."

His throat bobs with a swallow. "Fabes, I . . . I'm sorry for what happened that day."

"I was all right." My lips curve in a sad smile. "Just took a trumpet to the head, but it wasn't bad," I add, trying to bring some lightness back into the conversation.

His hand glides over Layla's head slowly. "I'm still sorry."

I nudge his toes with mine under the blanket. "Theo, you're already forgiven."

A deep breath rattles out of him. "Thank you," he whispers. "And thank you for being there for Mia when I couldn't. I appreciate that more than I could ever explain. You and I may not have been friends anymore, but you put twice as much friendship into her. She needed that."

A tear threatens to slip past my lashes, and I blink it away. "I don't think you're giving yourself enough credit for the role you played in helping her."

Through Mia, I've been lucky enough to see their friendship change and develop through all that life has thrown at them. And even when he was struggling, Theo always put her first. From little things like letting her choose the movie they'd watch or giving up the last slice of brownie, to big things like shifting his whole life to care for their grandparents so she didn't have to shift hers.

He's a caregiver. A protector.

Everything his father wasn't.

There's a distant look in his eyes. "I didn't . . . I should've done better."

"You were going through your own awful experience too. She doesn't blame you for any of it."

Thoughts seem to shudder behind his expression. His lips press into a thin, pained line.

Something pulls tight in my stomach, urging me closer to him, and it only takes me a heartbeat to decide. With a little rearranging, I tuck myself under his arm, the duvet draped over both of us. I rest my head on his chest and feel his deep sigh rumble against my cheek.

He smells like the woods in summer, and I savor it. Let it transport me back to a time when life was much simpler. When we were building forts in the trees behind the farm, promising our parents that the five of us would sleep out there all night. When we were racing to the river, delirious on sugar and sunshine after eating orange Popsicles on the porch, pink cheeks and sticky fingers.

Layla hops onto the couch and curls herself into a warm croissant at my feet. Knocks's judgmental glare burns into me from across the living room, but I ignore him.

The weight of the last few hours is heavy in my chest, but the longer I spend pressed to Theo's side, the more tension flows out of my muscles. And it seems to be the case for him too. He slowly relaxes, slumping farther into the couch with each exhale. This should feel strange—cocooned in his flannel and a blanket, with his fingers grazing my shoulder—but it's surprisingly cozy.

My eyelids are drooping by the time his deep voice breaks the silence. "How's your head?"

"A little better." I sigh. "I'm dreading going all the way upstairs though."

He shifts against me, almost like he's getting more comfortable. "Go to sleep, Fabes. I've got you," he whispers.

Distantly, I wonder if his fingers are slipping through the ends of my hair, but I'm asleep before I can figure it out.

## Chapter 17

*Theo*

*T*urns out, farm labor in the early morning is more of a workout than my usual run. Between chasing goats and hauling lumber, Fable's dad and I are working up a sweat, despite the cool, misty air. Layla's wandering the garden with Fable's mom, Mary, while Dave and I fix the fence on one side of the goat pen. He didn't seem surprised at all when I strolled up in place of his daughter—simply hugged me and put me to work.

His phone dings in his pocket, and he sets down his drill to grab it. A snort of laughter barrels out of him. "Seems Fable's finally awake. She says, 'Sorry I'm late! Be right there.'" He peers at me under the brim of his blue cap. "Should I give her a hard time for sleeping in?"

I can't help smiling as I remember the sight of her in bed this morning. Long lashes fanned over her cheekbones. Hair in a wild tangle on her pillow. Sleeping so soundly I couldn't wake her. "Nah." I toss a broken fence board into the trash pile. "She was exhausted."

Dave types a response, then almost immediately, my phone buzzes.

**Fable:** Really?! Why didn't you wake me up?

**Theo:** You looked so peaceful, sleeping beauty.

**Fable:** Did you carry me to my bed last night?!

**Theo:** No, that was Layla.

**Fable:** 😳

**Fable:** I'm coming over there.

**Theo:** You want to explain how you got that bandage on your head? 👀

I snap a selfie of me crouched by a fence post and Dave in the background, both of us thumbs-up, grinning.

**Theo:** We're almost done. Don't worry about it.

That goes unanswered. I imagine her scowling down at her phone. Letting out that adorable, stubborn growl of hers.

It's a shame I'm not there to hear it.

Dave and I get into a groove for a bit. I grab boards and hold them in place, he drills in the screws, then we move to the next.

"Is Fable doing all right?" Dave asks after a few minutes.

I'm so startled by the question that I nearly drop the next board. It's strange to be the one who might know the answer to that. In some ways, I barely know her, and in other ways . . . well, I feel like I always have.

But I don't know how much she shares with her family. I have a hard time believing Dave knows about the broken stairs or the unsafe railing, because he'd be over there fixing them right now. Do they know she's barely moved into that place? That Gramps's things are still in boxes, and she only has the bare minimum of her stuff taking up the cabinets and drawers? Do they notice how sad her eyes get every time Gramps comes into the conversation? Do they know how hard she is on herself? How many times I've seen her cry in the last week and a half?

None of that is for me to share, though. "She's doing okay. We've been working together on the A-frame, you know, in exchange for her helping me with this Arthur stuff," I tell him, trying to shift the conversation.

He takes the bait. "How's that going? Mary said you're hoping to buy the practice?"

"Yeah, I'd love to buy it with Garrett. Both of us run the place." I shrug. "But Arthur is hesitant to include me. He doesn't think I'll be sticking around here long enough."

"But you will?"

I nod. "I'm staying. Being away made me realize—this is home." I hold up the next board. "I just have to show Arthur this is my dream."

Dave screws another board into place, then pauses. "You have a gift with animals, Theo. They trust you. They know you're one of the good ones. If you need anything from me to help prove that to Arthur, I'm here. Whatever it is."

Animals have always been a source of comfort for me, but my father hated the idea of having a pet. He had every excuse in the book—they're dirty, loud, annoying—and we were never allowed to have one. But I would befriend every animal I met, desperate to fill that space in my heart that wanted one.

Then, on a random Thursday evening—after the divorce was final and we'd moved into our new house—Mom showed up with a dog. She'd found him behind the dumpster at the elementary school. He was sad, untrusting, hurt in ways we couldn't see—so similar to how I felt at the time, and I had an instantaneous connection to him.

I like to think we healed each other in little ways for years. Chance was there to hug when I needed him in the middle of the night. He showed me that despite the fights I was getting into, I knew how to be gentle. He taught me that I could do this one thing—take care of him. And that became enough.

The job at the clinic is the one place I trust myself, and maybe that's why Arthur's doubt hurts so much. It feels like he's stripping away the one real thing I let myself have, and that means I'm going to dig my nails in and grip onto it with everything I've got.

I take a steadying breath and nod. "Thank you."

\* \* \*

As I WALK up the steps to the A-frame, I spot Fable through the glass. She's cross-legged on her couch, with a mug of tea in one hand, and scrolling through something on her computer with the other.

I turn the knob and . . . it's locked. *Good girl.*

She gives me a sassy little grin before snapping her laptop shut and carrying it to the kitchen counter. Taking her sweet time, she shuffles to the door and eyes me through the window, the mug tucked between her hands. She's wearing a form-fitting white shirt, light-wash jean overalls, and fuzzy socks. Looking cozy and warm. I have the overwhelming urge to wrap my arms around her and breathe her in.

"Good job locking the door," I call as Layla jumps up, her one front paw balanced on the glass.

Her brows arch. "Learned my lesson last time."

*Oh shit.* Does that mean—? The memory of her with that toy between her thighs burns behind my eyes again. Something hot and achy shoots through me, and my heart speeds up. She can probably hear it through the window.

Her eyes go wide, and she whips the door open. "Oh my *god*, Theo. I was taking a *shower*! Stop looking like"—she waves a hand vaguely in front of me—"*that!*"

Layla zips in the door and I hear a distant screech from Knocks. Apparently, their temporary truce from when they slept curled up together on the couch with me has ended.

I bite the inside of my cheek. "What am I looking like?"

She leans on the doorframe and narrows her eyes over the rim of her mug. Sunlight reflects off the gold hoop in her nose and brightens the strands of damp hair around her face.

"Like you were thinking about last night," she says matter-of-factly. "Which can't happen. We need to pretend those few minutes didn't exist. Okay?"

Ah, so I'm supposed to completely forget it was *my* name she moaned while she was getting herself off? Fuck if that's ever going to happen. Those two breathy, desperate syllables will be burned into my brain for the rest of my life.

"It's totally normal. Everyone does it. We're moving on," she announces with finality. But I can see the pink painted beneath her freckles. The way she's chewing at her bottom lip and avoiding eye contact.

"Right." My voice is gravelly. "Doesn't matter at all."

"Nope."

"Never think about it again."

"Easy." She takes a sip of tea, still not looking at me.

"We'll be very chill about it."

"Arctic tundra chill."

"Absolutely."

The space between us pulses with heat. There's nothing *chill* or *arctic* happening here. I step closer and her breath hitches. My fingers graze her chin as I tilt her head and inspect the bandage, enjoying the way I can feel her breath against my throat. I tuck her hair behind her ear, and she shivers under my touch.

*Oh, sweetheart, I can see right through this charade.* She's stubborn enough to never admit the truth, but it's written all over her—she's not nearly as unaffected as she wants me to think.

Clearing my throat, I step back, and Fable spins away before I can say a word. I smother a grin, following her to the kitchen, where we discover Layla and Knocks lying on the floor together.

"Have you decided about the coaching position?" I ask, needing to shift the conversation away from last night. If I keep thinking about it, all my blood will be pooling in inappropriate places.

She casts me a long, weighted look. "It's gonna cost you a *free space*."

Hope ignites in my chest. "Can I get us matching shirts?"

"Hell no."

"Come on," I beg, shamelessly using my best puppy eyes. "They're the Unicorns. We *need* a shirt with a unicorn on it."

Her shoulders drop, and she glares up at the ceiling, begging the universe for something. "Fiiiiiine," she groans, not sounding happy about it at all.

"You won't regret it. I'm going to make sure yours says 'district champ.'"

"I already regret it."

"Too bad. It was a *free space*—dealer's choice! Only stipulation was that it follows the plot, and given the gossip around our town, I'd say it does." I don't give her a chance to argue. "Now, come on. I need supplies. It's steps-replacement day," I announce, tugging her after me toward the door.

She drags her feet. "I have to work."

"Me too." I tip my head toward the stairs. "I'll knock it out while you're gone today. Then you don't have to worry about it."

There's a huff of annoyance as she pulls her still-wet hair into a bun and secures it with a green scrunchie. She loops a bag over her shoulder and across her body. "No touching my stuff though."

"Yes, ma'am." I nod, walking backward toward the door. "Should I look for a bookshelf too? Finally gets these books out of boxes?"

She seems taken aback by my question. Her feet stall on the hardwood floors. "They're Gramps's."

"Yeah, I know. Are they going to live in these boxes forever? We could get them out. Let them see the world!"

Her fingertips graze the nearest box. She stays quiet for so long I don't think she's going to answer. Then she whispers, "Maybe one day."

And that's good enough for me. I know exactly what to get for her birthday.

## Chapter 18

*Fable*

**Fable:** Things you left at the A-frame this week:

**Fable:** <photo of Layla's extra dog food>

**Theo:** In case we get to spend the night again!

**Fable:** <photo of red toothbrush>

**Theo:** Would you rather me have not brushed my teeth the other night?

**Fable:** I'd rather you took it HOME with you.

**Fable:** You're not moving in here. We're in a FAKE relationship.

**Theo:** Thing you left in my heart just now: 🗡️

Theo has always been unreasonably attractive. He effortlessly stands out as the most handsome guy in the room every time. Maybe it's the way his chestnut hair always seems to be the perfect amount of charmingly messy. Or those eyes that sparkle with so much mischief. Or the sharp jawline and annoyingly big muscles he stole right from a Greek statue.

Right now, though, he's at least tripled his attractiveness. He's running around with ten five-and-six-year-olds, in a lavender T-shirt with a sparkly white unicorn on the front, a matching flag tied around his neck, and the biggest smile I've ever seen. He's beaming sunshine straight out of his face, leading the girls in a curvy, loopy jog through the field.

"Follow the unicorn," he shouts, sounding like he's having the time of his life.

He got those shirts made so quickly, he must've bribed Brenda at the screen-printing shop. Or at the very least, flashed those dimples at her. They say *Coach Theo* and *Coach Fable* across the back, with a logo from the team's sponsor, Carlos's Taco Truck.

Dammit if these shirts aren't the cutest thing ever.

He spent all last Saturday replacing the broken steps while I was at work. The stairs are mismatched now, some with new, raw boards, and some the finished older ones, but Theo is going to gradually replace them all to match.

The rest of the house was exactly how I left it other than a note taped to the downstairs bedroom door. On a torn piece of notebook paper, he'd scribbled, "DO NOT ENTER! Birthday present loading!!" with a little hand-drawn loading symbol. Then at the bottom in tiny letters: "I'll know if you peek, Fable Oaks!"

I'll be honest—I almost peeked. Even turned the doorknob. But I didn't push it open. Something in my gut told me not to, and I'm pretty proud of myself for listening.

"Water break!" Theo calls, leading the giggling girls to the sideline. The crew of parents behind me pushes closer, handing out water bottles and telling the girls how amazing they're doing. Theo sits beside me in the grass, long, tan legs stretched out in front of him. "You coming back out there with us?"

I tip my head, staring out at the field. "The view's better from here."

He clears his throat pointedly, highly unimpressed with my excuses. "When was the last time you kicked a soccer ball? Are you allergic now or something?"

The grass prickles under my palms as I lean back on my hands. The reality is, I *love* soccer. For many years of my life, I lived and breathed it. On any given night in high school, you could find me watching recaps on my laptop. I followed all my favorite players on social media, kept up with their stats, and knew who was looking good for the next Olympics. My life consisted of soccer and books. The end.

Then I went to college and everything changed. I wasn't good enough to earn a soccer scholarship, but I did get a spot on the team. Once I got there, though, I felt overwhelmed by all of it. I was a tiny fish in a big pond, and there were so many people who were better than me. Faster on their feet, more consistent at scoring, exceptional at moving the ball where it needed to be. There were amazing, kind people on my team, and watching them shine so bright made me feel dim in comparison. And ultimately, useless.

I couldn't find the joy in it and didn't feel like there was any point in me being there. Between the two or three practices a day, time in the gym, eating a strict diet, and letting it consume so much of my time . . . I started to wonder if it was even worth it at all.

So . . . I quit. Things felt hard so I left, which became a trend for me.

I definitely haven't earned the right to teach these girls how to play. What kind of example am I to look up to? *Here's Coach Fable. Soccer got hard, so she quit and ran away. But, hey, do as she says and not as she does, and all that.*

When I still haven't answered, Theo bumps my shoulder with his. "Come on. You could stand out there and laugh at me for all I care."

I exhale sharply. "I can do that from here."

His gaze burns my cheek as he appraises me, but I don't meet his eyes. I set my jaw and stare out at where a few girls are kneeling beside the goalpost, plucking tiny flowers from the grass, just like Mia and I used to do. Mom and Eva would hold on to every flower we brought them during practice, then we'd press them into the pages of books when we got home.

"Enjoy the show," he says, patting my thigh before he stands and jogs toward the goal.

A few minutes later, I'm watching Theo in the center of the field, wondering who the hell decided he was qualified for this.

"Yeah, like that," he instructs, squatting to position Priya's foot to where her toes are pointed at the sky. "You're gonna kick with the bottom of your foot."

My head tilts. *What the fuck is he doing?*

He rises and steps away. "All right, go!" Her foot draws back then punches forward, her heel catching on the grass. She makes enough contact with the ball to move it a few inches.

Voices murmur behind me, the parents probably wondering the same thing I am—has Coach Theo never kicked a soccer ball in his life?

He takes the ball and tries the technique himself, then laughs when it barely makes it to the goal. "Just need a little practice," he assures them, the wind whipping the flag on his back.

A mom comes to stand beside me, her arms crossed as she watches him line up another child's foot. "What the hell?" she mumbles.

The little girl side-eyes the parents, her expression clearly asking, *Are you seeing this?*

Blowing out a sharp breath, I stand and cross my arms to match the woman beside me. Theo glances over for a beat, eyes dipping down my frame, then looks back at the kid. His instruction gets her another failed attempt.

"That's okay. We'll get there," he says, waving the next player forward, a girl named Emmy. "Sometimes you can even try with your heel. If you can get your toes pointed up enough, and the back of your foot pressed into the ball—"

"For fuck's sake," I grumble under my breath and take a step over the sideline. For a moment, I freeze, looking down at my blue tennis shoes against green grass. They're startlingly out of place. I should back up, hope no one noticed, and sit down. Let Coach Theo figure this out himself.

But then I hear *oh no* in the sweetest, little disappointed voice, and it snaps me back into gear. I jog toward them, ignoring the nerves itching under my skin.

"Hold on." I kneel at the front of the line and look up at Emmy. "Okay if I help you?" She nods and I smile. "Perfect. So, listen. We're actually not going to kick it the way Coach Theo said." I shoot him a pointed look. He shrugs. "There are a lot of ways to kick a soccer ball, but none of them are with the bottom of your foot. Let's start with this one."

With her hand on my shoulder for support, she lets me position her foot correctly and swing it back to show her where she wants to hit the ball. Then I stand and let her try. All the girls let out a whoop of victory when the ball travels much farther than before.

"That's amazing!" I give her a high five, and the next player steps forward. Moving to stand beside Theo, I scowl over my shoulder at him. "The bottom of the foot? Really? Have you ever even *seen* someone play soccer?" We all clap and cheer again as the ball rolls into the goal.

When he turns my way, his eyes are glittering, mischief dancing over his expression. "I used to watch this one girl play. She was breathtaking out on that field."

Something swoops and dips in my belly. I don't know what to make of that, how to file that information away in my mind, or what to say back. So instead, I turn and help the rest of the line of players practice kicking a ball into the goal.

When our hour is up, and we're walking back toward the sideline with our team, Priya reaches for my hand. Most of her dark hair has fallen out of her ponytail in the last hour, and a streak of dirt is smudged on her cheek, but there's a wide grin on her face. "Did we do a good job pretending?"

"Pretending what?" I ask, squeezing her hand.

"Coach Theo said if we pretended to kick with the bottom of our foot, you'd come help us."

I choke on a breath. My eyes meet his across the group, and his smile is absolutely shameless. That asshole knew exactly what he was doing, and I don't know whether to be impressed or angry about it.

*Annoying little shit*, I mouth, and he winks.

\*\*\*

"What time is your dinner?" Logan asks, poking his head around the corner from aisle three. He's been there for five minutes, rearranging the same screwdrivers over and over.

The entire afternoon has been filled with questions. *What are you doing tonight for your birthday? Who's going? What are you having? Do you need to leave work early? Did you bring a change of clothes? How are you getting there?*

On the surface, that sounds like normal conversation, but paired with Logan's behavior the rest of the day? It's suspicious. Like the fact that he asked me to come with him on his afternoon drink run (a honey and dragonfruit concoction from Mabel that he winced his way through), he shut down the whole shop to take me to lunch at the diner (which we've never done), and then he hasn't been hiding out in his office once today. The only time I've been by myself was for a trip to the bathroom. He has been hanging around the shop like he's waiting for something.

When Mrs. LaGrande showed up with a box of cupcakes, I thought that might've been it. But after singing "Happy Birthday" with her and shoving a cupcake into his mouth, Logan has still been on his hovering routine.

Other than my family serenading me in a giant group call this morning, my phone has been surprisingly quiet too. I haven't heard from Mia (which is weird) or Theo (which wouldn't have been weird a few weeks ago, but given our now-regular texting habits, seems weird).

Birthdays have never been my thing, but this year feels extra uncomfortable. I'm twenty-nine today. Staring down the barrel of thirty. With no plan for my life. Not even a hint of direction. I've distracted myself with fixing up the A-frame—but then what? Compared to everyone else around me, I'm spinning my wheels.

Today doesn't really feel like a celebration at all. It feels more like the walls are closing in.

I'm going to have a stiff drink—or two—later.

Logan moves to the window, watching out the glass for a few moments. He shuffles one way, then the other, trying to get a better view.

Something weird is going on. I feel it in my bones.

Suddenly, his shoulders perk up and he whirls toward me. "Fable . . . um . . . don't move. Stay right there," he says, waving to the register.

"Okaaaay." He's so adorably nervous that I can't help but play along.

He wrings his hands. "Maybe close your eyes too."

I bite back a laugh. "All right." *Finally*, we're getting to the bottom of this.

His shoes squeak against the floor as he paces, waiting for whatever this delivery is. Maybe he got me flowers? I hear him clear his throat, then the bell over the door jingles, and a familiar voice squeals, "Surprise!"

My heart leaps up my throat. I open my eyes to see Mia running toward me, her arms spread wide and a giant smile on her face. She's *here*. My best friend is *here*, and I can't think of anything I need more today. I dart around the counter and into her arms.

"Happy birthday!" She hugs me, and I get a face full of her long black hair, but I don't mind at all.

"How? What . . . ?" I soak her in. "I was about to be so mad at you for forgetting my birthday."

"Told you she would be." Theo chuckles, but I can't see him on account of the hair.

"You know me too well. I couldn't call. You'd figure it out," Mia says.

"I forgive you because you're here," I exclaim.

Mia pulls back, and I see the moment she spots the tiny bruise still on my forehead. It's mostly faded, only a tinge of yellow left, but she zeroes in on it. "What happened?"

Blood rushes to my cheeks. I give her the same answer I've doled out for the last week. "Bumped into an open cabinet."

Instinctively, my gaze bounces to Theo. He's standing by the door, the tiniest smirk pulling at his lips, looking downright delicious as always—hands shoved into his dark-wash, fitted jeans, broad shoulders taking up all the air in here, and a nice button-down shirt with his sleeves rolled up to reveal those thick forearms.

The audacity of this man for coming here, looking like *that*. I hate how much I want to bite him. Respectfully. Disrespectfully. Somewhere in between.

"Damn. That must've hurt," Mia coos, steering us toward where Logan and Theo are waiting. "Bree's here, too, but she got a work call right as we pulled into town. Fancy lawyer shit and all that."

I narrow my eyes on Logan. "Is this why you've been suspicious all day?"

He paws at his beard. "This guy didn't tell what time they'd be here," he grumbles, tipping his head toward Theo. "Just told me to, 'Make sure she stays around the shop.' Feels like I've been babysitting all day."

A laugh tumbles out of me. "Lucky for you, I was on my best behavior."

"Except when you were too pushy with Mabel." He grimaces. "Trying to get us to go see the botanic gardens together."

Mia wiggles her shoulders. "That sounds like a great date idea."

"Right? That's what I said!" Logan scoffs, but color rises on his cheeks. "You're coming to dinner, right?" I ask him.

"Oh, no." He shakes his head. "I've got stuff going on."

Mia straightens to her full height—all six feet—and levels him with a stern look. "You're coming to dinner."

He ducks his chin to hide a grin. "Well, okay then."

Once I grab my stuff—and offer Theo the last cupcake, which he devours in two bites—Mia steers me out the door. "I need to make one quick stop at the coffee shop," I say, turning us in that direction. "We've got to convince Mabel to come to dinner too."

## Chapter 19

*Theo*

"Wait. You two are coaching soccer now?" Mia shouts over the country music playing through the Branch.

Fable's smile is the widest I've seen it in a long time. She's two margaritas deep, and the bartenders here make a mean drink, so she's adorably tipsy at this point—all giggly and uninhibited. "You should see your brother on that field. Running around, decked out in sparkly rainbow unicorn gear, with his little unicorn-minions running around behind him." She titters into her glass. "He looks ridiculous."

"—ly handsome," I finish for her, slinging my arm over the back of her chair. "I caught you smiling a few times."

She glares up at me, but there's no heat behind it. "Fine," she says to Mia and Bree. "It's so cute, actually. Those girls love him already."

"Knew it." I clink my water cup with her now-empty glass. "Thank you, Ethan, for this magical truth serum."

Mia flips her hair over her shoulder. "Who would've thought we'd see the day when you two were working *together* on something?"

That catches Mary's attention. She leans over and nudges Mia's shoulder. "Maybe I should sneak over to a practice and see them in action?"

Mom perks up beside me. "I'll come with you!"

"Bring the fancy camera," Dave adds. "Get some good photos."

Mia pounces on that idea instantly. "Yes. Send them to me."

"Looks like I'll be sitting out the next practice then," Fable announces.

I shrug a shoulder. "I don't know. I was pretty fucking convincing last time."

"*Language*," Mom scolds.

Fable tries to conceal her smile, but I catch the corners of it. That alcohol has gone straight to her cheeks. They're practically glowing pink.

"Ohhh, do tell," Bree says, leaning forward and perching her chin on her fist.

Fable side-eyes me. "I wasn't participating in soccer time, because... *reasons*. Then your brother did the most annoying—"

"—ly adorable," I interject.

"—thing." She elbows me in the ribs. "He teamed up with all his unicorn-minions and they made a plan that if they acted like they didn't know how to kick the ball, I'd get up and help."

"And did it work?" Bree asks.

Fable rolls her eyes. "He was teaching them to kick the ball with the *bottom of their foot*." She steals a handful of my fries, and I let her. "Of course it worked. He was embarrassing the both of us."

Mia grins at me affectionately. "Well, what else is new, really?"

Fable pats my thigh, her expression dipping into something soft. "But did you see Ariana by the end? She really had the hang of it."

"She was so proud." I curl my hand around her shoulder, pulling her an inch closer.

In the back of my mind, I know I should stop touching her so much, but it's like a compulsion at this point. I'm trying to rationalize it. Tell myself it's normal to feel this way about her. She's beautiful and kind and magnetic and soft in surprising ways. It's bound to happen—this rush of . . . wanting. It's growing in tendrils, reaching for any tiny bit of her it can get. It's spinning around me so much I'm dizzy with it.

I'd hoped that spending time with her would quench my thirst for more of her, but it only seems to be multiplying. I *want* so much it hurts. I *want* in a way that's treading dangerously close to something deeper than I'd planned, and I'm fighting a losing battle to put those thoughts back in the cage where they belong.

Mia sets her elbows on the table. "I heard we're going house-hunting tomorrow."

"Fabes and I are. I didn't invite *you*." I give her the kind of withering smile specifically designed for siblings.

Her gaze narrows threateningly.

Leaning into Fable's ear, I whisper, "Oh, she's big mad. Look, her nostrils are flaring."

Her hair tickles my cheeks as she laughs. "And that vein is popping out in her forehead, see?"

Mia tosses a fry and it hits me in the jaw. "Please, Theo. It'll be like real-life Zillow creeping. Bree and I have been training for this for years—hours of time spent on that app when we weren't even trying to buy a house."

Bree looks wistful. "You remember that cottage in Scotland? I think about it all the time."

"Yes." Mia gasps patting her fiancée's arm. "With the little garden in the back? We should look that up again." She pulls out her phone and distractedly asks, "How many houses do you have lined up?"

Apparently, we're bulldozing past her lack of invitation. "Cathy sent me two or three, I think."

"Fuck's sake, Cathy," Fable and Mia chirp. We all look down the table to Logan, who takes a break from staring dreamily at Mabel to raise his beer bottle proudly in our direction.

Behind him, the main door opens, and my stomach knots when Arthur appears, strolling toward the hostess stand with his wife.

Things were busy at the clinic this week. Garrett and I have been working hard on the adopt-a-thon planning, and I got in touch with most of the rescues and shelters in the area. There's going to be a big turnout if we can gather enough volunteers to help transport animals. Everything is looking really good, except that I'm on edge every time Arthur is around.

I feel like I'm putting on a show for him. Like this is all a performance, and it's an unsettling sensation. I've never tolerated lying—it probably stems from my experience growing up but lying and secrets always make me uncomfortable. And this feels like the biggest lie I've ever told. I'm doing things I wanted to do anyway but doing them for this reason . . . it's sitting weird in my stomach. I can't figure out how to come to terms with it.

"Let's dance," Fable says, standing and grabbing my hand.

A beat of stunned silence. "What do you mean?"

"It's a thing people do when there's music." She sways her hips to the peppy beat, and my gaze drops to catch the movement. "You know you want to," she says, tugging me up.

*She* wants to dance with *me*. One hundred percent, we can blame this on the alcohol. She's unfiltered and unconcerned. But it's dancing and she's asking.

Hell yes, I want to.

As I stand, I meet Mia's eyes across the table, and her expression is smug, like she's somehow the mastermind here. "Have fun," she singsongs. Fable leads me away, and I distantly hear my sister whisper something about soft pretzels.

Fable's fingers are folded around mine until we get to an open spot on the dance floor, and she spins my way. "How do I look?" she asks, hands perched on her hips.

I grin, taking her in. Her honey-blond hair is in a messy knot at the back of her head after she was laughing so hard an hour ago that she got marinara on the tips. A low-cut dark-green dress with tiny, delicate flowers hugs the curves of her breasts, then flairs at the waist and fans out above her knees. That freckle I love is there, along with the tattoo peeking out at her shoulder and wrist. Bare legs and black Converses and small gold hoops in her ears.

She looks like a dream I'd never want to wake up from.

"You always look beautiful, Fabes."

I get an eye roll. Somehow that wasn't the answer she was hoping for. "But do I look like Theo's girlfriend?"

My heart pauses for a beat. What does *Theo's girlfriend* even look like? I've never really let myself picture it. But that gaping, achy *thing* inside my chest—the one that keeps drawing me closer to the woman before me—whispers faintly that if it was anyone, it would be her. Lazy mornings and bare skin. Sharing fries and sharing secrets.

Fable doesn't give me a chance to answer as she lifts one hand to my shoulder and links her other with mine. "Because I'm contractually obligated to put on a show here." She looks toward the edge of the dance floor where Arthur and his wife are seated at a table. "I signed on the dotted line."

*Oh.* That reality check burns on its way down, blanking my mind for a moment.

"Put your arm around me," she instructs.

Despite the pinch in my chest, I follow her lead, my hand covering the velvety fabric at her waist. The material is so thin it's almost nonexistent.

I breathe in her flowery scent. It's not a factory-made flower smell, poured into a bottle and slapped with a label. No, it's straight-from-the-garden—like she planted them, watered them, picked them, and set them in her kitchen window. It's intoxicating and real.

Fable steps into me and her breasts brush my chest. Longing coils around my spine. I love the way she feels against me. In my hands and in my lungs. But it's taking all my concentration to remember she's pretending right now. I'm tipping over the edge of . . . *something*, losing my stomach in the process, and she's still on sturdy ground.

I force myself to move us around the dance floor, and she falls into rhythm with me. Our toes bump a few times, and she snickers under her breath.

She looks up at me through golden lashes. "Are you okay? You look like you're in pain."

"I am."

"To which part?"

My hand flexes against her waist. "Both?"

Her head tilts. "Why are you in pain?"

I almost don't reply. My brain says to keep the status quo, make it through this dance, go home and have a cold shower. Or two.

But my heart says fuck it. She's half drunk on alcohol, I'm half drunk on her. She's putting on a show, I'm very much not. How can the truth make this any more complicated?

"I'm in pain because a stunning woman is in my arms, and I can't remember how to dance properly. Or even function, really." I trip over her toes on our next step, proving my point.

Color flashes over her cheeks. "Want me to teach you how?"

"To dance or to function this close to you?"

"Whichever one is more important."

"I'd say the functioning."

A grin curves her pretty pink lips. "Here's what I do. When my brain is going all fuzzy because you look exceptionally bitable or your mind-melting dimples show up, I try to remind myself of all the annoying things you've done."

A small laugh bursts out of me. "Bitable?"

She smacks my chest lightly. "Do not laugh at me."

"Sorry, yes, this is very serious." I school my features. Let my thumb trail over her side. "What exactly are you trying to bite?"

"Nothing." But her eyes betray her by dipping to my forearm.

I'm having trouble not grinning like a fool. "A love bite or a draw-blood bite?"

"Enough to leave a mark, I guess."

Heat pools in my stomach at that thought. I want that. Very much yes. She can mark me up any way she pleases. A low, deep groan pulls from the back of my throat.

She shivers. "See, you can't do that either. Add that to the list of things that make it hard to function."

I almost do it again, just to see what happens. "Ah. What annoying thing are you thinking of to cancel it out?"

She swallows. Thinks. Sighs. "It's hard to find one right this second."

"On account of the dimples?" I ask, smiling so I know they're showing.

"And your smell and the irritatingly firm muscles." Her nails dip into the hair behind my ear. "And this. How does it always look adorably unkempt?" My eyes fall shut under her touch, but then it's gone, her hand back to my chest. "Mostly, though, it's you in general. How you always see me and seem to know what

I need. How you take care of me in little ways, even though you don't have to."

Warmth infuses my muscles. I don't know how much of this conversation she'll remember tomorrow, but I'll never forget it. She sees *me*, even if she's cranky and glowering, she knows my intentions, and that soothes something inside me.

As the song fades away, Ethan's voice flickers over the speaker to announce that someone ordered soft pretzels. "You all know what that means," he says, then the first few notes of Billy Joel's "Just the Way You Are" drift through the bar. Out of the corner of my eye, I see Mabel pulling Logan to the dance floor.

I spin Fable twice, savoring the way her dress twirls around her pretty thighs. She laughs as she lands against my body, tucking herself closer this time. My hand spans her lower back, and I ease us into a slow rhythm.

"What about me?" she asks, eyes glittering under the bar lights. "What makes it hard to function?"

The tension thickens between us. I can practically taste it in the air. I stare down at the freckles sprinkled over her cheeks. That perfect pink mouth I'd give anything to taste.

"Everything," I admit, sliding a loose strand of hair behind her ear.

She pouts. "That's not fair. I told you real things."

"You're right." I take a breath and bring my thumb to her cheekbone. "First, it's this blush. The way it flashes over your cheeks when you're angry or happy."

Her face goes scarlet like I'd hoped. Her breath hitches. The bar feels light-years away at this point. It's just me and Fable here, floating in each other's arms.

"Then, it's when your eyes get fiery. Gold blazes in the center, and *god*, I want to burn right there. Makes annoying you so fucking worth it."

Her gaze holds mine, unflinching. She's lost that giggly state from the table. Shifted into something serious, and I don't know if that means she's sobered, or if the tension between us has stolen away the humor.

I dip my chin to look between us where that freckle sits in the subtle slope of her cleavage. "And this damn freckle. You don't know it, but you torture me with that freckle. I search for it every time I see you."

Her chest moves with a breathy laugh. "Really?"

"I *dream* about that freckle." I trace my thumb over the edge of her mouth. "It's also the smiles you try to hide from me. I love catching a glimpse of them when you think I'm not watching." A smile blooms under my touch. "But mostly, it's you in general," I say softly. "Your big, stubborn heart and your friendship and the way you make me feel safe with you."

Her smile hitches wider—raw and open and beaming. My knees go wobbly at the sight of it.

She tips her head, assessing me. "Are we flirting?"

I move my hand back to her hip. "Yeah, we are."

"Is it weird for you?" Her gaze dips to my mouth. "'Cause it's . . . not for me."

"Not weird at all." My thumb slides against the material of her dress. "Feels like the most normal thing in the world."

She nods. "Fun, even."

"Why do you think I've been doing it for so long?"

Her eyes flash, something wild and reckless dancing in their depths. I'm having so much trouble untangling my own thoughts that there's no chance of figuring out hers.

She licks her bottom lip. Clenches her fist in the front of my shirt. "Theo." Those two syllables strum right over my heart. Send something molten rippling through my blood. "What if we—"

Her words are cut off when the bar erupts in a round of applause, as it does every time this song ends. Everything around me surges back into focus. The people. The smell of stale beer and fried food. Someone cheering from a table.

Fable looks away. The moment shattered.

What if we . . . *what*? I'm about to ask her to finish the rest of that sentence when she pats my chest and steps out of my arms.

# Chapter 20

## *Fable*

**Oaks Folks**

**Millie:** Sorry we couldn't be there for your birthday, Fabes!

**Tessa:** Me too!

**Dad:** You all missed a hell of a party.

**Dad:** There was a beer slip-n-slide.

**Dad:** And balloon monsters.

**Dad:** Everyone dressed up as their favorite farm animal.

**Mom:** We did none of that.

> **Tessa:** Dad, your ideas of a good time are bizarre. Not inviting you to any of my future parties.

> **Dad:** You'll be missing out.

> **Dad:** Ask your mom about that party in 1982.

> **Mom:** I will not be answering ANY questions about that.

> **Millie:** please

> **Tessa:** pleeeeeeease

"That third margarita might've been a mistake," I announce as Theo guides me up the steps to the A-frame. It seemed like a good idea at the time—a cold drink to cancel out the hot feeling in my belly after that dance with him.

Did it help? No, Your Honor, in fact, it did not. That hot feeling is still eating me alive from the inside out.

Maybe I'm hungry. That must be it—drunk and hungry. I need food.

"I'm no expert," Theo says with a laugh. "But maybe it was also the shots you and Mia did before you danced to 'It's Gonna Be Me'?"

"Oh yeahhhh. I remember that." I trip up the last step and he steadies me. "Still can't believe Ethan played *NSYNC."

A deep chuckle sounds behind me. "Don't think it was his first choice, but Mia wasn't letting it go."

I stumble again. Damn these two left feet. "I love Mia. She's the best friend ever."

"Good, because I think you're stuck with her." The world stops moving and keys jangle at my side. He must be unlocking the door. Thank goodness, because I think I'm tilting.

"Whoa." I land against a warm wall of muscle and let it hold me up for a minute. It smells nice here. Like trees and manly things. I could live here on this wall, I decide. I'm never moving from this spot. Doesn't matter if *NSYNC shows up in the flesh and tells me I must move, I'm not doing it. This wall is my home now.

The wall pushes into me. "In you go," it says.

I resist the urge to stomp my foot like a toddler. "I am *not* leaving this spot."

"Did you just stomp your foot?" Theo asks, grabbing my arms to steer me inside.

"No, I didn't. I'm twenty-nine years old." I transform my voice into an absolutely horrendous rendition of a Jane Austen–era heroine. "I have no money and no prospects." I hiccup once. I'm butchering this, but I keep going anyway. "I'm a burden to my parents and . . . and I'm *frightened*. So don't judge me, Theo. Don't you dare judge me!"

"The fact that you can quote the 2005 *Pride and Prejudice* but not walk in a straight line is really an accomplishment," he says, herding me around the couch.

I whirl to face him. "You've seen that movie?" The room keeps spinning even when he grabs my elbows.

"Yep. You and Mia watched it a lot growing up, remember?" *Oh, yeah.* Knocks pushes himself against my ankle and Theo bends to pick him up. "This little guy needs food, I bet."

I gasp. "Food! Yes! I need that too." I tumble toward the kitchen and rip open the fridge. Damn past-me for not going grocery shopping again. As much as I want to be able to survive on tea and audiobooks, it's just not cutting it. "Where are the *snacks*?"

Theo chuckles as he flips on the light and scoops out food for Knocks. "We're going grocery shopping tomorrow."

"We?"

"We." He rummages around in the cabinet for a moment. "I'm taking you. To make sure you actually do it. You can't live on hazelnut spread and Ritz crackers."

"Excuse me, *sir*," I say, reaching into the cabinet beside him. "You take that back. I absolutely *can*." I tear into the cracker package like a starving raccoon. The silverware drawer screeches as I yank it open and pull out a butter knife. Then I sit on the counter, swinging my feet, as I spread the chocolate-y, hazelnut-y goodness on crackers and shove them in my mouth.

Theo watches me, his eyes crinkling on the edges with amusement.

"You wanna try?" I offer, dipping the knife into the jar.

"Sure." I fix it up for him, and he chews with a thoughtful expression. Finally, he says, "All right. I concede. It's really good."

"Dark chocolate is where it's at," I inform him, holding up the container.

"We'll be sure to get some more at the store tomorrow, then." He reaches around me for a water glass, fills it, and hands it to me. I down half of it in one go.

Tipping my head, I stare up at the ceiling. The beams sway a little, making me feel even more dizzy, so I look back at Theo instead. He's watching me intently, dimples carved out in his cheeks and mocha eyes dialed-in. I have all his attention.

But that makes me feel swirly and upside down, so I focus on my snacks again. Snacks are safe. Snacks are good. Snacks don't have lopsided grins that make my stomach curl into knots. I eat two crackers in a row without looking up.

All of a sudden, Theo is on his knees in front of me. One hand grabs my ankle and my drunk-lizard brain screeches in the back of my head. *What is happening? Is he about to lift up my dress?*

*Ohhhh. He's unlacing my shoes. Cool.* I am very cool and not at all warm at the sight of him on his knees in front of me.

I need to get a grip.

He unties both of my shoes and pulls them off, leaving me in short wool socks, before he leans against the other counter.

"Thank you," I whisper. Or croak, rather. I don't know, it comes out weird. I clear my throat, trying to think of something funny to say to alleviate this tension somehow. "It's been a long time since I drank this much, but you're pretty lucky. Normally after alcohol, I'm hungry, turned-on, *and* crying." I shake my head, shoving one more cracker into my mouth and garbling around it, "Tonight it's only two out of three."

A choking sound leaves the back of his throat. Then silence drenches the room, only punctuated by the slow crunching inside my mouth. Maybe that wasn't nearly as funny as I thought. His pupils are blown wide, which is odd because I'm the drunk one—he was nursing a water glass all night. His knuckles are white as he squeezes the edge of the counter.

I swallow hard and wash it down with the rest of my water. "There's still time for tears though." I laugh, twisting the lid onto the hazelnut spread.

He scrubs his hands down his face and groans behind them. "Come on, Fabes. You can't tell me stuff like that."

"It's okay. The crying will probably happen after you leave. I tend to get emotional when I'm drunk. One time, Mia had to take my phone away because I couldn't stop sobbing over videos of these two penguins that fell in love. The zoo even had a wedding for them!"

He tilts his head up, like he's pleading the swaying beams for help. "Not the crying part, Fabes."

I try to think of what he means, but that was more than thirty seconds ago, so I'm not sure I remember. Then it hits me. "The part about being turned-on?"

He looks like he's in pain. "*Yes*. That's exactly the part."

I roll my eyes. "You saw me . . ." I wave a hand vaguely in the direction of upstairs, trying to remind him about that time he walked in on me with a vibrator. "I think we're past that."

"Are we?" His arms cross over his chest. "Because Sober-you told me a few days ago that we were going to forget it ever happened. We were going to be as chill as the arctic tundra."

"Sober-me is *so* boring." I let out a dramatic groan and hop down from the counter. The room shifts under my socked feet, and I almost fall, but Theo curves one strong arm around my waist.

He sounds amused when he says, "Okay. Let's get you to bed, birthday girl."

I hum in agreement, and he turns off the light, guiding me toward the stairs, his hand warm on my lower back. "What about my birthday present?" I ask, pointing toward the downstairs bedroom door. "I still haven't peeked. Are you proud? You should give me a gold star."

His laugh is a rush of air by my ear. "I'm very proud. You can see it tomorrow."

"Promise?"

"Cross my heart."

"And you'll get me a gold star?"

"A whole pack."

When we reach the bottom of the stairs, I glare up at them. They're a little blurry and overwhelming, so instead, I sag back against Theo and relish the way it feels to let him hold me up. I'm so tired, and I bet he would make a really good pillow. We could lie down right here for the night.

He laughs softly, his hands sliding up from my elbows to my shoulders. "I think you have plenty of pillows upstairs."

*Oh, shit. My brain needs to stop thinking out loud.*

I go up one step, then turn to look at him. Most of his face is cast in shadows, the smallest bit of moonlight from the big windows dancing over his cheekbones, illuminating his grin.

My blood feels like champagne, bubbly and sparkling with possibilities. He's right here—broad shoulders and perfect composure. Cool, calm, and collected.

I want to take him apart. Rip that composure away and see what he looks like wrecked and undone, when my hands have been sifting through his hair and his lips have been touching mine. Messy and disheveled because of me.

Something pulls in my stomach. A tug, urging me closer. Maybe this is the perfect time to give in. Theo doesn't do real relationships, and honestly that sounds fabulous. A fling. A temporary arrangement. Orgasms with a hot guy? What an amazing birthday present, actually.

I'm doing it.

His expression sharpens slightly as I lean forward and crash into him—my arms around his neck, our bodies pressed together. He absorbs my momentum, keeping us upright, but he doesn't put him arms around me.

"Theo," I whisper into his hair—his soft, silky hair that smells like something my brain is too fuzzy to identify, but it smells *good*. Incredible. I could sleep in *there*, actually.

With a deep sigh, he finally wraps his arms around me. My toes are barely touching the ground, and we soak each other in for a few moments before I pull back in the circle of his arms.

Our breaths mingle, our mouths only inches apart. There's heat brimming in his gaze when his eyes drop to my lips.

*That.* That right there is my signal. He wants this just as much as I do.

Head full of confidence and heart full of bravery, I bring my mouth to his.

But they never connect. Theo's hand slips between us and his fingertips cover my lips. "Fabes," he says firmly. "No."

My stomach bottoms out. Embarrassment flames through me. I pull away and almost trip up a step. But Theo catches me again. Strong hands on my waist. An apology in his eyes.

"Sorry, I just wanted—" I drag a hand down my face. "I don't know what I wanted, but for some reason I thought you wanted it too."

A pained noise rushes out of him. "It isn't a matter of *wanting*," he says with a tortured expression. "The way I want you, Fabes . . . the way I've always wanted you." He drops his forehead to mine, subtly shaking his head back and forth. "Of course I've dreamt of kissing you. Thoroughly and enthusiastically."

I sigh, folding my hands in the front of his shirt. "Then why aren't we kissing right now? I bet we'd be great at it. We'd have good chemistry. I feel it in my bones." Kissing him sounds exhilarating. Just the right amount of reckless.

He groans, a bitten-off, jagged sound from the back of his throat. "Because you've been drinking." His head lifts, his heavy gaze meeting mine. "And if we're going to do this—give in to this thing between us—I want it to be a conscious choice. I don't want to be something you regret tomorrow morning. My heart couldn't handle that."

"But . . . I've been wanting you longer than just tonight."

His fingers graze my cheek and tuck a strand of hair behind my ear. "Then tomorrow. If you still want this. Okay?"

My whole body droops as exhaustion sweeps in. "Okay."

A ghost of a smile flickers over his mouth. "Time for bed." He nudges me to turn and continue upstairs.

I trip over the next step, and he mutters under his breath—something about *fucking railing* and *unsafe*. He keeps one hand anchored on my waist the whole time, like he's worried I might fall at any moment.

When we reach the loft, he sits on the edge of the bed while I go the bathroom. I drop the toothpaste once and bang my elbow on the wall while trying to get my bra off, but I manage. By the time I reemerge—sans makeup and wearing my favorite shorts-and-tank sleep set and socks—Theo's elbows are on his thighs, his focus on the ground.

As I step out, his eyes lift. It's a slow drag, all the way from my toes to my face. His throat bobs on a swallow. His gaze falls behind me, to the lacy bra and panties set lying on the ground. He squeezes his eyes shut.

"I'm going to get some water." I take a step toward the stairs, and he jumps up.

"No. No way in hell I'm letting you walk down those steps in your current state. They're basically a death trap." He points to the bed. "Sit. Stay."

I arch a brow. "Woof?"

One dimple appears. "Lie down," he orders before descending the stairs.

I'm half asleep by the time he returns but sit up long enough to take a big drink of water before falling back to the mattress. I catch his hand after he sets the cup on the nightstand. "Sit. Stay."

He gives my fingers an affectionate squeeze. "I can't."

"I might try to go down the steps again."

"That wouldn't be very wise."

I try pleading with my eyes now. "Lie down. You already know I'm prone to crying while drunk. You don't want that, do you?"

A muscle ticks in his jaw. "Sweetheart, *please*."

The endearment lodges somewhere in my chest. He says it like that word was made for him and me. Like it never existed before it dripped from his lips, syrupy and thick. I have half a mind to tell him I'm not sweet at all, but the way he's looking at me—full of affection and longing—I think maybe I could be.

If he thought that *sweetheart* was going to make me give up, he was so wrong. I pull harder, wrapping both hands around his elbow and yanking him over me. He falls easily—like he's a house of cards tumbling over—landing sideways across my body.

It takes a minute for him to get situated. He kicks off his shoes and sends a quick text before he lies flat on his back beside me, on top of the covers. Long legs stretch down to the end of the mattress. I don't think he's breathing.

"Theo?"

"Mm-hmm?"

A yawn. "Thanks for staying."

His pinky slides over and curls around mine on the blanket. "Fabes?"

"Theo?"

"Happy birthday."

\* \* \*

I WAKE UP in a straitjacket.

Which shouldn't be that surprising, given the memories that filter back into my mind as I come into consciousness. I think Mia and I danced on the karaoke stage? A fantastic lemon vanilla cake was in attendance, maybe? There's a vague vision of me smearing icing on Mia's cheek and Bree licking it off, and I think I was showing my parents videos of miniature donkeys and telling them they should get some for *the vibes*.

All those moments are hazy on the edges, but a few flicker in crystal-clear. Theo twirling me on the dance floor. His thumb sliding over my bottom lip. Late-night snacks in the kitchen. Dimples in the moonlight.

*Are we flirting? Yeah, we are.*

The straitjacket tightens. My pillow shifts. A soft, contented hum hits the nape of my neck.

I barely contain a gasp as my eyes flash open. Holding my breath, I peer down. Thick, tan forearms greet me—one banded across my collarbone, the other around my waist. Time slows as I take inventory of everything else I can feel. A cozy blanket wrapped around me. Kitten curled at my thighs. Breath puffing against my bare shoulder. Warm bicep under my head. A long body pressed to my back, curved behind my legs.

*He stayed.*

My pulse is like an accelerating drumbeat, building into a big crescendo. It's a wild, feral thing inside my chest, and I don't know how to slow it down. Another hum leaves Theo's throat, and he pulls me even closer.

That's when a new memory drops into my mind. An almost-kiss. Fingers blocking my mouth. An apologetic smile.

*Fabes. No.*

Oh, god. I tried to kiss him. No, worse than that. I tried to kiss him, and he turned me down.

Embarrassment washes through me. This is awful, actually. I need space. Wait, I need more than space. I need to move towns. I need to move planets. I don't know how I can look him in the face ever again.

My mouth feels like it's full of cotton balls, there's an elephant-size pain in my head, and my heart is racing like we're in the Kentucky Derby. I need to get away from here. I try to wiggle, squirm, and shimmy my way out of his arms, but every inch I gain, he steals back, pulling me closer. His breaths are steady, like he's still asleep, and every time he tugs me in, his muscles relax again.

I'll be honest, it'd be really damn adorable if my heart wasn't crumpling with humiliation and my bladder wasn't fighting for its life.

Finally, I whisper, "Theo."

I hear him swallow. "You can't go down those stairs, sweetheart."

Goose bumps prickle over my shoulders. *Oh my god*, Theo's voice first thing in the morning is more than I can handle. It's rough and delicious and I want to—fuck, I'm getting distracted.

"I promise I won't go downstairs. Just the bathroom."

A low sound—maybe a hum, maybe a growl—leaves his throat as he loosens his arms, and I wiggle my way out. At the bathroom door, I turn back and *dammit*, it's a mistake. He looks soft and rumpled, still in last night's clothes. Sexy layer of scruff on his jaw. Little cowlick in his hair. Pillow creases on his cheek.

In my bed. Theo is *in my bed*. And, sweet hell, does he look good there.

*Get a fucking grip*, my brain whispers. *You made a fool out of yourself trying to kiss that man last night, and he let you down as nicely as he could. Have you no shame?*

I start to shut the door but pause when he leans up on one elbow. "Fabes?"

"Yep?" I chirp, a little too high-pitched.

A slow blink. "You still want to come house-hunting? If you don't feel up for it, it's okay."

"Mm-hmm. I can do it. I'm just going to . . . uh . . . take a shower first."

He runs a hand through his hair. "Sounds good. I'll find us some breakfast."

I slam the door before I die of embarrassment.

## Chapter 21

*Theo*

"As you can see, everything is very modern. Very sleek." Cathy waves her hand in a sweeping arc through the kitchen. "All the appliances are brand-new, and the counters are only about a year old."

"What do you think?" I ask Fable, trying to catch her eye but it doesn't work.

"It's . . . nice." She looks like she'd rather be getting a root canal.

I don't know what happened between dragging me onto her bed and when she woke up this morning, but *something* did. I spent all night burrowing myself as close to her as I could. Meanwhile, she was apparently dreaming up a new list of reasons to hate me.

I thought stopping to get her favorite chocolate chip scones from Wildwood Bakery would help, but it didn't. She has been icy and distant all morning, hiding behind Mia and only faking a smile when Cathy looks her way.

My sister slides her fingertips across the slate-gray countertop. "Everything is beautiful, but I don't know. Something feels off for you two."

This place is all sharp angles and straight lines—none of the charm I'm looking for in a home. I want warm wood. Exposed beams. Character and quirks. I don't want the fanciest house on the block, I want the most comfortable and welcoming.

The first house didn't have that, either, and I'm realizing maybe I didn't accurately explain to Cathy what I was looking for. Or perhaps I didn't know until I was here and could definitively say this is not it.

Cathy clears her throat. "Let me show you the master suite. That may change your mind. The Jacuzzi tub is to die for."

When she turns to steer us out of the kitchen, I block Fable's path and bend to meet her gaze. "What's going on?"

"Nothing. I'm fine." It's the kind of *I'm fine* that comes out of a woman who's actively plotting your death.

Cathy's voice echoes from the living room. "And isn't this the perfect window to frame your Christmas tree?" Fortunately, Mia's there to *ooh* and *aah* appropriately.

"It sure doesn't seem like you're *fine*," I tell Fable. "You're barely looking at me."

She purses her lips. "I'm looking at you right now."

"This"—I motion motion to all of her. Crossed arms, cocked hip, sharp scowl—"is mad-looking. Last night, you were—"

"Please." Her eyes squeeze shut. "Do not bring up last night."

My lips part as I try to piece the problem together, but I must be missing important information. Twelve hours ago, she was warm, relaxed, trying to kiss me. Now she's distant and cold.

Mia calls our names, and Fable steals the opportunity to escape this conversation, leaving me standing in the kitchen.

While we're touring the master suite, I can't even focus on Cathy's sales pitch because I'm too busy replaying the events of last night, trying to catch the moment that might've upset

Fable. I remember every detail. Her infectious excitement as she smeared hazelnut spread over crackers. The adorable grin when she realized I'd seen *Pride and Prejudice*. Her sleepy, half-lidded eyes when she begged me to stay with her. The sound of her soft sigh once I curled behind her in bed.

I'm not sure where it went wrong.

By the time Cathy is done showing us around the master bathroom, I know this isn't the house for me. I don't need to see the rest of it. What I *need* is to know what's going on with Fable.

So, as everyone turns to leave, I call Fable's name from the bathroom. She reluctantly traipses in with her arms crossed.

"Please tell me what's up." I shake my head. "You've gone from begging me to stay with you, to not speaking to me. What did I do wrong?"

"I didn't beg," she insists, scowl still in place.

"You did. Yanked me into your bed, in fact."

A head tilt. "You weren't complaining."

"I'm still not." Luckily, Mia and Bree slept in my guest room last night, so I'm sure Layla had the time of her life cuddling in bed with them. "I had no idea it was going to come with that bedtime serenade. I think it was a Fleetwood Mac song, but you were half asleep, so it was hard to tell." Her cheeks turn scarlet, and something clicks into place. "Wait, is this because you're embarrassed? Fabes, everyone does something silly when they're drunk." That only seems to make her angrier. "Honestly, if you made it all the way to your twenty-ninth birthday without drunkenly embarrassing yourself, I'm impressed. So don't worry about it. You sang yourself right to sleep."

Her lips tighten. "That's not it."

"The British accent, then? We can work on that."

"No, Theo," she grits out.

"The mess in the kitchen? It only took me thirty seconds to sweep up the cracker crumbs. It's fine."

She covers her face. "Please stop. You're making this *so* much worse."

I grab the back of my neck, thinking. "If it's about you and Mia dragging your dad out on the dance floor, I think he's—"

"It's the kiss, okay?" she whisper-yells, hands stretched wide in the air between us. "The almost-kiss. Whatever it was." I'm stunned speechless. I can't even find a response before she continues. "It's all the flirting and dancing and looking at me with that *look* you do sometimes . . . my drunk brain was confused. Hence why I flung myself at you. And I'm sorry, okay? Sorry I was so messy last night. Sorry I tried to kiss you."

I shake my head. Words finally come back. "What? Why would you be *sorry*?"

Her feet shift. "The wires got crossed somewhere, but it's fine. I need to brush it off and move on. Obviously, you're allowed to not want to kiss me—"

"Not *want* to?" I drag a hand through my hair. "What do you mean?" And then it *finally* makes sense. "You don't remember, do you?"

She goes still. "Remember what?"

My throat feels tight as we stare at each other. Rain pelts the window over the Jacuzzi tub, and in the dreary, dim bathroom, my mind whirls me right back to that almost-kiss. Her arms around my neck. A hum against my ear. Hazel eyes in the moonlight. How could she not remember that? It felt like the most destabilizing moment in my life—admitting to the *want* coursing through my veins.

She searches my face, a hint of uncertainty creeping in, but then Mia's voice ricochets into the space between us.

"Fable? Theo?" She rounds the corner to find us in the middle of the bathroom. Her dark eyes narrow, sensing something's off. "What's going—"

"So, you love the bathroom, huh?" Cathy says, rejoining us. "I knew you'd be a fan of that tile work," she carries on, giving her Realtor spiel at full volume.

I hold Fable's gaze for a moment, willing her to remember last night. Remember what I said. Remember how it felt to be in that moment. Confirm it really existed and wasn't a dream.

But she looks away. Mia watches me carefully as Fable hooks their arms together and steers her out of the bathroom.

"Oh, moving on then?" Cathy asks excitedly. "Let's go see the dining room."

I trail after them in a daze. We tour the dining room, where Cathy points out we could fit a table big enough for both our families, the laundry room, which is large enough to hold a party in, and the garage, where Mia teases that I can keep an extra bed for when Fable kicks me out of the house.

A sassy *hmm* comes from Fable. "Not a bad idea."

I smirk, enjoying the way that seems to piss her off more. "As long as Layla and Knocks get to sleep with me."

"Uh, no," she snaps. "They'd rather sleep with me."

"Maybe your *memory* is a little fuzzy," I say pointedly, "but Knocks slept on top of my head last night. He loves me."

Her eyes narrow. "When I woke up, he was cuddling *me*. My memory is fine, thank you very much."

"You're welcome."

"You're *not* welcome."

I bite the inside of my cheek. "Good one."

Cathy gives an awkward laugh beside us. "Maybe we should move on to the—"

"We *are* moving on," Fable interjects, crossing her arms as she follows Cathy back into the house. In the doorway, Fable pauses and turns to whisper, "We're forgetting it happened. Not bringing it up anymore. Got it?"

"But I think we have very different interpretations of how it went. One of us was completely sober, sweetheart."

Her pointer finger presses into the center of my chest. "Don't you *sweetheart* me."

Behind me, a snort bursts from Mia. "Are we still talking about Knocks, or . . . ?"

Tension soaks the garage. Fable's glaring at me. I'm grinning at her. Everything is right with the universe, and I have the most intense urge to kiss that glower right off her pretty face.

"See. Stop looking at me like *that*," Fable says sharply, pointing at my face before spinning on her heel to follow Cathy.

"Trouble in paradise?" Mia whispers, marching up the stairs behind me.

"Nah. Just a minor disagreement," I reply with a smile. "We'll sort it out."

The bedrooms are all the same. Empty and cold. I'm still barely paying attention as I search for a place to pull Fable aside again and clear this up. I don't want another moment to pass without her remembering what really happened.

Finally, when Cathy leaves the third bedroom and Mia trails after her, I seize my opportunity. I tug Fable into a tiny closet, leaving the door open. Gray light from the bedroom window filters in to reveal her expression. Arms crossed, shoulders back, chin tipped up—a mad little hellion.

She could take me down in a heartbeat. I'd let her.

"Do you remember what I said after you tried to kiss me?" I ask softly.

An annoyed grumble. "You don't have to do this. I promise."

"Do. You. Remember?" I clasp her cheeks, desperate at this point. I *need* her to know the truth.

Her eyes meet mine, searching. I watch her think through it, several emotions flickering over her features quickly.

I clear my throat. "I'd spent all night watching you laugh, dance, twirl around in that short, flirty dress. Bare legs. That freckle on display." Her breath hitches. "You were trying to kill me, I think."

She gives me a sly look. "I've been threatening to for a while."

"I'm an easy target when it comes to you, sweetheart."

In a flash, she moves out of my reach, glowering at me again. "*Don't* call me sweetheart. You have to stop flirting with me."

"Don't think I could stop even if I wanted to."

She groans and points to my face. "See, you're doing it again. That *look*."

I can't help but smile. "This is just my face."

"No." She squeezes her eyes shut for a moment. "It's not just your face. It's the way you look at *me*. I don't know what it is, but it makes me feel . . ." She cuts herself off.

"Good? Warm? Greedy?" I finish for her. "Because that's how it feels when I'm looking at you this way. Like I want to hold you close and keep you all to myself. Like I might finally know peace if I press my lips to yours."

That catches her off guard. She freezes, eyes wide, lips parted.

I step closer. "What did I say after you tried to kiss me? Think about it." Slowly, I lift my hand to cup her face, thumb at the corner of her mouth, palm spanning her jaw. "You were only inches away. Your tongue darted out over your lips, and you got this adorable little line between your brows—like you were so focused and intent on what you were about to do." My thumb slides over her bottom lip. "I had to stop you, but what did I say?"

Rain patters loudly against the house, and I don't know where Cathy and Mia are, but I couldn't care less. The entire world has narrowed to this closet. There's a buzzing, electric tension gathering in the air between us. Pressing into my skin. Coiling in my muscles.

I see the moment the memory returns. Her eyes spark, twin flames in the dim closet. "Oh," she whispers.

"What did I say?" I ask again.

Her throat works on a slow swallow. "You said . . . you've dreamt of kissing me. Thoroughly and enthusiastically."

My heart beats faster. "And?"

"And you didn't want me to regret anything."

"Right. It was never about not wanting to kiss you. I *want* you so much it hurts. It consumes me, takes up all the space in my brain. I can't get away from it, no matter how hard I fucking try." I thread my fingertips into her hair. "You're allowed to be as grumbly about last night as you want to, but I stopped you because it was the right thing to do." I shake my head, wondering how we got this so mixed-up. "And to be completely honest, the crankier you are, the more I want to kiss you."

She licks her lips. A faint blush rises on her cheeks. "So, this . . . tension . . . you feel it too?"

My free hand folds around her waist, and I step toward her. "Yes. Fuck. All the time. I don't know how to make it go away."

Her gaze flickers to my mouth. "Maybe we just try it. See if it helps."

"Maybe we should." A deep, warm feeling unfurls in the pit of my stomach. "Fabes, do you still want to kiss me?"

She nods, moving closer.

"I need to hear you say it, sweetheart." I tilt her chin up to meet my gaze. "Do you want to kiss me? Check yes or no."

Amusement flickers in her eyes. "Yes. I want to kiss you. If you want—"

I don't even let her finish that last sentence. Fuck yes, I want.

My lips crash with hers and her shoulders land against the wall, my hand cradling the back of her head. Whatever tethers were holding us back *snap*, like we've waited long enough for this and can't stand another second without it. Her lips part, and when her tongue brushes mine, something bursts inside my chest. I'm charged to full power. Illuminating the closet.

It's hot and hungry and all-consuming. A swarm of need that steals every bit of my focus. A low hum of satisfaction vibrates between us. She's so warm, so soft, so pliant in my arms. She grabs a fistful of my shirt, keeping me anchored against her. My fingers pulse on her waist, knit into her hair.

She teases me, I tease back. I push hard, she pushes back. We meet each other at every beat, like we were perfect for this all along. Her nails graze my scalp, and I grip her hair, tipping her head so my tongue can dive farther into her mouth. I want to devour her, leave no space unclaimed. We're not quiet at all, greedy grunts and moans traveling between our mouths.

This kiss is a feral thing. A desperate thing.

Her fingers hook into my belt loops, and she pulls my hips to hers. "*Fable*," I groan into her lips as she presses herself against where I'm hard for her.

A whimper crawls up her throat. "You said my name," she whispers, breathless. "Say it again."

She's been *Fabes* since we were kids. It's a safe space. A boundary I've kept between us. But that boundary feels irrelevant with her lips against mine and her fingers tucking under my shirt.

A heartbeat before I say it again, Mia's voice echoes toward us. "I wonder if they got lost," she calls, stilted and loud, like she's purposely trying to get our attention.

Fable pulls back, her laughter twirling around me. I bury my head in her throat, chuckling as quietly as I can. We stay like that for a moment, trying to catch our breaths. Her flowery scent hits something in my brain and relaxes the tension in my body, just like last night.

"One more," she begs, shoving my shoulders away until she can grab my face again and pull me in for another kiss. It's slower this time. Leisurely and deep, and I let myself get lost again. I feel the kiss *everywhere*—aching in my chest, sweeping up my spine.

A throat clears beside us and Fable pushes me away. She lifts her hands in surrender, like she's been caught stealing government secrets.

Fuck, she looks *beautiful*. Kiss-bitten lips. Mussed hair. Unbridled lust blazing in her eyes.

"I've distracted her as long as I can," Mia says, crossing her arms at the bedroom doorway. "Think you two can participate now?"

Fable lifts off the wall immediately, combing her fingers through her hair.

I reach for her arm before she leaves the closet. "I'm going to need a moment," I admit softly. She makes it worse when she dips her chin and stares right at where I'm straining against my jeans. "That's not helping. Get the hell out of here." I laugh, nudging her to leave the closet.

When Fable reaches the bedroom door, Mia sighs dramatically. "The things I do for the people I love. Fuck's sake, Cathy can talk . . ." Her voice trails off as she walks down the hallway.

At the door, Fable turns back my way. There's a small, secret smile on her lips and pink glowing on her cheeks, and I realize I'm absolutely and irrevocably fucked.

## Chapter 22

*Fable*

*I* don't know if I've taken a steady breath in the two hours since that kiss. Have my lungs forgotten how to function normally? That's my best explanation. Because it makes way more sense than the second option, which is that Theo kissed away my ability to breathe. Stole it right from my lungs.

That kiss should've been strange. I've known him for eighteen years. We've cried together while watching *The Land Before Time*. I know he used to put Goldfish on his peanut butter and jelly sandwiches, and that puke-green was his favorite color for about six weeks. I was there when he face-planted into the mud at school, and I wiped blood off his face with my shirt after a bike wreck when he was eleven.

All of that should've equaled *not* wanting to kiss him. It should've meant overwhelming awkwardness when our lips touched. But instead . . . the math isn't working in my head, because instead, I want to kiss him *more*.

This is a problem. A huge problem. Because that man is supposed to be my *fake* boyfriend. Emphasis on the *fake*. This thing between us isn't going anywhere. *Can't* go anywhere.

Yet that kiss was . . . incredible. I think it altered something in my brain chemistry, and all I can think about is doing it again.

Out of the corner of my eye, I peek over at him in the driver's seat. His focus is on the road, but a smirk crosses his lips, like he knows I'm looking.

"I don't feel like any of those houses were *it*," Mia says from the back seat. After touring the final house, we picked up Bree, who was doing some work at Coffee Cottage. She and Mia wanted to see whatever birthday present Theo has hiding at the A-frame.

Theo hums in agreement, turning the steering wheel to pull us into the driveway. "Me either."

"It's still helpful to see places you don't like," Bree says. "Then you get closer to figuring out what you do."

The truck comes to a stop in front of the A-frame and Theo shuts it off. No one moves for a moment as his gaze travels over the cabin. I watch his eyes trace the peaked roof and porch, a muscle flickering in his jaw. "Yeah," he murmurs, sounding almost in a daze. "I'm starting to figure it out."

I follow his gaze and sweep my eyes over A-frame. The rain has stopped, but the skies are still a gloomy gray, painting the view in the same muted tones. But even though the world around it appears dull, the cabin seems to glow. A lamp got left on inside, and the golden light cascades over the front windows, making it seem soft and cozy—almost alive in there.

On the way inside, I cast a sad, quick glance at the empty flower beds around the porch. I've been weeding, giving the soil extra nutrients, and sending as many good vibes to those little tulips bulbs as I can—even whispering happy things to them on a regular basis—but they still haven't broken through the ground, and on the tulip timeline, they're behind. They might really be gone.

We take a brief intermission in the living room for Mia and

Bree to love excessively on Knocks before walking to the bedroom door. The sign that has been here all week greets me, but Theo pulls it down and tosses it aside.

"Ready?" he asks.

I whisper a *yes*, and he reaches past my hip to open the door and let it swing wide.

The sight before me makes my legs turn to jelly. I tilt back a bit to find Theo right behind me, and I lean against him at the threshold, absorbing as much as I can.

The atmosphere has completely changed. He has rearranged the room to build bookshelves along one wall—five long boards attached with brackets underneath. Gramps's reading chair has been uncovered, and his favorite lamp is illuminating the dark green fabric.

Mia and Bree gasp behind me.

"Theo," I whisper, more to myself than to him. "It's . . ." *It's everything.*

The room calls to me in a visceral way, and I step inside. In the foggy back of my brain, I remember a few weeks ago when I couldn't walk in here. When this room felt like a tomb. Cold and lonely.

But *now*. It's brimming with possibilities. Even without the books, it feels warm. Welcoming. Homey.

Running my fingers along the wood, I walk the length of the room, sensing everyone's eyes on me.

"I can paint them if you want," Theo offers, his voice soft. I turn back to find him standing in the middle of the room, golden lamplight dancing across his features. His hands are shoved in his pockets. Shoulders by his ears. Dark gaze trained on me. A shy smile hooking the corner of his mouth.

"No, they're perfect," I tell him. "The wood matches the A-frame."

That lopsided smile widens as he leans on the edge of the table he has pushed against the wall. Beside him on the surface sit the six water-damaged books and the metal box of photos. "Thought you might want to organize the books yourself. I can carry boxes in for you."

My heart leaps into my throat. Theo has built me this birthday gift in a house that isn't mine, and I'm not sure how to reply.

"Come on," Mia says, already carrying in a box. "It'll take the four of us no time at all."

Before I can reply, Bree is handing me a knife to cut through the tape. I don't think I'm emotionally prepared to see more of Gramps's books, but there's no time for my emotions to catch up as everyone heads to the living room to grab another box.

This is fine. I can get Gramps's books out and give them some fresh air. They deserve better than cramped cardboard boxes, and they're probably safer on shelves anyway, given my house-flooding tendencies.

With my hands planted on the top of the nearest box, I draw in a deep breath. Nerves skitter under my skin, but I cut through the tape anyway and pull out the first book.

It's a worn, hardback copy of *My Side of the Mountain* by Jean Craighead George. What a book to start with. Gramps read this to me countless times. Tears gather in the corners of my eyes as I open the front cover. I glance around the room to make sure I'm alone, then pull the book to my nose, close my eyes, and inhale. It smells exactly the way I remember—exactly the scent I associate with Gramps—like old books that absorbed a little of his tea aroma over the years.

It hurts *deep* in my chest when that smell hits my lungs, like it's digging right into the tender part of my heart. But I drag in another hit of it and my lips curve into a sad grin.

When I lower the book, Theo's there, his gaze caressing my face. "You okay?"

I swallow the lump in my throat. "Thank you for this," I whisper. "All of it."

His lips brush my temple in a soft kiss. "You're welcome. Thought it might be time to get them out of boxes."

My lungs constrict as I glide my hand over the title page, the old paper smooth under my fingers. "Other than the flood incident, I haven't looked at these books since he died. Haven't even read a paperback because . . ." I fade out, feeling my face pinch with grief.

But Theo must hear the words I left out. "Want me to help you?"

At first, I don't answer. Mia and Bree drop off two more boxes, but Theo's gaze never leaves me. He waits. Watches. Lets me think.

This is painful—digging into these boxes, seeing books that meant something to Gramps, touching the same pages he did. It's going to be emotionally taxing and heart-wrenching, but if I've learned anything from crying in front of Theo several times in the last two weeks, it's that I'm safe with him. Sure, he knows how to tease me and push my buttons, but I can trust him with these emotions.

Nodding, I whisper, "Yes, I'd love your help."

\* \* \*

"That's the last one," Bree says, sliding an old poetry book into place.

I step back and lean against the table on the opposite wall, surveying the shelves.

Mia, who oversaw the color-coded organization, perches

herself next to me and loops our arms together. "Turns out my brother is handy sometimes."

"Every once in a while," Theo agrees from Gramps's reading chair, a smug grin on his mouth.

"Which one are you going to read first?" Bree asks.

I think about it for a moment—imagine sitting down in Gramps's chair and opening a paperback. It's been so long since I felt the desire to do that but after holding them in my hands and seeing them on the shelves . . . maybe it would be nice to open them up and discover what memories are tucked inside.

"I don't know. Definitely nothing from the nonfiction section." I wave a hand toward the left corner, where the history books got placed. "Who wants to read about the real world?" I ask with a laugh.

Bree raises her hand. "Me?"

Aghast, I look to Mia. She shakes her head. "I know. It's her only red flag."

Bree purses her lips. "Well, it seems like *Gramps* would've appreciated that about me."

Mia kisses her on the cheek. "For sure. You two could've read World War II books and talked about cardigans to your heart's content."

"Oh, he appreciated a good cardigan too?" Bree asks.

"He did." My heart goes achy behind my ribs. I reach for the tin box behind me. The lid makes a loud *pop* when I open it and grab the stack of pictures inside. Bree's eyes light up as I hand them to her, but I can't watch her go through them. Instead, I walk over to the shelves and peruse the book collection.

Behind me Mia and Bree giggle over Gramps's adorable hats and sweaters, the ice cream cones that made a frequent accessory, and how I slowly grow up through the photos.

"What's the story with the *Our Bookshop* notes on the back?" Mia asks.

Still facing away from them, my eyelids fall shut. "He always wanted to open a bookshop. Said we'd do it together one day." Two sad *aww*s sound behind me. "So every time we went somewhere, he'd track down the perfect spot in that town and take a picture."

"Did he ever open one?" Bree wonders.

I scrunch up my face even though they can't see it. "No. A dream that didn't come true."

Theo's voice is deep and adamant when he adds, "Yet."

Over my shoulder, I shoot him an unimpressed glare. It's a *stop saying things like that* look.

His returning lopsided grin says, *no chance*.

"Have you ever checked up on these places?" Mia asks.

"What do you mean?" I turn back to see her dropping to the ground beside Theo.

"How cool would it be if one of them got turned into a bookstore. Maybe it was *fate*," she whispers with a hint of drama. She places a photo on her outstretched legs and swipes through her phone. "We can just do some minor stalking of the buildings to see what happened to them."

I don't quite know if I would be happy or devastated if one of them is a bookstore now. But I'm too curious not to sit beside her and watch as she opens the maps app and types in the town written on the back.

I pick up the photo and Theo leans over me to see it. "Definitely looks like it was downtown."

Gramps and I are standing in front of a redbrick building, with similar structures attached on each side. He's in a maroon cardigan, with brown corduroy pants, his signature loafers, and his favorite newsboy cap atop his head. My chest pinches at the sight of him. I remember him like he's sitting in the room with us now—his deep belly laugh, his calming presence, the way he'd squeeze my hand when he knew I needed reassurance.

Mia swipes and zooms on her phone, scooting the view down a road until—she freezes. It takes all three of us a moment to glance back and forth between the photo and the screen, but then.

"That's it," I whisper. "Look at the lines of darker brick."

"Even the awning is the same," Theo adds.

"Let me see," Bree says, joining us on the ground.

Once we've all given our confirmation that she's found the spot, Mia says, "Not a bookstore, then."

"An antiques shop?" Bree asks, squinting at the screen. "Okay, that's still cute though." She hands over another picture. "Try this one."

Mia flips it over and types in a new town, this one in northern California. She and Theo argue about where to search, trying a few different roads before they land on one that looks similar.

"I have a good feeling about this one," Mia says, but when they finally spot the same building, a collective sound of disappointment swoops through the room. "Looks like a realty office."

Bree hands her another and another after that. Theo grabs my laptop from the kitchen so we have a bigger screen, and we search through towns all over the Pacific Northwest, sometimes giving up when we can't find the right location. But we do find several: a pottery shop, an art museum, architects offices, a Pilates studio, an ice cream parlor.

We've made it through a third of the stack when Mia lands on a location in a small town in Oregon. My heart stutters to a stop when I see the sign overhead: **BARB'S BOOKS**.

"A bookstore!" Bree cheers, but I can't even smile.

"It's so adorable, isn't it?" Mia clicks the link to their website. She presses on the About Us in the corner and scrolls down, reading Barb's bio. "Oh my god, I love her already."

There's a heavy, achy pressure in my body, and I don't know what it means. I draw my legs up and tuck them close. It feels like I've lost a competition I didn't know I was participating in. A missed chance I didn't take. A dream I handed over to someone else.

The shop truly seems perfect—exactly the kind of place Gramps would've loved. My heart hurts at the thought that I can't go visit it with him. Someone saw the same vision he did, and he'll never get to witness it.

I can feel Theo's eyes on me, and I give in to the urge to look his way. His expression is gentle. He can see exactly what I'm feeling, and for the first time, I'm grateful for it. Thankful someone else is in this emotional space with me.

"*Holy shit!*" Bree's outburst snaps my attention away from Theo. "This one's in Fern River." She flips over a new photo, back and forth to confirm.

My heart beats unsteadily. "What?" I reach for the photo and stare at the handwriting on the back. *Fern River, Washington.* How did I miss this?

I turn the picture over slowly, and what greets me on the other side has my mouth going dry. An electric current zips up my arm, locks into my chest, and I can't breathe. The world feels like it's tilting underneath me. *I know this place.* I work two doors down from it every day.

"Is that—?" Theo starts.

"Yes," I croak, then swallow hard. Mia types something into the computer, but I stop her. "You don't have to look this one up. I know where it is and . . . and . . . it's empty right now."

Sandwiched between the thrift shop and Wildwood Bakery sits a rental space. No one has been there since the music store moved into a bigger lot two roads over a couple of years ago.

In the photo, Gramps is in a short-sleeved shirt and vest, and I'm so tiny beside him—maybe five or six. I'm wearing a pair of denim overalls and a dark green bucket hat, but instead of looking at the camera, like all the rest of the photos, we're smiling at each other. The photo is grainy, but I can feel the connection between our gazes and his hand on my shoulder. I can see the mirth in his green eyes as clearly as if I'm standing right there with him.

Something stirs in the back of my mind, just out of reach. I can't quite identify it, but I'm very aware of its presence.

Mia is constantly finding signs from the universe. *It was fate*, when she tried a new coffee shop and overheard her now-boss discussing the fact that she needed a last-minute graphic designer. *It was meant to be*, when she was getting "weird vibes" about a party in college, so she canceled, and we ended up at a bar where she met Bree. *It was destiny*, she said, when her gut told her to take a new route to dinner, and she found a box of abandoned kittens on the way—one of which is now curled up in Bree's lap.

Honestly, I'm jealous of that ability. If the universe is sending me signs, I'm either not seeing them or I have no idea how to translate them.

But something about this photo feels *heavy*, and I wonder if I'm supposed to be paying attention to that sensation.

Mia's phone comes to life on her lap, her mom's face appearing on the screen. She mutters a curse. "We're late for dinner."

Bree stands and sets the rest of the photos back in the box. "Eva's gonna swat you two with a kitchen towel."

Mia gives her fiancée a simpering smile. "And probably give you all the credit for getting us there."

"Someone has to be the favorite," Bree singsongs.

Mia rolls her eyes and answers the phone as they leave the room. "We're almost there, Mama."

Theo stands and offers me a hand. "Come to dinner with us."

I set the photo down and let him pull me up, feeling inexplicably drawn to him. Like some invisible force is shrinking the space between us. His gaze darkens as I step closer and lift onto my toes, wrapping my arms around his neck while his circle my waist.

Pressed fully against him, I savor every detail of the hug—my fingers curling into the hair at his nape, his face buried in my neck, my toes barely touching the ground.

"You smell *incredible*," he whispers against my pulse.

"So do you. Your hair . . ." I fade out, closing my eyes to inhale again.

There's a smile in his voice when he informs me, "Last night, you said you'd like to sleep there."

A laugh slips out of me. "I said that out loud?"

"Mm-hmm." Fingers flex on my back, and my insides flutter with something hot and effervescent and *awake*. It pulls me right back to that closet.

"We kissed," I whisper, unable to keep the thought to myself.

He leans back and looks over every inch of my face. I feel the appraisal like fire on my skin. Every part of me, from my toes to my ears, prickles with anticipation as his gaze falls to my lips. "We did."

I curve my hands to his jaw, his stubble deliciously rough against my palms. "Is it something you're interested in doing again?"

The golden flecks in his irises glow bright. A line appears between his brows. "Fable," he whispers, and my lashes fall to my cheeks. "I don't know how to explain what a ridiculous question that is."

A hand dips into the back pocket of my jeans, and warmth swirls up my spine. My restraint is burning away so quickly that I wonder if it ever even existed. I want to wrap my legs around his waist. Hear him groan into my skin. Dig my nails into his shoulders. Feel him press into me. Watch him come undone.

"Your heart's beating pretty fast," I whisper, leaning closer until our noses brush.

His smile curves against my cheek. "You make me nervous."

I can't hold back anymore. I press my lips to his, and a low, unconscious sound leaves the back of his throat. My breath disappears again, and I'm melting from the inside out. He kisses me like I've offended him by asking if he wanted this—like he needs to make it very clear how much he does. It's hot and hungry, wet and delicious. His grip tugs me impossibly closer, and his tongue dives into my mouth.

It's as if he knows kissing has been boring for me in the past, and he's determined to prove otherwise. He's going to fight to change my mind with every slide of his tongue, every guttural groan, every nip of his teeth. And it's working. He isn't *just* kissing me; he's lighting me aflame. It might be difficult for any of my future partners to beat him at this.

My toes leave the ground. His hand grasps my thigh, and I'm about to koala myself onto him when—

"Hey, um, guys?" Bree's apologetic voice filters down the hall. "Mia sent me in to tell you we need to go. She said she'd steal your keys if she has to."

Theo shakes his head and calls, "Be right there."

My feet touch the ground again, and I step back to see his expression. He looks properly kissed. Perfectly disheveled. Puffy lips and messy hair. I wish I had a picture of it.

He cups the back of my neck, fingers and thumb tucked behind my ears. "Do you get it now?" he whispers against my forehead. "How much I want to kiss you? How desperate I am for more of you?"

"I think—" I laugh shakily. "You made a very good argument."

We take a second to help each other look presentable—me raking my fingers through his hair and him straightening my shirt—before we leave the room.

And on our way out of the house, I sneak over to stick the new photo of Gramps and me to the fridge. If this picture is a sign, I want to make sure I can see it.

## Chapter 23

*Fable*

The gazebo in the middle of downtown Fern River has seen and heard a lot of things. Secrets to Santa are whispered under its eaves during the holiday festival, Logan's famous *fuck's sake, Cathy* took place in the grass right beside it, the winner of the annual pie baking contest is crowned on its steps, and Tessa's first kiss—with a boy in her theater class—took place on the bench inside.

But for the last three days, the gazebo has been forced to bear witness to hours of my mental roller coaster over that rental space. Every lunch break, I scurry out the door of Hawkins Hardware and plant myself on this bench with a book. I try my best to read Gramps's worn copy of *My Side of the Mountain*, but the building across the street steals all my attention.

The ornate double doors. The windows partially covered in paper from the inside. The cracked sidewalk. The small, red For Rent sign.

As much as I want to walk over there, I haven't let myself. I don't feel brave enough for that. So, instead, I sit. I think. And I try my best to ignore that the bookshop idea is burrowing under my skin, headed straight for my heart.

"Want some company?" The familiar voice startles me as Theo appears in my line of vision, dark green scrubs stretched over those broad shoulders. He's clutching a bag from the taco truck on the corner. "Or am I interrupting your staring contest with that building?"

The gazebo now witnesses at least five seconds of me gazing longingly at those damn lips—the ones that kissed me three days ago. *Really* kissed. Like the kind of kiss that lit up my entire body and had me finally giving up on the vibrator ban I instated after the hospital incident.

It might actually be unhealthy how much time I've spent thinking about those lips.

"I'm not having a staring contest," I lie as he sits on the bench beside me.

"This is the third time I've seen you doing this on your lunch break."

*Shit.* "So you've been spying on me from the clinic windows, then?"

Instead of answering, he hands me a drink. "Thought you could at least be hydrated and fed while you stare," he says, offering me two foil-wrapped tacos.

Suddenly ravenous at the sight, I peel back the foil and take a huge bite. The spice sparks on my tongue, and I sigh with pleasure. When my eyes cut over to Theo, his focus is pinned to me.

"Thank you," I mutter around my bite.

A warm grin curves his lips. "You're welcome," he replies, leaning over to press a kiss to my temple.

These temple kisses are going to have to stop. The kisses on the lips are hot and horny and all-consuming. But the soft kisses? The ones he whispers against me, gently and intimately. Those are the ones that feel out of my control. They feel so unfake that my heart can't sort them out.

Theo has told me real relationships aren't on the table, but when he kisses me like that, I wonder if he's forgetting too. It's easy to get swept up in the moment, but I'm trying my best to hold on to the boundary between us. Honestly, I don't have the capacity for a relationship right now either. I'm barely keeping my life together, and I know for sure that romantic distractions wouldn't help me focus one bit.

*Physical* distractions, though? Well, I might be able to make time for that. My body won't stop *wanting* him. I'm drawn to him in a way that seems threaded into the fabric of who I am. It's a twisted, knotted feeling in my gut, pulling me closer to him all the time, and I'm starting to wonder if I might actually be more productive if I gave into that part.

Maybe it's because I've known him for so long? Maybe it's just that I know I'm safe with him? I trust Theo, and I know that whatever limits and boundaries I ask for, he would follow them explicitly.

I'm not quite sure I know how to have a *just physical* relationship. Hell, I don't even know what to call that. I've had one-night stands, and I've had relationships, but this would fall somewhere in between. Some sort of no-strings, friends-with-benefits situationship?

"Ran into Ethan at Coffee Cottage this morning," he says, wadding up the foil from his first taco. "He told me the drive-in is doing a fundraiser this weekend. They're trying to get a better sound system before the summer movie series, so they're hosting an all-night marathon. The concession stand will be open, the Branch is setting up a bar, Mrs. LaGrande is bringing cupcakes. The whole nine yards." His brows bounce in a *we should go* motion.

"What movies?"

"It'll be fun," he says, ignoring my question.

"What movies, Theo?"

He winces. "*Scream* one through four?"

My lips press into a thin line. "Remember when I hid under the coffee table during *The Sixth Sense*? I can't handle scary movies."

"Right, but is *Scream* really *scary*? Or is it hilarious and . . . campy?"

"Scary!"

"But you *love* murder," he insists, and I'll give him half credit for that.

"I like murder *mystery*. True crime. The puzzle part, not the gory part."

He nods like we're talking about the same thing. "And I'll be there to protect you." He gives me a cocky grin, and dammit, he's so fucking cute it hurts to look at him sometimes. I want to kiss that smirk right off his face.

That desperately horny part of my brain takes over and decides that cuddling up next to Theo all night sounds lovely. "Fine," I concede. I can close my eyes during the scary parts.

His thigh presses against mine as he unwraps his next taco. "Perfect, now, we need to strategize for soccer practice this afternoon. How can we get Priya to come out of her shell a little?" He's giddy with excitement. "I just know if we got her to kick that ball, she'd send it two fields over."

\*\*\*

"This is a wild idea," Theo starts, collecting our trash into the paper bag. "But we *could* walk over there and look at it." His head tips toward the vacant storefront I've been peeking at through our entire lunch.

I slurp down the last sip of my drink, glancing to those beautiful double doors again. While things are much safer if I stay away from that building, my curiosity is pretty much consuming my brain at this point, and I worry the only way to squash the idea is to go over there. Maybe from a closer distance, it'll seem ridiculous and irresponsible. Then I can let it go.

"Want to walk over there with me?" The words come barreling out of me, sounding less like a question and more like a threat.

A delighted grin hooks the edge of his mouth. "Thought you'd never ask."

We walk side by side across the street, my pace so quick that even Theo's long legs are stretching to keep up. When I step onto the sidewalk in front of the building, though, I pause. Clear my throat. Nerves are suddenly dancing under my skin, but I push through and walk forward to peer in the window.

Through the spot where the paper has peeled away from the glass, I can see what looks like a construction zone. It's as if someone got halfway through a makeover before leaving everything behind. Paint buckets along one wall, scaffolding with drop cloths hanging over it, some long pieces of lumber in one corner, and about half the floor has been ripped up to reveal the concrete underneath.

It needs a lot of work before it could ever house a business again.

But the thing is—the *problem* is—I can immediately see it. As I stare through the dirty glass, I can see what Gramps would've dreamt up. Rows of shelves, a seating area in the front by the window, seasonal decorations throughout, a place for community meetups and children's story times. Any moment Meg Ryan is going to pop into view inside, The Shop Around the Corner from *You've Got Mail* coming to life right before my eyes.

It's perfect, actually. Frustratingly, thrillingly perfect.

"Dammit," I whisper, pressure building in my throat.

"What's wrong?" Theo moves closer.

"This was supposed to make me not want to think about it

anymore. The plan was to come over here and prove this is a dumb idea." I step back and shake my head. "But even though it's a mess in there . . . I can see the possibilities."

He reaches for my hand and gently folds his fingers around mine. "What's so bad about that?"

I give a sarcastic laugh. "Are you kidding? It's terrifying!"

"What is?"

"Hoping?" I shrug. "My track record is not great—when things get hard, I quit. I can't trust my instincts with something like this."

A sympathetic smile curves his mouth. "What if you weren't quitting, you were making space to find your true calling?" There's a roller-coaster dip in my stomach. "It's not a bad thing to keep searching for what makes you happy. You're allowed to change your mind."

My brain is going a hundred miles an hour, trying to rearrange what he's saying and make it make sense. I wave toward the building. "How do I know if *this* is the thing?" It's so tangled up in my grief for Gramps that it's hard to tell.

"Only you can answer that," he says, tilting his head. "But the good news is you don't have to decide right this second. This place has been empty for what, two years? You have time to think about it."

I turn to look at the faded For Rent sign and the phone number scrawled in black ink. I can practically hear Gramps's excited voice in my ears saying, *This is it, Fable. This is the one.*

Goose bumps rise over the back of my neck. Something clenches in my stomach. An awareness. A rightness that feels impossible to ignore.

*What would Millie do?* She would think on it, let the idea soak in a little at a time. Weigh the options and assess.

"Okay. I'm going to think about it," I tell myself out loud.

"Hell yeah!" Theo shouts down the street, pumping a fist in the air. "She's going to think about it!"

I hide my face behind my hands. "Stop yelling or I'm also going to think about hurting you."

"Don't threaten me with a good time." He wraps his arm around my shoulders and steers me toward the hardware store.

\* \* \*

WHEN I PULL up to the A-frame that evening, I sit in the silent Bronco for longer than necessary, my mind a whirlpool of thoughts. All afternoon, I've been hyperfixated on the thought of the bookstore. I found myself behind the counter at work googling things like: *How to open a bookstore. Do I need a business degree to run a bookstore? Small business loans.* I made a mood board on Pinterest—full of cozy, adorable bookshop vibes. I jotted down random thoughts in the Notes app on my phone: *Also sell puzzles? Dad would be great at story time. Stickers. Sage-green walls? Plants in the front window. Knocks—bookstore cat? Mom can help decorate.*

There's a gentle, swelling excitement in my heart every time I think about it. Not that I know all the answers, but my chest feels like it's brimming with . . . *something*.

Heartburn? Is this the fire-breathing dragon sensation Mia was referring to?

I don't know how to tell.

My gaze traces the peaked A-frame roof, the porch, where two empty chairs sit in the corner, to the flower beds around the—

I blink. Gasp. Throw open the door before I've even remembered to unbuckle my seat belt. I hiss a *shit* and *fuck*, wrestling to untangle myself, then tumble out of the car and run to the flower bed. My jeans sink right into the wet earth as I drop to the ground, gaping down at the tiny sprouts breaking through the soil. Tears tingle behind my eyes.

*The tulips.* Right here, finally, bright green and healthy.

"I thought you were gone," I whisper, gliding my finger gently over the side of one. It's sturdy and strong already.

Last year, I spent weeks walking over here from my parents' house. I'd approach with hope ballooning my chest, but every time, it would pop and deflate when I found nothing. I had to stop checking because the disappointment was too heavy.

I don't know what it is, but *something* has changed. The weather? The compost? The universe? Whatever it is, I've never been so happy for a glimmer of hope.

"You're going to be beautiful," I tell them, emotion bleeding through the words. A tear falls and lands on my thigh. I wipe my cheeks with the back of my hand and sniffle.

A wet laugh trickles out of me when I realize I'm crying over tulip sprouts, but something about these sprouts feels like a message. And I don't know what that message is yet, but I'm paying attention. It *means* something. I can feel it in the earth beneath me, right up into my bones.

"I'm listening, Gramps," I whisper, rubbing my hands up my arms to fight the sudden chill in the air.

## Chapter 24

*Theo*

"She's probably just trying to convince you she needs a second dinner," I inform Mom.

Her voice crackles through the phone as she checks with her boss for the night. "Are you still hungry, Layla girl?"

This happens every time Mom babysits, and I'm starting to wonder why Layla even wants to come home with me after. She gets new toys, extra treats, and apparently a second dinner at Mom's house. Mom sighs.

"She looks awfully sad."

"That's because she knows you're a softie." I round the corner to the concession stand, and Fable comes into view. She's ordering our food, her head tipped back laughing.

"I'll just give her a half serving. It'll be like dessert," Mom decides.

"I'm sure she'll love that. Give her a kiss for me. One for Mr. Maxwell too."

"Have fun. Love you."

"Love you too," I tell her before tucking my phone away and walking toward Fable.

I expect to find the owner of the concession stand, Fran, on the other side of the glass, but instead it's her son, Tony, and the way he's looking at Fable with hearts in his eyes right now . . . well, I'm not proud of that little stab of jealousy. But it's there nonetheless.

"How long are you in town?" Fable asks. I set our beers down on the small counter and pull out my wallet.

He types a couple things on the register. "Only the weekend. Wanted to help out with the fundraiser. What are you up to these days?"

"Just working at Hawkins Hardware," she replies.

"Oh, I'll have to stop by tomorrow," Tony says, a bit too excited for my liking. "You visited me, I'll visit you."

Fable laughs softly. "Please. It gets boring around there sometimes."

Tony types a few more things. Shuffles some napkins around. Clears his throat. "Well, you look really good. Really happy." He scans her face, his eyes doing a hopeful, flirty thing.

"Thanks. You too." Fable's eyes do it back, and I grind my teeth. "And do you mind making the fries extra crispy?"

He grins. "My pleasure."

I *bet* it's his pleasure. That's enough of that. I toss my arm around my girlfriend's shoulder and pull her closer. "Mine, too, please."

"How much do we owe you?" Fable asks, her fingers coming around to pinch my side playfully.

He waves that off. "Nothing. On the house tonight. For an old friend."

"Nope. No." I hand him a twenty-dollar bill. "Isn't this supposed to be a fundraiser?"

His cheeks flush. "Right." He takes the cash and pops the register open. "It'll be ready in a few minutes."

"Thanks, Tony," Fable calls as I shepherd her away.

We pick a spot at the edge of the crowd to wait for our food.

"What was that?" she asks.

"What?"

"That thing back there. You were getting a little caveman."

An annoyed grumble leaves my chest. "I was not."

"You were." The opening scene of *Scream* is playing on the big screen behind her, and she glances over her shoulder for a moment.

"He was flirting with you. Right in front of me."

A disbelieving laugh bursts out of her. "He was not."

"And you were flirting back."

Her arms cross, the beer bottle dangling from her fingers. "Who gave you the right to get all possessive about me talking to men?"

I ignore that. "He's practically a child."

"He's only two years younger than us!"

"Really?!"

"Yes!"

A noncommittal hum is all I can muster.

"You know, one day, this'll be over, and I'll be back on the market, dating whoever I want."

There's an awful, bitter taste in my mouth. I take a swig of my beer, hoping it'll wash it away.

Tony saves me from having to reply when he calls, "Fable! Order up!" from the window.

With our food and beers in hand, we make our way through the grass toward my truck in the back corner of the lot. It's not the ideal spot for movie watching, but we got here a little late. After Fable's shift at Hawkins, she wanted to run home to change into something comfortable, which turned out to be an oversize Arctic Monkeys tour hoodie and a pair of navy sweatpants.

## No Place Like You

"Have you uh . . . been dating a lot before this?" I ask, hating myself even as the words are still tumbling out.

Fable rearranges the items in her hand to grab two french fries and shove them in her mouth. Ominous music filters from the movie as we weave between two cars. "This is the first date-date I've been on in a long time." She lowers her voice to whisper, "Even if it's fake, it's the closest I've gotten." She tips her beer back for a sip. "By the way, this is our last *free space*."

*Wait.* "Really?" I'd apparently lost track.

"Unless you're looking to add some more renovations." Her gaze cuts to me, a question in her eyes.

"There is some siding that needs to be replaced," I offer, dipping my voice into something very businesslike.

She plays along, copying my tone. "And the washing machine is having trouble draining."

"Of course."

Her lips twitch. "We need to make sure Arthur is convinced." But I think her eyes are saying, *I'm having fun with you.*

"Wouldn't want you to run into any more problems with the A-frame." My eyes reply, *I'm having fun with you too.*

When we reach the back of the truck, we set our food on the tailgate. It turned out the air mattress I had fit perfectly in the back, so I set that up with a few quilts and a bunch of pillows, and quite frankly it looks like the coziest movie-watching experience in the world.

Fable climbs up first. "When was your last date?" She gets herself settled cross-legged on the mattress before I hand her our food.

"Well, we went to Maddox and Vivian's," I remind her, lifting myself up into the truck.

"You know what I mean. Before me."

"I'm pretty sure the right boyfriend response is to say, *there was no one before you, pookie*," I tease, avoiding the question. My dating history (if you can even call it that) isn't exciting or noteworthy. I've been on many dates in my adult life, and all of them were for one purpose—a hookup. It's not a very interesting story to tell.

"No, the right response is the truth. Or your *pookie* is going to hit you with a pillow." We shift the blankets and food around so we can both get comfortable leaning against the cab's back window. She tips sideways, bumping her shoulder into my bicep. "I'm genuinely asking."

"I've been on dates, but it's always very casual," I explain, unwrapping my burger. "Never more than one evening, really."

"So, hookups." She opens her ranch and dunks three fries.

"There was one woman I . . . met up with regularly for a little while. We were both looking for"—I take a sip of beer to wet my throat—"physical release, and we provided that for each other. No guilt, no emotions. It worked out perfectly until she met the love of her life at the laundromat one day."

"Friends with benefits?" she asks.

"Minus the *friends*. We didn't really spend time together outside of sex."

Her thoughtful hum threads between us. "My last relationship—or situationship, I guess—was Philip."

Surprise jolts through me. "Philip?! The same one who knocked you into me at the Branch?"

"The very same."

"The one who didn't even acknowledge you?"

She grabs a chicken tender. "We were together-ish for about four months, but he wanted it kept a secret the whole time."

The rage that fills me is instantaneous and hot. "What the fuck?"

Fable swallows, staring down at her food. "I'm over it. Really. The other night confirmed he was such a waste of time and emotional effort. No point in letting it bother me."

I scrub a hand over my jaw. "We really should've slashed his tires, Fabes."

"Yeah," she sighs. "It would've been fun."

We eat in silence for a few minutes, watching a particularly creepy scene on the screen. She shivers and I scoot closer, bringing my side up against hers.

"Anyone serious before Philip?" I ask, my curiosity getting the better of me.

"Not really. I always seem to hit a wall around the two-month mark and lose interest. Some random thing gives me the ick. Or I'm bored. Or I've found myself not caring whether I see them or not. Broke up with someone because he didn't believe in climate change. Another when they were rude to our waiter." She huffs a laugh. "One guy hated animals."

"Ultimate red flags."

She stays quiet for a minute, twirling a fry in her ranch. "It's possible I wasn't giving those relationships enough time to really mean something." With a soft *huh*, she sits back. "I guess I've been quitting those too?"

I plant a hand on her bent knee, pulling her attention to me. "Realizing you deserve better doesn't make you a quitter. If you open a door, and it doesn't feel right, don't stay in that room. Turn around and look for the next one. The one that'll make you happy."

Her eyes search my face. I'm not sure what she's looking for, but my skin warms under her gaze. Softly, she asks, "Why are you against relationships? Why do you not trust yourself?"

Something turns in my stomach, forcing me to set the rest of my burger down. I watch the screen for a moment, debating how extensively to answer her question.

A part of me wants to brush it off. Distract and deflect. Crack a joke to ease the tension.

But when I look her way, her expression is so open, so tender. She has trusted me with a lot over the last few weeks—left tears in my shirt and let me see the soft, vulnerable parts of her that I suspect not many people get to see.

And in the face of that, I can't bring myself to be anything but honest.

Swallowing the lump in my throat, I start with, "I've always had this . . . fear lurking in the back of my mind that anger is sitting right below the surface of my skin, waiting to jump out at any moment."

Her hand curves around my wrist. "Theo," she says, her voice barely above a whisper. "You're not an angry person."

I almost laugh. "Fabes, you were there the first time. You saw me in high school—in fights on a regular basis. I was an angry kid."

Her forehead scrunches. "That was a long time ago."

"I nearly hit Philip the other night." Needing something to do with my hands, I fiddle with my beer bottle. "And I wouldn't have felt guilty about it. It has always been so easy for me to hit someone. That rage is right there, on a hairpin trigger."

Fable's silence feels like it's clawing its way inside my chest. She appears to be working through her response, but I don't want her pity. I just need her to understand where I'm coming from.

I clear my throat and sit up straighter. "I've found other ways to control my emotions—running, deep breathing, cold showers, talking to Maddox. But the biggest thing that makes me feel in control is to keep a wall up so everyone stays safe. I don't want to get into a relationship with someone, fall in love and build a life together, only for that rage to bubble to the surface when I least expect it. I saw what that did to Mom and Mia—the emotional and physical trauma they went through—and I can't risk that."

Her eyes are glassy as she simply says, "You're nothing like him, Theo."

I wish I could believe her—ignore this nagging feeling and separate myself from him. But he made sure that was impossible when he wrote me the letter that still echoes in my mind daily.

It arrived at my grandparents' house in a plain white envelope a few years after he'd been released from jail. There was no return address, but I recognized his handwriting immediately. I shoved the letter in the back of my closet and spent weeks debating whether I should open it or burn it.

But one dark day, my curiosity got the best of me.

With shaky hands, I tore into it, and bits and pieces etched themselves into my brain without my permission. *I'm so proud of the man you are. You've always taken after me. From the moment you were born with my eyes, I knew we would be close. I bet you look just like me now.*

All of it felt like a warning. A sentencing. A giant flashing red sign—*he approves of you, which is the most damning information you could receive.*

And I've been carrying that knowledge with me since.

"How do you know?" leaves my throat before I can stop it.

Her gaze is unwavering. "Because I know *you*," she says, her voice steady.

I shake my head. "I've hurt people, Fabes. I've hurt you."

A sad smile curves her mouth. "Why did you punch Graham in tenth grade?"

"Kylie was crying, and he was forcing her into his car. He wouldn't stop." I can still feel the satisfaction in my veins from when I gave him that black eye.

"And what about Porter?" she asks.

My fingers tighten around the bottle. "He called Mia a bitch in front of the football team."

Now she looks slightly nervous as she asks, "And Blake?"

I hold her gaze, my mind slipping right back to that night. When I showed up at that New Year's Eve party to find Fable's swollen eyes and tearstained cheeks, all it took was one look from my sister to know whose fault it was.

"Because he cheated on you."

"You didn't know that at the time," she points out softly.

"Knowing he hurt you was enough for me."

A long moment passes, the movie a dull background noise compared to my pulse in my ears. Fable's expression is full of tenderness and warmth—the kind that can only be found in the hazel depths of her eyes.

Finally, she says, "You're right that you probably shouldn't have hit them, but it sure sounds like you've learned better. You were a kid, going through hell, and your emotions were all over the place." She sighs, shaking her head. "How long has it been since you actually fought with someone?"

I swallow thickly. "Since freshman year of college."

She nods like she expected that answer. "I think you should forgive younger-Theo for the choices he made. Because the truth is, you're protective and kind and trustworthy. You stand up for the people who need help. You're a safe space, and I've *never* thought you weren't." A few beats pass before she adds, "I'm not trying to convince you to be in a relationship, get married, have kids . . . any of that. I just don't want you to have to carry that guilt anymore. It's gotta be heavy."

I picture younger-Theo, with that dark cloud around his head and his heart. He was so lost and betrayed and confused. I wish I could give him the hug he desperately needed. That guilt was heavy then, and I don't think it's gotten any lighter, even after years of carrying it.

"Hey," Fable says a few minutes later, mouth full of the last of her fries. "You didn't actually punch Philip. That's an improvement, see?"

I force a laugh, trying to bring us back to something lighter. "I did take his phone, turn it off, and hide it behind the dumpster, though."

"You did not," she gasps, eyes wide.

"Definitely did."

"Personally, I think that shows remarkable self-control." She lifts her bottle to mine, the glass clinking as they tap together. "Think he ever found it?"

"He probably just bought a new one."

"It's nice to imagine about him rooting around in the dumpster for it though," she says, smiling fondly at the thought. Picking up her cup of ranch, she places it between us on the blanket. "We can share this, if you want."

It's a generous offer. Fable sharing her ranch is pretty much an invitation to be her best friend.

But then she reaches over me to steal a handful of my fries. "And we can share these."

I burst out laughing, snagging her beer in retaliation. She giggles, stretching under my arm to grab the whole container of fries and hide it behind her back, and I'm helpless to stop her, too busy trying to keep the ranch from tipping over.

"Thank you," she says sweetly, the picture of innocence as she dunks two fries in the ranch.

## Chapter 25

*Fable*

I'm learning something about myself this evening: I don't mind scary movies when the setting is right. And the setting is *right* when I'm reclining back against Theo in the bed of his truck, my hips between his spread thighs.

All it took was one brief mention that the ridges on the back of the cab were digging into my shoulders, and before I knew it, Theo was grabbing me by the waist, pulling me into his lap, and tossing the quilt over us.

He seems to have relaxed since our conversation earlier. That sad, haunted look in his eyes had my heart breaking for him. I didn't realize how much his father's actions were still impacting his life, and it makes me wonder if he shares that piece of himself with anyone else. Do Mia and Eva know he's still struggling so much? Is he able to be honest with Maddox? Is he going to therapy?

But I keep those questions to myself for tonight, because his demeanor has lightened significantly, and I don't want to bring him back down. We've been laughing and bickering about the characters' decisions, sharing cupcakes, and finishing off a couple more drinks. I had a brief moment of wondering if we've lost the plot on this event, because it's feeling startlingly date-like and not nearly fake enough, but I've been having too much fun to overanalyze it.

It must be close to midnight now and *Scream 3* has just started. About half the other cars have gone home, leaving us all alone in the back row, tucked into the dark corner, and my body is hyperaware of that information. I'm way too distracted by his hand resting on my thigh beneath the blanket to be scared of this ridiculous movie. I can't sit still—my blood is close to boiling simply because of Theo's proximity, and every muscle is coiled, waiting for *something*. I just don't know what.

My heart is thumping loudly against my ribs, and it doesn't have anything to do with the movie. I adjust my hips again, planting my hands on his thighs.

Theo's lips graze the shell of my ear as he murmurs, "Why are you squirming so much?"

"I don't know," I whisper.

A low hum rumbles against my cheek. "I think you do."

I clear my throat. Squirm again. But don't reply.

"Is it because you're scared of the movie?"

I shake my head. We've been making fun of it more than anything.

A smile pools in his voice when he asks, "Is it because you're tired?"

"Wide awake, actually."

"What is it, then?" His hand splays wider on my thigh, like he already knows the answer.

Leaning a bit, I turn my head to look up at him. Flashes of light from the screen dance over his features, but he's not watching the movie at all.

"What is it, then?" he repeats, his smirk full of challenge.

I take the bait. It's now or never, and my body is definitely screaming *now*.

My attention dips to his lips. "What if we . . ." I swallow and work up the nerve to blurt, "What if we did more than kissing?"

His smirk hitches wider. "What if?"

I turn a little farther. A sudden surge of shyness threatens to hold me back, but I push on. "It could be something like the friends-with-benefits thing you had in Oregon. What did you say? 'No guilt, no emotions'? We could do that." I think. I've never done it before, but this is Theo. I trust him. "Responsibly, of course. We'd have rules."

Something seems to shift behind his expression as he searches my face. "What sort of rules do you have in mind?" One hand spans my jaw while the other slips under my hoodie to curve around my waist.

I feel so held, cradled against him, that my body relaxes. I'm finding it hard to even *want* to set rules. My instincts are screaming to just go with the flow here, but I've learned those bitches don't know what they're talking about.

"Fable." My name is soft but precise. "Rules?"

"Right." I clear my throat. "Um. No sleepovers." That seems good. Smart. I don't know if I could handle seeing him in my bed again—with sleepy eyes and mussed hair and pillow creases on his cheeks.

"All right." The fingers on my waist swirl slow circles against my skin. "What else?"

"I'm not sure. I can't think with your fingers doing that." They pause. "Don't stop though."

His grin is hot and predatory as he starts again. "Yes, ma'am."

"So, no guilt, no emotions, no sleepovers?" I ask, my breath hitching when his fingers graze the waistband of my sweats.

His gaze dips to watch his thumb trace my lower lip. "And no more flirting with other people."

"A little possessive," I tease.

His sigh borders on a growl. "Yeah," he admits, not looking ashamed in the slightest, and that's okay. I'm feeling a little possessive over him right now too. If this is the only time I get with him, I'm going to be greedy about it.

Tense music echoes from the movie, and I tilt my head toward the screen. Theo seizes the opportunity to readjust us, spreading his legs a little and letting me lean farther against him.

"Do we have a deal?" he murmurs, voice low and husky.

"Yes." My heart races, and I'm not sure if it's from the movie or Theo.

"Then you just keep watching that movie, sweetheart."

Which is the most absurd request, because he has a hand on my waist and one on my upper thigh, and I don't know how I could concentrate on anything else. I think he must know that, though, because he tortures me by just continuing those slow circles on my stomach.

It seems like a subconscious movement, but it turns me to wildfire. I'm focused on every breath he takes, every warm pad of his fingers on my waist, every millimeter of space his hand covers on my thigh. Even through the thick fabric of my sweatpants, I can feel the heat of his palm there.

I fidget and wriggle, begging him for more. "Theo," I whisper.

"Fable." He sounds steady, unconcerned.

It's annoying. "I need . . ." I start to sit up, but he holds me firmly in place.

"Relax. I've got you," he assures me, pulling me closer. His hardness presses into my ass, and my mind goes blank. "I'm going to take care of you. I promise. I just need a minute to calm myself down."

My gaze sweeps over the cars in front of us. I've never done anything like this, but as long as I can stay quiet, I feel safe here in the dark corner, with everyone's attention on the movie.

Theo's lips graze my neck. "Do you know how long I've thought about touching you like this?" His hand slides up my thigh agonizingly slow, fingers tracing the inner seam of my pants. But before he reaches where I'm achy for him, he slips back down. "How much I want to kiss you when you glare at me? How hard I get every time you say something snarky? How desperate I've been for you to want me like this?"

Heat pools in every corner of my body. I dig my nails into his thighs, and I spread mine wider as his hand slides up again. But he bypasses my core and glides all the way up to dip beneath my waistband. *Finally.* My stomach tightens with anticipation.

When he reaches the lace of my thong, a pained noise leaves the back of his throat. "Fable." My name sounds like a reprimand this time. "What are you wearing?" His fingers travel over the top of the fabric like he's analyzing every detail. "Describe them."

I bite back a grin. "Lacy. Maroon. Thong."

He fists the thin band at my hip. "Fuck," he says, sounding like this is awful news.

"Matching bra, too," I tell him, pushing his other arm up.

"I want a picture of you in only this." He cups my breast, then strokes his thumb over my nipple. I moan louder than I mean to. "Shh, sweetheart. This is our secret back here. You can be quiet, right?"

"Mm-hmm." I can feel my pulse pounding in my neck, my stomach, my core.

He presses a kiss to my jaw. "Good, because I really want to make you come." His fingers finally—*fucking finally*—dip into my thong and slide down where I need them. With a low groan, he parts me, gliding his touch over my clit. "Oh, Fable. You're so wet already."

A hot, electric feeling blooms in my stomach, and I melt into his leisurely movements. He explores me slowly, like he has all the time in the world, but I could combust at any moment. I whimper, sounding so desperate it's almost embarrassing.

"Your little sounds," he murmurs, bringing his lips to my throat. "God, they're fucking perfect."

My hips twitch, grinding me between his hand and his cock, and a sharp grunt leaves his chest. Pleasure swirls through me as he glides a finger inside, satisfying that empty feeling that's been plaguing me for weeks.

"Please tell me you're still okay," he whispers. "I don't think you're breathing."

"I . . . I can't breathe, but it's— It feels good." I move my hips again, chasing the friction. "Don't stop."

The air mattress squeaks a bit as he shifts, sliding almost all the way out and then back in, his thumb working over my clit in slow circles. His other hand slips up under my bra and palms my breast, dragging a low moan out of me.

I try to wedge my hand back between us, needing to touch him, make him feel this good, but he presses closer against me with a teasing, "Nuh-uh. This is about you."

Fine. If he won't let me touch him, I'll keep grinding back against him until he gives in.

When I do, he chuckles, like he knew that plan before I did. "Oh, the claws are coming out. You gonna punish me?"

"I don't have claws." I gasp when he pushes into me with two fingers, and the pressure grows exponentially.

"Hey, I love your claws. Scratch me the fuck up. I can take it." He does some curling movement and hits a spot that makes me whimper. "Oh, right there, huh?"

Everything is too good. His touch. His words. The arrogant smile I can hear in his voice. Twitches of pleasure are barreling down my limbs. It's going to be over too fast.

Frustrated, I grind against his erection, and this time, he lets a moan slip out.

"Right there, huh?" I tease back, breathless.

With a dark chuckle, he doubles down, working me with the kind of precision that tells me he was just playing with me before. I tilt my head back, trying to delay the orgasm I can already feel building. I silently curse myself for being so fucking desperate that Theo's hands have me this close to the edge within minutes.

But, of course, he realizes what I'm doing. He nips at my earlobe. "Don't fight it." Velvet lips coast over my jaw. "Let me have it."

"I—" When his fingers curl again, I lose my ability to speak.

"You what?" he coaxes playfully.

"I don't want it to be over," I admit.

He hums, fingers still moving in a smooth rhythm. "Let me have this one, nice and easy, and then you can make me work for the next one. How's that sound?"

Heat infuses my cheeks. The answer tumbles out of me. "Yes. Yeah. Okay."

My eyes fall shut as he moves more firmly. I dig my fingers into his thighs, trying to grip anything I can. His lips are against my throat. Fingers pinching my nipple. Rumbly murmurs in my ear. Until he sends me careening into ecstasy.

I muffle a cry with my hand. My back arches away from him, pleasure shooting all the way down to my toes as I come apart.

"That's it. Just like that," he whispers, my muscles fluttering around his fingers.

Relief sweeps through me. I'm panting, arms limp and shoulders loose, but he doesn't let me catch my breath. Doesn't even pull his fingers away before he murmurs, "One more."

I shake my head. "I can't."

His smile curves against my cheek. "You can. You're gonna give me one more. Make me work for it."

The ache rekindles in my belly. And when his hand leaves my breast to splay over my thigh, pulling my legs open farther, I don't fight it. My core throbs with need, and I bite into my bottom lip. I use my grip on his thighs to circle my hips against him, seeking every bit of pleasure I can for both of us.

This time, he's rougher. Grittier. "Can you feel how bad I want you?" he asks, grinding against my ass. "So fucking bad it hurts, sweetheart." His teeth drag over my throat.

My feet search for purchase against the slippery air mattress, but I finally hook them on the outside of Theo's calves to get better leverage. I'm coming undone, trembling against him, and if anyone looked back here right now, they'd know exactly what was happening, but I can't find the will to stop.

"Theo," I whimper. I need more of him, so I reach back and tangle my hand in his hair, nails against his scalp.

He groans, his breath ragged. "Attagirl. Hold on to me." His hips are punching into me with every stroke of his hand, and when I tip over the edge a second time, his teeth clamp down on my neck. A low, almost feral grunt rolls from his chest, and tiny unconscious thrusts press and then *hold* against me as he finds his own pleasure.

After a moment, the rest of the world comes back into focus. My hand slips from his hair and his fingers glide out of me. *"Fable,"* he hisses, lips grazing my cheek.

I turn to see his face. His eyes are gleaming, skin flushed in the light from the screen. He's never looked more beautiful.

His rapid pulse thrums against my ear as he lifts the fingers that were inside me, and with slow, deliberate movements, he paints my lips with my arousal. I watch, entranced by the heat in his gaze. Then he brings his mouth to mine, and we groan into the kiss. He cups my face firmly, lapping at my lips and into my mouth until I'm ready to start all over again.

"Fuck, you taste good," he murmurs against my mouth before pulling back. With an arrogant grin, he adds, "Told you you could give me one more."

"Is this really the time to be smug?" I tease, shifting my hip against where he's still half hard.

He lets out a breathy laugh, cheeks going redder. There's some rearranging as he slides me out of his lap and cocoons me back on the pillows with the quilt tucked around me.

Then he presses a kiss to my temple and promises, "Be right back." And I don't think I make it one minute before my eyes are slipping closed, and playful dimples and soft lips flood my dreams.

## Chapter 26

*Theo*

**Fable:** Things you left at the A-frame:

*I*'m walking out of an exam room when the text appears, and I swipe it open without thinking. When the photo of Fable brightens my screen, my feet stumble over each other. A choked *oh, fuck* slips out as I step inside my office and shut my door to fully soak in what I'm seeing.

She's standing in front a full-length mirror in nothing but maroon lace. It barely covers her tits, her rosy nipples visible through the fabric. Thin straps—the ones I almost ripped off her the other night—sit high on her hip bones, right over a tattoo I've never seen before. A cascade of flowers down her side and upper thigh.

My mouth falls open. I want to bite her right there. Leave fingerprints on her skin. Trace the dark lines with my tongue.

I zoom in, shamelessly trying to absorb every detail. That freckle in the swell of her breast. The exact curve of her bare shoulder. Smooth line of her collarbone. Honey-blond hair in wild waves around her head, like she's just woken up looking this perfect.

Her expression is smug. She knew exactly what she was doing by sending this to me at nine in the morning on a random fucking Wednesday.

> **Theo:** Is this how you kill me?
> Because I think I'm dying.

I can still hear every stuttered breath from Saturday night. Her soft whimpers. Her husky voice moaning *Theo* as she came.

A text appears at the top of the screen.

> **Fable:** See you at soccer later. ☺

A soft knock rattles against my office door, and I click off my phone and shove it in my pocket. "Come in!" My voice sounds hoarse and too high at the same time.

Garrett pushes the door open. "Have a second?"

"Of course. What's up?" I scoot closer to my desk, trying to hide how Fable in lacy lingerie has left me with a semi in the middle of my workday. My flustered brain scours the office for any sign of the photo. I didn't accidently print ten copies and hang them on my wall, right?

With a smile, Garrett takes a seat across from me. "Wanted to see if we could have an impromptu check-in about the adopt-a-thon. Only two more weeks," he says excitedly.

"Absolutely." I bring up my email, scanning through them until I find one from yesterday. "I did get a reply from Havenbrook, and as of right now, they're coming with eight dogs and three cats."

"That's great. And any word from that rescue in Juniper?"

"They'll be here too."

"Perfect."

"I did get an email that the Robinsons won't be able to make it. And they were bringing most of the animals from the Paws Out rescue, so I'm a little worried we're going to need more volunteers. With the number of animals we potentially have, we may have to scavenge for more help." I tap my fingers on my desk, trying to think of where we could find them.

"Also, I'm concerned about food," Garrett adds. "The taco truck will already be at the event, but I think we need to organize lunches from somewhere else for our volunteers. I want Carlos to get to concentrate on orders from the public. So we should place an order with someone else."

"I can work on that," I offer.

Arthur appears in the doorway, a half-eaten glazed donut in his hand. He shuffles in, sneakers squeaking on the buffed floors. "Sounds like you two are working well together."

Mentally tracking back through the last few minutes, I rehash everything we talked about. From what I remember it was all fine, but I feel slimy even worrying about it. I hate lying and being on edge, and I wish I didn't have to overanalyze everything around Arthur. I wish he just trusted me enough without this whole performance.

Garrett chuckles. "We make a great team."

"Everything ready to go?" Arthur asks, taking a bite of donut and looking to me for an answer.

I sit up straighter. "We've run into a couple small issues, but we've got it figured out."

"Good, good." Arthur nods in acknowledgment, licking glaze from his thumb. "And will we be seeing Fable at the event?"

A hint of nausea rolls through my stomach. "Yep. We'll be there together," I assure them, even though I'm just digging my nails in further with the lie.

\*\*\*

"Yes!" Fable shouts, giving Priya a high five. "That was a great kick!"

I jog around the goal to grab the ball she just kicked hard enough that it went flying to the other field, and when I punt it back to Fable, she catches it easily and lines it up for the next player.

Despite the dreary skies and drizzly spring rain, she's shining bright. It's almost like someone turned up the saturation on her over the last few weeks. The same woman who was sitting on the sidelines for most of our first practice is now running around in her unicorn T-shirt, mud splattered on the fabric and a huge smile on her face. And those little girls are obsessed with it. Obsessed with *her*.

I can't blame them.

"Goalie ready?" she calls to me.

Positioning myself in front of the net, I give a thumbs-up. "Come on, Emmy! Can you get it past me?" So far, the balls are either not making it to me or missing the goal entirely. I think I'm getting more exercise here than anyone, with all the running I'm doing to fetch balls. But we'll get there.

Emmy steps to the front of the line, pushes her bangs back, and kicks as hard as she can, letting out a feral scream. But the ball rolls to a stop about five feet in front of me. Her bottom lip pokes out in a pout.

Fable gives her a hug. "That's okay. You'll get him next time."

I kick the ball back to her and she catches it under her foot, waving the next player forward.

But Emmy pauses and stares in my direction. "Can you get him, Coach Fable?"

Fable's eyes tighten playfully. "Oh, heck yeah."

"Betcha can't," I taunt, crossing my arms to goad her.

Her tongue presses into her cheek. She nudges the ball a few inches, positioning herself.

"Nuh-uh." I wave toward the middle of the field. "You have to kick from back there, Coach."

With a cocky grin, Fable leans over and whispers something to the girls. They squeal and giggle as Fable walks to center-field.

Once she's lined herself up, the Unicorns start chanting. *Coach Fable. Coach Fable.* And I'm not going to lie—my nerves ratchet up a few notches. She shimmies her shoulders to the beat of their chant, and I don't even have time to realize she's pulling her leg back before the ball is flying forward and whooshing into the tiny goal behind me. I dove too low and didn't even touch it.

By the time I look up, the girls are tackling her to the ground, everyone whooping and hollering with delight.

It's the morale boost everyone needed, because for the rest of practice, the girls are full steam ahead on trying to get the ball past me, and even if someone misses, they cheer enthusiastically.

When our hour ends and the girls are on their way home—mud-stained and exhausted—Fable helps me pack up. We're the only people left at the soccer fields, and the misty rain is amping up a few notches as we carry the gear bags to the storage room behind the concession stand.

"You didn't even see that soccer ball coming," she teases, bumping her shoulder into me.

"Psh. I *let* that ball go through," I lie, unlocking the door and flicking on the dim overhead light. "Didn't want you to embarrass yourself."

She laughs, dropping the bag of soccer balls in the corner. "You never stood a chance."

"Rematch next time?" I ask, turning to find her waiting by the door. She's in baggy shorts and dirty sneakers. Little stray pieces of blond hair have fallen out of her ponytail and are curling around her cheeks. There's a splatter of mud on the side of her neck and a green tinge on her shirt from when she got tackled to the grass.

She's messy and happy and so fucking beautiful it hurts.

"You're doing that *look* again," she points out, licking her lips.

"What look?" I ask, even though I know. It's the look of a man who's slowly becoming obsessed with the woman he's only temporarily allowed to have. I'm playing with borrowed time at this point but fuck if I know how to stop it.

"Like you want something," she replies.

I let out a low hum, stepping closer. "Oh, I *want* all right." Her breath hitches. "I want to slide my hand down these shorts. Feel that lace you teased me with." I bring my lips to her ear. "That picture got me so damn hard I should punish you for it."

She shivers. "I . . . that sounds . . . nice." She steps back, her shoulders bumping against the door to shut it.

"Nice? I don't know if *nice* is the right word to describe what I want."

Her eyes spark with flames as she reaches for the waistband of my shorts, tucking the tips of her fingers inside to pull me closer. "That's okay. I can handle not nice."

I follow the tug, my hands curving around her waist, my head dipping to her neck. I don't think I'll ever be over knowing her like this. The exact curve of her hip. How her pillowy soft lips feel against mine. That breathy sound of pleasure she makes. All the tiny intimate details of Fable are going to be tattooed on my brain permanently.

"Can I touch you, Theo?" she whispers, and *that*—that will also be tattooed there.

"Yes." I move my hand under the hem of her shirt to feel her soft skin against my palm. "Can I touch you?"

"Please," she begs. Her teeth graze my throat, biting lightly, and I. Lose. My. Damn. Mind.

I lean to the side so I can slide my hand against her stomach and into her shorts. "Is this the same set you had on in that picture?"

"It is," she says, a whimper chasing the words as I tease her through the lace.

"Oh, sweetheart." I groan when I reach the soaked fabric. "You need it, don't you?"

A breathy *yes* drifts from her lips, and she fumbles with the button on my shorts. I pull back in a daze, watching her work. The zipper buzzes and she tugs the fly open and when she palms me through my briefs, heat curls down my spine.

I reward her by pulling the lace to the side and sliding two fingers into her center. She cries out, clenching around me as I pump them and move my thumb over her clit. The rain picks up on the other side of the door, providing a low, drumming soundtrack to complement the sounds of pleasure rolling through the closet.

With quick movements, she tugs down my waistband and fists my cock firmly in her warm hand. My mind goes utterly blank. I feel myself swell in her grip.

"*Fuck.*" My forehead falls to the cool metal door, my fingers pausing inside her because I can't think straight.

"You okay?" she teases, rolling her thumb over the bead of pre-cum gathered at the tip.

I shake my head. "I don't think so. I'm dizzy. You feel so fucking good."

Her laughter is a gust of air against my throat. "I need you to move again, though," she says squirming against my hand, searching for friction.

I bring my lips to hers and murmur against them, "This was supposed to be your punishment."

"Then do it," she orders, tightening her fist around me. "Don't make promises you can't keep, Theo."

The way she taunts me is my awakening. I thrust my fingers and curl them the way she likes, and I'm rewarded when she tips her head back. Eyes to the ceiling, she moans in that husky, sweet voice.

Gripping her wrist gently with my free hand, I pull her away from my cock and lift her palm between us. "Spit on it, sweetheart," I tell her.

Lust dances through her eyes as she watches me and dips her chin, spitting into the center of her palm.

A thrum of pleasure pounds through me. "That's my girl." My gritty voice is unrecognizable to my own ears.

Fable's lashes flutter against her cheeks, and she lowers her hand, sliding her palm against me. She grips me so confidently, firm and sure of herself, like she knows exactly how I need it.

The truth is, she could do anything, and it would ruin me completely because it's *her*.

My breath goes ragged as she slides and twists, slides and twists. "Look what you do to me, Fable," I whisper, both of us watching her hand move up and down my length. "You make such a mess of me."

Her laugh curls into a moan. "I'd say we're both pretty messy right now," she points out, trying to blow her hair out of her face.

We're muddy and mist-soaked, making this moment feel primal. Desperate. Consuming.

Her core flutters around my fingers, and I let myself grind harder into her grip. "You're close, aren't you?"

"Yeah. Yes. It feels"—she moans—"so good."

Face to her throat, I breathe her in, getting a faint hint of sweat and soap and dirt, and I've never smelled anything more perfect. My grin curves against her pulse. "Should I stop? Punish you for teasing me?" I move my thumb away and she makes a hiccuping sound.

"No. Please." Her whole body trembles. "You can punish me after. I need it."

"Promise?"

"Promise," she slurs.

I pull back to watch her, moving my thumb firmly over her clit and curling my fingers inside her. Her eyes are heavy-lidded and hazy, her lips parted in pleasure, and then she's calling out my name, clenching around my fingers, tightening her fist around me, clawing at my shirt. She shudders against the door, and I kiss her fiercely, needing to *feel* every bit of pleasure that leaves her body.

As she catches her breath, a ghost of a smile tugs her mouth. Her gaze lifts to mine as I pull my fingers out and suck them into my mouth. I lick them clean, savoring her taste. Her grip tightens around my cock, pumping me again, but I drag her away.

She watches me strip out of my damp shirt and place it on the ground between us. Hazel eyes rove over my body, and I let her look her fill. Then I grab her chin and tip her head back to murmur, "On your knees, sweetheart."

There's unbridled heat in her expression as she follows my orders and drops to the ground. She blinks up innocently, tugging my shorts down farther, and I'm already unraveling.

I scour her features, devouring every fucking detail of her. "You look so pretty," I rasp, pushing a few strands of hair away from her face. "All dreamy eyes and flushed cheeks from coming on my fingers." Those soft pink lips are only centimeters away from where I want them, practically taunting me. I smooth a hand over her cheek, fisting myself with the other. "You want to taste me, Fable?"

Her only response to my question is to open her mouth and stick her tongue out flat, waiting for me to snap.

"That's perfect. Just like that. I want to see some tears in those fiery eyes. Got it?" My nerves skitter as she slides her tongue over me, teasing me.

"Tell me what you like," she whispers, and my knees buckle. She stares up my body and takes the tip into her warm mouth. A low hum of pleasure vibrates around me, and I'm not sure if it's from me or her or both.

"That's it." I groan. "It doesn't matter what you do—" I choke on my words when her nails dig into my thigh. "Yeah. I like all that. I like everything."

Her lashes fall as she slides me a little farther into her mouth.

"Eyes up here, sweetheart." I grab her ponytail and tilt her head back. "I've been dreaming about this for so long. Let me see those hazel eyes while you take me down your throat."

That gaze holds a little snarky defiance when it meets mine again, but that's perfect. Exactly what I want. I'm a riot of sensations, electricity sparking in my veins and pulsing in my spine.

Her fingers flex on my thighs as she works me all the way to the back of her throat. My legs threaten to give out, so I press one hand on the door to hold myself up while the other cradles her cheek. "You're doing so fucking good, Fable."

She slides back, swirls her tongue over the tip, and then pushes forward again, and I'm crumbling rapidly. My hand fumbles to her ponytail, twisting her hair around my fist, like it has a mind of its own. I'm shaking with the effort of holding myself back from fucking her hot mouth.

As if she can hear my thoughts, she pulls away enough to whisper, "Do it. I can take it."

She doesn't give me a chance to argue before her mouth is on me again, and she's reaching behind her head to show me what she wants. And what she wants is for me to be rougher. More desperate. More greedy.

Her eyes hold a hunger I'll never forget as she tilts her head back and I tentatively thrust farther. "You like that?" I grit out. "When I'm so desperate for you I can't control myself?"

She hums in pleasure as I slide back in, harder this time. One hand to her cheek and one gripping her hair, I hold her still, savoring the way her lips circle me and her cheeks hollow out with every pull.

Her nails dig crescents into my hips, but the little burst of pain only spurs me to thrust harder. When tears drip from the corners of her eyes and run down her temples, I come undone. Pressure ricochets through my bones and zips up my spine. I groan her name, holding myself still, watching her blink rapidly as I pulse down her throat.

She takes it all so perfectly, and when I pull away, her lips close with a smug smirk. Her throat bobs on a heavy swallow.

"Fucking hell, Fable," I manage, voice hoarse as I devour every detail of her appearance. She's disheveled in the most erotic way—hair mussed and clothes askew, a drop of my cum on the corner of her lips.

I've never felt so satisfied in my life.

I reach out to slide my thumb over the drop and she sticks out her tongue to catch it. "Fable Oaks, you greedy girl," I murmur, watching her lick it off. "Come here." I pull her up and collapse back against the door, tugging her with me until our bodies are pressed together. I'm delirious and blissed-out and don't want to stop touching her. "Come home with me. I'll clean you up. Put you in my clothes. Cook you dinner. Tuck you into my bed."

"Can't," she says, pressing a quick kiss to my lips then stepping away.

"And why's that?" I ask, pulling my shorts back into place and grabbing my shirt.

She opens the door and walks out into the drizzling rain, squinting back at me. "Promised Logan I'd help him inventory some things tonight."

I follow her and lock the door behind us. "Funny, he didn't mention that when I talked to him earlier."

"What—" She starts, but I grab her hand and run toward our vehicles.

When we reach her Bronco, it takes her a couple tries to get the door open, but when she finally does, she tumbles inside and looks back at me. Rain sluices down my face as she asks, "What did you need to talk to him about?"

"Mmm. That's a secret," I tell her. "Just be ready at eight tomorrow morning."

She lets out an annoyed sound—something between a scoff and a whine. "For what?"

"You need an overnight bag!" I say before shutting her door and jogging around my truck.

Through the window, I see her throw her arms up and shout something to me, but I just wink, and that pisses her off so much that she throws her vehicle into gear and pulls out of the parking spot.

A few minutes later, I get a string of quick texts.

**Fable:** Where are we going?

**Fable:** And why?

**Fable:** No sleepovers, remember??

**Fable:** Theo. Answer me.

**Theo:** New phone, who dis?

**Fable:** 🔪

## Chapter 27

*Fable*

"That was unhinged," Theo announces, popping a pink Starburst into his mouth.

"Right?!" I pause the closing remarks of the podcast and unwrap another Starburst. We've been on the road for almost three hours now. Destination: Unknown (by me at least), but we did pass by a Welcome to Oregon sign a few minutes ago.

"How was that podcast any less creepy than *Scream*? This shit really happened!" He shivers and I laugh. "She re-gifted the belongings of her previous victim to her new victim!"

"Hence why she's called the *Re-Gifter*. And it's not less creepy . . . it's just more fascinating. It's fun to figure out the puzzle of it all. The whole time you're wondering why she would do that, and then you find out it's because her aunt had been doing it for years before and taught her. Like the family business!" I say excitedly.

He side-eyes me. "You scare me."

"Good." I set my feet on the dash and pop a Starburst into my mouth—a red one. As kids, we would fight over the reds, but I guess Theo's tastes have changed because he left them on the console between us. "How much longer do we have?"

Scanning the next sign, he says, "About five minutes."

A disappointed hum. "No time for the next podcast episode, then. It's called 'The Tailor of Taylorsville.'" I give him a wicked grin.

"Sadly, no," he says, not sounding very sad at all.

"Oh well. We have to save something for the drive home." I look down at the pile of red Starburst and offer him one. "Why are you skipping the red? You used to love them."

He cuts me a look before taking the next exit. "Because you love them. Saved 'em for you."

Unwrapping the last red, I offer it to him, and he takes it with a smile. He turns left at a sign proclaiming that Glendale, Oregon, is one mile away. That name ricochets around in my brain for a moment before I can place it. Then it settles—Gramps's cursive on the back of a photo coming to mind. Glendale, Oregon, is the home of Barb's Books.

My throat goes dry.

"Theo. What are we doing here?" I croak.

His gaze shoots to mine. For a beat, he takes in my expression, and it must be giving away my thoughts, because his hand lands on my thigh. "We're going for a visit."

A colorful blanket of wildflowers lines the road on both sides as we enter the city limits. Theo steers us toward downtown, and when the brick building comes into view, with Barb's Books written in blue above it, my heart beats out of my chest.

The truck comes to a stop as we park on the street, and all I can do is stare out the windshield at the bookshop. It's warm, welcoming, bright. Benches and plants line the sidewalk. There are books displayed in the bottom of the window, flowers painted along the edges, and a huge Pride flag hanging across the top. When the door opens, a man pushes a stroller out, and two kids follow him with books in their little hands.

An older Black woman catches the door from inside and waves goodbye to them. She has short, curly gray hair, bracelets lining her wrists, glasses hanging from a beaded chain around her neck, and she's wearing a long, flowy skirt with an oversize cardigan.

"That's Barb," Theo whispers.

I force my shoulders to relax. She looks kind. Absolutely huggable. She's probably never met a stranger.

Dammit, I want to be her best friend.

"We don't have to go in if you don't want to," Theo says gently. "I got us a place to stay tonight, and we could just explore Glendale instead."

Barb's eyes meet mine through the windshield, and I don't know what she can read on my face, but her smile hitches wider in response. And I feel that smile urge me forward. "No, let's go in."

"Are you sure?"

"Yes," I decide, unbuckling my seat belt.

By the time we make it to the sidewalk, Barb has gone back inside and Theo holds the door open for me. Stepping into the bookshop is like walking into a dream. It's even more magical in person than the pictures online. Cozy, colorful, with the perfect scent of old books and coffee.

"Welcome in," someone sings from the back of the store.

The wood floor creaks in the most nostalgic way. Somewhere between the shelves, a child is giggling. I want to live here. I could sleep curled up in that sunny armchair.

Winding my way through the shop, I slip my hand over the edges of shelves and lines of spines. I soak in every detail I can, trying to view the shop as a reader but also as a potential bookseller myself. I note the way it's organized, the end-cap displays, the little trinkets like key chains, bookmarks, and decorations on display.

Half my mind is overwhelmed by it all—like I could never absorb enough information. But the other half is inspired. The thought of creating a space like this, with community and overflowing warmth, feels possible.

By the time I reach the children's book section, I realize I've lost Theo somewhere. But all thoughts of trying to track him down vanish when I spot an older man in the corner of the shop. He has a young girl in his lap, a book held before them. I can't see the cover, but as his words filter to me, I recognize what he's reading. I remember the first chapter of *The Hobbit* like I heard Gramps read it to me yesterday.

Instead of looking at the book, the little girl is peeking up at the man adoringly. I feel like I'm intruding on a private moment, but I can't make myself look away. My heart pinches behind my ribs.

Sometimes my grief is dark and hollow. A hole in the middle of my chest. But other times, like now, it's warm. It's a sweet, achy memory that I can't repeat, but at the same time I'm so grateful I got to have it at all.

A tear slips down my cheek, and a steadying hand caresses my back. The smell of summer and sunshine hits my lungs.

I press my lips together. "Gramps"—a tight swallow—"would've fallen in love with this place." His instincts were right. This spot made a perfect bookshop.

A melodic voice sounds from my other side. "You two need help finding anything?" I turn to see Barb, a stack of romance books in her arms and a friendly, crinkly-eyed smile on her face.

Before I can answer, Theo reaches for the books and offers, "Do *you* need help?"

"Well, thank you, young man," she says, handing him the stack.

"I'm Theo, by the way." He shifts the books to one arm so he can shake her hand.

"*Theo!*" She brightens like they know each other. Then she turns to me. "So you must be Fable."

"I am." I shake her hand as well, giving Theo a look that asks, *How do you know each other?* His returning wink reveals very little.

"Well, I'm Barb, and it's so lovely to meet you." She waves for us to follow as she heads down the narrow gap between two shelves. "Theo called yesterday and said you'd be stopping by." She pauses at the romance shelves and pulls the first book from the stack in Theo's arms. "Let me get these shelved, and then we'll chat all things bookshops!"

My gaze meets Theo's and his brows bounce excitedly. While Barb neatly slots books into place—murmuring authors' last names as she goes—Theo and I have a silent conversation with our eyes.

*What did you do?* I ask.

*Go with the flow*, he insists.

*Where is it going?*

*Relax, Fabes. We've got this.*

When all the books are sorted, Barb clasps her hands together. "Okay. So, Theo told me you're in the early stages of thinking about opening a bookshop?"

I manage to hold back the wince that naturally wants to come out. This feels incredibly uncomfortable to admit out loud, but I push through the awkwardness. "Yes. Very, *very* early, but yes."

Excitement practically billows out of her. "Well, first of all, congratulations. Even realizing that dream is a huge step."

I don't know that I've fully realized that, but I thank her anyway.

"Should we do a tour?" she asks.

"I . . . guess?"

"Perfect! Let's grab a drink first." She leads us over to the small bar on one side of the shop. "Elliot's working today. They make the best tea and coffee."

We place our orders with Elliot, and when I pull out my wallet to pay for our drinks, Barb stops me. "Oh, no. This is on me."

"You don't have to do that," Theo insists.

She gives him an unimpressed look. "And yet, I am." Theo thanks her as she turns to me. "Now, Fable. What makes you want to open a bookstore? Other than the fact that your name is perfect for it."

I bite my lip, suddenly nervous and put on the spot. I don't have a reply prepared for this. But . . . something feels soothing about Barb, like she isn't going to judge a single thing that comes out of my mouth.

Elliot offers my cup over the counter, and I take it, letting it warm my palms. "It was my grandfather's dream. Growing up, he was always talking about the bookstore we would open together one day. But he passed away a couple of years ago, without that dream coming true."

Her eyes are full of sympathy. "I'm so sorry."

"That's okay. It's just always lived in the back of my mind—but I've never felt like I could do it on my own."

"Ah, but then this guy came along," she says, patting Theo's arm.

I tip my head, smiling up at him. "He did. I also found some pictures of my grandpa's. Every trip we took, he would photograph places he thought would make a great bookshop. And this building was one of them. We have a picture right out front, from maybe twenty years ago?"

She gasps, a hand to her chest. "Here?"

I nod. "It's the only location we could find that actually became a bookshop. I wish he'd been able to come see this place. He would've loved it."

Surprise jolts through me when Theo pulls the photo out of his back pocket and offers it to her.

Barb inhales a sharp breath and slips her glasses on, gawking at the image. "Oh, my goodness. This is wild." Flipping it over, she takes in the words on the back, then looks at me, eyes glittering. "So you're opening a bookshop?"

I shuffle on my feet. "I'm still not one hundred percent. I'm thinking on it." Barb and Theo exchange a knowing look. Doubt wraps its grubby hand around my lungs. "I don't know. What if I can't do it?"

"Oh, honey, you won't know until you try." She waves around the store. "Things could go belly-up at any moment, but the important thing is: Did I have fun while I did it? Was my heart happy? And if the answer's yes, then I have no regrets."

Damn, Gramps would've loved her.

"Can I give you a hug?" Barb asks, spreading her arms wide.

I don't even need a second to consider. I barely know this woman yet hugging her seems like the most natural thing in the world. She squeezes me just shy of too tight—the kind of embrace you can feel all the way down to your bones. My eyes fall shut, and I hug her back with the same strength.

And it's inside the arms of a stranger that I miss Gramps more than I ever have. He used to hug me like this, wholeheartedly— like he might be able to fix all my worries with that hug.

Tears spring to my eyes and I shudder a breath.

"Oh, honey. It's okay," Barb murmurs, holding me for a few more moments.

When I pull away, I shake out my shoulders and try to smile. "Thank you. I needed that."

Barb squeezes my arm. "Anytime. Hugs are my love language." She grabs her drink from Theo, then waves us toward the shop. "Shall we?"

There's a pep in her step as she guides us through the store, first to the seating area tucked in the back corner, then to the community room where they host story time, author signings, and other events. We thread our way through the children's area, where there's a giant forest animal mural on the wall, along with a few toys and tables with coloring supplies. Then Barb leads us through the shelves, where she explains why she laid them out the way she did and what she'd do differently.

The books are amazing, the collection enviable. But what makes this place really come to life is the atmosphere. It's the people and the community space and the inclusive warmth. What makes it shine is everything *besides* the books.

Once our tour is over and we've said goodbye to Barb—with the promise of being back soon—Theo and I step outside. The warm, spring air caresses my cheeks as I turn to look back at the shop. I can easily see Gramps falling in love with this place. It's exactly what he described to me every time, and Barb has turned it into a reality without even knowing him.

There are so many things to figure out, probably an endless to-do list and a roller coaster of emotions ahead of me, but for the first time, the possibility seems within reach. And I wonder if I really might be able to do this.

## Chapter 28

*Fable*

"I think you forgot we have a No Sleepovers rule," I remind Theo as he opens the hotel room door.

"I did, in fact, remember that." He waves for me to walk in first. "Which is why I requested two beds."

Well, look at that. He did. Yet, for some annoying reason, a sharp pang of disappointment burns through me. I'm the one who set the rule, yet I'm the one annoyed about it? Make it make sense.

The only way to fight that feeling is to give Theo shit for it. "I don't know. Isn't it technically still a sleepover because we're sleeping in the same room?"

He gives me an unimpressed look before setting our containers of leftover shrimp scampi in the tiny fridge. "It's a gray area."

I cross my arms. "If one of us is sleeping in the same space as the other, it's a sleepover."

"Then we don't need to worry about it, because we've already broken the No Sleepovers rule when you slept sprawled across me at the drive-in." *Gotcha*, his expression says.

*Dammit.* Between my birthday and the drive-in, I've slept

extremely well cuddled up to him twice now. I fear it's going to become an addiction if I keep letting it happen.

I motion toward the bed closer to the door. "Fine. You can have that one."

Walking to the dresser, I set my phone and crossbody bag on the surface. I kick off my shoes, watching Theo in the mirror in front of me as he slips out of his.

Today has felt very couple-y. After Barb's Books, we had lunch on a breezy patio, where Theo and I shared two meals because I couldn't decide which I wanted more. We visited a thrift store, where I tried to talk him out of getting a lamp that looks like a tower of puppies in a trench coat. ("This is literally me," he'd said, holding it up beside his face. And he's not wrong, so it's sitting in the back seat of his truck now.) Then we took a walk in a nearby park (with a not-so-brief pause to make out against a tree) before having dinner on another beautiful patio, where he let me steal bites of his pasta the entire meal.

It's been effortless and easy, and I hope that means we have a chance of staying friends once this is over—that we haven't blown it all to shreds with our friends-with-benefits arrangement.

His gaze meets mine in the mirror, and he gives me a curious look. "You okay?"

My voice comes out wobbly as I blurt out my thoughts. "Do you think we'll still be friends when this is all over?"

That question seems to surprise him. "Why wouldn't we?" He walks closer, watching me in the mirror.

"I don't know." I scan our reflection. "After all the different chapters we've been through, it's hard to picture what that would look like."

His chin comes to rest on my shoulder, arms around my waist. "In an ideal world, what would it look like to you?"

Color seeps into my cheeks. "Today was nice."

A soft hum. "It was."

"So something like that? Without the kissing at the park?"

Something seems to shift behind his dark eyes. After a moment, he says, "Right. Friends, minus the kissing."

"Friends, minus the kissing," I repeat. "Once this is over."

His lips drag over the soft spot between my neck and shoulder. "But until then?"

*No guilt, no emotions.* "Until then"—I tip my head back to give him more access—"we take full advantage."

A deep, needy sound rumbles out of him. His hands slip under the hem of my shirt to wrap around me and pull me right against him, igniting a pool of heat low in my belly.

Some foggy part of me wonders if I'll even be able to give this up. Will this *wanting* feeling fade right away? Or ever? I've never wanted like this—so greedily and viscerally that I feel like I'm drowning in it. Is this how he felt in his last friends-with-benefits situation? I don't know what I'm doing here or what it's supposed to feel like. Is it always so consuming?

My breaths are quick with anticipation. He grips the bottom of my shirt and steps back to pull it off and toss it aside. I watch his reflection as he devours the sight of me, his gaze trailing down my neck, to the green lace covering my breasts.

"You're beautiful, Fable." His eyes are shining with something I can't identify, but it shoots straight into the chambers of my heart and glows there.

Slowly, his fingers curl around my bra strap, then pause, waiting for permission. I nod, breathless, before he slips it down my shoulder. He does the same with the other side, then unhooks the back, and the bra falls to the floor. Cool air sweeps over my skin and tightens my nipples.

"I can't . . . I . . . *Fuck*. Look at you." Theo lets out a low groan, gaze flickering everywhere at once. His hands hover but don't touch, almost like he can't decide what to do first.

I'm topless in front of the mirror, my breasts practically begging for his attention, but he chooses to focus on my tattoo first. With the lightest touch, he starts at my wrist, trailing his fingers up, swirling and curving around the flowers, caressing them like he wants to be gentle with the delicate petals, and it lights me aflame.

"I love this tattoo," he murmurs, his eyes tracking his path. There's a twitch in his jaw, desperation in his eyes. "Do you have plans for more?"

Swallowing thickly, I barely manage to form words. "I want some tulips, I think."

His deep hum sends goose bumps up my neck. "More flowers?"

"I love them," I whisper.

"Me too." When his fingers reach my shoulder, he replaces them with his lips, brushing kisses over the dark lines as his hands finally cup my breasts.

I whimper, tipping my head back to his chest. He caresses me, molds me, teases my nipples. That achy feeling pounds hot and heavy in my core and spreads out through the rest of my body. I look desperate, cheeks flushed and chest heaving. That infuriating, cocky grin pulls at his mouth, but I don't hate it this time. It promises me things I *need*.

Lips graze my throat, and he lowers his hands to my jeans. "Can I take these off, sweetheart?"

"Mm-hmm," I reply, and he unbuttons them with a flick of his wrist. The zipper rasps through the quiet room, revealing a bit of green lace in the mirror.

He tucks his fingers into the waistband and drags them down

my hips, kneeling behind me to help me step out of the denim. When only my thong remains, a low, gritty sound leaves his throat.

The carpet is soft under my bare feet as he turns me to face him, his hands curved around my hips. Dark lashes lift, and he stares up the line of my body. As I slide my fingers into his hair, my memory flashes back to the storage closet yesterday. Rough hands and dark eyes and whispered praise.

I may have been the one on my knees, but he worshipped *me*.

His palms glide slowly over my hips, down my thighs, up to my ass, like he's memorizing every inch of me through his reverent touch. He leans forward, grazing his lips over the sunflowers tattooed at my right hip. "I get the whole *bitable forearms* thing now. I want to bite this tattoo so bad I might die."

A breathy laugh tumbles out of me. "Go ahead."

"Really?" His eyes flare, hopeful and bright. Palms on my ass to hold me steady, he pulls me to his mouth and grazes his teeth over the flowers. It's not even sharp enough to sting, but then he soothes it with his tongue and lips before moving to another spot, leaving a trail of little nips. A deep, possessive groan rumbles against my skin.

When his mouth makes it to the lacy band at my hip, I nearly jump out of my skin. His eyes crash with mine as his teeth clamp onto the fabric and drag them down. My heart is a drum in my ears, pounding with every millimeter he moves them. At my knees, his hands take over until he helps me out of them.

Shadows play over his grin. "Mine now," he whispers, shoving them into his back pocket.

"Thief," I grumble, but there's no heat behind it.

He sits back on his heels, fists clenched tightly on his thighs.

"You all right down there?" I ask, grinning.

"Fuck's sake, Fable. You make me nervous."

A pleased hum. "Well, you look damn good on your knees." I thread my fingers through his hair. "Such a good boy."

His eyes get impossibly darker. One hand lands low on my stomach and he pushes me back until my hips bump the dresser. Then he grips my thigh and lifts, propping my knee on his shoulder. "You're going to need something to hold on to, sweetheart."

A wave of sharp desire crashes through me. I follow his directions, gripping the edge of the surface behind me.

He takes in the sight of me above him. "You should see yourself right now. A fucking goddess." His voice is a strained whisper, barely in control.

And I believe him. I really do. It's etched into his expression. He looks at me like I'm someone special. Someone to be treasured.

His attention lowers as he slips his free hand between my thighs. Just one, slow touch through my arousal and my hips shift uncontrollably.

A downright devilish grin takes over his face. "You sure do like me on my knees for you."

I can't even argue. The evidence is currently soaking his fingers.

Gaze fused with mine, he draws closer and slides his tongue through me. I whimper, my nails digging into his hair like an anchor to keep me from drifting away. His eyes close, a low groan bleeding out of him as he plays with my clit, licking and swirling and teasing like he's been desperate to do just this for years.

It's too much and not enough at the same time. I'm pretty sure I'm not breathing again. My hips push toward him, begging for more. And he gives it, swearing against my pussy and sucking at my clit. A long, low moan tears out of me, bouncing off the walls of our room.

He pulls away, breaths stuttered, lips glossy. "Can I do this every day?" he asks, a whimper chasing his words. "Please. I'll be so good."

"Mm-hmm," I mutter mindlessly, gripping his hair to push him back where I want him. *Need* him. I might cry if I don't get to experience the orgasm waiting just out of reach. "Yes. *Please*. Right there," I whisper, his tongue swirling over my clit again.

His grip tightens on my thigh, holding me in place as he dips two fingers into my core. I clench around him, my hips squirming greedily, chasing the pleasure that's just out of reach. It's *so close*. I'm a burning fuse, about to erupt—

But Theo drags his mouth away. His fingers slip out of me, leaving my body pulsing around nothing.

I audibly whine, not caring at all how I sound. "*What* are you doing?"

He licks his lips, flashing that annoying lopsided grin. "Oh, did you want to come?"

## Chapter 29

*Theo*

*She's going to kill me.*

Eyes blazing, she shifts her leg, but I catch it before she can move. I want her to stay exactly where she is, so I glide my fingers back into her, keeping her still.

"Y . . . Yes. P-Please," she stammers, breathless.

"What do you need, Fable?"

Instead of telling me, she tugs at my hair, bringing me closer. The little burst of pain morphs into pleasure, but this close, I can't stop myself from tasting her again. Her *yes* is a breathy whimper. I flick my tongue over her, pumping my fingers, as she cradles the back of my head, holding me in place.

I wind her back up, focusing on getting her to the edge again, licking and sucking until I can feel her legs trembling beside my head and her muscles fluttering around my fingers. Her back arches, her grip in my hair tightens—

"Sweetheart?" I pause, keeping my fingers inside her.

She dips her chin to glare at me. "*What?* I was so close," she whines.

"I know," I soothe, circling my thumb slowly over her clit, giving her just enough to keep her in place. "But I have a question." I don't, really. I just want to annoy her until she's begging for it.

Nostrils flaring, she shakes her head. "You can ask after I come." She grabs my hair again, pushing me toward her.

With a dark chuckle, I resist, not bringing my mouth back. "Awfully bossy when you're desperate, huh?" I wait until her eyes burn like hazel embers and her cheeks turn scarlet.

*Perfect.*

"Fuck. You. Theo," she growls.

I laugh, hearty and loud. "Keep being mean, sweetheart. It only makes me harder."

She lets out an exasperated sigh. "Please. I need . . ." She squirms, grinding herself against my hand. A startled *oh* leaves her lips as she realizes she can chase her own pleasure, and she works herself more firmly.

*Dammit.* She won this round.

I reward her by curling my fingers and bringing my mouth back where she wants it, and her satisfied moan burns through my ears. Just as I hoped, she tastes even sweeter when she's annoyed with me.

She writhes against my tongue, begging for more. I wait until her hips are canting and her moans are getting longer, and fuck, this is agony for me, too, but I pull away, ready to rile her up again.

"You're the *worst*." She tips her head back, bumping the mirror.

"But I thought I was a good boy?"

Gripping my hair, she glares down at me. Wildfire burns in her dark eyes. "Theo Nikolaou. Be a good boy and make me come."

The thrill I feel at that *good boy* is unrivaled. More endorphins than all the runs I've ever been on combined. Her nails dig into my scalp and all the air rushes from my lungs, and this time, when I bring my mouth to her, I don't stop.

I *can't* stop.

It only takes a few moments before she's screaming, soaking me in her pleasure, and I lap up every bit of the reward I worked for as she moans my name and pulses around my fingers.

Her leg falls from my shoulder, and her other one gives out. But I stand and catch her, scooping her into my arms and carrying her to the bed.

She lands against the mattress with a whoosh, and all the air in the room vanishes as I look at her. Honey hair fanned out on the bedding. A flush on her cheeks and down her throat. A sated curve to her lips. Gorgeous tits and rosy, peaked nipples. I want to play with her, tease her, make her ache for me as much as I ache for her.

She lifts onto her knees and waves me closer until she can unbuckle my belt. "I got tested after my last partner, and there was nothing to report." She unbuttons my jeans and pushes them to the floor so I can step out of them.

I tuck a loose strand of hair behind her ears. "I went a few months ago, and everything was clear. I can show you my results on my phone, and I haven't been with anyone since."

"That's okay. I trust you." She tugs my shirt over my head and tosses it away. With a coy grin, she lifts her knuckles to graze my cock through my briefs and a ragged sigh rattles out of me. "Do you have a condom?" she asks, eyes bright with lust.

My heart beats so hard I can almost hear it. Is this right? Should we be doing this? No matter how much I try to pretend this is only a physical arrangement, this is *Fable*.

I've kept my feelings for her locked in the cage for so long, and this was supposed to be like dipping a toe into the water. Only letting myself have the tiniest bit before I pull back. But I can't help feeling the water is already over my head, and I didn't even take a breath before I dove in.

Touching her chin, I tilt her face up. "We can stop if you want," I whisper. "It's okay if this is too much."

"I don't want to stop." She dips her fingers into my waistband.

"Me either." My shoulders hunch as I press my forehead to hers. "Fable. This is—I can't—fuck, it's so hard to think."

An amused huff coasts over my lips. She tucks her fingers in farther, dancing them over the head of my erection. "Then why are you trying to? I thought we were just chasing what feels good."

*Right.* I push away the doubts and center myself back to the plan. No guilt, no emotions. I've done that before, I can do it again.

"I want this," she whispers, her voice steady.

I drop my mouth to her throat. "Are you sure?"

Her answer is to tug at the waistband of my briefs, pulling them down my hips and wrapping her fingers around my hard length.

"Fable." The word is an agonized rasp as I fold my hands around her waist. My whole body is tense, barely hanging on to the last threads of my control.

"I want you to fuck me, Theo," she breathes, twirling her thumb over the tip of my cock. "I *need* you to."

Her plea untethers me. I reach for my jeans, grabbing the condom out of my wallet, before sitting at the top of the bed, legs spread out and shoulders against the headboard. She waits, on her knees at my feet, her gaze dragging down my body, arousal staining her cheeks red.

I fist my cock, giving myself a firm tug that has her lips falling open. "Come here," I instruct, my voice deep and gravelly.

Crawling up the bed, she places her palms on my shoulders and slings a leg over mine, straddling my thighs. She sits back, my erection between us as I tear open the condom.

"Put it on for me," I request.

The wrapper crinkles as she pulls it out and then I watch her slide it slowly over me. My hands shake, and I grip her thighs tighter with every inch. When she reaches the base, I shudder.

Our eyes meet. "Are you sure? Tell me again," I whisper.

She props her hands on my chest, her heartbeat hammering in the side of her neck. "I'm positive." She leans forward and presses her mouth to mine. I seize the opportunity, cupping her cheeks and diving into the kiss, letting every bit of doubt and worry evaporate between us. Her fingers dig into my shoulders, and she kisses me as wildly as I kiss her.

I pull away just enough to murmur against her lips, "Then please, sweetheart, show me how perfectly we fit together."

My lips part as she lifts up on her knees and scoots forward, her bright, flowery scent filling my lungs. She reaches between us to notch me at her entrance, and the tip of my cock slips into her warmth. My breath tumbles out of me. My vision goes hazy. I don't know how I'm going to hold myself together for this.

Gaze pinned to mine, she sinks down an inch. My fingers flex on her hips as she stretches around me, the pressure tight and heavy and perfect. We groan in unison, her nails digging into my chest.

"That's it—oh, *fuck*. Just like that," I soothe, feeling myself throb inside her. "You're doing so good, taking me so well." My voice is strained as I watch us come together.

Sliding her hands up my neck, she threads her fingers into my hair and tilts my head back. When our gazes connect, she drops the rest of the way down until I'm fully seated inside her.

We both gasp at the feeling. Something in my chest locks into place. I search her eyes. For what? I'm not sure. But I know it's not supposed to feel this . . . consuming. It has *never* felt like this.

Neither of us moves our hips, but I wrap my arms around her back, pulling us closer together. "Fable," I breathe into her neck, peppering kisses against her skin.

My fingers tangle in her hair. She squirms with tiny movements, seeking more friction, but I hold her still in my embrace, trying to wrap my head around why this feels so different. I don't know if I can handle it. I feel as if I've been flayed open and taken apart from the inside. Everything is new and hypersensitive, too exquisite to ever be this good again.

"Theo... please." She circles her hips, begging for movement.

With a sharp exhale, I lean back against the headboard. "You okay?" I whisper, letting my thumb roll over my freckle on her chest.

"Yeah. Are you?" Her grin is full of affection. "Your eyes are a little wild."

"I *feel* a little wild," I admit, my hands roaming down to her hips.

"Don't forget to breathe," she teases, digging her knees into the mattress to slide up and dip back down in the most delicious way.

I groan, watching where I disappear inside her. "I can't. My lungs aren't working."

"Need me to stop?" she taunts, fingers dragging over my scalp.

I shudder, my entire body tense and taut. "Fuck no. Please never stop." I think I might die if she did.

She laughs, stealing my breath as she writhes above me. I'm too overwhelmed to figure out where to focus my heavy-lidded eyes. Maybe on the way the flowers on her hip shift with every movement. Or her incredible breasts bouncing only inches away from my mouth. Or the wisps of hair swaying at her cheeks. Or that confident smirk on her pretty lips.

Everywhere I look is a new detail I want to spend hours memorizing. No, *days. Years.*

She's stunning above me, chasing her own pleasure, using me however she needs.

"That's my girl," I murmur, pushing my hips up into hers. "That's my good fucking girl."

I'm unraveling faster than I expected, pleasure rolling through my thighs. My body is rioting with the need to feel her come around me. To spill inside her. To bury myself so deep she can't forget this.

I give in to the feeling, letting our movements become frantic. A layer of sweat coats my skin, and I grip her hips, tight enough to press little bruises into her skin as I grind up. Her back arches and she mutters a string of incoherent words, hands trembling on my shoulders.

"Give it to me, sweetheart." I move a hand between us to circle her clit. "I'm right there with you."

When she gasps out my name and her walls clench around me, the building pressure whirls up my spine and beams out through my limbs. My body tightens and tenses, and I shout her name, pulsing inside her. I reach around her back to grab her shoulders and crush her to me, low, breathless grunts leaving my chest with every pump of my hips.

"*Fable*," I mumble. I'm floating somewhere faraway, where my bones are limp, and my mind is full of a distant humming pleasure. "Say my name again."

I manage to hear her whisper, "Theo." Then even softer, "Theo."

Cradling her against me, I drag my hand up and down her back in soothing movements, letting our bodies settle. "That was—I'm never going to recover." I sigh into her hair.

"I'm . . . just . . . yeah," she says, making us both chuckle.

When she pulls away a few moments later, my hands itch to hold on to her. But she sends me a soft smile as she walks to the bathroom. Then we switch places, and I return to the room to find her tucked under the blankets in the bed she chose.

Even though my mind *screams* at me to slide in beside her, I throw myself onto the other one—completely naked and right on top of the covers.

Hands tucked under her cheek, she watches me across the space between our beds. I copy her position, watching her too.

I pretend the distance isn't there and we're right beside each other. Our pillows side by side. Our knees touching. Her lips mere inches from mine. If I close my eyes and pretend hard enough, I might be able to trick myself into sleep.

"Goodnight, Theo." Soft, golden light coasts over her features.

"Goodnight, Fable," I whisper back, then reach over to turn off the lamp.

Sheets rustle as she readjusts in the dark. I clear my throat. A loud sigh rattles out of her.

It's only a few heartbeats later—honestly, much quicker than I expected—when I hear a mumbled "Goddammit." More sheet rustling. "Get over here."

I hold in my laughter as I settle into bed behind her, relishing the feel of her warm skin against mine. "You little rebel. Breaking rules all over the place."

A tiny growl. "Stop talking and go to sleep."

"Yes, ma'am." I kiss her bare shoulder. "Dream of me, sweetheart. I'll be dreaming of you."

## Chapter 30

*Fable*

### Oaks Folks

**Mom:** Fabes, I know you're off on an overnight adventure with Theo but just wanted you to know that Knocks is doing great.

**Tessa:** OVERNIGHT??!!

**Tessa:** Answer your phone, right this instant.

**Millie:** Leave her alone, Tess. They're probably sleeping!

**Millie:** Or other things!

**Dad:** Things we should keep out of these texts . . .

> **Millie:** Like eating breakfast?

> **Tessa:** Or eating someONE! Amiright?!

> **Dad:** I'm still wondering how I get out of this group chat.

*H*ere you are, sweetie." Mom hands me a blueberry muffin before sitting on the porch swing beside me and tipping us into motion.

"Thank you." I peel off the wrapper and take a big bite, watching Theo and Dad in the goat pen as they try to drain a particularly muddy spot. Layla is at the fence, mud coating her torso, trying to convince them to let her help.

It has been a week since we woke up tangled in each other in Oregon, and the No Sleepovers rule has officially dissolved into nothing. We've spent every night together since, splitting our time between his house and the A-frame. When we stay here, he gets up every morning to come work with Dad. I can't help but tease him about it—leaving me in bed to hang out with my dad is objectively hilarious—but I also love it. Seeing them together warms my heart.

"Your dad doesn't even care if I come out to help with the morning chores anymore," Mom says, following my gaze.

"Aw, are you feeling replaced?" I laugh. "Want me to tell Theo he can't come over to play anymore?"

Early morning sunshine dances over her cheekbones, accentuating her soft wrinkles as she grins. "Absolutely not. I love it. So does your dad." She picks off a piece of her muffin. "And I think it's good for Theo."

"Me too."

"You should've seen Eva's face light up when I told her he'd been coming over. She had tears in her eyes." Wrapping her arm around my shoulders, she pulls me closer and asks, "How's my baby?"

There's something about Mom holding me, my cheek to her thin sweater, her head tipped to mine, that brings everything to the surface instantly. Maybe it's her years as a school counselor or maybe it's just who she is, but she's adept at pulling the truth out of me.

"I'm okay," I try, but my voice cracks.

"Want to talk about it?" Her fingers rub gently on my upper arm. She waits patiently while I think, chewing through a bite of muffin.

"I just don't know what I'm supposed to be doing with my life," I finally admit.

A soft, thoughtful hum. "I don't know if any of us really do."

"It seems like everyone else does. Like you all figured it out way quicker than me, and I'm behind."

"Are you in a hurry?"

Truthfully, everything feels so heavy right now, like if I don't make a decision, I might crumble under the weight.

I kick my feet to swing us again. "Seems like it's now or never."

"I promise it's not. You have plenty of time to find out what makes you happy." She pulls me closer and kisses the top of my head. "You can't be behind in your own life. It's easy to get caught up in where you think you should be, but this is your timeline. You make the rules."

A groan rumbles through me. I lean over and rearrange myself to lay my head in her lap. "Then I might not be grown-up enough for this. It would be much easier if someone else made the rules for me."

She laughs. "Well, I've actually retired from making the rules. That's all on you now."

Mom drifts her fingers through my hair, just like she always did when I was younger. Everything from soccer to school to boys—all of it could get sorted out while I was curled up next to my mom, letting her play with my hair.

"Be kind to yourself," she insists. "You're getting there. One day you'll *know* it's right, and you'll leap for it."

"I think that's part of the problem. I don't know that I'm brave enough to leap. Everything is so risky, and I've fallen so many times at this point—ideas and jobs and decisions that I thought were going to work out and didn't. And I have no way of knowing if this will end the same."

She sighs. "Life is risky. All our decisions risk *something*, but that doesn't mean it isn't the right one. It also doesn't mean the path is easy. You might want to give up a thousand times in the process, but that doesn't make it the wrong path." Her nails drag gently over my scalp. "You remember the story of how I met your dad, right?"

I grin. "Yeah." My sisters and I used to beg for this story, never tiring of hearing about the moment they met on a train in Seattle. Mom had her nose in a book, one hand wrapped around a post. When the train stopped abruptly, she fell forward, right into Dad's arms. He invited her to dinner, and the rest is history.

"But did I ever tell you why I was on that train?"

Rolling onto my back, I look up at her. "Not that I remember."

She smiles, her gaze drifting out to where Dad is working. "I'd moved to Seattle for this one job—left my family in Colorado, packed up my car with all my belongings, and driven all the way up there—just to find out I hated the job. I *despised* it, so I quit. I was in tears on a daily basis as the reality set in that I'd taken this huge risk and failed. A few weeks later, I hadn't found another job yet and I was running out of money, so I sold my car. As I drove to meet the buyer, I was sobbing into the steering wheel, heartbroken over getting rid of the last valuable thing I had. But I left it with the buyer and took the train home." She shrugs a shoulder. "Lo and behold, the man I was going to marry was on the very same train. I'd taken a lot of risks and failed at a few things to get to that day, but if I hadn't, I wouldn't have met your dad."

My lips twist with emotion. Tears prick behind my eyes. "Sounds like fate."

"That's exactly how it felt that night. Like everything had actually gone perfectly to plan."

It's easy to put myself in her shoes because I've done it so many times—made a big decision and regretted it—but I've never thought about what I gained through those perceived failures.

If I hadn't quit those other jobs, I wouldn't have ended up at Hawkins, where my employee discount has made it much easier to renovate the A-frame. If I hadn't messed up the leaky pipe, I never would've unpacked Gramps's boxes. If I hadn't needed Theo's help with the drywall, I wouldn't have found the photos from the bookshops.

Everything has woven together to bring me to this very moment.

She pulls back and scans my expression. "Is there a certain risk you're thinking about taking?"

Nerves bubble in my stomach. "I don't know if I'm quite ready to share it yet."

"Well, let me know when you're ready." The porch swing squeaks as we go back and forth a few times. "But no matter what, your dad and I will be cheering for you the entire way." Her hand curves around my cheek. "And you never know what's waiting on the other side—whether things work out the way you planned them or not. Everything will be all right in the end. And if it's not all right, it's not the end."

## Chapter 31

*Theo*

"Can you keep a secret?" Dave asks, slamming the end of his pick into the ground.

We're fixing a muddy spot by the barn, digging out a temporary path for the water to drain, then later this week we'll create a more permanent solution. Mud is caked onto our boots, splattered up our jeans, and there's even some in Dave's gray hair. But we've got warm coffee Mary delivered a little while ago, a belly full of her delicious blueberry muffins, and a crackly radio playing Jefferson Starship. It's a great morning.

"Is it about Fable?" I glance back to where she and her mom are sitting on the porch swing.

"I'm smart enough to know you shouldn't be keeping secrets about your partner." He winks and my ears feel hot. It's one thing to be in a fake-relationship-with-benefits with Fable; it's an entirely different thing for her father to call attention to it. "No, this is about Finn and Millie."

"Then yes, please."

"Finn took the day off work yesterday to drive down and tell us he's going to propose to Millie."

A smile streaks across my face. "That's exciting!"

Dave tosses away a clump of mud. "They planned a trip to visit his family in Italy in August, and he wants to do it there. Came down to give us the details in hopes that we could make it to surprise her."

"Are you all going?"

"Yep. We're buying our tickets this afternoon." He pauses, turning to look my way. "We're getting tickets for Tessa and Fable, and I wanted to see if you'd like to come with us."

I freeze, my shovel halfway into the dirt, completely taken aback. If everything works according to plan, this agreement between Fable and I will be over in August.

That doesn't stop the hopeful beat in my chest, though. I give myself a breath to imagine what that would look like—me a part of the Oaks family, traveling and celebrating milestones with them. Fable and I in the beautiful streets of Italy, our arms around each other, color on her cheeks from a day spent in the sun. She'd taste like chocolate gelato when I pressed my lips to hers.

But in the next breath, I cut myself off. I can't keep dreaming about more than I can have. It's bad enough when I'm with her—my mind is constantly trailing into places it shouldn't, trying to work around the rules and make exceptions.

But I can't risk her like that.

"Tessa's fiancé can't make it," Dave continues. "But I'd love for you to be there if you want to."

"I, uh . . ." My brain scavenges for a good explanation. "I don't know if I'll be able to with everything going on at work."

He nods, his expression thoughtful. "If anything changes, let me know. We'd be happy to have you with us."

"Will do," I assure him, getting back to work. It takes me a few moments to realize Dave hasn't joined me.

I look up to find him leaning his pick against the nearby fence.

"You know, I've always loved that I had three daughters. I think I was meant to be a girl dad." He steps closer and squeezes my shoulder. "But damn if I haven't lucked out in the son department too. I couldn't ask for better than you and Finn."

It's shockingly instantaneous, the pressure behind my eyes. The second he says those words, I can barely keep my face from scrunching up with emotion.

My voice comes out wobbly on the edges when I whisper, "Thank you. That . . . that means a lot to me—to be included in that."

He tilts his head. "You *are* an exceptional man. You know that, right?"

I can't lie to Dave and pretend to agree with him, so I stay quiet.

It takes two seconds for him to see the truth somewhere in my face. "Then I haven't done a very good job making sure you know." He steps in front of me, taking up all the space in my line of vision as he folds his hands around my shoulders. "I'm proud of you and so grateful you're part of this family. No matter what's to come between you and Fable, you'll always be a part of it, okay?"

Then he wraps his arms around me, and even inches taller than him, I feel small inside his embrace. I'm fourteen again, desperately needing a hug from a kind, gentle man.

He seems to realize that. Maybe he hears my hard swallow. Maybe he feels the subtle shake in my shoulders. But he doesn't comment on it. He just holds me, even though my shirt is damp with sweat and mud is caking both of us.

Birds sing in the distance. The wind blows through the trees. A horse whinnies in the field. While he holds me tight. Like he knows I need it.

\* \* \*

## *No Place Like You*

THAT EVENING, I'M in my office, finishing up a report on a surgery, when a FaceTime call from Mia appears on my phone. The clinic is silent, everyone else has gone home for the day, so I swipe to answer it.

"Hey!" Mia beams excitedly from her home office. "Whatcha doing?" Bree leans over her shoulder to see the screen as well.

"Working." I flip the phone around to show her my desk before setting it back down. "Writing a report on Beans's surgery this afternoon."

Bree sticks her bottom lip out. "Poor Beans."

"Don't worry. He's going to be better than ever." I tilt my head. "What are you two doing?"

"Making pasta," Bree replies.

"Aaaand." Mia's practically bouncing in her seat. "We just had a meeting with our wedding planner!"

"Oh yeah?" I lean back. "How's that going?"

"Great," Mia says. "We got the gardens reserved for the ceremony, and I think we found a bakery we want to use." She waggles her brows. "Their lemon raspberry cake? You're going to want to eat the whole thing." Her expression smooths into something serious. "But I wanted to ask you a question. Do you have a second?"

"Absolutely. What's up?"

"We've been thinking through the logistics of the ceremony for a few weeks and"—Mia grabs her fiancée's hand—"I wanted to ask if you would walk me down the aisle? I'd be honored if it was you."

My heart stutters to a stop, completely startled by the question. "I, uh ... you don't want *me*."

She looks offended. "What do you mean? I'm *asking* you."

I shake my head. "Mia. I'm—" I pause, trying to find the right words. *I don't deserve that. I'm not the person you want for that role. I didn't protect you when I should've.*

I mean them—down to my very bones I mean them—but I can't bring myself to say them out loud. To admit them to my sister.

Instead, I settle on, "You don't have to do that."

Mia's face contorts with pain, like I've hurt her somehow. She turns to Bree and murmurs something too soft for me to hear. Bree kisses her cheek and says, "Love you," before leaning into the phone and telling me, "I love you, too, Theo."

For some reason, that statement burns in the back of my throat as she leaves the room.

Mia scoots closer, tightening the bun atop her head. "I want you to listen to me. And you're not going to like it, but I *will* fly down there and make you listen in person. Don't put it past me. I'll tie you to a chair if I have to, so you really hear me."

I manage to crack a smile. "All right."

Her throat works on a swallow. "You're pushing away the thought of walking me down the aisle because you don't think you deserve it."

My muscles tense. I press my lips together, unable to come up with an argument because she's exactly right.

"I want *you* to walk me down the aisle, Theo," she insists. "*You*. And quite frankly I won't take no for an answer."

I feel as if an anvil has dropped on my chest. "I'm just your brother."

Her jaw shifts. "Don't say that. Without you . . ." There's a glassy sheen to her eyes that I feel mirrored in mine. "I wouldn't have made it without you. You made sure Mom and I felt loved and taken care of. You've stopped at nothing to make sure I'm happy all these years."

My voice cracks when I say, "Your happiness is the most important thing to me."

"I know. You gave up your job to live with our grandparents, so I didn't feel the need to. You take care of Mom while I live hours away." She shakes her head. "Now it's your turn."

"For what?" I ask, genuinely confused.

"To take care of you. To let yourself be happy. You pretend you are—put on a good show, really—but you're not. You're too busy worrying about everyone else and not giving yourself the life you deserve."

The floor wobbles under my feet. "I . . . happy."

Her face falls. "No, you're pretending to be because you think it'll be easier on me. And, god, I'd love to say, 'Do it for me. Be happy because it makes me happy.' But that's bullshit, Theo. I want you to be happy for *you*." A tear tumbles down her cheek. "And I don't think you'll be able to truly be happy until you can talk about what happened."

My shoulders shudder with a deep breath. "Talking about it is hard."

She shakes her head, her face full of sympathy. "But pushing through the hard part is what helps you get better. I'm not going to sugarcoat it. It sucks. But you come out better on the other side. I promise. I'd love if you talked to me—I'm always going to make time to talk about it with you. But I think it's even more important for you to stop canceling therapy appointments. Talk to someone who can help you."

Those appointment nudges come through on a monthly basis, and they're piling up in the junk folder of my email. Every reminder feels like a punch to the gut, but I haven't been able to bring myself to block the email—like my subconscious is trying its hardest to push me in the right direction.

"I can see it—you're keeping everyone at a distance, punishing yourself for something you didn't do." Mia shrugs. "And I'm sure it's hard to hear, but I need you to help yourself. It's not something we can do for you. You have to decide you want something different."

My eyes fill with tears. Combined with the conversation with Dave this morning, my emotions are boiling over. I can't keep a lid on them.

Then Mia delivers the final blow. "How much more are you going to let him take from you? We've lost so much to him. He doesn't deserve any more of us."

The dam breaks. A tear tracks down my cheek and Mia makes a devastated noise through the phone. "Dammit, we should've had this conversation in person. I need to hug you."

I sniffle. "You can owe me one."

Her laugh is watery. We're quiet for a few beats before she tips her head. "Next time I see you, I'll hug you extra hard."

"Not if I do it first."

Mia nods and shifts to talk about wedding plans. She sends me pictures of the dresses she picked out—one for the ceremony and one dancing-friendly option for the party—and tells me all about the pop-up tattoo station she wants.

"You could finally get a tattoo," she says, eyes mischievous. "*My sister is a genius*, right across your neck, so everyone knows."

I grin. "As soon as you get *my brother is the best* across yours."

"Wonder what Fable and Bree would have to say about that." Her laughter lightens something in my chest. "Who are we kidding? They'll be right there taking pictures of the whole thing."

"I'll tell Fable to charge her phone."

A smirk tugs at her lips. "Huh. I just realized, Fable will be there. You'll be there. You two could come to my wedding *together*."

My smile falters. "Our arrangement will be over by then." The thought of seeing her there, maybe even with someone else, constricts something in my chest.

"Hey, Theo?" Mia says gently.

"Mm-hmm?"

"You know you can admit you're in love with her, right?"

The floor whooshes out from under me. I'm not *in love* with her. I'm... infatuated. I'm... borderline obsessed. But I'm not in love. I can't be. I'm not allowed to be.

Mia must see my panicked expression because she laughs softly. "Don't hide from it because you're scared. Let yourself be happy."

## Chapter 32

*Fable*

"How was your day?" I swipe a portion of dark chocolate hazelnut spread across a cracker and shove it in my mouth.

Theo's across the kitchen from me, leaning against the island—the same positions we took that night of my birthday party. In a lot of ways, I feel exactly the same, half-drunk and giddy, but this time it's not alcohol-induced. That heart-bursting, happy feeling is all Theo.

"Good. We had a surgery that took up a lot of the afternoon, but everything went well. Beans will be back to himself in no time." His gaze drifts away for a beat before coming back to me. "And Mia called."

"Oh, yeah? Did you get to see the dress pictures?" She sent them to me yesterday, and I think that's when it really set in that my best friend is getting married. She and Bree shopped for dresses together—because according to them, "fuck traditions"—and I can't wait to see the dresses in person. They're going to be stunning.

"I did. They were beautiful." A hint of discomfort seeps into his voice when he adds, "She also asked me to walk her down the aisle."

A gasp jumps out of me. "Theo! That's amazing!" He doesn't seem to be on my level of excitement, though. "What's wrong?"

Something heavy settles into his expression. "I don't know. I feel"—he sighs—"a lot."

I hop down from the counter and wrap my arms around his waist. Propping my chin against his chest, I look up at him. "Do you not want to?"

"No, I want to." He folds his arms around me. "It just feels like such an honor," he mumbles.

Understanding seeps in. "One you don't think you deserve?" He doesn't reply, which is answer enough. "Theo," I whisper, cupping his scruffy cheeks to tip his eyes down to me. "You absolutely deserve it. She wants *you*. She trusts *you*. She's showing you how important you are to her."

"You think so?" His voice is so full of insecurity. I wish I could zap it all out of him somehow.

Lifting onto my toes, I press a soft kiss to his lips. "I do. No doubt in my mind, I assure him, and his chest relaxes with a deep breath.

As he washes our dinner dishes and I dry them, his mood seems to lighten. We laugh about the joke book Priya brought to soccer practice and Knocks's inability to leave Layla alone while she's sleeping.

This is probably the thing I'll miss the most when this is over—the simple moments with the two of us. Everything's soft and intimate when we're in the A-frame together. The outside world is distant and unimportant, and I get so busy enjoying *this*, I forget it's going to end one day soon.

We tuck ourselves into our usual corners of the couch, me with Gramps's copy of *The Hobbit* and Theo with one of Gramps's favorite sci-fi books. We've been reading together at night—or at least I've been trying to—but I tend to get distracted by Theo's serious eyes and focused brows while he reads. He makes the cutest faces.

"Any reading actually happening over there?" he asks, not looking up from his book.

"Some," I mumble, bumping my toes with his beneath the blanket.

He sets the book on his knees. "How are you feeling about the bookshop?"

"I'm feeling like . . ." I wince. Shit, I'm scared to even say it out loud.

I've spent the last week researching everything I can get my hands on—small business loans, other local bookstores, market data, and plenty of other things I don't completely understand. Barb is probably very sick of my emails, but she has been gracious and helpful anyway. I've done everything I can think of *before* taking any steps, but the rental space's phone number has been burning a hole in my pocket, and I think if I don't do something soon, I might lose all my nerve.

"I'm feeling like I'm going to call the rental company," I announce, my voice as steady as it can be.

Theo's eyes sparkle. "Hell yeah." He sets his book on the ground and crawls over me, kissing me fiercely. "You're going to be amazing."

"You think so?" I'm not completely sure of myself, but I'm more confident than I was a few weeks ago.

"I do. No doubt in my mind," he assures me, echoing my words from earlier.

\* \* \*

"You know, I *can* traverse the stairs safely now that you've fixed the railing," I point out as Theo carries me over his shoulder, up the stairs.

"And you know, I get off on touching you, so I'll take every opportunity I can," he says, tossing me onto the bed.

I giggle as he leaps after me, catching himself before he lands completely. "Hey," he whispers, his knuckles gliding over my cheek

"Hi." I curve my hand to his jaw. "Wanna play a game with me?"

"What kind of game?" His eyes dance with mischief. So devastatingly beautiful and charming.

I give him a devilish grin. I've been thinking about this for weeks. Slipping a hand under the pillow on my side of the bed, I pull out the pink vibrator. "One where we reenact that time you caught me with this." His eyes flare and my body goes hot, arousal flooding my veins. "No head injuries or hospital trips this time," I clarify.

"Yes. Please. Yes. This is my new favorite game." He lowers his mouth to where my tight nipples are pressing into my top. The thin fabric soaks through instantly, and I'm already losing my breath when he snatches the vibrator from me.

"First, I want to see you spread out like that night. Then I'll let you play with it," he says, rising to stand at the end of the bed, exactly where he was that day.

I'm wearing the same soft pajama set with nothing underneath as I take position, letting my knees fall wide and staring at him down the line of my body. "You've got a little drool right there," I tease, pointing toward his mouth.

He drags the back of his hand across his lips. "I'm sure I do. Just look at you." The mattress dips beneath his weight as he kneels between my feet. "Touch yourself for me, Fable."

My breath hitches. With my gaze on his, I slip my hand inside my shorts and down to stroke my center. It's almost embarrassing how turned-on I already am—how turned-on I always am around Theo. Fire blazes in my cheeks at the wet sound of my fingers sliding through me.

His eyes darken. "You're always soaked for me, aren't you?" He presses a button, and the device buzzes to life, the sound ratcheting up my arousal. "Show me how you play with it while you think about me," he instructs.

My hips jolt at the feeling as I position the suction over my clit. The steady pulse has my eyes rolling back, a heavy pressure settling low in my belly.

I look up to find Theo stripping out of his clothes, his focus pinned to me. While I squirm and writhe against the toy, he drags my shorts down and throws them aside, giving him a full view of everything.

He's so goddamn gorgeous I don't think I'll ever be able to picture anyone else when I'm getting myself off. He's the standard from now on, and that's equal parts infuriating and exhilarating.

As the pressure builds in my spine, my thighs try to clench closed, but he grabs my knees, prying them apart. "Keep them wide open for me," he says roughly.

With a breathy whimper, I let my legs fall back to the mattress, baring myself for him.

"Attagirl," he praises with a wink. He spits into his palm and strokes himself once. "Is this what you were imagining that day?"

A laugh stumbles out of me. "I was actually trying my best"—I moan when he tugs the neckline of my shirt down and his mouth finds my nipple—"to *not* picture you."

He hums against my breast. "Oh, sweetheart, that's the wrong answer." In one swift move, he flips me over and yanks my hips up and back. I catch myself on my arms, the vibrator falling to the mattress. With a dark chuckle, he reaches between my thighs and moves my hand to hold the toy over my clit. "You stay just like that. And don't come until I say so," he murmurs in my ear.

Then he's gone, and I'm on my hands and knees on the bed, so close to coming I might scream. Tension is coiling in every muscle, begging me to let it snap. The arm holding me up trembles, and that flickering suction over my clit is fantastic, but I need something inside me. Something to clench around.

"I need you," I whimper.

The mattress shifts again as he settles behind me, and I hear him tear open a condom. "Where do you need me?" he asks, a hand stroking over my hip, squeezing right where the flowers are etched.

"Everywhere," I offer, which isn't entirely helpful, but it feels very accurate. I need him inside me and all around me and everywhere at once. I don't think it'll ever be enough.

"This where you want me, sweetheart?" he asks, but the way his cock notches at my entrance, I think he already knows.

"Please. Fill me up," I beg.

In one thrust, he does. With his hands tight around my hips, he pushes into me exactly the way I need. My arm almost gives out, but Theo reaches around to hold the toy as he moves inside me, allowing me to keep myself up with both arms.

"Is that what you wanted?" he asks, deep and gritty. A whimpered *yes* is all I can manage as he picks up his pace. "Fuck, I want to stay buried here forever."

My body pulls tight, my back arching, toes curling. "Theo. I'm so close. Please can I come?" A scream lodges in my throat. I'm already pulsing around him, barely able to hold it back.

And then, thank fuck, he murmurs, "Yeah," in my ear. "Come for me, sweetheart."

In an instant, I detonate. It's an earth-shattering, mind-numbing orgasm that starts in the farthest corners of my body and bursts into my core. I pulse and tremble and my arms finally give out, my shoulders falling to the bed.

Theo pulls out and flips me onto my back. He sets the vibrator aside, and my core is still fluttering when he slides back into me.

"Fuck," he groans, his eyes clouding with an emotion I can't identify. "You feel so perfect around me." He buries his face in my throat, his weight a delicious pressure over my body.

His movements are slower now—he thrusts into me in deep, achy strokes that I feel all the way in my toes and fingers. My hands rove over his back, pulling him even closer, trying to feel as much of him as I can, desperate to remember every dip and curve of his body.

"I can't . . . I don't . . ." He shakes his head, not making any sense. "I didn't know it would be like this."

When he pulls back, there's a deep crease between his brows. I try to untangle his words and his expression, but it's all knotted. His gaze searches my face, as if he's piecing something together, his eyes holding a mixture of longing and confusion? I can't be sure.

My breath stutters. Something is pooling in the air between us, and it feels a whole lot like the emotions we promised wouldn't come into this. They're rising from somewhere deep, insistent and unrestrained, begging to be acknowledged. And Theo doesn't look entirely sure what to do about them.

I'm not sure either.

He pauses, his thumb sliding gently over my cheekbone. "Fable, I don't know if I can . . ." His eyes fall shut, and I hear the words he left unsaid.

I don't know if I can let this go either. I don't know if I can follow the terms I promised I would. I don't know if I was meant for *no emotions* with him. On some level, they've been there all along.

"It's okay." I pull him closer, trying to stop whatever is unraveling between us.

He's trembling as he lets out a needy groan against my throat. Then his pace picks up, deep and relentless. I imagine him reaching a piece of me that'll never be touched again, like he's staking a claim that only I'll know about. It'll never be as good as this ever again.

And when his mouth comes to mine in an all-consuming kiss, I don't think I'll ever be kissed like this again either. Theo will be the keeper of all my favorite kisses.

His lips stay fused to mine as I tumble over the edge and euphoria pools in my lower back and stretches out to my limbs. He mutters a string of words I can't understand before his grip turns rough and tight, and I feel him pulse inside me.

Our bodies are damp, muscles loose, as he wraps his arms around me and pulls me over with him. He nuzzles against my neck and trails his fingers over me, leisurely drawing lines on my skin.

When my heart rate settles, I whisper, "Theo."

"Fable," he whispers back.

"I like you," I admit, my brain too muddled, my heart brimming with too many emotions to make sense of it all. But I know this one thing. I like him. More than I planned to. Enough to hurt. "A truly maddening amount, I'm afraid."

A deep exhale—so deep his lungs must be the size of the whole house. "I . . . like you too," he says, lips against my temple. "The perfect amount, I'm afraid."

## Chapter 33

*Theo*

*I* think my feelings for Fable started as a slow wave, way out at sea—so far I could barely see them beginning. Over the last few weeks, they've picked up weight and speed and force, and on a Monday afternoon in May, they hit me like an unannounced tsunami.

I'm driving Fable's Bronco home from soccer practice. Her feet are on the dash, toes bouncing to the beat of "Everywhere" by Fleetwood Mac as it blares through the speakers. The windows are down, cool wind billowing into the cab and swirling her hair in tendrils, the golden rays of sunset making the strands glow.

She slides her hand across the bench seat between us, and when she laces our fingers together, she looks my way. A small, secret grin curves her lips. Hazel eyes glitter with happiness, her cheeks flushed pink beneath her freckles.

It's the kind of image that imprints permanently into my mind—a core memory downloaded into place. I'll see this wild, effervescent version of her every time I close my eyes, until the day I die.

Something travels between our gazes—a message that doesn't

need words. It's a warm, cozy feeling that nestles itself right into my heart, like it had a spot there all along.

*I love her.*

In theory, it should be a foreign feeling I don't recognize right away. I've never been here before.

But it doesn't strike me as unfamiliar at all.

It's Fable. It feels like the most natural thing my heart could experience. Like our souls are linked together somehow, and mine has just found the place it was meant to settle.

Home.

I've spent years avoiding it, fighting it, keeping walls in place to never let this feeling in, hoping it would protect everyone around me. But now that it's here, a living, breathing thing woven inside my chest, I don't know how I'd ever be able to remove it.

There are still plenty of doubts and fears tangled up with this feeling, but the way Fable looks at me—like she's experiencing all the same things I am, like I'm important to her, like she feels safe with me—it gives me hope that I might be able to make her happy.

For weeks, I've been the one to calm her tears and the one to make her laugh. I know what sounds she makes when she's unraveling for me and how bright her freckles look against her skin when she comes. I got to witness her raspy morning voice and the little sigh that accompanies her first sip of tea. I know how hot she likes the water in her shower, the myriad of facial expressions she makes when she's concentrating, and that she's one hundred percent likely to steal a bite of my food.

Somewhere along the way, she chose to let me in. She chose *me*. And I want nothing more than to be worthy of it.

This feeling is too big to contain. Too right to question. Too encompassing to fight.

There are no people, no places, no life worth trading for her. I just have a lot of work to do to be worthy of it.

My eyes are already back on the road when Fable squeezes my hand. "You okay?" she calls over the music.

My heart replies, *I think I just realized I'm completely in love with you.*

"Perfect," I say instead, squeezing her hand back and making a mental list of everything I need to do.

\* \* \*

"Four o'clock sounds great." I nod, tapping my fingers on my desk.

The receptionist on the other line says, "Okay, you should get a confirmation email in just a moment, and we'll see you then."

"Thank you." I hang up and set my phone down, relief rushing through me.

It just so happened that my old therapist had a cancellation for tomorrow afternoon, which is much quicker than I was prepared for. But I've avoided this for too damn long—staying stagnant and letting the wound fester—and I'm grateful to finally be moving in the right direction, one phone call and one appointment at a time.

Step two is next, and while it's going to be an uncomfortable conversation, I force myself to walk to Arthur's office. This forward momentum might stall out if I don't keep making progress.

Arthur is at his desk when I arrive and knock lightly on his open door. "Mind if I come in for a minute?"

"Not at all," he says, setting his glasses on a stack of papers.

Unease sweeps into my stomach as I take a seat across from him. "I need to talk to you about something."

"All right."

Dropping my elbows to my thighs, I lean forward, unsure where to start. Now that I'm here, I don't know how to sugarcoat it. But maybe that's the point. I can't.

"I'll just come out and say it," I decide. His brows crease, but I barrel onward, not wanting to slow down. "Fable and I have been . . . pretending that we're together."

He looks like I've just told him I'm moving to Mars. "What? Why?"

My voice takes on an apologetic tone. "Mainly, I wanted to impress you. I wanted you to think I was here to stay." His expression sharpens. "When Cathy took a picture of us at the Branch, the situation sort of appeared and snowballed from there. You seemed excited about the prospect of us together, and I really wanted to be taken seriously as an option to buy the practice."

A muscle ticks in his jaw. "So you lied."

I swallow through my sandpaper throat. "I did, and I've been really uncomfortable about it. My only consolation was that Fable was getting something out of the deal, too—I've been helping her fix up her A-frame in exchange. But I've felt extremely guilty about lying to you."

He sits with that for a moment. Then says, "That's not the kind of trustworthy behavior I expect from an employee."

Embarrassment tightens something in my chest. "That's why I'm here. I'm sorry."

His fingers press into his brows. "Do you even want to stay in Fern River or was that also a lie?"

Rolling my shoulders back, I straighten in my seat. "That wasn't a lie. This is my home. It's where I grew up, and I love this community. I didn't know how much I wanted to be here until I was gone. While I'd appreciate if you still considered me for this position—it would be a dream to continue working here with Garrett and keep this place thriving—I completely understand if I've ruined my chances."

A heavy silence fills the office. Arthur holds my gaze the entire time, and I can't get a read on what he's thinking. "This doesn't seem like something I should overlook, though," he finally says.

"I don't expect you to." I lace my fingers together and stare down at them. "If this means the end of my chances at buying the practice, I understand. But I had to be honest with you anyway."

There's a hint of respect in his eyes as he nods. "I'll think about it. Give me a few days, okay?"

I stand, not wanting to take up any more of his time than necessary. "I appreciate it."

In the hallway, I take a deep breath, feeling that weight lift from my shoulders. It may result in losing out on one dream, but I know I did the right thing.

## Chapter 34

*Fable*

It's midafternoon when Logan steps out of the store for his Coffee Cottage excursion. He has given up the front that he's in it for the drinks and instead announced, "Going to say hi to Mabel" before he left.

Clutching my phone in my hands, I pace the paint aisle. I've been working up the nerve to call the owner of the rental space all day. I promised myself that if I was brave enough to do it by the end of today, I could go to the Branch and gorge myself on fries and ranch as a reward.

*What would Tessa do?* She'd say the only way to get to the next step is to push through this one. Get it over with. *What would Millie do?* She'd hold my hand and tell me to take a deep breath.

I pull a little strength from my sisters and imagine them here with me as I push the call button.

Nausea rolls through me with every ring. One. Two. Three. Four.

Until finally the call connects. "Callum Properties. How can I help you?" asks a voice through the line.

I freeze, forgetting everything I'm supposed to say.

"Hello?"

My stomach swoops, but I manage to form words. "Hi. My name is Fable Oaks, and I'm interested in finding out more information about a rental property at 416 Main Street in Fern River, Washington."

"Ah, yes. Just a moment. Let me bring it up," he says, typing something.

My unease spurs me to fill the quiet. "I'm looking to open a bookstore, and it seems like the perfect location. I saw there was some work that needed to be done, but that doesn't scare me." I'm rambling, giving him more information than he needs this early in the conversation, but he doesn't say anything, so I keep going. "It seems perfect, and I grew up here in Fern River. I promise I would—"

"Miss?" he interrupts.

I swallow down the rest of my speech. "Yes."

"It looks like that space isn't available anymore. We're drawing up the contract with a new tenant this week."

My mind goes utterly blank—no idea how to proceed past this barrier.

"But don't worry," he adds animatedly. "You're really going to love what they're opening: a Smoothie Bro. Have you been to one? They're a huge hit."

The ground tilts under me. All the anticipation leaves my body in a rush, and I slump against the end cap of aisle four. A few empty plastic buckets clatter to the floor.

"Are you there?" the man asks.

I croak out a "Yeah."

"I can send you over to our website where we have a lot of other rental listings." His voice is so chipper it grates on my nerves. "We have quite a bit in Seattle and Portland, and all the way into California too. A lot of options for you."

"Mm-hmm. Thanks," is all I can muster.

"I'll text you a link when we get off the phone, and we hope to hear from you soon."

I don't even manage a goodbye before I hang up and walk to the stool behind the counter. Sadness and grief swirl in my chest, stealing my breath.

My mind drifts to that picture of me and Gramps pinned to the fridge at home. His huge smile and hopeful heart. I thought it was a sign. I'd already daydreamed about hanging that photo in the bookstore. I'd imagined waking up every morning and feeling as though I was going to work with Gramps, making him proud.

How did I get it so wrong?

Tears burn behind my eyes. I'm merely *days* too late. If I'd just called earlier. If I'd tried harder. If I'd jumped sooner.

If I hadn't been so distracted by Theo.

The bell rings over the door. "Have you ever heard of a pineapple latte—" Logan's words cut off when he sees me. "What's wrong?"

"I'm, uh—" I haven't breathed a word of this idea to anyone but Theo and explaining it from start to finish sounds miserable. There's no way I can do it. "I'm not feeling well."

Sympathy washes his features. "Go ahead and take the rest of the day off, then. I can handle everything here."

"You sure?"

"Absolutely."

I give a faint nod. "Thank you," I mutter, and seconds later, I'm out the door to where Baby Blue waits for me on the street. It takes me four frantic tries to get the door open, and with every attempt I can feel the tension in my body pulling tighter. I'm a rubber band, being stretched to capacity.

When I finally get inside and stick the key into the ignition, she doesn't roar to life. The *click-click-click* echoes ominously through the cab as I try again. And again. And again.

Baby Blue quits on me, and something in my chest *breaks*. It's sharp and jagged, and it hurts so damn much I can't breathe through it.

I try again, cursing myself and begging her to please work for me. But she just gives me a few more clicks and nothing else.

That's the final straw. I drop my forehead to the steering wheel and burst into tears.

Which is how Theo finds me a few minutes later. He jerks open the driver's door in one try and wraps his arms around me. "What's wrong? What happened?" he asks, breathless.

"Everything is falling apart," I cry into his neck, unable to make any more sense than that.

"What do you mean?" He rubs gentle circles on my back.

I pull away to see his face. "I just talked to the rental space owner."

"What did they say?"

I toss my hands up. "Add it to the list of things falling apart."

"Huh?" He's more confused than ever.

"They already have a renter," I explain. "A *Smoothie Bro* is going in, and if that's not a giant *fuck you*, I don't know what is. I quit working at one in Seattle because they wanted me to add 'bro' to the end of everything I said to the customers." He bites back a smile, and that only enrages me more. "It's not funny! A fucking Smoothie Bro, Theo!"

Gently—like I'm made of fragile glass—he cups my cheeks and wipes my tears with his thumbs. "It's okay. I promise. We can figure this out."

I shake my head, spiraling further with every breath I take. "There's nothing to figure out. This wasn't meant to be."

His expression takes on that sympathetic look that my family always has when I've failed at another thing. "That's not what this means. It's simply a roadblock we have to work around. It's not a big deal."

But everything feels like a very big deal. The dream is disintegrating before it even took its first breath.

I'm suddenly too hot. Too frustrated. Too angry. Pushing him out of the way, I scramble out of the cab and pace the length of the Bronco. "It's a sign that it's time to quit thinking about this."

"What about all the signs that you were on the right track?"

"I misread them. Maybe Barb's Books was the sign! You know, that sometimes dreams pass you by because they're meant for someone else," I continue, trying to convince myself. "The Smoothie Bro sign is going to be clear as day when it's hanging there!" I jab a finger in the direction of the rental space. "I can't live here and see that every time I drive through town."

Theo shakes his head. "Or maybe you're looking for a sign from someone else to tell you what to do, when really you need to look in here to figure it out," he says, walking closer to lay his palm to the center of my chest.

Stepping out of his reach, I stare up at him, my breaths quickening with every inhale. I feel irrational. Barely held together. But I don't know how to fight against it. Years of self-doubt are coming back up my throat and choking me.

"How am I even supposed to know what *this*"—I point to my chest—"is saying? I can't trust that either." I've never been able to.

His expression hardens. "If this is your dream, I'm not letting you quit. Don't give up just because things get hard."

I make a short, frustrated sound. "It's my life, Theo. Not yours." Groaning, I press my palms to my face. "Fuck, I should just leave town." The rental space isn't mine. The A-frame isn't mine. There's nothing tying me down here other than reminders of all the ways I've fucked up. I could just *go*.

"What?" His voice is eerily calm.

I lower my hands and find confusion etched on his features.

"What do you mean *leave town*?" His focus is intense. Locked-in. "Where are you planning on going?"

There's an uncomfortable twist in the pit of my stomach. I've taken a wrong turn somewhere and I don't know how to get back on track.

I shake off the feeling and press on. "Well, Baby Blue isn't going anywhere, apparently. Can't even get her back to the A-frame." I glance around, suddenly realizing we're having this very public disagreement. Fortunately, there are only a few people walking through downtown. "This probably isn't looking good for your bullshit with Arthur."

"I don't give a fuck about that." His jaw ticks, his entire body tense. "You'd leave? Just like that?"

"Yes," I blurt, exasperated. "Remember? I'm an expert at giving up. Gold medal quitter."

Hurt pinches his face. "What about me?"

"What about you?" I blink up at him, trying to slow my racing pulse. "This is fake, Theo," I whisper. "What, I'm supposed to be your fake girlfriend forever?"

His brows crash together. "This is not fake, and you know it."

The space between us seems to pulse. The rest of the world is startlingly quiet.

I can't pull my gaze from his. "No emotions, remember?" It's a bold-faced lie, but with everything that's happened in the last fifteen minutes, I can't think straight. I'm careening out of control, and I don't know how to stop the momentum.

In one big step, he reaches me. Warm hands cup my cheeks,

and he dips his mouth to mine. It's less of a kiss and more of a reckoning. Warmth infuses my body as he parts my lips, and his tongue slips into my mouth. He tips my head and pushes me back against the truck, and I go willingly. The kiss is thorough and deep, like he's working to undo every bit of doubt I might have. Attempting to unravel every thread of tension in me.

I let him try, loosening and melting in his arms for a moment before he pulls away. Too soon. And in the wake of that kiss, I realize tears are dripping down my cheeks.

"Did that feel fake to you?" His throat bobs on a heavy swallow. "Did any of the other times? When I made love to you, did it feel like we were pretending?"

The next tear falls before I can stop it. I'm having trouble finding the right words. My body feels like it's spinning in three different directions, and I don't know how to gather myself back together.

His palm presses to the center of his chest. "Because I wasn't pretending. This is the most real thing I've ever felt."

A knot tightens in my stomach. "You didn't want anything real," I remind him, scrambling for solid ground to stand on.

"Sweetheart, I was wrong. Real is all it's ever been." He gives me a half smile. "I changed my mind. *You* changed my mind."

My heart jumps into my throat. I've been fighting my feelings for weeks, gaslighting myself into thinking they weren't there, and now he just gets to decide to completely change the plan?

I turn away, avoiding his gaze and walking to the hood of the Bronco to pop it open. Nothing under here makes a bit of sense, but I stare at it like I might be able to solve why it's not starting.

I need to get out of here. The urge to run is working its way down my body, consuming every thought. All I want is to fix Baby Blue so I can drive away. For hours. Days. Weeks. I want to not have to think about Theo or Gramps or bookshops. Or feelings or tulips or dimples or anything else that hurts.

My brain is an absolute mess of thoughts that I can't make sense of, and I'm losing myself in the chaos.

"Well, I didn't change mine." I wipe the tears from my cheeks, shaking my head. "I can't live here and see a fucking Smoothie Bro in the spot where Gramps's bookshop should be."

Theo's arms cross, frustration practically steaming out of him. "So, what? You're just going to run away from me?"

"Yep. Just like you did fourteen years ago," is what slips out.

As soon as the words land between us, I wish I could scoop them out of the air and shove them back in. Bringing up that moment is a low blow that neither of us saw coming. Shame curls up my throat.

Theo flinches so hard that he stumbles back a step. All the fight leaves him in a rush, his entire body slumping with the weight of my words. He's closing in on himself, trying to protect what he can, and *I* did that.

My brain hastily backpedals, attempting to twist it into something else. He wordlessly joins me at the hood, his jaw hardening as he searches the motor for any sign of what's wrong.

Drawing in a shaky breath does nothing to help the feeling that my lungs are caving in. "I'll still come to the adopt-a-thon."

"You don't need to." Theo's voice is lifeless and cold, sending a shiver down my spine. "I told Arthur the truth today."

That stuns me speechless for a beat. My lips part. "Why?"

He reaches for the battery, adjusting the cables attached to it. "I wanted to come clean about the whole thing. Lying was eating away at me," he says, before turning and jogging to where his truck is parked behind mine. He returns with a screwdriver, tightens a few screws on the cables, then mutters, "Try her now."

My stomach is somewhere in my ankles as I climb into the driver's seat. This time, she starts easily, and I don't even have the energy to be grateful. Theo doesn't meet my eyes when he closes the hood and walks to the open door. There are no dimples and no lopsided grins, and I miss them terribly.

"I'm sorry," I whisper, hoping he hears me over the rumble of the engine. A tear slips down my cheek, and I try to secretly wipe it away as I reach for my seat belt.

I wish I could figure out what's going on inside me right now. Nothing feels right. Nothing *is* right. This is mangled and backward and so fucking confusing. How can I have so many doubts crash into me in such a short span of time?

"I'm sorry too." His tone makes it a final statement, not the beginning of something. It sounds like *the end*. When he finally meets my eyes, his expression knocks the wind out of me. There's a lifetime worth of pain on his face and I wish I could undo everything from the last ten minutes. Take all the broken pieces and glue them back together.

But before I can figure out how, he dips his chin once. "You go first so I know the truck is okay."

He doesn't wait for a reply. I watch through the side mirror as he stalks back to his truck, dragging a hand through his hair.

It isn't until I put Baby Blue in gear that the weight of what I've done really hits me, and that's when I shatter. The warm wind flows in through the windows, whipping my hair against my skin as I drive with no destination in mind, and a well of endless tears pours out of me. I cry for Gramps, for Theo, for the A-frame, for the bookshop.

Mostly, though, I cry for me, because I think I just quit the one thing I could've been good at.

## Chapter 35

*Fable*

"I brought supplies" is the first thing Tessa says as she barrels into Millie and Finn's kitchen door, fresh off her flight from Chicago.

*What would Tessa do?* Apparently fly halfway across the country last-minute when her sister needs her.

I had no idea where Baby Blue and I were headed until the forest-green door appeared in front of my windshield. My subconscious had steered me straight to Millie's doorstep, and into the arms of my sister and nieces.

Millie noted my puffy eyes and tearstained cheeks immediately. "What can I do?"

Six hours later—after a much-needed evening of dance parties and coloring with Avery and Eloise—Tessa's here with several bags full of snacks and two bottles of wine that she must've made Finn stop to get on their way from the airport.

Leaving my perch on the kitchen barstool, I let her pull me into a hug. A heartbeat later, Millie's there, too, her arms around me for the hundredth time today. My body relaxes into the embrace. This is exactly what I needed—to be sandwiched between the two people who've had my back since the day I was born.

And as I breathe in their familiar scents and feel their arms tangled around me, I finally let out a sigh of relief.

"It's going to be okay." Tessa's voice is so sure that I can't help but believe her.

Thirty minutes later, my sisters and I are sitting cross-legged around a giant charcuterie board, with glasses of wine and *10 Things I Hate About You* playing on the television. Avery and Eloise helped us set up an air mattress in the middle of the living room, complete with a fluffy duvet and at least ten pillows, for what we called a *sisters' sleepover*.

"Can we have a sisters' sleepover too?" Ave had asked as she climbed onto the mattress.

Eloise stuck her bottom lip out and flashed some puppy eyes that almost had me giving in. But Finn promised their own sleepover upstairs, and I swore to take them to the park in the morning. Which garnered enough excitement that they were running to their bedroom, their dog, Pepper, bounding after them.

"Okay, catch me up." Tessa pops a grape into her mouth. "What did you already tell Millie?"

I roll my eyes. "We waited for you to get here."

"Knew how mad you'd be if you missed anything." Millie gives her a knowing look.

Tessa grins. "You two get me."

"Or we're scared of you," Millie murmurs into her glass.

"Whatever works." Tessa flutters her lashes. "So fill us both in, Fabes."

I sip my wine and sigh. "It's a whole lot of things that seem unrelated, but they're somehow tangled up together."

"Then give us the pieces and we'll sort them," Tessa assures me, which is exactly what I need—someone to make sense of this for me.

Grabbing a slice of cheese, I tell them, "I think I messed everything up with Theo."

Millie's smile is sympathetic. "I find that hard to believe, but tell us what you mean."

The emotions from earlier prickle behind my eyes again. There's no great way to explain everything, so it tumbles out in a messy string of sentences.

"I finally worked up the nerve to call the property owner for the bookshop, but it's already rented to someone else. So I was falling apart, and I wanted to leave. Just run away and not think about it anymore. But the Bronco died—which ended up being a stupid battery cable issue, but I was already losing it at that point—and I just . . . wanted to quit everything."

They exchange a look, but I can't stop to clarify. I'm on a roll, and if I pause, I may never get going again.

"Then Theo shows up and says he won't let me quit. We've been doing this fake dating thing—with a contract and rules. It's supposed to be casual, but out of nowhere, he says he has *real* feelings for me. He's the one who's been telling me this can't be real—that he doesn't trust himself enough. This whole time I've been keeping a wall up, trying not to let myself fall for him, but then he said that and"—my hands go wide, frazzled—"I was trying to leave, and he didn't want me to, and then I . . . said something awful." I gulp in a deep breath and let it out slowly.

Millie's eyes are full of concern. "What did you say?"

I swallow against my dry throat, not wanting to repeat it. But at the same time, I think the only way to face it might be to let it out and be honest. I can't hide it if I want to fix it. "I said I was leaving just like he did at the parade."

Both of their faces confirm what I feared—the jab was unnecessarily cruel. Guilt gnaws at my insides.

"Okay." Tessa takes a big swallow of wine. "A lot to unravel there."

"We should've taken notes," Millie chimes in.

"Sorry," I mumble.

"Don't apologize," Millie says quickly. "This is a safe space. No sorries needed. This is what we're here for."

"Makes me feel useful. I live for this kind of stuff," Tessa assures me, tying her long hair into a bun, like she means business. "Let's chat about Theo, then we'll circle back to . . . a bookshop? Did I hear that right?" I nod, my cheeks heating. "Coming back to that, then."

"First, nothing is beyond repair." Millie rubs a hand over my back soothingly. "People say things they regret all the time in the heat of the moment."

"Absolutely." Tessa stacks some cheese and prosciutto on a cracker and hands it to me. "The important part is apologizing and trying to do better next time." She shrugs. "At least that's what I've been trying to tell Harrison, not that he takes my advice."

My gaze meets Millie's for a beat. Harrison and Tessa have been together for a few years and recently got engaged on a trip to Bali. The photos were beautiful and everything in their relationship seems to be progressing exactly how Tessa hoped it would. The only problem is, we have yet to meet him, and in a tight-knit family like ours, none of us know what to make of that.

Tessa shakes her head, seemingly clearing away her train of thought. "Did you really not know he had feelings for you?"

"There were times I wondered. Times I hoped." I grab a grape and twirl it between my fingers. "But he insisted he didn't trust himself in relationships. He has a lot of leftover trauma from his dad, and I didn't know how to convince him they are nothing alike."

Millie hums. "Poor Theo."

"I want to give him a hug," Tessa agrees.

"But it's not your job to convince him of that," Millie says. "You can be a piece of that puzzle, but not the whole thing. There are a lot of other parts that need to come into play."

"Do you have real feelings for him?" Tessa asks. "Because the pictures I've seen in the group chat make it pretty clear that—"

"What group chat?" I interrupt.

My sisters have a silent conversation with their eyes. "The one you're not part of?" Millie says with a wince.

"Who's in it?"

Tessa gives me a look that says, *Oh, sweet summer child.* "Everyone else."

"The two of us, Finn, Mom, Dad, Eva, Mia, Bree." Millie ticks them off on her fingers.

"And Logan," Tessa adds.

I gape at them. "My boss too?!"

"Really, it's just us gossiping about how to make you two realize you have feelings for each other. And sometimes we share pictures," Millie supplies. At my frown, she adds, "How else are we supposed to know how adorable you two are when we don't get to see it in person all the time?"

Tessa's expression goes dreamy. "Remember the photo Logan sent?" She pulls out her phone and swipes until she finds it.

PROJECT THABLE is entered across the top as the group chat's name.

"Thable?" I glare down at the screen. "That's awful, actually."

Tessa waves a hand in the air. "It was between Thable and Fabeo."

"Fair enough." I take in the photo Logan sent last week. It seems he snuck the picture when Theo came to visit on his lunch break and ended up following me around the store while I changed price tags for some items Logan was putting on sale.

In the image, my focus is on the sticker gun in my grip, but Theo's is all on me. He's leaning a shoulder against the shelves, one ankle crossed over the other, and even in the grainy quality, I can tell he's giving me *the look* I keep teasing him about. Like he finds me adorable and wants to scoop me up and take me home. Like there isn't a damn thing in the world that could pull his attention away.

Logan's text says, the boy is quite smitten.

Tessa reaches over and swipes down to a photo from Mom. In this one, Theo and I are in our Unicorns shirts after our first soccer game. The girls convinced me to help them dump their water bottles over his head, and even though he's tall enough for it to not work, he pretended not to see us coming and let us pull him to the ground. His mouth is wide open with faux shock, water darkening his hair and shirt. Our soccer team is all around him, laughing their butts off, and I'm looking at him with hearts in my eyes, smiling so big I almost don't recognize myself.

Mom's message below the image says, she's smitten too. Followed by a text from Mia: this is totes working.

I fold my lips together to suppress a grin. "I can't believe there's a secret group chat."

Tessa makes an amused sound. "We've had to witness the tension between you for years. Of course we're going to celebrate when you two idiots come to your senses." She grabs the phone and zooms in on my smiling face. "You can't look at this and tell me you don't have very real feelings for that man."

Millie leans her head on my shoulder, looking at the image with me. "You've fallen so hard that you're silly and giddy around him."

There's a soft, glowy feeling tucked in the middle of my chest, and her words make it flare brighter. It's almost too easy to remember the other giddy moments I've had over the last few weeks. The day I made a show of getting the soccer ball past him and got tackled to the ground by the Unicorns. Last week, when we were laughing so hard at his attempt to make a cat and dog pancake that there were tears in my eyes. When we were lying in bed one morning, Theo's arms wrapped securely around me like always, and I gave into the urge to finally take a bite of his forearm.

He has brought out a side of me that's been dormant for so long—that comfortable, childlike joy I've been missing.

I think about laughing into the warmth of his chest. About hazelnut spread on crackers in a dark kitchen. Toes touching under a blanket, red Starburst saved for me, a bookshelf to help me heal. His hands on my skin and his sighs in my ears. The way he supports me, cheers for me, pushes me to believe in myself.

Judging by the way my heart is simultaneously aching and cheering, I might've also failed at the whole casual arrangement.

"I think," I start, my voice hitching. "I think I have very real feelings for that man."

"Finally!" Tessa shouts, throwing her hands in the air.

Millie shushes her. "Quiet celebration! Think of the children!"

We all burst into a fit of giggles, trying our best to lower the volume.

"You *like* like him," Millie says, pressing one of my hands between hers.

Tessa's eyes are glassy. "I'm so happy for you. Truly. You deserve someone who's as obsessed with you as he is."

I scoff. "I don't know if he's *obsessed*."

Millie bumps her shoulder with mine. "Theo's been all-eyes-on-Fable since we were kids, babe."

Footsteps echo down the stairs before Finn comes into view, in plaid pajama pants and a T-shirt Millie got him for Christmas last year. It has an image of Spock surrounded by pink hearts that had Finn blushing bright red when he opened it.

"Speaking of obsessed," Tessa murmurs under her breath, sending us into giggles all over again.

A tiny smirk hooks his mouth as he circles the back of the couch to reach Millie. "Sounds like you three are having a great time." He drops a sweet kiss to the top of her head.

"Did we wake the girls?" Millie asks, tilting her chin to look up at him.

He brushes her auburn waves behind her ear. "No, they're sleeping soundly. Don't worry about them; just enjoy your sisters' night."

The air practically sizzles around them. Finn seems like he's in a trance as he lowers his lips to hers, and I have to look away. The sight of them is making something sharp prick at my insides, and it feels an awful lot like *longing*.

Tessa's gaze crashes with mine, and she points a thumb over her shoulder, mouthing, *Should we go?*

But then Finn clears his throat, adjusts his glasses, and reaches an arm out to me. "Want a refill?"

"Yes, please." We hand him our empty wineglasses and he goes to the kitchen to open a new bottle.

Voices from the movie fill the quiet as I try to decide what these newfound feelings mean. I don't want to run from them. I want to turn around and run right back *to* them.

"Do you think I royally fucked everything up?" I ask warily.

"Not at all," Millie assures me.

The air mattress squeaks as my sisters lean toward me for a group hug, our obliterated charcuterie board on the mattress between us.

"We've all said a lot of mean stuff over the years, and we still like each other," Tessa points out.

A laugh bubbles out of me. "We're sisters. It's kind of unavoidable."

When Finn returns—with three fresh glasses of wine and the eye masks Tessa brought tucked into his arm—he passes everything out and we relax back against the pillows. He helps us open the packages while balancing our wine, then collects the trash, drops another kiss to Millie, and says, "Have fun. Let me know if you need anything," before leaving us to our sisters' sleepover.

"Okay," Millie says, patting my thigh. "Tell us about this bookshop."

\*\*\*

"How 'bout you give me the number of the property owner?" Tessa requests.

I slouch a little farther between them. "No way."

"But it sounds *perfect*," Tessa says adamantly. "The photo alone is a blatant sign, straight from Gramps."

"If anyone can get you that spot, it's Tessa," Millie adds through a yawn.

Tessa nods. "I'll have those Smoothie Bros on their knees. That building will be yours."

"I appreciate that." I laugh, reaching for their hands. "But I wanted this to be something I accomplished on my own."

Tessa gives me an unimpressed look. "Like the A-frame? I know you're the queen of stubborn, but we're your family."

"You didn't tell us it was falling apart." Millie sighs, disappointed. "He was our Gramps too. We would've loved to help."

Guilt burrows its way behind my rib cage. "It's not that I didn't want to tell you." I pause to think about it. "Okay, maybe I didn't want to tell you. But that's because you all would've given me an out, and I think I knew that if you did, I would take it. I'd throw in the towel and let Mom and Dad sell the place." My throat constricts around the words. "And I wanted to fix it so badly. For Gramps. You know how much he loved that cabin."

A long moment of silence passes between us. I suspect we're all thinking about Gramps now, picturing him in his reading chair, sock-covered feet propped on the coffee table, a book in his hands, a steaming cup of tea nearby.

"We loved it, too, though." The edges of Tessa's lips curve down. "I have a lot of amazing memories there. Remember when we helped him turn the living room into a life-size Candy Land board?"

Millie smiles fondly. "Nobody wanted that bowl of licorice."

"I'm sorry I didn't tell you." Looking back, I can see how stubborn that was—trying to take everything as a personal mission. When, really, they should've been there too. It could've been a project that brought us closer instead of putting distance between us.

"You know, Fabes," Millie says, squeezing my hand. "You can absolutely do this on your own. I wholeheartedly believe in you. But the thing is, you don't have to. Why carry all the weight when you could split it with us? That's what family is for."

I try to stop my lips from quivering. "But you all never ask for help. I feel so messy compared to you two."

"Oh, Fabes. We ask for help all the time." Tessa leans her head on mine. "Remember our caravan of cars when everyone helped me move to Chicago?"

"How about when I made Mom and Dad come stay with me when I had the flu for a week?" Millie says.

Tessa nods. "Or that time in college when the entire backstage crew got mono, and you all spent the weekend building the sets with me?"

A soft laugh seeps out of me. "Still wondering how they *all* got mono."

"I blame Rick, the cheating bastard," Tessa grumbles.

Millie laughs, wrapping her arm around me. "The point is, we all help each other. Right?"

I nod, and Tessa pulls out her phone, opening the Notes app. "So tell me, what still needs to be done?"

I wave her off. "You really don't have to—"

She sits up and gives me a sharp look. Tessa in serious mode is a little scary. In a good way. I try to tame my smile. "Look," she says. "I have five days here. Hand me a paintbrush, I'll paint the shit out of something. Hand me a power tool, I'll look up how to use it, then power-tool the shit out of it. You hear me? I'm not taking no for an answer."

My smile bursts free. "Yes, ma'am."

Millie sits up, too, copying Tessa's expression. "What she said!"

Laughter trickles between us, and as I list what the A-frame needs—burrowed under a quilt, wedged between my sisters—the tension bleeds out of my body. The knot in my chest loosens, and I feel lighter than I have in years.

## Chapter 36

*Theo*

I've been coming to the Branch since fifth grade. It was the baseball team's favorite spot to grab dinner after a game, I had my first kiss in the bathroom hallway one Friday night, and my first drink at the bar the day I turned twenty-one. This place is full of memories, but all I can recall as I sit here with Maddox are the ones that include Fable.

Like when she fell into my lap, completely rerouting the course of our relationship. Her birthday, when I got to hold her in my hands and spin her around the dance floor. Last week, when she ordered soft pretzels even though she doesn't like them, just so we could dance again.

She's everywhere here. I should've told Maddox to pick a different place for dinner.

The solid oak door creaks open behind me, and my heart skips a beat. *Maybe it's her. Turn around and see.*

My thoughts must be written all over my face, because Maddox glances behind me and shakes his head with a sympathetic half grin.

We've just finished putting out a fire in a shed outside of town, so with my sweat-stained clothes and the smell of smoke clinging to every inch of me, it's probably for the best that I don't run into her right now.

But I miss her something fierce, and I'm finding it hard to focus on anything else.

I miss how she takes up the entire bed when she sleeps and the feel of her bare skin against mine. How her lashes flutter when she's dreaming. Grilled cheese with our toes pressed together on the middle cushion. I miss her stealing bites of my food and the tiny twitch of her mouth when she's secretly proud of herself. The exact color of her eyes when she's about to say something snarky. The way she smells and tastes. The sound of her laugh and her little growl. My lips on her tattoos and her hands in my hair.

I miss her. Period.

So I'll probably keep checking that door. I can't help it.

"Are you finally ready to admit you're down bad?" Maddox arches a brow.

All I can offer in response is a sigh. I know I am. He knows I am. I don't have to say it out loud.

The days of silence are wearing on me. Even soccer practice—my one chance at seeing her—got rained out yesterday. My fingers are itching to open our text thread and send her random updates on my day, ask her how she's doing, find out if she's remembering to eat something other than cereal.

But every time I pick up my phone to contact her, something heavy drops in my stomach. Our conversation is still rattling around in my head constantly. She wanted to leave, and that hurts all the way down to my bones. I know that seems to be her track record when things get hard, but I didn't think I would be included in that. She's battling all kinds of doubts and insecurities and grief, but my heart aches when I think about how easily she pushed me away.

I was ready to tell her I'm in love with her. She was ready to run.

And the fact that she knew right where to stab me . . . it fractured something I thought we had mended.

Dave called me yesterday and said his bowling league had an opening—apparently his friend Steve is moving—and I jumped at the opportunity to join them. I won't lie, I went there hoping to dig up some information about Fable, but once I heard she was with her sisters, I let it go. At least she has people with her and she's not driving across the country without a word to anyone.

For the record, I ended up having a blast at bowling. Those old guys know how to have a good time and letting go of the last few days to enjoy myself with them was more freeing than I expected.

Maddox tips his head. "You doing okay?"

I swallow a sip of water, trying to decide on my answer. I'm surprised when "I started therapy this week" comes out of my mouth.

His brows lift slightly. "That's great. How was it?"

That's a bit of a loaded question. Therapy should really come with a warning label: *Beware! Gets worse before it gets better!* Turns out I have to pick open every scab and prod at what's underneath to make any progress.

"It's certainly not fun to dredge everything back up." I shrug. "But my therapist said if I want the wounds to heal the right way this time, we have to give them some attention. And I've been ignoring them for too long."

Pride flickers behind his eyes. "How can I support you in this?"

There's a rush of pressure in my throat. It's such a simple question, but so profoundly thoughtful. My voice comes out watery when I tell him, "Thank you for even asking."

With a nod, he stands and comes to my side of the table, pulling me up and into a hug. And in the middle of the Branch, both of us smelling like smoke and sweat, we hold each other tightly.

"I'm proud of you," he murmurs.

"Me too," I admit. I'm proud that I'm going for *me*. Not because it will make Mia or Mom happy and not because I think it'll fix anything with Fable. I'm going for myself, and at the core of it, I think that's the most important part.

When we're both back in our seats, Maddox lifts his water glass and I meet it with mine. "Now, tell me how I can support you."

I down a sip. "It might be helpful if you wanted to check in and make sure I'm attending my appointments. We're starting with a two-a-week schedule for the foreseeable future. In the past, I've brushed them off or made excuses that there were more important ways to spend my time. So, some casual check-ins might keep me on track."

"I'm on it," he assures me.

My face scrunches up. "You might be 'on it' for a while. According to my therapist, this is a long-term thing."

Earlier this afternoon, he explained, *"Healing* is an ongoing process for the rest of your life. I don't have a stamp in my office where I give you a seal of approval that you're healed. Your goal is not to check off 'therapy' on your to-do list and then go about the rest of your life. As hard as it is to hear, we're in this for the long haul."

Maddox grins. "You know I'm not going anywhere. You're stuck with me."

I let out a breath of relief. "Perfect. You're stuck with me too."

Our conversation meanders for a while. We talk about his boys and Vivian, Mia and Bree's wedding plans, and rehash the fire we got called to this afternoon.

Then Maddox asks, "You ready for Saturday?" as I get out my card to pay for dinner. We used to argue about who was buying, but we've settled into a routine of switching off and calling it even.

"Mostly. Still wishing we had more volunteers, but I've reached out to everyone I can think of. We have a lot of people helping transport animals, but I'm still worried it isn't enough."

Arthur hasn't mentioned our conversation from Monday, so I'm continuing to prepare for the adopt-a-thon. I figure, if he's angry enough to fire me, he'd probably be better off doing it after the event.

"The fire department could volunteer," Maddox offers. "That's ten or fifteen more people who could be helping. Plus . . ." His eyes sparkle with mischief. "People love a firefighter-animal combo. Those are big on social media. We could even wear some gear, play up the whole thing."

I twirl my straw through the ice in my glass. "That's a great idea, actually."

"We'd draw in a crowd." His brows waggle.

"Think we can put that together in two days?" My mind spins with possibilities.

He pulls out his phone. "I bet we don't even need one. You just tell me where to send people."

I open the spreadsheet on my phone where I'm keeping most of the transfer and volunteer info, and within ten minutes, we have five firefighters and two of their partners on board to help.

As we get up to leave, Ethan's voice rings through the bar. "Got an order of soft pretzels, folks!"

Cheers erupt around us, then the first few notes of "Just the Way You Are" start up. My mouth feels full of sand as I walk toward the door, weaving through couples on their way to the dance floor. Dancing with Fable out there is still so fresh in my mind—her pink cheeks and messy bun. The way that flowery dress flirted with her knees when she moved.

The pain of it must be etched on my face by the time we get to the parking lot, because Maddox leans closer and bumps his shoulder with mine. "It'll work out, Theo. I know it will."

I clear my throat and give a voice to the thought that's been plaguing me for days. "And if it doesn't?"

"Already told you—I'm not going anywhere. You're stuck with me."

## Chapter 37

*Fable*

"They're beautiful, Fable," Dad says, kneeling in front of the orange, pink, and yellow tulips to take a few close-up pictures.

Mom loops her arm through mine. "I wish Gramps could see them."

"Me too." I sigh.

When Dad turns to stand, though, his eyes glassy and his lips pressed together, I realize I got the next best thing. He hugs me close, a soft "Thank you" whispered into my ear. "Can you get a picture of us?" he asks, handing his phone to Mom.

She waits for us to get into position, both sitting right in front of the tulips, Dad's arm around my shoulders. It reminds me so much of my photos with Gramps that I promise myself I'm going to frame this one too.

"I'm already weepy and I haven't even been inside yet," Dad says as we walk toward the porch.

I shove my hands in my pockets. "We don't have to go in," I offer. Now that we're here, do I even want him to see everything? I tidied up the best I could, but with the tools and renovation supplies tucked into the corners, it's still messy.

Something flashes behind his eyes. "Are you kidding? Of course we're going in. I want to see all the work you've been doing."

Holding my breath, I lead the way.

* * *

THE LAST TIME the A-frame was this full was Gramps's eightieth birthday. He hosted a party, inviting everyone he could think of—even a man he'd met at the market that morning. We had streamers, balloons, a hand-cut banner Millie and I had made that said HAPPY BIRTHDAY, GRAMPS, and the biggest cake I'd ever seen from Wildwood Bakery.

I remember listening to everyone sing "Happy Birthday," our voices echoing beautifully off the wood plank walls, while Gramps sat at the center of it, beaming with joy and tears in his eyes.

Today, I feel like he's here, among the chorus of people who have shown up for me. There aren't any streamers or banners, and we've replaced "Happy Birthday" with a Disney Hits playlist, but the voices and laughter filling these walls would make Gramps happy.

Dad and Finn are working on the siding, replacing pieces that are weatherworn and crumbly. Finn is pretty clueless about the process, but he makes up for it with sheer enthusiasm. He's wearing the hell out of those safety goggles as he runs the saw, and Millie seems to be a huge fan of the tool belt he brought.

Tessa is staining the new railing and steps from the top down. A jumpsuit she borrowed from Dad sits baggy over her frame, and a bandanna is tied around her head Rosie the Riveter style to keep her bangs out of her face.

Millie and Mom worked together to get the washer and dryer out of the laundry room, and now they're deep cleaning it before painting the walls. Dad had leftover paint in his workshop, and he thinks it'll be enough for a fresh coat.

Avery and Eloise are trying their best to assist, but their attention spans have them bouncing between tasks. For now, the front and back doors are propped open for air flow, so they're taking laps through the house, giggling and singing the whole way. Occasionally they stop to check on Knocks, who's been left in the library, sleeping in Gramps's chair, for his own sanity and safety.

My heart feels full enough to burst as I watch the people who showed up for me. Even when I kept them at arm's length for months, they were right there, ready to jump into action when I asked.

The only problem is, I'm missing one person—a key ingredient to this cabin. He's become such an irreplaceable part of my life that it doesn't feel complete without him.

I could fill an entire photo album with the bits and pieces of himself he has left behind. His flannel is still here, and I wear it around like a robe. The sci-fi book he started is on my nightstand with a receipt from the taco truck tucked inside as a bookmark. Three socks, gray sweatpants, and a pair of scrubs—the sexy green ones. An extra container of dark chocolate hazelnut spread he tucked in the back of the cabinet, *for emergencies* scrawled on the lid. In the bathroom, his toothbrush and razor sit beside mine. In the library, that hideously adorable puppies-in-a-trench-coat lamp is perched on a shelf.

Theo's *everywhere*, and yet I find myself wishing there were even more signs of him.

There has always been an element of mystery about romantic love for me. I can *see* it in the people around me—in the way Mom and Dad have cherished each other for years, in the way Mia and

Bree seem to always be on the same wavelength, and in the way Millie and Finn celebrate life together, sharing secret smiles and heated glances.

But *feeling* it is an entirely different sensation. I don't know the exact moment when the switch flipped from platonic love to romantic love. Maybe it was a gradual shift, little moments pushing me into new territory over time—so slowly I didn't feel the difference at first.

Now, though, I'm realizing the difference. This love is all-consuming. It's gut-wrenching and soothing. It's wild and soft in the same moment. It's a visceral need to be closer to him, a yearning to hear every detail of his day. It's safety in being myself. The security of knowing I can take a leap because someone will be there to catch me if I falter. It's peace. Comfort. Wholehearted acceptance.

And I miss it. I miss *him*. So much.

If the last few days have taught me anything, it's that I was a complete idiot. I don't know a lot about what the future holds, but I know one thing for sure: I want Theo there with me.

Tessa's voice startles me out of my thoughts. "This sure is looking like a home," she says, wiping her forehead with her sleeve.

She's right. For the longest time, this was Gramps's home that I was staying in for a bit. I was an interloper, too unsettled to take up much space.

But somewhere along the way, that changed. Inside these walls, I've found myself. Taken risks. Opened my heart. Learned to believe in myself. Fallen in love.

And I'm wishing I could stay. In Fern River. In this cabin. Instead of calling it *Gramps's A-frame*, I'd really love to call it *home*.

The urge to run from the other day is long gone, and I'm so thankful I didn't fully give in to it. Even if I can't open that exact bookshop in that exact location, that doesn't mean there isn't a life for me here. The possibilities are actually endless, because Gramps saw his vision in a hundred different locations. All I need to do is adopt his level of creativity.

And I have a feeling he'd be proud of me no matter where I made that dream come true.

Dad's soft gaze meets mine, the creases beside his eyes deepening with a smile. Something unspoken dances between us, and then he winks. "You're taking up the whole attic at our house. 'Bout time we bring all that stuff over so I can make space for my new yoga room."

My throat tightens at his words. I'm starting to wonder if everyone knows what I want way before I do.

From the laundry room, Mom shouts, "How about you actually come to a class with me before you build out a whole room?"

Over the sound of everyone's laughter, my phone starts ringing. When I slide it out of the back pocket of my overalls, I nearly drop it.

Callum Properties blinks across the screen.

"Shit," I whisper, darting out the front door. I jog all the way to Baby Blue, somehow manage to open the door on the first try, and duck inside, catching the call just in time with a croaked, "Hello?"

"Ms. Fable Oaks?" asks a female voice.

"Hi. That's me." I flex my free hand nervously.

"Good afternoon. This is Jessie with Callum Properties. I was calling about your interest in the rental space in Fern River, Washington. We've had some changes to that property that we wanted to reach out about."

My stomach is making its way up my throat. "Okay."

"Our previous potential tenant has fallen through, and we wanted to see if you were still interested."

For a heartbeat, I wonder if this is real. Am I actually sleeping and having a fabulous dream about winning against a Smoothie Bro? "Yes . . . Yes, I-I am," I stutter out.

There's a smile in her voice as she says, "That's great. Before we take it any further, I want to tell you that the main reason our previous tenant fell through was due to the work needed in the building, so we'd love for you to visit the property as soon as possible."

I nod. "Yes. Absolutely."

"Once you see it, we can have a bigger discussion, but in general, we're willing to build a contract around the possibility of you doing some of the work that needs to be done in place of cheaper rent on the space." Hope inflates my chest. "Unfortunately, my colleague is out this week, and my schedule is pretty booked. So, if you're willing to view the space by yourself, I can give you the code for the back door. We'd love for you to look at it and let us know if you'd like to move forward with figuring out the next steps. How does that sound?"

I'm barely breathing. This is it—the moment to turn back or keep going. There are a million obstacles still to come. This is only the *space*. I haven't begun to tackle a small business loan or permits or any of the financial details.

But in a heartbeat, I know the answer.

I bring that small photo on the fridge to the front of my mind. Gramps's wide smile, that hopeful light in his eyes. His assured voice as he said, *This is the one.*

And I leap.

## Chapter 38

*Theo*

As I hop out of my truck, Maddox opens one of the crates in the back and helps a puppy down from the tailgate. "Good morning, little lady," he says, petting the top of her head. The young husky mix's tail whips excitedly. "Ready to find a home today?"

True to the plan, Maddox and I, along with the rest of the fire crew, are dressed in bunker pants, suspenders, and tight black shirts. We're definitely playing up the image, but with the crowd already gathered around our adoption area, I'd say it's working.

Maddox hands the leash off to Margo, one of our other firefighters, then moves to the next animal. We had a couple of volunteers drop out at the last minute, leaving at least fifteen animals that needed transportation from local rescues. It took quite a bit of coordinating with vehicles and crates, but with the added help from the fire department, I think we've made it work.

A chorus of yips and barks greets me as I walk past the dogs and carry a small crate toward the banner that reads CATS AND KITTENS, decorated with paw prints.

"This gal's a little nervous." I hand the crate to a volunteer from our local shelter. The tabby cat's amber eyes peer at me from the back corner of the enclosure. "We're going to find you a good home. Don't you worry," I promise before hurrying back to my truck to move it out of the way.

The roads nearby are closed for the parade, and an unbelievable number of people have already gathered downtown. It takes a bit of help from the police department to thread my truck through the crowd, but once I finally get to a parking spot, I jog back the way I came, hoping I have enough time to catch the parade. Maddox and Vivian's boys will be walking with their preschool, and it's bound to be adorably chaotic.

Weaving my way to Main Street, I curve around the taco truck and the stage that's been set up on the south side of the square, where a local band is plugging in their sound equipment. There are booths with small business vendors, and Coffee Cottage has a line out the door. Almost all the tables and chairs Garrett set up are full of people, eating and visiting and sipping coffee, and children are chasing one another through the playground. Laughter and chatter are echoing all around me.

I've never seen this many people gathered for the Thimbleberry parade. Maybe, just maybe, there's a chance we can actually pull off our adoption goals.

The urge to search for Fable in every face in the crowd is overwhelming. I keep hoping I'll catch a glimpse of her blond hair or hear her laughter over the roar of voices. Her Bronco was back in front of the A-frame when I ran down her street yesterday morning, and I had the tiniest bit of hope she might get a hold of me.

No luck, though. I'm starting to worry about what that means for us.

"Hey, you!" calls a voice to my left. I turn to find Philip Fucking Anderson beside the puppy corral, waving me over. He's in a long-sleeve button-down, slacks, and a tie, which looks terribly out of place on a warm spring day at a parade.

Of course he wouldn't recognize me. We went to the same small-town high school for three years and had at least five classes together during that time. But, sure, call me *you* instead of my actual name.

"Do you have any purebred dogs?" he asks as I step closer. "I want to get my wife a wedding gift, but these are all . . ." He sneers down at the gaggle of puppies. "They're not what we're looking for."

I have the sudden desire to knock the back of his knees and send him tumbling down. As we learned at the Branch, he looks great sprawled out on the ground.

Clearing my throat, I put as much disdain into my grin as I can. "See, the whole point of this adoption event is that we're trying to find homes for rescues—animals who've been in shelters for various reasons. If you're looking for a purebred dog, this isn't the event for you." I'm actually pretty proud of myself for how calmly I said all that.

But his displeased grunt ratchets up my annoyance again. "Seems dumb. You might actually make decent money if you had something more valuable out here."

I'm too stunned to speak. My molars grind together. What the fuck is this guy's problem?

As I look around for someone—*anyone*—to save me from this conversation, a flash of honey-blond hair catches at the corner of my eye.

My heart trips over a beat as I turn, then it picks back up at four times the speed.

The sight of Fable sucks all the oxygen from my system. She's glowing in the sunshine—her hair wrapped in those two adorable buns I've become obsessed with and a crown of thimbleberry flowers atop her head. She's wearing a tank top with an open, flowy shirt over it and fraying denim shorts with tiny flowers embroidered on them that show off her gorgeous legs, tipped in her black Converse sneakers. There's a smile flirting with her pretty pink lips. That tattoo is peeking out at her collarbone, begging me to drag my lips there, and my freckle is on display, like a secret message just for me.

She looks like springtime and home and forever. So beautiful my heart aches.

When my eyes meet hers, her expression turns desperate, and she breaks into a run. In real time, it's only a few seconds, but I watch it in slow motion. The loose shirt dances in the air behind her, her smile beams brighter, and her eyes get glassier, until her feet leave the ground, and she *leaps* into my arms.

I can finally breathe again when her legs circle my waist, her arms around my neck. She fits perfectly right there against me, held so tightly we might never let go. She smells incredible—like flowers and bare skin and everything I've missed.

"Theo," she whispers, nuzzling into my throat.

"Fable," I whisper back, squeezing my eyes shut to ignore every other person around us. The noise of the festival fades away until all I can hear is her soft breath.

Her fingers tuck into the hair at the nape of my neck. "I'm so sorry," she murmurs. "I regretted it as soon as I said it." She pulls back, blinking away tears as she cups my face. "That wasn't fair. I shouldn't have thrown that at you. I'm sorry."

A sigh of relief gusts out. "I'm sorry too."

She presses her thumbs to my lips. "No apologies from you. You've already done that, and you're not going to keep doing it."

I nod, grinning behind her fingers.

She buries her face in my neck again and breathes me in. "I missed you."

I tighten my grip. "Not nearly as much as I missed you."

## No Place Like You

A throat clears beside us. "Fable?" Philip's grating voice filters back in.

*Huh.* Forgot that guy existed.

Fable looks his way but doesn't try to lower herself from my arms. Thank goodness. "Oh, I didn't see you there," she says airily.

He glances back and forth between us, still not appearing to recognize me. "It's been a while."

"Not that long." Fable tilts her head. "Last month, you ran into me at the Branch. Remember when you fell?"

His brows dip. "That was you?"

Fable just nods, her jaw tightening.

"Oh."

"*Oh?*" I blurt. "That's it?" Still no apology from this asshole. He'd look really good with a black eye and a busted nose.

Fable distracts me by slipping her nails over the back of my neck. I have to swallow down a hum of pleasure. "Luckily, though, Theo was there to catch me."

My name must trigger his memory. Recognition alights in his eyes. "Oh, Theo. We went to school together," he comments like I'm the one who needed the reminder.

We both give him a blank stare, which seems to make him fidget. Good. I hope he feels so uncomfortable he leaves this conversation. This town. The whole state.

"Looking for a dog?" Fable asks.

He glances back at the corral of puppies. "There isn't a great selection here," he remarks, and I swear a few of the dogs pause their playing to glare at him. "I was hoping to find something with better breeding and—"

Fable cuts him off with a short, sarcastic laugh. "God, you really are a snob."

"Aunt Fable!" shouts a little voice as Eloise comes into view beside us. She has a giant bright-blue ice cream cone—which is quite a treat for ten in the morning—and a matching blue stain around her lips.

Fable drops to the ground and kisses the top of her niece's head. "Hey there."

Behind them, the rest of the family waits at the edge of the crowd. Avery has a pink ice cream cone, Tessa and Millie are telling secrets behind their coffee cups, and Mary has her phone out, pointed in our direction. Beside her, my mom waves and Dave dips his chin in greeting, a smile in his eyes.

"What's a snob?" Eloise asks.

Fable scrunches her nose. "Oh, just someone who thinks they're better than everyone else."

Eloise peers up at Philip, looking just shy of predatory. Her cunning gaze sweeps over him from head to toe, then, with a tiny smirk, she lifts her ice cream. She takes one huge bite from the top before unceremoniously dropping the entire thing.

Or maybe she tosses it? I can't be sure.

But we all watch with wide eyes as a mound of bright-blue ice cream plops onto Philip's leather shoes. For a moment, none of us react, we're all frozen in place.

"Oops," Eloise says, her mouth so full I almost can't tell what she said.

Philip lets out the most childish whine I've ever heard. "Are you kidding? These are expensive!" He jumps back, trying to kick the ice cream off his shoes.

Millie and Finn are there in a heartbeat, apologizing and herding Eloise away, but judging by the smug grin on her face, I'd say that went exactly how she intended.

That little troublemaker sacrificed her ice cream for that stunt. I'd better go buy her a new one.

## *No Place Like You*

A burst of cheering sounds from Main Street, and Fable slips her hand in mine. "The parade is starting. Let's go." She tugs me in that direction, leaving a pissed, cursing Philip in our dust.

We manage to wedge ourselves into a spot in front of the hardware store with a perfect view of the parade. I keep Fable pressed to the front of my body, my arms around her the entire time, unable to let her go.

As expected, the preschool walk is adorable. All the kids carry their favorite stuffed animal and Maddox and Vivian's son Carter needs an entire wagon for his. There are homemade floats, a group of children with colorful flower crowns, and a bike procession from a local nature club.

And as the high school athletics teams go by, I pull Fable closer, savoring how far we've come since that day. How much life has taken us on a meandering, winding path to bring us right back here. Together.

When the parade is nearly over, she curls her hand around my wrist and pulls me to follow her. "Come on. I need to show you something before the adopt-a-thon starts."

And I let her lead me through the crowd, because I'd follow her anywhere.

## Chapter 39

*Fable*

A warm breeze billows through the alley behind my future bookshop. Theo's surprisingly quiet while I find the number in my phone, then type it into the keypad. The lock clicks, but before I open the door, I look up at him.

"Callum Properties called back yesterday."

"To ask you what kind of smoothie you like at Smoothie Bro?" There's a teasing glint in his eye.

I grin. "No, the bros fell through."

He reaches out to lace our fingers together. "And what does that mean?"

"It means"—I push the door open with my free hand and lead him inside—"the space is available."

My legs feel wobbly as I step over the threshold and into what appears to be a storage room. Or maybe a trash room? A construction zone? It's a mess—a crumbling shelf full of cardboard boxes against one wall and several sheets of drywall and plywood along another.

"They're willing to work with me on fixing up the place and taking it out of my rent," I explain, stepping over a pile of boards and around some paint buckets.

"That's great. You have a lot of helpers."

"I do." A whole crew of people who would help me with anything. I'm not nearly as alone as I thought I was.

We reach another doorway, which opens into the main part of the store, and my feet pause at the view. It's still a mess, but it's *beautiful*. The doorways are arched with intricate trim details. Decorative light fixtures hang throughout the space. The crown molding around the ceiling gives the room an old, charming feel.

There's history here, and I can't wait to learn every detail of it.

This storefront was never meant to be a Smoothie Bro. It was meant to be a bookstore—the kind of place that feels like a home away from home. Where you grab a cozy seat and find new adventures between the pages of a book.

I wish Gramps could see it. He'd be in love.

Tears press at the backs of my eyes as I let go of Theo's hand and stroll to the front door. The crowd is loud on the other side. I peek through a tiny gap in the paper to see everyone milling about.

"Next year, we'll have the doors wide open during the festival," Theo says from close behind me. "People spilling in and out of the shop."

I smile at the thought. "I'll plant tulips in pots on the front stoop, and we'll have ferns hanging by the windows."

"I can't wait to see it."

Spinning in a slow circle, I point to different spots. "We'll have a seating area over here. The register here. Shelves lining all the walls, then shorter ones throughout the store." I skip toward the back corner, narrowly avoiding a ladder. "And a story time and book club over here. What do you think?"

I turn to find Theo standing in the middle of the room. He's unreasonably attractive in his fire crew pants and a tight black shirt that molds over every curve of his muscular build. His arms are crossed over his chest, that lopsided smile hooking his mouth, and happiness sparkling in his eyes.

In a space full of mess and chaos, he's calm and unwavering in the center. Full of possibilities and steadfast faith in me. He's watching me with the kind of intensity that makes me feel like I'm floating.

That look is for me. It's mine and no one else's.

He always says a lot with that look. *I want to kiss you. You're adorable. You have no clue how much I want you.*

But right now, it's saying something else. I can see it clearly. *I love you.*

"Theo." His name is an unconscious, breathless murmur on my lips as I walk toward him.

He doesn't take his eyes off me. "Hm?" he asks, a raspy hum.

"I'm so sorry." I wrap my hands around his suspenders. "You've been a safe space for me—comforting and encouraging and patient when I need it. And I didn't do the same for you. I threw that moment at the parade like a weapon, when that's not how I feel at all."

A deep breath gusts out of him. His hands curve to my waist. "I know you don't, sweetheart."

I pause, working through it in my head. "I shouldn't have threatened to run away. Leaving just felt like the easy solution—like it always has."

His expression is somewhere between cautious and hopeful. "And how are you feeling about leaving now?"

"I don't want to. At all." His eyes brighten. "I'm trying really hard to believe in myself. To trust that I can figure it out. But I'm also learning there are a lot of people around who are willing to help me see my dreams come true. I thought I had to do it on my own to be successful at it, but—" I fade out, my throat tight.

"But it's not a bad thing to ask for help. We all *want* to be part of something you love," he finishes.

"We?" I ask, needing to make sure. "You haven't changed your mind?"

*I love you*, his eyes say again. I'm realizing it might be less of an *again* and more of an *always*.

"Sweetheart." The endearment shoots straight to the warm, glowy spot in my chest. "I'm not changing my mind. My heart is yours."

My breath of relief is audible. There's an electric hum beneath my skin. "I was hoping you'd say that." Holding his gaze, I pull a piece of paper out of my back pocket.

"There was a doubt in your mind?"

"It was small. Tiny. Microscopic," I admit, carefully unfolding the paper and presenting it to him.

My heart flares as bright as the sun while I watch him read the words. *Do you love me? Check yes or no. [ ] yes [ ] no*

Dimples bracket his wide smile. "Fable, I need—"

"Oh!" He needs a pen. I whip out the one tucked in my pocket and offer it to him.

But he can't grab it because he's busy opening his wallet. "I need to show you—I have one too." He slips out a piece of notebook paper. It doesn't make a sound as he unfolds it—too old and worn and touched to crinkle in his fingers. "It's eighteen years old, written by a lonely boy who really wanted to be friends with the girl who sat beside him in math class. He didn't know it at the time, but that note would change his entire life."

"Theo," I rasp, tears welling in my eyes as I take the soft paper from him. The letters are barely there, faded over the years, but I know them by heart. *Do want to be my best friend? Check yes or no. [ ] yes [ ] no*

He reaches up to caress my cheek. "Little did I know, that girl would be my soulmate, my best friend, the love of my life."

A breathy cry bursts out of me. "Love of your life, huh?"

He doesn't answer yet, just slips the pen from my fingers and walks over to the wall, using the surface to write something on the paper.

As he returns, he says, *"Do you want to be my best friend?* and *Do you love me?"* A slow smile stretches across his face as he turns the paper to show me his answer. "They feel like the same question when it comes to you."

The note is blurry through my tears, but I can see a green heart sitting over the yes box and beside that he's written *thoroughly and enthusiastically*, a callback to how he told me he wanted to kiss me.

The joy of his reply cracks me wide open, all the contents of my heart spilling out in the best way.

I grab the paper, and Theo tucks the pen in his pocket to cup my face. "That little boy got so lucky. Once-in-a-lifetime lucky."

"Maybe not *that* lucky. She's kinda mean sometimes." I try to laugh, but it comes out watery.

"And he loves every second of it. Wouldn't trade it for anything." His lips pinch and his voice dips into something sad. "I wish I could offer you this perfect version of myself, trauma-free and healed. You deserve that."

I tip my head back, needing to see his eyes when I tell him, "You don't have to be healed to be loved. You don't have to carry all that alone. I love you just the way you are. *You* deserve *that.*" Something seems to shift inside him. A broken breath stutters out and he melts against me. "Healing doesn't have to happen before we love each other. It gets to happen *because* we do. We can walk that path together."

He searches my face. "You love me?"

"A truly maddening amount," I whisper.

Leaning in, he brushes his lips over my forehead. "That's the perfect amount, actually."

I curl myself into his arms, our notes tucked together in my hands. The echoes from the crowd outside fade away as his heartbeat hammers in my ear.

"I heard it's the dimples and the bitable forearms," he murmurs.

"Those definitely." I look up at him. "But also your friendship. Your big heart and the way you make me laugh even when I think I don't want to."

He presses a kiss to the top of my head, my temple, my cheek. "Am I allowed to kiss you?"

I nod eagerly. "I really wish you would. I'm dying here."

"Seems like apt punishment for what you do to me."

When he brings his lips to mine, something unfurls inside me. It's a slow, gentle pressure, warm and comfortable and everything I've been missing. A hum of pleasure pours out of me as his palm slides over the side of my neck, and I lean into it, tilting to deepen the kiss. He takes advantage, tightening his grip and devouring me, a hot, desperate moan pooling in the back of his throat.

I'm seconds away from jumping up into his arms and begging him to press me against the wall when his phone goes off. He keeps kissing me, like nothing else in the world matters, but a loud ruckus outside the shop brings me back to my senses.

I pull away, and his mouth falls to my throat. "Theo, we have to go."

"Mm-hmm." He lazily trails his lips over my collarbone. "My freckle demands attention," he says, kissing the spot.

"I promise we're going to pay a whole lot of attention to each other later. In fact, I insist," I tell him as he wraps his arms around my waist. "But right now, there are a bunch of animals that need adopting."

That seems to break him out of his spell. He lifts his head, kiss-bitten and dreamy-eyed and blissed-out. "Come with me. I don't know if I can let you out of my sight today."

Once our notes are safely tucked away, he slips my hand in his and we walk toward the exit. Looking back, I cast another glance over the space that will house Gramps's bookshop one day. *Our* bookshop.

He may not be here to see it, but he'll be in every decision and every corner of the space, and I can't wait to bring it to life for both of us.

We stop at the back door. Theo tips my chin up, his eyes tracing my features. He studies me, touches me, like I'm something precious to him. Like I always have been.

"You know what this means?" I ask.

"That I get to leave a lot more stuff around the A-frame?"

I roll my eyes playfully. "Yeah, but something else."

"That you get all the red Starburst forever?"

"I'd better, but not that either." He gives me a quizzical look. "It means you have to listen to true crime podcasts for the rest of your life. Especially the creepy, gory, unhing—"

He cuts me off with a kiss. "A win is a win," he says with a wink and that lopsided grin that has had my attention since day one.

# Epilogue

*Theo*

*Three months later*

"Can you grab the salsa?" Fable calls, stepping out the front door with one arm wrapped around a basket of chips and the other holding a platter of tortillas.

Balancing the salsa jar in my grip beside the fajitas, I follow her, stepping out into the warm summer evening. In the grass before the A-frame are three long tables Dave and I built, full of people we love. Our crew is too big to actually fit inside our finished cabin, but the weather's perfect for an outdoor picnic.

Our parents are sitting together at one, quietly chatting (and probably scheming) about something. Finn and Millie are here, the latter sporting a shiny new rock on her finger that I got to see Finn give her in Italy last month.

Tessa, Mia, and Bree all flew in for the weekend, and even Maddox and Vivian and their boys have joined us. Layla is running circles around the house with Avery and Eloise and Millie's dog, Pepper, while Mr. Maxwell lounges on a plush porch chair and Knocks keeps tabs on everyone from the A-frame window.

It's a perfect night, and at the center of it all is the woman of my dreams. The woman who showed me I didn't have to be fixed to be loved. That I'm as safe with her as she is with me. And that our love is as steadfast and sturdy as our friendship.

She's glowing in an orange sundress that showcases the flowers on her arm and my freckle nestled in the swell of her breasts.

I'm obsessed with this dress. I can't wait to take it off her later.

After setting the salsa and fajitas down, I wrap my arms around her waist, lifting her into the air. "Hey, sweetheart."

She grins, looping her arms around my neck. "Think we have everything?"

There's an adoring *aw* beside us, and Mia says, "This is going in the group chat for sure." I glance over to see her camera pointed in our direction.

"You know, we could be *in* the group chat now," Fable points out.

"Nah." Tessa sighs. "It's way more fun to talk about you without you there."

"Hold on, though." Maddox raises a hand. "Can I get an invite?"

"Oh, for sure." Tessa nods. "You, too, Vivian?"

Fable shakes her head and murmurs against my lips, "Might as well give them something to talk about." And she kisses me again, igniting a burst of rowdy cheers and applause beside us.

\* \* \*

## *Fable*

*Three more months later*

"Come on! We're going to be late!" I shout up to the loft.

"We have an hour," Theo calls back. A drawer slides shut, followed by several footsteps, a door closing, and then he appears at the top of the stairs, buttoning up—

"A flannel? Really?" I pretend to be unimpressed. Secretly, though, I didn't know it was possible to love an article of clothing more. There's something about that plaid pattern stretched over his broad shoulders that really does it for me.

I've been stealing them for myself since he moved in. I'm pretty sure he knows.

Theo struts down, smug as ever. "This is my *nice* flannel, thank you very much."

"For a wedding though?"

Coming to a stop in front of me in the kitchen, he finishes the bottom button. "They're getting married in the gazebo downtown. Logan told me *he's* wearing a flannel, and if the groom can wear one, I can too." He points to my outfit. "Besides, it matches you perfectly."

I look down at my dress—dark green with gold, yellow, and orange flowers. It'll fit right in for a fall wedding. Arching a brow, I point to his maroon-and-gray shirt. "Oh yeah? There's no maroon in my dress."

His grin is slow and lavish as he reaches for the bottom hem of my dress. He slips his hand underneath, sliding up past my thigh-highs to twist his fingers in the lace at my hip. "We both know where the maroon is, sweetheart."

My breath catches, cheeks flushing to match the color of my lingerie.

A smooth hum drifts from his chest, and he tugs the band higher up my hip. The shift pulls the lace tighter against me, pressing into my clit in a way that makes my legs falter. Heat pulses in my core, pounds through my blood. I lean back against the kitchen island to steady myself.

"You sure we don't have a few extra minutes?" he asks, shoving his thigh between mine, only increasing the pressure against my core. "Because I'd sure love to spread you out on the counter."

He lowers his mouth to my ear and murmurs, "Please. I want to sit through that wedding with the taste of you on my tongue."

"Um . . ." My eyelids get heavy. I can't stop myself from grinding against his thigh. "Maybe a few—"

I don't even get the words out before his hands are around my waist, hoisting me onto the counter. My arousal flashes, hot and bright. He pushes me gently back to my elbows and flips my dress up to my hips, feasting with his eyes first.

"Hm." There's laughter in his tone as he slips his thumb beneath the lace to circle my swollen clit. "This where you want me, sweetheart?"

Too distracted by his thumb, all I can do is nod and let out a breathy moan.

His deep, knowing chuckle vibrates through me. Hands on my thighs, he splays me wide open. I whimper at the delicious stretch of my muscles. I'm trying my best to relax, but the anticipation is killing me.

He knows it, too, because he takes way too long teasing—rolling his fingers over my clit, breathing me in and blowing cool air across my heated skin. Slowly, he builds me up, plays with me, like we don't have somewhere to be.

I'm whining and moaning and begging by the time he shoves the lace aside and slides his tongue where I need it.

A moan rattles out of him. "Fuck, I'm so addicted to this," he murmurs, lapping at my arousal.

With a hand on my hip, he holds me in place and slips two fingers inside, working them in tandem with his mouth. He's eager. Thorough. Groaning and sucking like he can't get enough. I fall back, clawing at the counter, searching for something to hold on to. I settle for a handful of his flannel and another of his hair, and a long, drawn-out *"Fuck"* rumbles over my clit.

The pressure building in my spine feels like it might split me apart. "Please," I beg. "Yes. Right—"

I can't even finish my words before I'm convulsing beneath him. With a strangled moan I tumble into ecstasy, pulsing around his fingers. He keeps working me, wrenching every bit of pleasure from my body until I melt against the cool counter.

My legs are still shaking when he helps me sit up. I reach for his belt buckle, but he stops me with a hand over mine.

"No, sweetheart. This was just a taste. I couldn't make it through the wedding without it." His eyes are flaming as he licks his lips. "The rest comes later. I want you desperate and thinking about it—fantasizing about it—all evening."

I can't even form a response before he slips the wet lace back into place, taunts me with one more lazy roll of his thumb, and pulls me down from the counter. "Come on, you tease. We're going to be late," he murmurs.

\*\*\*

## Theo

*Three more months later*

"Best behavior, okay?" I scoop up the tiny puppy from the passenger seat and hold her in front of my face. She plants a paw on my cheek, her glassy amber eyes staring back at me.

When Garrett and I bought the practice together a few months ago, we started regular visits to the shelter for spays and neuters. This afternoon, a park ranger brought this little gal in after finding her in the nearby national park. She's about four months old—probably a beagle mix—with long, floppy ears and white and tan fur. Sweet, cuddly, and kissable. I fell head-over-heels. Had to adopt her on the spot.

"She's going to love you," I assure her, tucking her under my chin and zipping up my jacket until only her little black nose is sticking out of the opening.

I wince against the cold wind as I walk to the house. But there's a plume of smoke billowing out of the chimney, welcoming me to the warmth of the A-frame.

Layla's the first to greet me after I kick off my boots. She bounds over, immediately smelling our new family member and jumping up to investigate, tail wagging excitedly. Knocks is probably off doing cat things—jumping to the top of the fridge or tumbling breakable shit to the ground—and couldn't care less about my arrival.

But the family member I don't see is . . . "Fabes?" I kick off my shoes by the door and readjust my coat companion.

"Uh . . . in here," she calls, sounding very unsure about her answer.

"Where's here, exactly?" There's a small bang from the downstairs bathroom, so I start that way.

As I reach the closed door, Fable shouts, "Don't come in!" Another bang and a scuffle, then a, "No, no, no. Please stay still."

Layla shoves her nose to the bottom of the door and sniffs hard. Knocks must've gotten into something. I duck my chin and press a kiss to the little black puppy nose. "Need help?" I ask Fable.

"Nope! No!" Another crashing sound. "Shit."

There's a sudden ruckus in the living room, and I glance over to see Knocks leaping from the couch to the end table, making the lamp on its surface wobble. Confused, I turn back to the bathroom door, lips parted to ask Fable who's in there, when she stumbles out, barely opening the door before slamming it shut behind her.

Her hands are clasped under her chin, water splashed all over her sweatshirt, hair in a messy bun and cheeks flushed. "Listen. He was in the road, shivering and cold and dirty and I couldn't leave him there, okay?"

I bite the inside of my cheek to suppress my smile.

"It's winter, for crying out loud, and he's old," she continues. "We can—" Her words cut off when my coat companion lets out a whine and licks the bottom of my chin. Fable's eyes go wide, mouth open in surprise. "What is that?"

I point toward the gray paw sticking out from under the bathroom door. "What is that?"

She bites her lips between her teeth before bursting into laughter. "Oh my god," she gasps, dragging the zipper down to reveal the puppy. "Who are you? What are you? I love you!"

I reach around her to open the door, and a medium-size gray dog comes barreling out, shaking and flinging water droplets all over us and the walls. "Hey, buddy," I greet, scratching him behind the ears as Layla gives him a once-over with her nose.

When I look up, Fable's smile is bright and entirely too adorable. The little puppy is burrowing into her neck, her tail whipping happily. "So, we're a family of six, now?"

\*\*\*

*Three more months later*

The tulips are blooming right on time. Early morning sunshine glitters over the pink, yellow, orange, and lavender blossoms that line the storefront in long, rectangular planters. A bench sits on either side of the double doors, and a large green and white sign hangs overhead, reading **OUR BOOKSHOP**.

From across the street, I scan the building, checking to make sure everything is perfect for our grand opening. The Thimbleberry Festival starts in a couple hours. Down the street, a team of people is hanging a banner over the road while another group decorates the gazebo. Vendors are setting up booths around the square; Theo, Garrett, and their volunteers are preparing for the adopt-a-thon; and the taco truck is pulling into place.

And our little bookshop is shining in the center of it all, ready for her debut.

It has turned into quite the family project—all hands on deck. Theo and Dad helped with the renovations and construction. Mom spent months planning the layout with me and scouring estate sales and auctions for every single thing we would put inside. Millie and Finn have been an integral part of helping me pick out the perfect collection of books to stock. Tessa stops in every bookstore she sees, sending me ideas and photos of things she likes, along with the contact information for every owner she meets, in hopes that we will become best friends.

Our logo, website, and social media accounts have all been designed and set up by Mia, and she sends me daily content ideas I need to start working on. Avery and Eloise made art and banners to decorate the shop walls and windows, and Barb has been on call for every question I could think of.

I couldn't have done this without them. I used to think I needed to accomplish something all on my own to be proud of it, but I've learned my lesson—the sweetest victories are shared with the people you love.

My gaze catches on Theo as he steps out of Coffee Cottage.

## *No Place Like You*

He walks toward me, eyes crinkling, with two cups in his hands, and that boyish grin curving his mouth.

His attention is pure sunshine, lighting me up and making me glow.

"Hey, sweetheart. How ya feeling?" He offers me a warm cup before looping an arm around my shoulder and tucking me to his side.

How am I feeling? I take a sip of tea and inventory my emotions. I'm excited, terrified, overwhelmed, relieved, giddy.

And sad, I think. Sad Gramps didn't get to see his dream come true. That he isn't here in his newsboy cap to take a photo with me in front of *our* bookshop. That I don't get to witness the awe in his expression as people step into the place he dreamt of. That he won't get to see all our framed photos decorating the walls inside.

My shoulders hitch as I draw in a deep breath and close my eyes, sending a message right from my heart to Gramps's. *This is it. We did it.*

"He'd be proud of you," Theo whispers. "I'm also proud of you." He turns us to face each other, his big hand tucked under my hair, a steady weight against the back of my neck. "I knew you could do it."

My smile is watery. "Good thing one of us was sure."

His thumb glides over my jaw. "Never doubted you for a second."

Yips and barks sound from the town square, drawing our focus to where a little boy is reaching into the fence of puppies, trying to pet them all at once. One side of the gate gives way, and a tumble of puppies pours from the opening.

"I'd better go supervise," Theo says with a laugh. "But once the adoption event is over, I'm all yours."

"You're all mine, anyway," I remind him.

He smiles, all dimples and charm. "From the moment you walked into math class."

# Acknowledgments

*M*y emotions are all over the place as I sit down to finally write the acknowledgments for the hardest story I've ever written. I put the most hours, the most tears, the most pieces of myself in between the pages of this book, and to finally have it going out to my lovely readers is making me burst into tears all over again. Thank you for reading my books and making space in your hearts for my stories. It's my greatest joy to bring you into these fictional worlds I've created, and I'm honored you want to be here.

To my grandfathers, who were gone too soon, thank you for inspiring Gramps. Papa Gene believed in me as an author before he even knew I wanted to be one. Every time I saw him, he insisted, "I just know you're going to be a writer." While it took years and years for me to believe in myself as much as he did, I'm so grateful I finally took the leap, and that he was here long enough to see my name on the front cover of a book. I'm going to have an ice cream in your honor to celebrate this one, Papa.

I'd like to send a big thank you to libraries and indie bookstores. The warm, welcoming spaces you create are changing the world one book at a time. Thank you for the community you build and the heart you bring to our literary universe.

To my husband and daughters (and puppies), thank you for supporting me always—and extra on the hard days. Sometimes

I'm not sure I deserve your unwavering faith in me, but you give it willingly anyway. Girls, it's such a privilege to watch you grow and see your kindness and empathy shine every day. I have the best little family in the universe. Thank you for being mine.

Priyanka and Grace, I'm so grateful to have you in my corner, shaping my stories into the best versions of themselves. Thank you for championing these books and believing in me. And to the entire team at Avon, I'm so happy my stories have found a home with you all. Thank you for your hard work to get my books into the hands of readers.

Lauren and Hannah, my agent team extraordinaire. I can't thank you enough for having my back, advocating for me, and helping guide my career in the right direction.

To my dear friend Ada—somehow, a DM about John Krasinski has turned into an invaluable friendship that I hold very close to my heart. Thank you for believing in me when I've forgotten how to do it myself. Your wildly genius idea for the vibrator self-care scene is now permanently out in the world, and I couldn't be prouder. Also, this *spit on it* is for you and only you. I appreciate you letting me steal all your unused baby names. And thank you for subscribing to my podcast. Let's get Crumbl cookies, what do you say?

MC, thank you for listening to my rambling messages and for being a safe space to laugh, cry, vent, and be myself. Everyone deserves a friend like you, and I treasure your kindness and generosity and love. Thank you for always making my day brighter.

I'm grateful every day for the beautiful author friendships I've made. Thank you, Ellie, Hannah, Ava, and Grace for holding my hand and cheering me on in this wild world we're a part of. Being each other's cheerleaders is my favorite thing.

Chloe, I am constantly in awe of your cover art. I'm so honored by how beautifully you bring my characters to life. Thank you for everything you do!

To my early readers: April, Wren, Katie, and Meg, I can't thank you enough for reading this story on its first round. Your unhinged comments and helpful feedback brought it to where it is now. I know a lot has changed, but I hope you enjoyed Fable and Theo even more this time!

I'd also like to lightning-round shoutout: Trader Joe's dark chocolate peanut butter cups, sparkling water, the dark chocolate hazelnut spread from HEB, Pedro Pascal, my espresso machine, the word *fuck*, croissants, my emotional support ghost, the 2005 version of *Pride & Prejudice*, and the 1995 miniseries version as well. You all know what part you played in making this book happen. Please remain on standby for the next book. ;)

And lastly, I want to thank me, just because I can. Eleven-year-old Jillian would be completely blown away by how I've made her dreams come true. With my heart in my throat and my eyes on the sky, I took a leap, and I'm infinitely proud of that.

# About the Author

**JILLIAN MEADOWS** writes cozy love stories that make you swoon, smile, and squeal. She lives in Michigan with her husband, four wild daughters, three unruly dogs, and her sparkling water addiction. When she's not writing, you can find her devouring a romance novel, playing board games, or enjoying the outdoors with her family.

If you want to learn more about Jillian and her books, please visit jillianmeadowswrites.com or find her on Instagram @jillianmeadowswrites.

# Discover More By
# JILLIAN MEADOWS

A sweet and spicy holiday romance between a spirited artist who returns to her small town for Christmas and her older brother's best friend, a serious architect who pushes all her buttons—but whom she can't seem to stay away from.

A swoony, steamy, STEM romance in which two curators at a science museum—a handsome but grumpy astronomer and an anxious but sunshine-y entomologist—realize they are the perfect match.

DISCOVER GREAT AUTHORS, EXCLUSIVE OFFERS, AND MORE AT HC.COM